3 0012 00013936 9

B

Michael Moorcock

Behold the Man
and other stories

Behold the Man

Constant Fire

Breakfast in the Ruins

PHOENIX HOUSE

LONDON

Behold the Man was first published in Great Britain by
Allison and Busby Ltd., 1969
Constant Fire was first published in Great Britain as *The Transformation of Miss
Mavis Ming* by W. H. Allen & Co. Ltd, 1977
Breakfast in the Ruins was first published in Great Britain
by New English Library, 1971

This collected edition first published in Great Britain in 1994 by
Phoenix House, Orion House, 5 Upper St Martin's Lane, London WC2 9EA

A CIP catalogue record for this book is available from the British Library

ISBN csd 1 89758 036 3 cased
ISBN pbk 1 89758 041 x paperback

Printed in Great Britain by
Clays Ltd, St Ives plc
Designed by Peter Guy

Behold the Man

To the memory of Angus Wilson
and with respect and thanks to Peter Ackroyd –
two generous friends

Behold the Man
and other stories

Behold the Man

For Tom Disch

Part One

1

THE TIME MACHINE IS A SPHERE full of milky fluid in which the traveller floats enclosed in a rubber suit, breathing through a mask attached to a hose leading into the wall of the machine.

The sphere cracks as it lands and the spilled fluid is soaked up by dust. The sphere begins to roll, bumping over barren soil and rocks.

Oh, Jesus! Oh, God!
Oh, Jesus! Oh, God!
Oh, Jesus! Oh, God!
Oh, Jesus! Oh, God!
Christ! What's happening to me?
I'm fucked. I'm finished.
The bloody thing doesn't work.
Oh, Jesus! Oh, God! When will the bastard stop thumping!

Karl Glogauer curls himself into a ball as the level of the liquid falls and he sinks to the yielding plastic of the machine's inner lining.

The instruments, cryptographic, unconventional, make no sound, do not move. The sphere stops, shifts and rolls again as the last of the liquid drips from the wide split in its side.

Why did I do it? Why did I do it? Why did I do it? Why did I do it? Why did I do it? Why did I do it?

Rapidly Glogauer's eyes open and close, then his mouth stretches in a kind of yawn and his tongue flutters and he utters a groan that turns into an ululation.

He hears the ululation and thinks absently: The Voice of Tongues, the language of the unconscious . . . But he cannot hear what he is saying.

Air hisses and the plastic lining begins to sink, until Glogauer lies on his back against the metal of the wall. He stops crying out and looks at the jagged crack in the sphere; he has no curiosity concerning what is beyond it. He tries to move his body, but it is completely numb. He shivers as he feels the cold air that blows through the ruptured wall of the time machine. It seems to be night.

His passage through time has been difficult. Even the thick fluid has not wholly protected him, though it has doubtless saved his life. Some ribs are probably broken.

Pain comes with this idea and he discovers that he can, in fact, straighten his arms and legs.

He begins to crawl over the slippery surface towards the crack. He gasps, pauses, then moves on.

He faints, and when he recovers the air is warmer. Through the crack he can see harsh sunlight, a sky of shimmering steel. He pulls himself half-way through the crack, closing his eyes as the full strength of the sunlight strikes them. He loses consciousness again.

Christmas term, 1949

He was nine years old, born two years after his father had reached England from Austria.

On the grey gravel of the school playground the other children were screaming with laughter; they were playing a game. At the edges of the playground there were still little heaps of dirty ice. Beyond the fence the grimy South London buildings were black against the cold winter sky.

The game had begun earnestly enough and somewhat nervously Karl had suggested the role he play. At first he had relished the attention, but now he was crying.

'Let me down! Please, Mervyn, stop it!'

They had tied him with his arms spreadeagled against the wire netting of the playground fence. The fence bulged outwards under his weight and one of the posts threatened to come loose. He tried to free his feet.

'*Let me down!*'

Mervyn Williams, the red-faced boy who had proposed the game, began to shake the post so that Karl was swung heavily back and forth on the netting.

'Stop it! Somebody help me!'

They laughed again and he realized his cries only encouraged them, so he clenched his teeth. Tears fell down his face and he was full of a sense of bewilderment and betrayal. He had thought all of them were his friends; he had helped some of them with their work, bought others sweets, sympathized with some of them when they had been unhappy. He had thought they liked him, admired him. Why had they turned against him – even Molly, who had confided her secrets in him?

'*Please!*' he screamed. 'This wasn't in the game!'

'It is now!' laughed Mervyn Williams, his eyes bright and his face flushed as he shook the post harder.

For a few more moments Karl endured the shaking and then, instinctively, he slumped, pretending unconsciousness. He had done much the same thing before, to blackmail his mother from whom he had learnt the trick.

The school ties they had used as bonds cut into his wrists. He heard the children's voices drop.

'Is he all right?' whispered Molly Turner. 'He's not dead, is he . . . ?'

'Don't be silly,' Williams replied uncertainly. 'He's only kidding.'

'We'd better get him down, anyway.' It was Ian Thompson's voice. 'We'll get into awful trouble if . . .'

He felt them untying him, their fingers fumbling with the knots.

'I can't get this one undone . . .'

'Here's my penknife – cut it . . .'

'I can't – it's my tie – my dad'll . . .'

'Hurry up, Brian!'

Deliberately, hanging by the single tie, he let himself sag, still keeping his eyes tightly shut.

'Give it to me. I'll cut it!'

As the last tie gave way, he fell to his knees, grazing them on the gravel, and dropped face-down to the ground.

'Blimey, he really is . . .'

'Don't be a fool – he's still breathing. He's just fainted.'

Distantly, for he was half-convinced by his own deception, he heard their worried voices.

Williams shook him.

'Wake up, Karl. Stop mucking about.'

'I'm going to fetch Mr Matson,' said Molly Turner.

'No, don't . . .'

'It's a lousy game, anyway.'

'Come back, Molly!'

Most of his attention was now on the chips of gravel that dug into the left side of his face. It was easy to keep his eyes closed and ignore their hands on his body. Gradually he lost his sense of time until he heard Mr Matson's voice, deep, sardonic and unruffled as usual, over the general babble. There was silence.

'What on earth were you doing this time, Williams?'

'Nothing, sir. It was a game. It was partly Karl's idea.'

Heavy masculine hands turned him over. He was still able to keep his eyes shut.

'It was a play, sir,' said Ian Thompson, 'about Jesus. Karl was being Jesus. We've played it before, sir. We tied him to the fence. It was his idea, sir.'

'A bit unseasonable,' Mr Matson murmured, and sighed, feeling Karl's forehead.

'It was only a game, sir,' Mervyn Williams said again.

Mr Matson was taking his pulse. 'You should have known better, Williams. Glogauer isn't a strong boy.'

'I'm sorry, sir.'

'A really foolish thing to do.'

'I am sorry, sir.' Williams was almost in tears now.

'I'll take him along to Matron. I hope for your sake, Williams, that there's nothing seriously wrong with him. You'd better come and see me in the common room after school.'

Karl felt Mr Matson lift him up.

He was satisfied.

He was being carried along.

His head and side were so painful that he felt like vomiting. He had had no chance to discover where exactly the time machine had brought him, but, turning his head and opening his eyes, he saw from the dirty sheepskin jerkin and cotton loincloth of the man on his right that he was almost certainly in the Middle East.

He had meant to land in the year AD 29 in the wilderness beyond Jerusalem, near Bethlehem. He wondered if they were taking him to Jerusalem now?

He was probably in the past, for the stretcher on which they carried him was evidently made of animal skins that had not been too well cured. But perhaps not, he thought, for he had spent enough time amongst the small tribal communities of the Middle East to know that there were still people who had hardly changed their living customs since the time of Mohammed. He hoped he had not got the cracked ribs for nothing.

Two men carried the stretcher on their shoulders while others walked beside him on either side. They were all bearded and dark-skinned and wore sandals. Most of them carried staffs. There was a smell of sweat and animal fat and a musty odour he could not identify. They were walking towards a line of hills in the distance and had not noticed his awakening.

The sun was not as strong as when he had first crawled from the time machine. It was probably evening. The surrounding ground was rocky and barren and even the hills ahead seemed grey.

He winced as the stretcher lurched, moaned as the pain in his side once again became sickeningly intense. For the second time he passed out.

Our Father which art in heaven . . .

He had been brought up, like most of his schoolfellows, paying a certain lip-service to the Christian religion. Prayers in the mornings at school. He had taken to saying two prayers at night. One was the Lord's Prayer and the other went God bless Mummy, God bless Daddy, God bless my sisters and brothers and all the dear people that surround me, and God bless me. Amen. That had been taught to him by a woman who looked after him for a while when his mother was at work. He had added to this a list of 'thank-yous' ('Thank you for a lovely day, thank you for getting the history questions right . . .') and 'sorrys' ('Sorry I was rude to Molly Turner, sorry I didn't own up to Mr Matson . . .'). He had been seventeen years old before he had been able to get to sleep without saying the ritual prayers and even then it had been his impatience to masturbate that had finally broken the habit.

Our Father which art in heaven . . .

His last memory of his father concerned a seaside holiday when he had been four or five. The war had been on, the trains had been crowded with soldiers, there had been many stops and changes. He remembered crossing a railway line to get to another platform, asking his father some questions about the contents of the trucks being shunted past in the sunlight. Had there been a joke? Something about giraffes?

He remembered his father as a tall, heavy man. His voice had been kind, perhaps a bit sad, and there had been a melancholy look in his eyes.

He knew now that his mother and father had been breaking up at that time and his mother had allowed his father this last holiday with him. Was it in Devon or Cornwall? What he remembered of the cliffs, rocks and beaches seemed to correspond with scenes of the West Country he had seen on television since.

He had played in an orchard that had been full of cats and a broken-down Ford in which weeds had grown. The farmhouse they had stayed in was also crammed with cats; seas of cats that had covered chairs and tables and dressers.

There had been barbed wire on the beaches, but he had not

realized it spoiled the scenery. There were bridges and statues of sandstone carved by the wind and the sea. There were mysterious caves from which water ran.

It was almost the earliest, and certainly the happiest, memory of his childhood.

He never saw his father again.

God bless Mummy, God bless Daddy . . .

It was silly. He didn't have a daddy, didn't have any brothers and sisters.

The old woman had explained that his daddy was somewhere and that everyone was a brother or a sister.

He had accepted it.

Lonely, he thought. I am lonely. And he woke up briefly thinking he was in the indoor Anderson shelter with its sheets of reddish steel and its wire grating sides, thinking there was an air raid on. He had loved the security of the Anderson. It had been fun getting into it.

But the voices were speaking a foreign language. It was probably night, for it seemed very dark. They were no longer moving. He felt hot. There was straw beneath him. He touched the straw and, without knowing why, felt relieved. He slept.

Screaming. Tension.

His mother was shouting at Mr George upstairs. Mr George and his wife rented the two back rooms of the house.

He called up the stairs to his mother.

'Mummy! Mummy!'

Her hysterical voice: 'What is it?'

'I want to see you!'

He wanted her to stop.

'What is it, Karl? You've woken the child up now!'

She appeared on the landing above him, leaning dramatically on the banister, pulling her dressing-gown about her.

'Mummy. What's the matter?'

She paused for a moment as if in decision, then collapsed slowly down the stairs. She lay at the foot now, on the dark, threadbare carpet. He sobbed and tugged at her shoulders but she was too heavy for him to move. He was panic-stricken. 'Oh, Mummy!'

Mr George came heavily down the stairs. He had a resigned expression. 'Oh, hell,' he said. 'Greta!'

Karl glared at him.

Mr George looked back at Karl and shook his head. 'She's all right, son. Come on, Greta, wake up!'

Karl stood between Mr George and his mother. Mr George shrugged and pushed him aside, then bent and pulled Karl's mother to her feet. Her long, black hair was all over her beautiful, harassed face. She opened her eyes and even Karl was surprised that she had woken up so soon.

'Where am I?' she said.

'Come off it, Greta. You're all right.'

Mr George began to lead her back upstairs.

'What about Karl?' she said.

'Don't worry about him.'

They disappeared.

The house was silent now. Karl went into the kitchen. There was an ironing board set up with an iron on it. Something was cooking on the stove. It didn't smell very nice. It was probably something Mrs George was cooking.

He heard someone descending the stairs and he ran through the kitchen into the garden.

He was crying. He was seven.

2

In those days came John the Baptist, preaching in the wilderness
of Judaea, And saying, Repent ye: for the kingdom of heaven is
at hand. For this is he that was spoken of by the prophet Esaias,
saying, The voice of one crying in the wilderness, Prepare ye
the way of the Lord, make his paths straight. And the same
John had his raiment of camel's hair, and a leathern girdle about
his loins; and his meat was locusts and wild honey. Then went
out to him Jerusalem, and all Judaea, and all the region round
about Jordan, And were baptized of him in Jordan, confessing
their sins.

MATTHEW 3: 1–6

THEY WERE WASHING HIM.

He felt the cold water running over his body and he gasped. They
had stripped off his protective suit and there were now thick layers
of sheepskin against his ribs, bound to him by bands of leather.

There was less pain, but he felt very weak and hot. The mental
confusion of the weeks preceding his entering the time machine, the
journey itself and now the fever made it difficult for him to begin to
understand what was happening to him. Everything had had, for so
long, the quality of a dream. He still could not really believe in the
time machine. Perhaps he was just high on something? His hold on
reality had never been particularly strong; through most of his
adolescence and adult life only certain instincts had enabled him to
preserve his physical well-being. Yet the water pouring over him,
the touch of the sheepskin round his ribs, the straw beneath him, all
had a sharper reality in their way than anything he had known since
he was a child.

He was in a building – or perhaps a cave, it was too gloomy to tell –
and the straw had been saturated by the water.

Two men in sandals and loincloths sluiced water down on him
from their earthenware jars. One wore a length of cotton pushed
back over his shoulders. They both had swarthy Semitic features,
large dark eyes and full beards. Their faces were expressionless,
even when they paused as he looked up at them. For several moments they stared back, holding their water jars to their hairy
chests.

Glogauer's knowledge of ancient written Aramaic was good, but he was not sure of his ability to speak the language in order to make himself understood. He would try English first since it would be ridiculous if he had not moved through time and he tried to speak an archaic tongue to modern Israelis or Arabs.

He said weakly: 'Do you speak English?'

One of the men frowned and the other, with the cotton cloak, began to smile, speaking a few words to his companion and laughing. The other answered in a graver tone.

Glogauer thought he recognized a few words and he began to grin himself. It was ancient Aramaic they were speaking. He was sure of it. He wondered if he could phrase a sentence they might understand.

He cleared his throat. He wet his lips. 'Where – be – this place?' he asked thickly.

Now they both frowned, shaking their heads and lowering their water jars to the ground.

Feeling his energy begin to dissipate, Glogauer said urgently, 'I – seek – a Nazarene – Jesus . . .'

'Nazarene. Jesus.' The taller of the two repeated the words but they did not seem to mean anything to him. He shrugged.

The other, however, only repeated the word Nazarene, uttering it slowly as if it had some special significance for him. He muttered a few words to the other man, then moved away, out of Glogauer's field of vision.

Glogauer tried to sit up and gesture to the remaining man, who looked at him with brooding puzzlement.

'What – year,' Glogauer said slowly, 'doth – the Roman emperor – sit in – Rome?'

It was a confusing question to ask, he realized. Christ had been crucified in the fifteenth year of Tiberius' reign, and that was why he had asked the question. He tried to phrase it better.

'How many – year – doth Tiberius rule?'

'Tiberius!' The man frowned.

Glogauer's ear was adjusting to the accent now and he tried to imitate it better. 'Tiberius. The emperor of the Romans. How many years has he ruled?'

'How many?' The man shook his head. 'I know not.'

At least, thought Glogauer, he had been able to make himself understood. His six months in the British Museum studying Aramaic had been useful, after all. This language was different – perhaps two thousand years earlier – and had closer affinities with

Hebrew, but it had been surprisingly easy to communicate with the man. He remembered how strange it had seemed when he had had none of his usual difficulties when learning this particular language. One or two of his crankier friends had suggested that it was his race memory that served him. At times, he had been almost convinced by the explanation.

'Where is this place?' he asked.

The man looked surprised. 'Why, it is the wilderness,' he said. 'The wilderness beyond Machaerus. Know you not that?'

In biblical times Machaerus had been a large town lying to the south-east of Jerusalem, on the other side of the Dead Sea. It had been built on the flanks of a mountain, guarded by a magnificent palace-fortress constructed by Herod Antipas. Again Glogauer felt his spirits rise. In the twentieth century few would have known the name of Machaerus, let alone used it as a reference point.

There was almost no doubt at all that he was in the past and that the period was some time in the reign of Tiberius, unless the man he spoke to was completely ignorant and had no idea who Tiberius was.

But had he missed the crucifixion? Had he come at the wrong time?

If so, what was he to do now? For his time machine was wrecked, was perhaps beyond repair.

He let himself sink back on to the straw and closed his eyes, and a familiar sense of depression once again completely filled him.

The first time he had tried to commit suicide he had been fifteen. He had tied string round a hook half-way up the wall in the locker room at school. He had placed the noose around his neck and jumped off the bench.

The hook had been torn away from the wall, bringing with it a shower of plaster. His neck had felt sore for the rest of the day.

The other man was now returning, bringing someone else with him.

The sound of their sandals on the stone seemed very loud to Glogauer.

He looked up at the newcomer.

He was a giant and he moved like a cat through the gloom. His eyes were large, piercing and brown. His skin was burned dark and his hairy arms were heavily muscled. A goatskin covered his great barrel chest and reached to below his thighs. In his right hand he carried a thick staff. His black, curly hair hung around his head and face; his red lips could be seen beneath the bushy beard that covered the upper part of his chest.

He seemed tired.

He leaned on his staff and looked reflectively at Glogauer.

Glogauer stared back at him, astonished at the impression he had of the man's tremendous physical presence.

When the newcomer spoke, it was in a deep voice, but too rapidly for Glogauer to follow. He shook his head.

'Speak – more slowly . . .' he said.

The big man squatted down beside him.

'Who art thou?'

Glogauer hesitated. Obviously he could not tell the man the truth. He had, in fact, already invented what seemed to him a plausible story, but he had not planned to be found in this way and the original story would not do. He had hoped to land unseen and disguise himself as a traveller from Syria, counting on the chance that the local accents would be different enough to explain his own unfamiliarity with the language.

'From where do you come?' asked the man patiently.

Glogauer answered cautiously.

'I am from the north.'

'The north. Not from Egypt?' He looked at Glogauer expectantly, almost hopefully. Glogauer decided that if he sounded as if he came from Egypt, then it would be best to agree with the man, adding his own embellishment in order to avoid any future complications.

'I came out of Egypt two years since,' he said.

The big man nodded, apparently satisfied. 'So you are from Egypt. That is what we thought. And evidently you are a magus with your strange clothes and your chariot of iron drawn by spirits. Good. Your name is Jesus, I am told, and you are the Nazarene.'

Evidently the man must have mistaken Glogauer's enquiry as a statement of his own name. He smiled and shook his head.

'I seek Jesus, the Nazarene,' he said.

The man seemed disappointed. 'Then, what is your name?'

Glogauer had also considered this. He knew his own name would seem too outlandish to the people of biblical times and so he had decided to use his father's first name.

'My name is Emmanuel,' he told the man.

'Emmanuel . . .' He nodded, seeming satisfied. He rubbed his lips with the tip of his little finger and stared contemplatively at the ground. 'Emmanuel . . . yes . . .'

Glogauer was puzzled. It seemed to him that he had been mistaken for someone else that the big man had been expecting, that he had given answers that satisfied the man that he, Glogauer, was the man for whom he waited. He wondered now if the choice of name had been wise in the circumstances, for Emmanuel meant in Hebrew 'God with us' and almost certainly had a mystic significance for his questioner.

Glogauer began to feel uncomfortable. There were things he had to establish for himself, questions of his own to ask, and he did not like his present position. Until he was in better physical condition, he could not leave here, could not afford to anger his interrogator. At least, he thought, they were not antagonistic. But what did they expect of him?

'You must try to concentrate on your work, Glogauer.'

'You're too dreamy, Glogauer. Your head's always in the clouds. Now . . .'

'You'll stay behind after school, Glogauer . . .'

'Why did you try to run away, Glogauer? Why aren't you happy here?'

'Really, you must meet me half-way if we're going to . . .'

'I think I shall have to ask your mother to take you away from the school . . .'

'Perhaps you are trying – but you must try harder. I expected a great deal of you, Glogauer, when you first came here. Last term you were doing wonderfully, and now . . .'

'How many schools were you at before you came here? Good heavens!'

'It's my belief that you were led into this, Glogauer, so I shan't be too hard on you this time . . .'

'Don't look so miserable, son – you can do it.'

'Listen to me, Glogauer. Pay attention, for heaven's sake . . .'

'You've got the brains, young man, but you don't seem to have the application . . .'

'Sorry? It's not good enough to be sorry. You must listen . . .'

'We expect you to try much harder next term.'

'And what is your name?' Glogauer asked the squatting man.

He straightened up, looking broodingly down on Glogauer.

'You do not know me?'

Glogauer shook his head.

'You have not heard of John, called the Baptist?'

Glogauer tried to hide his surprise, but evidently John the Baptist saw that his name was familiar. He nodded his shaggy head.

'You do know of me, I see.'

A sense of relief swept through him then. According to the New Testament, the Baptist had been killed some time before Christ's crucifixion. It was strange, however, that John of all people had not heard of Jesus of Nazareth. Did that mean, after all, that Christ had not existed?

The Baptist combed at his beard with his fingers. 'Well, magus, now I must decide, eh?'

Glogauer, concerned with his own thoughts, looked up at him absently. 'What must you decide?'

'If you be the friend of the prophecies or the false one we have been warned against by Adonai.'

Glogauer became nervous. 'I have made no claims. I am merely a stranger, a traveller . . .'

The Baptist laughed. 'Aye – a traveller in a magic chariot. My brothers tell me they saw it arrive. There was a sound like thunder, a flash like lightning – and all at once your chariot was there, rolling across the wilderness. They have seen many wonders, my brothers, but none so marvellous as the appearance of your chariot.'

'The chariot is not magic,' Glogauer said hastily, realizing that what he said could hardly be understood by the Baptist. 'It is – a kind of engine – the Romans have such things. You must have heard of them. They are made by ordinary men, not sorcerers . . .'

The Baptist nodded his head slowly. 'Aye – like the Romans. The Romans would deliver me into the hands of my enemies, the children of Herod.'

Although he knew a great deal about the politics of the period, Glogauer said: 'Why is that?'

'You must know why. Do I not speak against the Romans who enslave Judaea? Do I not speak against the unlawful things that Herod does? Do I not prophesy the time when all those who are not righteous shall be destroyed and Adonai's kingdom will be restored on Earth as the old prophets said it would be? I say to the people, "Be ready for that day when ye shall take up the sword to do Adonai's will." The unrighteous know that they will perish on this day, and they would destroy me.'

Although John's words were fiery, his tone was perfectly matter-of-fact. There was no hint of insanity or even fanaticism in his face or bearing. Karl was reminded of an Anglican vicar reading a familiar sermon whose meaning for him had long since lost its edge.

'You are arousing the people to rid the land of the Romans, is that it?' Karl asked.

'Aye – the Romans and their creature Herod.'

'And who would you put in their place?'

'The rightful king of Judaea.'

'And who is that?'

John frowned and gave him a peculiar, sidelong look. 'Adonai will tell us. He will give us a sign when the rightful king comes.'

'Do you know what the sign will be?'

'I will know when it comes.'

'There are prophecies, then?'

'Aye, there are prophecies . . .'

The attribution of this revolutionary plan to Adonai (one of the spoken names of Jahweh and meaning The Lord) seemed to Glogauer merely a means of giving it extra weight. In a world where politics and religion, even in the West, were inextricably bound together, it was necessary to ascribe a supernatural origin to the plan.

Indeed, Glogauer thought, it was more than likely that John really did believe his idea had been directly inspired by God, for the Greeks on the other side of the Mediterranean had not yet stopped arguing about the origins of inspiration – whether it originated in man or was placed there by the gods.

That John accepted him as an Egyptian magician of some kind did not particularly surprise Glogauer, either. The circumstances of his arrival must have seemed extraordinarily miraculous and at the same time acceptable, particularly to a people who eagerly wished confirmation of their beliefs in such things.

John turned towards the entrance. 'I must meditate,' he said. 'I must pray. You will remain here until guidance is sent to me.'

He strode rapidly away.

Glogauer sank back on the wet straw. Somehow his appearance was bound up with John's beliefs – or at least the Baptist was attempting to reconcile that appearance with his beliefs, interpret his arrival, perhaps, in terms of biblical prophecies and so forth. Glogauer felt helpless. How would the Baptist use him? Would he decide, finally, that he was some kind of malign creature and kill him? Or would he decide that he was a prophet of some description and demand prophecies he would not be able to give?

Glogauer sighed and reached out weakly to touch the far wall.

It was limestone. He was in a limestone cave. Caves suggested that John and his men were probably in hiding – already sought as bandits by the Romans and Herodian soldiers. This meant that he was also in ordinary physical danger if the soldiers should discover John's hideout.

The atmosphere in the cave was surprisingly humid.

It must be very hot outside.

He felt drowsy.

The summer camp, Isle of Wight, 1950

The first night he was there an urn of scalding tea had been over-turned on his right thigh. It had been horribly painful, blistering almost at once.

'Be a man, Glogauer!' said a red-faced Mr Patrick, the master in charge of the camp. 'Be a man!'

He tried not to cry as they clumsily stretched plaster over the cotton-wool.

His sleeping bag was right beside an anthill. He lay in it while the other children played.

The next day Mr Patrick told the children that they had to 'earn' the pocket-money the parents had given him for safe-keeping.

'We'll see which of you children have guts and which haven't,' said Mr Patrick, swishing the cane through the air as he stood in the clearing around which the tents were grouped. The children stood in two long lines – one for the girls, one for the boys.

'Get in line, Glogauer!' called Mr Patrick. 'Threepence a stroke on the hand – sixpence a stroke on the bottom. Don't be cowardly, Glogauer!'

Reluctantly, Glogauer joined the line.

The cane rose and fell. Mr Patrick breathed heavily.

'Six strokes on the bottom – that's three shillings.' He handed the money to the little girl.

More strokes, more money paid out.

Karl became nervous as his turn came closer.

Finally he broke out of line and walked away towards the tents.

'Glogauer! Where's your spirit, boy? Don't you want any pocket-money?' came Mr Patrick's coarse, bantering voice behind him.

Glogauer shook his head, beginning to cry.

Glogauer entered his tent and threw himself on his sleeping bag, sobbing.

Mr Patrick's voice could still be heard outside.

'Be a man, Glogauer! Be a man, boy!'

Karl began to take out his writing-paper and ballpoint pen. His tears fell on the paper as he wrote the letter home to his mother.

Outside he could hear the sound of the cane smacking against the children's flesh.

The pain in his thigh got worse during the next day and he was generally ignored by the masters and the children. Even the woman who was supposed to be 'matron' (Patrick's wife) told him to look after himself, that the scald was nothing.

The following two days, before his mother arrived to collect him from the camp, were the most miserable he had ever suffered.

Shortly before his mother's arrival, Mrs Patrick made an attempt to cut off the blisters with a pair of nail scissors so that they wouldn't look too bad.

His mother took him away and later wrote to Mr Patrick asking for her money back, saying that it was disgusting the way he ran his camp.

He wrote back saying that he would not return the money and that if she asked him, madam, she had a weakling for a son. If you want my opinion, he said in the letter that Karl read when he got the chance, your son's a bit of a pansy.

A few years later, Mr Patrick, his wife and staff, were prosecuted and sent to prison for their various acts of sadism during the summer camps they ran on the Isle of Wight.

3

IN THE MORNINGS, AND SOMETIMES IN the evenings, they would pick him up on his stretcher and take him outside.

This was not, as he had first suspected, a transitory bandit camp, but an established community. There were fields irrigated by a nearby spring in which they grew corn; flocks of goats and sheep which were pastured in the hills.

Their life was quiet and leisurely, and for the most part they ignored Glogauer as they went about their daily business.

Sometimes the Baptist would appear and ask after his health. More rarely he would ask some cryptic question which Glogauer would answer as best he could.

They seemed a gentle people, given to considerably more minor religious rites than Glogauer would have thought normal for even such a community as this. At least, he gathered that they were religious rites that they were called to so frequently, for they were conducted where he could not see them.

Glogauer was left chiefly with his own thoughts, his memories and his speculations. His ribs healed very slowly and he began to fret, wondering if he would ever achieve the goal he had come here for.

Glogauer was surprised at how few women there were in the community. The atmosphere was almost that of a monastery and most of the men avoided the women. He began to realize that this was probably very much a religious community. Perhaps these people were Essenes?

If they were Essenes it would explain a number of things about them – absence, in the main, of women (few Essenes believed in marriage), John's particular apocalyptic beliefs, the preponderance of religious observances, the rigidly simple life these people led, the fact that they seemed deliberately to have set themselves apart from others . . .

Glogauer put it to the Baptist the next chance he got.

'John – are your people called Essenes?'

The Baptist nodded.

'How did you know that?' he asked Glogauer.

'I – I had heard of you. Are you outlawed by Herod?'

John shook his head. 'Herod would outlaw us if he dared, but he has no cause. We lead our own lives, harming no one, making no attempt to enforce our beliefs on others. From time to time I go out and preach our creed – but there is no law against that. We respect the commandments of Moses and only preach that others should obey them. We speak only for righteousness. Even Herod cannot find fault with that . . .'

Now Glogauer understood better the nature of some of the questions John had been asking him; understood why these people behaved and lived in the way they did.

He realized, too, how it was that they had accepted the manner of his arrival with so little fuss. A sect like the Essenes, which practised self-mortification and starvation, must be quite used to seeing visions in this hot wilderness.

He remembered, also, that he had once come across a theory that John the Baptist had been an Essene and that many of the early Christian ideas had been derived from Essene beliefs.

The Essenes, for instance, indulged in ritual bathing – baptism; they believed in a group of twelve (the apostles) who were the elect of God and would be judges on the last day; they preached a creed of 'love thy neighbour'; they believed, as the early Christians had believed, that they were living in the days immediately before Armageddon when the final battle between light and darkness, good and evil, would be fought and when all men would be brought to judgement. As with certain Christian sects, there were Essenes who believed that they represented the forces of light and that others – Herod or the Roman conquerors – represented the forces of darkness and that it was their destiny to destroy these forces. These political beliefs were inextricably bound up with the religious beliefs and although it was possible that someone like John the Baptist was cynically using the Essenes to further his own political ends, it was really quite unlikely.

In twentieth-century terms, Glogauer thought, these Essenes would be regarded as neurotics, with their almost paranoiac mysticism that led them to invent secret languages and the like – a sure indication of their mentally unbalanced condition.

All this occurred to Glogauer the psychiatrist manqué, but Glogauer the man was torn between the poles of extreme rationalism and the desire to be convinced by the mysticism itself.

The Baptist had wandered away before Glogauer could ask him any further questions. He watched the tall man as he disappeared inside a large cave, then turned his attention to the distant fields where a thin Essene guided a plough pulled by two other members of the sect.

Glogauer studied the yellow hills and the rocks. He was becoming eager to see more of this world and at the same time wondering what had become of his time machine. Was it in complete disrepair? Would he ever be able to leave this period of time and return to the twentieth century?

Sex and religion.

The church club he had joined to find friends.

A nature ramble, 1954

He and Veronica had lost the others in Farlowe's Wood.

She was fat and blowsy even at thirteen, but she was a girl.

'Let's sit here and rest,' he said, indicating a hillock in a little glade surrounded by shrubs.

They sat down together.

They said nothing.

His eyes fixed not on her round, coarse-skinned face, but on the little silver crucifix that dangled by a chain about her neck.

'We'd better start looking for the others,' she said nervously. 'They'll be worrying about us, Karl.'

'Let them find us,' he said. 'We'll soon hear them shouting.'

'They might go home.'

'They won't go without us. Don't worry. We'll hear them shouting . . .'

He lurched forward, reaching for her navy-blue cardigan-clad shoulders, his eyes still fixed on the crucifix.

He tried to kiss her lips but she turned her head away. 'Give us a kiss, then,' he said breathlessly. Even at that moment he realized how ludicrous he sounded, what a fool he was making of himself, but he forced himself to continue. 'Give us a kiss, Veronica . . .'

'No, Karl. Stop it.'

'Come on . . .'

She began to struggle, broke away from him and got to her feet. He was blushing now.

'Sorry,' he said. 'Sorry.'

'All right . . .'

'I thought you wanted to,' he said.

'You needn't've jumped at me like that. Not very romantic.'

'Sorry . . .'

She began to walk away, the crucifix swinging. He was fascinated by it. Did it represent some sort of amulet to ward off the sort of danger she probably considered she'd just avoided?

He followed her.

Soon they heard the shouts of the others through the trees and Karl inexplicably felt sick.

Several of the other girls began to giggle and one of the boys leered.

'What've you been up to, then?'

'Nothing,' said Karl.

But Veronica didn't say anything. Although she hadn't been prepared to kiss him, she was obviously enjoying the insinuations.

She held his hand on the way back.

It was dark when they returned to the church and had a cup of tea. They sat together. All the time he stared at the crucifix that hung between her already large breasts.

The others had all gathered together at the other end of the bare church hall. Sometimes Karl heard one of the girls giggle and saw a boy glance in their direction. He began to feel quite pleased with himself. He moved closer to her.

'Can I get you another cup of tea, Veronica?'

She was staring at the floor. 'No, thanks. I'd better be getting back. My mum and dad'll be worrying about me.'

'I'll see you home if you like.'

She hesitated.

'It's not far out of my way,' he said.

'All right.'

They got up and he took her hand, waving to the others.

'Cheerio, everybody. See you Thursday,' he said.

The girls' laughter grew uncontrollable and he blushed again.

'Don't do anything I wouldn't do,' shouted one of the boys.

Karl winked at him.

They walked through the well lit suburban streets, both too embarrassed to speak, her hand limp in his.

When they reached her front door she paused, then said hastily, 'I'd better be getting in.'

'Aren't you going to give me a kiss now?' he asked. He was still staring at the crucifix on her navy-blue cardigan.

She pecked hastily at his cheek.

'You can do better than that,' he said.

'I've got to be getting in now.'

'Come on,' he said, 'give us a proper kiss.' He was close to panic, blushing heavily and sweating. He reached towards her, forcing himself to hold her arms although now he was beginning to be nauseated by her fat, coarse face and heavy, lumpen body.

'No!'

The light went on behind the door and he heard her father's voice growling in the hall.

'That you, Veronica?'

He dropped his hands. 'Okay, if you're going to be like that,' he said.

'I'm sorry,' she began, 'it's just that . . .'

The door opened and a man in shirt-sleeves stood there. He was as fat and as coarse-featured as his daughter.

''Ullo, 'ullo,' he said, 'got a boyfriend then, have you?'

'This is Karl,' she said. 'He brought me home. He's at the club.'

'You could 'ave brought her home a bit earlier, young man,' said her father. 'Want to come in for a cup of tea or something?'

'No, thanks,' said Karl. 'Got to be getting back. Cheerio, Veronica. See you Thursday.'

'Maybe,' she said.

The following Thursday he arrived at the club for the Bible discussion group. Veronica wasn't there.

'Her dad's stopped her,' one of the girls told him. 'Must've been because of you.' She spoke contemptuously and he was puzzled.

'We hardly did anything,' he said.

'That's what she said,' the girl told him, smiling. 'She said you weren't much good at it.'

'What d'you mean? She wouldn't . . .'

'She said you didn't know how to kiss properly.'

'She didn't give me the chance.'

'That's what she said, anyway,' said the girl and glanced at the others.

Karl knew they were baiting him, even sensed that they were, in their way, flirting with him, were intrigued with him, but he couldn't stop himself blushing and he left the discussion group early.

He never went back to the church club, but his masturbatory fantasies of the next few weeks were filled with Veronica and the little silver cross hanging between her breasts. Even when he imagined her naked, the cross remained there. It was this, in fact, that began chiefly to excite him, and long after Veronica was gone from his dreams, he would think of girls with small silver crucifixes hanging between their breasts and the thought would arouse him to incredible excesses of pleasure.

4

In the beginning was the Word, and the Word was with God, and the Word was God. The same was in the beginning with God. All things were made by him; and without him was not any thing made that was made. In him was life; and the life was the light of men. And the light shineth in the darkness; and the darkness comprehended it not. There was a man sent from God, whose name was John. The same came for a witness, to bear witness of the Light, that all men through him might believe. He was not that Light, but was sent to bear witness of that Light. That was the true Light, which lighteth every man that cometh into the world. He was in the world, and the world was made by him, and the world knew him not. He came unto his own, and his own received him not. But as many as received him, to them gave he power to become the sons of God, even to them that believe on his name: Which were born, not of blood, not of the will of the flesh, nor of the will of man, but of God.

JOHN 1: 1–13

Lonely, lonely, lonely . . .
    Oh, Jesus . . .
        Stop!
                Fo-ol
STOP   fo
        STOP   ol   NO!
    Jes . . .
        STOP
        I love you . . .STOP.
Jesus, I . . .   STOP
        Lonely . . .
        Lonely . . .
        des . . .need . . .must lo –
        STOP
        lonely, lonely, lonely . . .
        Oh, lonely, lonely . . .

Acne. Washing. Lonely. Rationalism. Fucking a huge silver cross.

His ribs were mending.

In the evenings, now, he would limp to the entrance of his cave and listen to the chanting of the Essenes as they offered up their evening prayer. For some obscure reason, the monotonous chanting would bring tears to his eyes and he would begin to sob uncontrollably.

At this stage of his recovery, he was often filled with depressions that would make him think of suicide.

He had turned on all the gas fires in the house and had timed things to coincide with his mother's return from work.

Just before she opened the front gate and walked up the path to unlock the door, he lay down in the sitting-room before the main fire.

When she had come in she had screamed, picked him up, put him on the sofa and had broken every single window in the downstairs part of the house before she thought to turn the fires off and call the doctor.

When the doctor came, she had a story for him – about an accident. But the doctor had seemed to know all about it. He had been none too sympathetic with Karl.

'You're after the limelight, young man,' he said when Karl's mother was out of the room. 'You're after the limelight, if you ask me.'

Karl had begun to cry.

'We'll go on holiday,' his mother said, when the doctor had left. 'What's the matter? Not getting on well at school? We'll go on holiday.'

'It's nothing to do with school,' he sobbed.

'Then what is it?'

'It's *you* . . .'

'Me? Me? Why me? What have I got to do with it? What are you trying to say?'

'Nothing.' He became sullen.

'I must phone the people to come and put the glass in,' she said, hurrying from the room. 'It'll cost a fortune.'

Love me, love me, love me . . .

Lonely . . .

Our Father which art in heaven, hallowed be thy name, thy kingdom come . . .

LOVE ME!

★

Floating, bigger than the world, little circumcised cock in hand, silver clouds shaped like great, soft crosses, drifting, drifting, coming, coming . . .

LOVE ME!

Bill Haley and his Comets. See ya later, alligator. And for three and a half months, God was forgotten.

For a month, John the Baptist was away and Glogauer lived with the Essenes, finding it surprisingly easy, as his health improved, to join in their daily life.

He discovered that the Essene township consisted of a sprawling mixture of single-storey houses, built of limestone and clay brick, and the caves that were to be found on both sides of the shallow valley. Some of the caves were natural, and others had been hallowed out by previous occupants of the valley and by the Essenes themselves.

The Essenes shared their goods in common and some members of this particular sect had, as Glogauer had noticed earlier, wives, though most of them led completely monastic lives.

Glogauer learned to his surprise that most of the Essenes were pacifists, refusing to own or to make weapons. Their beliefs did not quite fit in with some of the Baptist's more warlike pronouncements, yet the sect plainly tolerated and revered John.

Perhaps their hatred of the Romans overcame their principles. Perhaps they were not absolutely sure of John's intentions. Possibly he had been deliberately obscure on this point – or maybe Glogauer had failed to understand him. Whatever the reason for their toleration of him, however, there was little doubt that John the Baptist was virtually their leader.

The life of the Essenes consisted of ritual bathing three times a day, of prayer with all meals and at dawn and at dusk, and of work.

The work was not difficult.

Sometimes Glogauer guided a plough pulled by two other members of the sect; sometimes he helped pull a plough; sometimes he looked after the goats that were allowed to graze on the hillsides.

It was a peaceful, ordered life, and even the unhealthy aspects were so much a matter of routine that Glogauer hardly noticed them after a while.

Tending the goats, he would lie on the hilltop, looking out over the wilderness. The wilderness was not a desert, but rocky scrubland sufficient to feed animals like goats or sheep.

The scrubland was broken by low-lying bushes and a few small trees growing along the banks of the river that doubtless ran into the Dead Sea.

It was uneven ground. In outline it had the appearance of a stormy lake, frozen and turned yellow and brown.

Beyond the Dead Sea lay Jerusalem.

Glogauer thought often of Jerusalem.

Obviously Christ had not yet entered the city for the last time.

John the Baptist (if the New Testament could be relied upon) would have to die before that happened. Salome would have to dance for Herod and the Baptist's great head would have to be severed from its body.

Glogauer felt guilty at the way in which the thought excited him. Should he not warn the Baptist?

He knew that he would not. He had been specifically warned before he entered the time machine that he should make no attempt to alter the course of history. He argued to himself that he had no clear idea of the course that the history of this time had taken. There were only legends, no purely historical records. The books of the New Testament had been written decades or even centuries after the events which they described. They had never been historically authenticated. Surely, then, it made no difference if he interfered with events?

But he still knew that he would make no attempt to warn John of his danger.

He realized dimly that the reason for this was because he wanted the events to be true. He wanted the New Testament to be right.

Soon he must begin to seek out Jesus.

His mother moved frequently, although she tended to remain in roughly the same area, selling a house in one part of South London and buying a house half a mile away.

After his brief phase as a rock-and-roll fan, they moved to Thornton Heath and he joined the choir of the local church. His voice was good and tuneful, and the curate who took choir practice began to show a special interest in him. Initially they discussed music, but soon their conversations would turn more and more to religion. Karl would ask the curate for advice on his rather general problems of conscience. How could he live an ordinary life of ordinary activity without hurting anyone's feelings? Why were people so violent to each other? Why were there wars?

Mr Younger's answers were just about as woolly and as general as Karl's questions, but he gave them in a deep, confident, reassuring voice that always made Karl feel better.

They went for walks together. Mr Younger would put his arm around Karl's shoulders.

One week-end the choir went to Winchester for a festival and they stayed at a youth hostel. Karl shared a room with Mr Younger.

Late at night Mr Younger crawled into Karl's bed.

'I wish you were a girl, Karl,' said Mr Younger, stroking Karl's head.

Karl was too disturbed to reply, but he responded when Mr Younger put his hand on his genitals.

They made love all that night, but in the morning Karl felt disgusted and punched Mr Younger in the chest and said that if he ever tried anything again he would tell his mother.

Mr Younger cried and said he was sorry, couldn't he and Karl continue to be friends, but Karl felt that somehow Mr Younger had betrayed him. Mr Younger said that he loved Karl – not in that way, but in a Christian way – and that he had enjoyed his company so much. But Karl wouldn't speak to him and avoided him in the coach on the way home to Thornton Heath.

Karl stayed in the choir for a few weeks more, but there was tension between him and Mr Younger.

At the end of an evening choir practice, Mr Younger asked Karl to stay behind and Karl was torn between disgust and desire.

Finally he did stay behind and let Mr Younger stroke his genitals under a poster which showed a plain wooden cross with the slogan GOD IS LOVE underneath.

Karl began to laugh hysterically and ran away from the church and never went back again.

He was fifteen.

Silver crosses equal women.

Wooden crosses equal men.

He often thought of himself as a wooden cross. He would have mild hallucinations between sleeping and waking where he was a heavy wooden cross pursuing a delicate silver cross through fields of darkness.

By seventeen he had completely lost interest in formal Christianity and became obsessed with pagan religion, particularly Celtic mysticism and Mithraism. He had had an affair with the wife of a sergeant-major who lived in Kilburn and whom he had met at a party given by a woman he had met through the correspondence columns of the short-lived magazine *Avilion*.

The wife of the sergeant-major (he was somewhere in the Far East) had worn a small silver Celtic cross, a 'sun cross', about her neck and that was what had first attracted him. It had taken him half a bottle of gin, however, before he had dared put his arm around her thin shoulders and later, in the darkness, put his hand between her thighs and feel her cunt beneath the satinette knickers.

After Deirdre Thompson, he had success after success with the plain-faced women of the group, all of whom, he discovered, wore exactly the same kind of satinette knickers.

Within six months he was exhausted, hating the neurotic women, loathing himself, bored with Celtic mysticism. He had been living away from home most of the time, mainly at Deirdre Thompson's house, but now he went home and had a nervous breakdown.

His mother decided he needed a change and gave him the fare to visit some friends he had made in Hamburg.

His Hamburg friends believed that they were the descendants of those who had perished when Atlantis was destroyed by atom bombs dropped from flying saucers by unsympathetic spirits from Mars.

There was a succession of plain-faced German women this time. Unlike their British sisters, they all wore black nylon lace panties.

It made a change.

In Hamburg he became militantly anti-Christian, claiming that Christianity was the perversion of an older faith, a Nordic faith.

But he could never quite accept that this faith in its purest form had been the faith of Atlantis, and at last he fell out with his German friends, found the rest of Germany generally unsympathetic, and left for Tel Aviv where he knew the owner of a bookshop specializing in works of occult lore, mainly in French.

It was in Tel Aviv, in conversation with a Hungarian painter, that he learnt of Jung and dismissed him as nonsense. He became even more withdrawn and one morning took a bus into the rural near-desert. Eventually he wound up in the Ante-Lebanon where the people spoke the closest thing to ancient Aramaic he had ever heard. He found them hospitable; he enjoyed living with them. He lived with them for four months before he returned to Tel Aviv and, in a receptive frame of mind, talked about Jung again with the Hungarian. In the occult bookshop and in the other bookshops and libraries of Tel Aviv, he could discover nothing of Jung's in English. He decided to leave for England and borrowed the fare from the British consulate.

As soon as he got back to South London he went to the local library and spent a lot of time there reading Jung.

His mother asked him when he was going to get a job.

He told her that he intended to study psychology and would eventually become a psychiatrist.

The Essenes' way of life was comfortable enough, for all its simplicity.

They had given him a goatskin loincloth and a staff and, except for the fact that he was watched all the time, they appeared to have accepted him as a kind of lay member of the sect.

Sometimes they questioned him casually about his chariot – the time machine they intended soon to bring in from the desert – and he told them that it had borne him from Egypt to Syria and then to here. They accepted the miracle calmly. They were used to miracles.

The Essenes had seen stranger things than his time machine.

They had seen men walk on water and angels descend to and from heaven; they had heard the voice of God and his archangels as well as the tempting voice of Satan and his minions.

They wrote all these things down in their vellum scrolls which were merely a record of the supernatural, as their other scrolls were records of their daily lives and of the news that travelling members of their sect brought to them.

They lived constantly in the presence of God and spoke to God and were answered by God when they had sufficiently mortified their flesh and starved themselves and chanted their prayers beneath the blazing sun of Judaea.

Karl Glogauer grew his hair long and let his beard come unchecked. His face and body were soon burned dark by the sun. He mortified his flesh and starved himself and chanted his prayers beneath the sun, as they did.

But he rarely heard God and only once thought he saw an archangel with wings of fire.

One day they took him to the river and baptized him with the name he had first given John the Baptist. They called him

Emmanuel.

The ceremony, with its chanting and its swaying, was very heady and left him completely euphoric and happier than he had ever remembered.

5

IN SPITE OF HIS WILLINGNESS TO experience the Essenes' visions, Glogauer was disappointed.

On the other hand he was surprised that he felt so well considering all the self-inflicted hardships he had undergone. Also he felt relaxed in the company of these strange men and women who were, he had to admit, undoubtedly insane by any normal standard. Perhaps it was because their insanity was not so very different from his own that after a while he stopped wondering about it.

Monica.

Monica had no silver cross.

They had first met when he was working at Darley Grange Mental Hospital as a male orderly. He had thought that he would be able to work his way up. She was a psychiatric social worker who had seemed more sympathetic than the rest when he had been trying to get someone to listen to him about the hardships the patients were made to undergo, the petty torments that other orderlies and nurses put them through, the blows, the shouts.

'We can't get the right sort of staff, you see,' she had told him. 'The money's so low . . .'

'Then they ought to pay more.'

Instead of shrugging, as the others did, she had nodded. 'I know. I've written two letters to the *Guardian* about it – not signing my name, you know – and one of them was published.'

He had left shortly afterwards and didn't see her for some years.

He was twenty.

John the Baptist returned one evening, striding over the hills, followed by twenty or so of his closest disciples.

Glogauer saw him as he prepared to drive the goats into their cave for the night. He waited for John to approach him.

At first the Baptist did not recognize him and then he laughed.

'Well, Emmanuel, you have become an Essene, I see. Have they baptized you yet?'

Glogauer nodded. 'They have.'

'Good.' The Baptist frowned then, as some other thought occurred to him. 'I have been to Jerusalem,' he said. 'To see friends.'

'And what is the news from Jerusalem?'

The Baptist looked at him candidly. 'That you are probably not a spy of Herod or the Romans.'

'I am glad you have decided that,' smiled Glogauer.

John's grim expression softened. He smiled and grasped him by the upper arm in the Roman fashion.

'So – you are our friend. Perhaps more than just our friend . . .'

Glogauer frowned. 'I do not follow you.' He was relieved that the Baptist, who had plainly spent all this time carefully checking that Glogauer was not in the pay of his enemies, had decided he was a friend.

'I think you know what I mean,' John said.

Glogauer was tired. He had eaten very little and had spent most of the day in the sun, tending the goats. He yawned and could not bring himself to pursue the question.

'I do not . . .' he began.

John's face clouded for a moment, then he laughed awkwardly. 'Say nothing now. Eat with me tonight. I have wild honey and locusts.'

Glogauer had not yet eaten this food, which was the staple of travellers who did not carry provisions but lived off the food they could find on the journey. Some regarded it as a delicacy.

'Thank you,' he said. 'Tonight.'

John smiled at him, a mysterious smile, then strode on, followed by his men.

Puzzling, Glogauer drove the goats into their caves and closed the wicker gate to keep them in. Then he crossed the clearing to his own cave and lay down on the straw.

Evidently the Baptist saw him as fulfilling some role in his own scheme of things.

All the grass, all the trees, all the sunny days with Eva, sweet, virginal, admiring. He had met her in Oxford at a party given by Gerard Friedman, the journalist who specialized in books on the supernatural.

The next day they had walked beside the Isis, looking at the barges moored on the opposite bank, the boys fishing, the spires of the colleges in the distance.

She was concerned.

'You mustn't worry so much, Karl. Nothing's perfect. Can't you take life as it comes?'

She was the first girl who had ever made him feel relaxed. He had laughed. 'I suppose so. Why not?'

She was so warm. Her blonde hair was long and fine, often falling over her face, hiding her large blue eyes that were always so candid, whether she was serious or amused.

For those few weeks he had taken life as it came. They slept together in his little attic room at Friedman's place, not even disturbed by Friedman's salacious interest in their affair, unbothered by the letters she sometimes received from her parents asking her when she was coming home.

She was eighteen, in her first year at Somerville, and it was vacation time.

It was the first time he could ever remember being loved by anyone. She was completely in love with him and he with her. At first her passion and her concern for him had embarrassed him, made him feel suspicious, for he could not believe that anyone could feel such love for him. Gradually he had accepted it, returned it. When apart they wrote not very good love poetry to each other.

'You're so good, Karl,' she would say. 'You'll really do something marvellous in the world.'

He would laugh. 'The only talent I've got is for self-pity . . .'

'Self-awareness – that's different.'

He would try to argue her out of her idealized picture of him, but this only convinced her of his modesty.

'You're like – like Parsifal . . .' she told him one night, and he laughed aloud, saw that he had hurt her and kissed her on the forehead.

'Don't be silly, Eva.'

'I mean it, Karl. You're looking for the Holy Grail. And you'll find it.'

He had been impressed by her faith in him, began to wonder if she were right. Perhaps he did have a destiny. She made him feel so heroic. He basked in her worship.

He did some research work for Friedman and earned enough money to buy her a small silver ankh to hang about her neck. She had been delighted by it. She was studying Comparative Religion and was at that time particularly enthusiastic about the Egyptians.

But he was not content for long to enjoy her love for him. He had to test it; make sure of it. He began to get drunk in the evenings, telling her dirty stories, picking fights in pubs – fights, he made it plain, that he was too cowardly to follow through with.

And she began to withdraw from him.

'You're making me nervous,' she explained sorrowfully. 'You make me feel so tense.'

'What's the matter? Can't you love me for myself? This is what I'm like, you know. I'm not Parsifal.'

'You're letting yourself down, Karl.'

'I'm just trying to show you what I'm really like.'

'But you're not really like that. You're sweet – good – kind . . .'

'I'm a self-pitying failure. Take it or leave it.'

She left it. She went home to her parents two days later. He wrote to her and received no reply. He went to see her and her parents said she was out.

For several months he was filled with a terrible sense of loss, of bewilderment. Why had he deliberately destroyed their relationship? Because he wanted her to accept him as he was, not as she imagined him to be. But suppose she were right? Had he deliberately rejected the chance to be something better? He could not tell.

One of the Baptist's followers came for him an hour later and led him to the house on the other side of the valley.

There were only two rooms in the house: one for eating and one for sleeping.

John greeted him in the barely furnished dining-room. He gestured for him to sit on the cotton mat on the other side of the low table on which the food had been placed.

He sat down and crossed his legs. On the other side of the table John smiled and waved his hand at the food. 'Begin.'

The honey and locusts was too sweet for his taste, but it was a welcome change from barley or goat meat.

John the Baptist ate with relish. Night had fallen and the room was lit by lamps consisting of wicks floating in bowls of oil. From outside came low murmurs and the moans and cries of those at prayer.

Glogauer dipped another locust into the bowl of honey. 'Why did you wish to see me, John?'

'Because it is time.'

'Time for what? Do you plan to lead the people of Judaea in revolt against the Romans?'

The Baptist seemed disturbed by the direct question. It was the first of its nature that Glogauer had put to him.

'If it be Adonai's will,' he said, not looking up as he leant towards the bowl of honey.

'The Romans know this?'

'I am not sure, Emmanuel, but Herod the incestuous has doubtless told them I speak against the unrighteous.'

'Yet the Romans do not arrest you.'

'Pilate dare not – not since the petition was sent to the Emperor Tiberius.'

'Petition?'

'Aye, the one that Herod and the Pharisees signed when Pilate the procurator did place votive shields in the palace of Jerusalem and seek to violate the Temple. Tiberius rebuked Pilate and since then, though he still hates the Jews, the procurator is more careful in his treatment of us.'

'Tell me, John, do you know how long Tiberius has ruled in Rome?' He had not had the chance to ask the question again until now.

'Fourteen years.'

It was AD 28 – something less than a year before the date when most scholars agreed that the crucifixion had taken place, and his time machine was smashed.

Now John the Baptist planned armed rebellion against the occupying Romans, but, if the Gospels were to be believed, would soon be decapitated by Herod. Certainly no large-scale rebellion had taken place at this time.

Even those who claimed that the entry of Jesus and his disciples into Jerusalem and the invasion of the Temple were plainly the actions of armed rebels had found no records to suggest that John had led a similar revolt.

Once again it occurred to him that he could warn John. But would the Baptist believe him? Would he choose not to believe him, whatever evidence was presented?

Glogauer had come to like the Baptist very much. The man was plainly a hardened revolutionary who had been planning revolt against the Romans for years and had slowly been building up enough followers to make the attempt successful.

He reminded Glogauer strongly of a type of resistance leader of the Second World War. He had a similar toughness and understanding of the realities of his position. He knew that he would only have one chance to smash the cohorts garrisoned in the country. If the revolt became protracted, Rome would have ample time to send more troops to Jerusalem.

'When do you think Adonai intends to destroy the unrighteous through your agency?' Glogauer asked tactfully.

John glanced at him with some amusement.

'The Passover is a time when the people are restless and resent the strangers most,' he said.

'When is the next Passover?'

'Not for many months.'

Glogauer ate in silence for a while, then he looked up frankly at the Baptist.

'I play some part in this, don't I?' he said.

John looked at the ground. 'You were sent by Adonai to help us accomplish his will.'

'How can I help you?'

'You are a magus.'

'I can work no miracles.'

John wiped honey from his beard. 'I cannot believe that, Emmanuel. The manner of your coming was miraculous. The Essenes did not know if you were a devil or a messenger from Adonai.'

'I am neither.'

'Why do you confuse me, Emmanuel? I know that you are Adonai's messenger. You are the sign that the Essenes sought. The time is almost ready. The kingdom of heaven shall soon be established on earth. Come with us. Tell the people that you speak with Adonai's voice. Work great miracles.'

'Your power is waning, is that it?' Glogauer looked sharply at John. 'You need me to renew your rebels' hopes?'

'You speak like a Roman, with such lack of subtlety!' John got up angrily.

Evidently, like the Essenes he lived with, he preferred less direct methods of expression. There was a practical reason for this, Glogauer realized, in that John and his men feared betrayal all the time. Even the Essenes' records were partially written in cipher, with one innocent-seeming word or phrase meaning something else entirely.

'I am sorry, John. But tell me if I am right.' Glogauer spoke softly.

'Are you not a magus, coming in that chariot from nowhere?' The Baptist waved his hands and shrugged his shoulders. 'My men saw you! They saw the shining thing take shape in air, crack and let you enter out of it. Is that not magical? The clothing you wore – was that earthly raiment? The talismans within the chariot – did they not speak of powerful magic? The prophet said that a magus would come from Egypt and be called Emmanuel. So it is written in the Book of Micah! Are none of these things true?'

'Most of them. But there are explanations – ' He broke off, unable to think of the nearest word to 'rational'. 'I am an ordinary man, like you. I have no power to work miracles! I am just a man!'

John glowered. 'You mean you refuse to help us?'

'I'm grateful to you and the Essenes. You saved my life almost certainly. If I can repay that . . .'

John nodded his head deliberately. 'You can repay it, Emmanuel.'

'How?'

'Be the great magus I need. Let me present you to all those who become impatient and would turn away from Adonai's will. Let me tell them the manner of your coming to us. Then you can say that all is Adonai's will and that they must prepare to accomplish it.'

John gave him an intense stare.

'Will you, Emmanuel?'

'John – there is no way in which I can help you without deceiving you, or myself, or the people . . .'

John looked at him thoughtfully. 'Perhaps you are unaware of your destiny . . .' he said musingly. 'Why should you not be? Indeed, if you made great claims I would be much more suspicious of you. Emmanuel, will you not take my word that you are the one whom it was prophesied would come?'

Glogauer felt defeated. How could he argue against that? For all he knew, he could be the one. Suppose there were men gifted with some sort of clairvoyant powers . . . Oh, it was nonsense. Yet what could he do?'

'John, you are desperate for a sign. Suppose the true magus arrives . . .'

'He has arrived. You are he. I have prayed and I know.'

How could he suggest to John that it was his desperate need for help which had probably convinced him? He sighed.

'Emmanuel – will you not help the people of Judaea?'

Glogauer pursed his lips. 'Let me think, John. Let me sleep. Come to me in the morning and I will tell you then.'

With some surprise he realized that their roles had changed. Now instead of wishing to keep the Baptist's good will, the Baptist was anxious to keep his.

When he returned to his cave he felt exhilarated, could not stop himself from smiling broadly. Without engineering it at all, he was now in a position of power. How should he use the power? Did he really have a mission? Could he alter history and be the one responsible for aiding the Jews to throw out the Romans?

6

'To be Jewish is to be immortal,' Friedman had told him a few days after Eva had gone back to her parents. 'To be Jewish is to have a destiny – even if that destiny is simply to survive.'

Friedman was tall and bulky with a pale, fat face and cynical eyes. He was almost completely bald. He wore heavy suits of green tweed. He was extremely generous to Karl and appeared to expect little in return – only Karl as an audience occasionally.

'To be Jewish is to be a martyr. Have some more sherry.' He crossed his study and poured another large glass for Karl. 'That's where you went wrong with her, my boy. You couldn't stand the success.'

'I'm not sure that's true, Gerard. I wanted her to take me as I was –'

'You wanted her to take you as you saw yourself, not as she saw you. Who's to say who's right? You do see yourself as a martyr, don't you? What a pity. A lovely girl like that. You might've passed her on to me instead of frightening her off.'

'Oh, don't, Gerard. I loved her!'

'Loved yourself more.'

'Who doesn't?'

'Lots of people have no love for themselves at all. It's to your credit that you do love yourself.'

'You make me sound like Narcissus.'

'You haven't the looks. Don't kid yourself.'

'Anyway, I don't think it's anything at all to do with being Jewish. You and your generation always make a big mystique out of being a Jew. You're over-compensating for what happened under Hitler.'

'Possibly.'

'Anyway, I'm not really a Jew. I wasn't brought up Jewish.'

'With that mother of yours, you weren't brought up Jewish! Maybe you didn't go to the synagogue, son, but you got the lot otherwise . . .'

'Oh, Gerard. Anyway, you're obscuring the issue – I'm trying to think how to get her back.'

'Forget her. Find yourself a nice Jewish girl. I mean it. She'll understand you. When all's said and done, Karl, these Nordic types are no good for what you want . . .'

'Christ! I didn't know you were a racialist.'

'I'm just a realist . . .'
'I've heard that before.'
'All right. If you want trouble . . .'
'Maybe I do.'

Father . . .
 Pained eyes.
 Father . . .
 A mouth moving. No words.

Heavy wooden cross struggling in a swamp while on a hillock a delicate silver cross watched.
 Hel . . .NO!
 Mustn't ask . . .
 Just want . . .NO!
 HELP ME!
 no

'Formal religion's no good,' Johnny told him in the pub. Johnny was an undergraduate friend of Gerard's. 'It just doesn't suit the times. You've got to find the answer in yourself. Meditation.'

Johnny was thin, with a perpetually worried face. According to Gerard, he was in his third year and doing very badly.

'You get the comforts of religion without the responsibility,' said Friedman from where he sat on a bar stool just behind Johnny.

Karl laughed.

Johnny rounded on Gerard. 'That's typical, isn't it? You don't know what you're talking about. Responsibility? I'm a pacifist – ready to die for my beliefs. That's more than you'd do!'

'I haven't any beliefs –'

'Exactly!'

Karl laughed again. 'I'll passively resist any man in this pub!'

'Oh, shut up! I've found something neither of you'll ever find.'

'Doesn't seem to have done you much good,' Karl said cruelly, regretted it and put his hand on Johnny's shoulder, but the young man shrugged it off and left the pub.

Karl became very depressed.

'Don't worry about Johnny,' said Gerard. 'He's always being baited.'

'It's not that really. He was right. He's got something he believes in. I can't seem to find anything.'

'It's healthier.'

'I don't know how you can talk about health, with your morbid interest in witch covens and stuff . . .'

'We've all got our problems,' said Gerard. 'Have another.'

Karl frowned. 'I only attacked Johnny because he embarrassed me, showed me up in a way.'

'We've all got our problems. Have another.'

'All right.'

Trapped. Sinking. Can't be myself. Made into what other people expect. Is that everyone's fate? Were the great individualists the products of their friends who wanted a great individualist as a friend?

Great individuals must be lonely. Everyone needs to think they're invulnerable. In the end they're treated less like human beings than anyone. Treated as symbols of something that can't exist. They must be lonely.

Lonely.

There's always a reason to be lonely.

Lonely . . .

'Mum – I want . . .'

'Who wants to know what you want? Been away nearly a year. Never wrote. What about what I want? Where were you? I could have died . . .'

'Try to understand me . . .'

'Why should I? Have you ever tried to understand me?'

'I've tried, yes . . .'

'Like hell. What do you want this time?'

'I want . . .'

'Did I tell you what the doctor told me . . . ?'

Lonely . . .

I need . . .

I want . . .

'You don't get anything in this world that you haven't earned. And you don't always get what you've earned, either.'

Drunk, he leaned against the bar and watched the little red-faced man talk.

'There's a lot of people don't get what they deserve,' said the publican and laughed.

'What I mean is,' said the red-faced man slowly.

'Why don't you shut up?' said Karl.

'Shut up yourself.'

'Oh, shut up both of you,' said the publican.

Love . . .

Delicate. Tender. Sweet.

Love . . .

'Your trouble, Karl,' said Gerard as they walked along the High towards the Mitre where Gerard had decided to buy Karl lunch, 'is that you're hung up on romantic love. Look at me, I've got all kinds of kinks . . . as you're so fond of pointing out in that hectoring voice of yours. I get terribly randy watching black masses and all that. But I don't go around butchering virgins – partly because it's against the law. But you romantic-love perverts – there's no law to stop you. I can't do it unless she's wearing a black veil or something, but you can't do it unless you've sworn undying love and she's sworn undying love back and everything's horribly mixed up. The damage you do! To yourself and the poor girls you use! It's disgusting . . .'

'You're being more cynical than usual, Gerard.'

'No! Not a bit of it. I speak with absolute sincerity – I've never felt so passionate about anything in my life! Romantic love! There really ought to be some law against it. Disgusting. Disastrous. Look what happened to Romeo and Juliet. There's a warning there for all of us.'

'Oh, Gerard . . .'

'Why can't you just fuck and enjoy it? Leave it at that. Take it for granted. Don't pervert some poor girl, too.'

'They're usually the ones who want it that way.'

'You have a point, dear boy.'

'Don't you believe in love at all, Gerard?'

'My dear Karl, if I didn't believe in some kind of love, would I be bothering to give you this warning?'

Karl smiled at him. 'You're very kind, Gerard . . .'

'Oh, good God! Don't, Karl, please! You see what I mean? If you look at me like that once more, I shall not buy you that expensive lunch. I'm serious.'

Karl sighed. The only man who had ever seemed to show him

any disinterested affection was the only man who refused to allow him any display of affection. It was ironic, really.

I want . . .
    I need . . .
    I want . . .

'Monica. There's something lacking in *me* . . .'
    'What sort of a lack?'
    'Well, perhaps it's more a sort of a lack of a lack, if you know what I mean.'
    'Oh, for Christ's sake!'

'You're sensitive,' Eva had told him.
    'No, I told you – self-pitying. It passes for sensitivity.'
    'Oh, Karl. Why don't you allow yourself some mercy?'
    'Mercy? I don't deserve it.'

'What are you looking for, Karl?' Gerard asked over lunch.
    'I don't know. Perhaps the Holy Grail. Eva seemed to think I'd find it.'
    'Why not? It'd be worth a fortune these days! Shall we have another bottle?'
    'You know, I'm not a martyr, Gerard, I'm not a saint, I'm not a hero, I'm not really a bum. I'm just me. Why can't people take me like that?'
    'Karl – I like you for being exactly yourself.'
    'So you can patronize me. You like me mixed up, you mean.'
    'You may be right. Another bottle?'
    'All right.'

Gerard had offered to pay his fees so that he could study psychology.
    'I'm only doing it because I'm alarmed at what might otherwise happen to you,' he said. 'You might enter the Catholic Church at this rate!'
    He had taken the course for a year before drifting out of it. All he had wanted to do was study Jung and they had insisted on his making a variety of studies. He found most of the rest of them very unsympathetic.

★

God?
  God?
  God?
  No reply.

With Gerard he was serious, intense, intelligent.

With Johnny he was superior, mocking.

With some he was quiet. With others, noisy. In the company of fools, he was happy as a fool. In the company of those he admired, he was pleased if he could sound astute.

'Why am I all things to all men, Gerard? I'm just not sure who I am. Which of those people am I, Gerard? What's wrong with me?'

'Maybe you're just a bit too eager to please, Karl.'

7

HE HAD MET MONICA AGAIN IN the summer of 1962, shortly after he had given up his studies. He was doing all sorts of temporary work and his spirits were very low.

At that time Monica had seemed a great help, a great guide through the mental darkness engulfing him.

They both lived close to Holland Park and it was there that they had met one Sunday, by the goldfish pond in the ornamental garden.

They went to Holland Park for walks almost every Sunday of that summer. He was by that time completely obsessed with Jung's strange brand of Christian mysticism.

She, who despised Jung, had soon begin to denigrate all his ideas.

Although she never really convinced him, she had soon succeeded in confusing him.

It would be another six months before they went to bed together.

He woke up to see John standing over him. The Baptist had an expression of anxious concern on his bearded features.

'Well, Emmanuel?'

Karl scratched at his own beard. He nodded his head. 'Very well, John. I will help you for your sake, because you befriended me and saved my life. But in return, will you send men to bring my chariot here as soon as possible? I wish to see if it can be mended.'

'I will.'

'You must not have too much faith in my powers, John . . .'

'I have absolute faith in them . . .'

'I hope you will not be disappointed.'

'I will not be.' John put his hand on Glogauer's arm. 'You shall baptize me on the morrow, to show all the people that Adonai is with us.'

He was still worried by the Baptist's faith in his powers, but there was nothing more he could say. If others shared the Baptist's faith, then possibly he could do something.

Glogauer felt the exhilaration of the night before, and the broad smile came uncontrollably to his lips again.

The Baptist began to laugh, uncertainly at first, but then more spontaneously.

Glogauer, too, began to laugh, unable to stop himself, every so often pausing to gasp for breath.

It was completely incongruous that he should be the one who, with John the Baptist, would prepare the way for Christ.

Christ was not born yet, however.

Perhaps Glogauer was beginning to understand this, one year before the crucifixion.

> And the Word was made flesh and dwelt among us, (and we beheld his glory, the glory as of the only begotten of the Father,) full of grace and truth. John bare witness of him, and cried, saying, This was he of whom I spake, He that cometh after me is preferred before me: for he was before me.
>
> JOHN 1:14–15

It was uncomfortably hot.

They sat in the shade of the cafeteria, watching a distant cricket match.

Nearer to them, two girls and a boy sat on the grass, drinking orange squash from plastic cups. One of the girls had a guitar across her lap and she set the cup down and began to play, singing a folk-song in a high, gentle voice.

Karl tried to listen to the words. At the college, he had developed a liking for traditional folk music.

'Christianity is dead.' Monica sipped her tea. 'Religion is dying. God was killed in 1945.'

'There may yet be a resurrection,' he said.

'Let's hope not. Religion was the creation of fear. Knowledge destroys fear. Without fear, religion can't survive.'

'You think there's no fear about these days?'

'Not the same kind, Karl.'

'Haven't you ever considered the *idea* of Christ?' he asked her, changing his track. 'What that means to Christians?'

'The idea of the tractor means as much to a Marxist,' she replied.

'But what came first? The idea or the actuality of Christ?'

She shrugged. 'The actuality, if it matters. Jesus was a Jewish troublemaker organizing a revolt against the Romans. He was crucified for his pains. That's all we know and all we need to know.'

'A great religion couldn't have begun so simply.'

'When people need one, they'll make a great religion out of the most unlikely beginnings.'

'That's my point, Monica.' He gesticulated intensely and she drew away slightly. 'The *idea* preceded the *actuality* of Christ.'

'Oh, Karl, don't go on. The actuality of *Jesus* preceded the idea of *Christ*.'

A couple walked past, glancing curiously at them as they argued. Monica noticed them and fell silent.

'Why are you so keen to knock religion, sneer at Jung?' he said.

She got up and he rose as well, but she shook her head.

'I'm going home, Karl. You stay here. I'll see you in a few days.'

He watched her walk down the wide path towards the park gates. Perhaps he enjoyed her company, he thought, because she was prepared to argue as intensely as he did – or almost, anyway.

Vampires.

We're quite a pair.

The next day, when he got home from work, he found a letter.

She must have written it after she had left him, and posted it the same day. He opened it and began to read.

Dear Karl,

Conversation doesn't seem to have much effect on you, you know. It's as if you listen to the tone of the voice, the rhythm of the words, without ever hearing what is trying to be communicated.

You're a bit like a sensitive animal, I suppose, who can't understand what's being said to it, but can tell if the person talking to it is pleased or angry and so on. That's why I'm writing to you – to try to get my idea across. You respond too emotionally when we're together.

He smiled at that. One of the reasons he enjoyed her company so much was because at most times her responses could be counted upon to be passionate.

You make the mistake of considering Christianity as something that developed over the course of a few years, from the death of Jesus to the time the Gospels were written. But Christianity wasn't new. Only the name was new. Christianity was merely a stage in the meeting, cross-fertilization, metamorphosis of Western logic and Eastern mysticism. Look how the religion itself changed over the centuries, reinterpreting itself to meet changing times. Christianity is just a new name for a conglomeration of old myths and philosophies. All the Gospels do is retell the sun myth and garble some of the ideas from the Greeks and Romans.

Even in the second century, Jewish scholars were showing it up for the mish-mash it was!

They pointed out the strong similarities between the various sun myths and the Christ myth. The miracles didn't happen – they were invented later, borrowed from here and there.

Remember those old Victorian dons who used to argue that Plato was really a Christian because he anticipated Christian thought?

Christian thought!

Christianity was a vehicle for ideas in circulation centuries before Christ. Was Marcus Aurelius a Christian? He was writing in the direct tradition of Western philosophy. That's why Christianity caught on in Europe and not in the East!

You should have been a theologian with your bias – not tried to be a psychologist. The same goes for your friend Jung.

Try to clear your head of all this morbid nonsense and you'll make a much better job of your life.

Yours,

Monica

He screwed the letter up and threw it away. Later that evening he was tempted to look at it again, but he resisted the temptation.

The time machine seemed unfamiliar. Perhaps because he had become so used to the primitive life of the Essenes, the cracked globe looked as strange to him as it must have done to them.

He touched the stud that would normally have operated the airlock from the outside, but nothing happened.

He crawled in through the crack. All the fluid had gone, as he already knew, and without that to cushion him, any journey through time would probably kill him anyway.

John the Baptist peered in, as if afraid that Glogauer was going to try to make his escape in his chariot.

Glogauer smiled at him. 'Don't worry, John.'

Everything was dead. The motors would not respond and even if he stripped off their casings, he wasn't engineer enough to fix them. None of the instruments was working. The time machine was dead.

Unless Headington built another machine and sent it after him, he was stranded in this period for good.

The understanding came to him as a shock.

He would probably never see the twentieth century again, could not report what he witnessed here.

Tears came to his eyes and he staggered from the machine, pushing John aside.

'What is it, Emmanuel?'

'What am I doing here? What am I doing here?' he cried in English, and the words came thickly. These, too, seemed unfamiliar. What was happening to him?

He began to wonder if this whole thing were not an illusion, some kind of protracted dream. The idea of a time machine now seemed completely ludicrous to him. The thing was an impossibility.

'Oh, God,' he groaned, 'what's going on?'

Again a sense of being completely abandoned came to him.

8

WHERE AM I?
  Who am I?
  What am I?
  Where am I?

'Time and identity,' Headington used to say enthusiastically, 'the two great mysteries. Angles, curves, soft and hard perspectives. What do we see? What are we that we see in a particular way? What could we be or have been? All the twists and turns of time. I loathe those ideas that insist on treating time as a dimension of space, describing it in spacial metaphors. No wonder they get nowhere. Time is nothing to do with space – it is to do with the psyche. Ah! Nobody understands. Not even you!'

The other members of the group had thought of him as a bit of a crank.

'I am the only one,' he had said quietly and earnestly, 'who really understands the nature of time . . .'

'And on that note . . .' Mrs Rita Blen said firmly, 'I think it's about time for a cup of tea, don't you?'

The other members agreed enthusiastically.

Mrs Rita Blen had been a little unsubtle. Hurt, Headington had got up and left.

'Oh, well,' she said. 'Oh, well . . .'

But the others were annoyed with her. Headington was, after all, well known and gave the group a certain prestige.

'I hope he comes back,' Glogauer had murmured.

He had suffered migraine since adolescence. He would become dizzy, vomiting, completely immersed in pain.

Often during the attacks he would begin to assume an identity – a character in a book he was reading, some politician currently in the news, someone in history if he had recently read a biography.

The one thing that marked them all would be their anxieties. Heyst in *Victory* had been obsessed with the three men coming to the island, worrying how to stop them, how to kill them if possible (as Heyst, he had become a somewhat less subtle character than Conrad's). After reading a history of the Russian revolution, he became convinced that his name was Zinoniev, Minister in charge of Transport and Telegraphs, with the responsibility of sorting out the chaos in 1918, knowing, too, that he had to be careful, otherwise he would be purged in a few years' time.

He would lie in a darkened room, his head full of nauseating pain, unable to sleep properly because he could find no solution for the completely hypothetical problems that obsessed him. He would lose track completely of his own identity and circumstances unless someone came to remind him of who and where he was.

Monica had been amused when he told her.

'One day,' she said, 'you'll wake up and ask who you are – and I won't tell you!'

'A fine psychiatric worker you are!' he'd laughed.

Neither of them worried about these mild hallucinations. In his day-to-day life he was not bothered by any abnormally schizoid tendencies, save that his role would sometimes change a little to suit the company he kept; he would find himself unconsciously imitating nuances of speech in other people, but he understood that everyone did that to some extent. It was part of life.

Sometimes he wondered about it, wondered at the accretions of other people's personalities upon his own.

Drunk in some pub, he'd suddenly got up from the table and waved his arms, jumping up and down and grinning at Monica. 'Look at me,' he'd said. 'Look – the original coral island . . .'

She had frowned at him petulantly. 'What are you on about now? You'll get us thrown out.'

'It's only me from over the sea, I'm Barnacle Bill the Sailor,' he sang.

'You can't hold your liquor, Karl, that's your problem . . .'

'I hold too much – that's my problem.'

''Ere, what d'you think you're playing at?' said a man at the bar whose elbow he had jogged.

'I wish I knew, friend. I wish I knew.'

'Come on, Karl.' She was up, tugging at his arm.

'Every man's life diminishes me,' he said as she dragged him through the doorway.

Pubs and bedrooms; bedrooms and pubs. He seemed to spend most of his life in semi-darkness. Even the bookshop would be dingy.

There had been days out, of course – sunny days and bright winter days – but all his memories of Monica were set against dark backgrounds of one kind or another. Tramping through muddy snow in the park beneath that particularly English sky, that heavy, leaden sky.

Whatever the hour, they had seemed to exist together in the twilight, after those first summer meetings before they slept together.

He had once said: 'I have a twilit mind . . .'

'If you mean a murky mind, I'm with you there,' she had replied.

He ignored the remark. 'It's my mother, I think. She never really had a firm hold on reality . . .'

'There's nothing much wrong with you if you'd face up to things – a trifle too much narcissism is all you've got.'

'Someone used to say I had too much self-hatred.'

'Just too much self.'

He would hold his circumcised penis in his hand and look at it with sentimental affection.

'You're the only friend I've got. The only friend I've got.'

Often it would take on a character of its own in his thoughts. A boon friend, the giver of pleasure. A bit of a lad though, always leading him into trouble.

Soft silver crosses spreading themselves against the surface of the shining sea.

Plonk!

Wooden crosses fell from the sky.

Plonk!

Disrupting the surface, shaking the silver crucifixes to pieces.

'Why do I destroy everything I love?'

'Oh, God! Don't give me that maudlin teenage stuff, Karl, please!'

Plonk.

Across all the deserts of Arabia I made my way, a slave of the sun, searching for my God.

★

Michael Moorcock

'Time and identity – the two great mysteries . . .'

Where am I?
  Who am I?
  What am I?
  Where am I?

9

Five years in the past.

Nearly two thousand in the future.

Lying in the hot, sweaty bed with Monica.

Once again another attempt to make normal love had changed gradually into the performance of minor aberrations which seemed to satisfy her better than anything else.

Their real courtship and fulfilment was yet to come. As usual, it would be verbal. As usual, it would find its climax in argumentative anger.

'I suppose you're going to tell me you're not satisfied again.' She accepted the lighted cigarette he handed to her in the darkness.

'I'm all right,' he said.

There was silence for a while as they smoked.

Eventually, and in spite of knowing what the result would be if he did so, he found himself talking.

'It's ironic, isn't it?' he began.

He waited for her reply. She would delay for a little while yet.

'What is?' she said at last.

'All this. You spend all day trying to help neurotics with their sex problems. You spend your nights doing what they do.'

'Not to the same extent. You know it's all a matter of degree.'

'So you say.'

He turned his head and looked at her face in the starlight from the window.

She was a gaunt-featured redhead, with the calm, professional seducer's voice of the psychiatric social worker. It was a voice that was soft, reasonable, insincere. Only occasionally, when she became particularly agitated, did her voice begin to indicate her real character.

Her features, he thought, never seemed to be in repose, even when she slept. Her eyes were forever wary, her movements rarely spontaneous. Every inch of her was protected, which was probably why she got so little pleasure from ordinary lovemaking.

He sighed.

'You just can't let yourself go, can you?'

'Oh, shut up, Karl. Have a look at yourself if you're looking for a neurotic mess.'

They used the terminology of psychiatry freely. Both felt happier if they could name something.

He rolled away from her, groping for the ashtray on the bedside table, catching a glimpse of himself in the dressing-table mirror.

He was a sallow, intense, moody Jewish cleric, with a head full of images and unresolved obsessions, a body full of conflicting emotions. He always lost these arguments with Monica. Verbally, at very least, she was the dominant one.

This kind of exchange often seemed to him more perverse than their lovemaking, where usually at least his role was masculine. At this time he had decided that he was essentially passive, masochistic, indecisive. Even his anger, which came frequently, was these days impotent.

Monica was ten years older than him, ten years more bitter. As an individual, he believed, she had more dynamism than he had. Yet she had a great many failures in her work. She plugged on, however, becoming increasingly cynical on the surface but still, perhaps, hoping for a few spectacular successes with patients.

They tried to do too much, that was the trouble, he thought. The priests in the confessional supplied a panacea; the psychiatrists tried to cure, and most of the time they failed. But at least they tried, he thought, and then wondered if that was, after all, a virtue.

'I did look at myself,' he said.

Was she sleeping?

He turned.

Her wary eyes were still open, looking out of the window.

'I did look at myself,' he repeated. 'The way Jung did. "How can I help those persons if I am myself a fugitive and perhaps also suffer from the *morbus sacer* of a neurosis?" That's what Jung asked himself . . .'

'That old sensationalist. That old rationalizer of his own mysticism. No wonder you never became a psychiatrist.'

'I wouldn't have been any good. It was nothing to do with Jung . . .'

'Don't take it out on me . . .'

'I wanted to help people. I couldn't find a way through. You've told me yourself that you feel the same – you think it's useless.'

'After a hard week's work, I might say that. Give me another fag.'

He opened the packet on the bedside table and put two cigarettes in his mouth, lighting them and handing her one.

Almost unconsciously, he noticed that the tension was increasing.

The argument was, as ever, pointless. But it was not the argument that was the important thing: it was simply the expression of the essential relationship. He wondered if that was in any way important, either.

'You're not telling the truth.' He knew that there would be no stopping now that the ritual was in full swing.

'I'm telling the practical truth. I've no compulsion to give up my work. To drop out. I've no wish to be a failure . . .'

'Failure? You're more melodramatic than I am!'

'You're too earnest, Karl. You want to get out of yourself a bit.'

He sneered. 'If I were you, I'd give up my work, Monica. You're no more suited for it than I was.'

She shrugged, tugging at the sheets. 'You're a petty bastard.'

'I'm not jealous of you, if that's what you think. You'll never understand what I'm looking for.'

Her laugh was brittle. 'Modern man in search of a soul, eh? Modern man in search of a crutch, I'd say. And you can take that any way you like.'

'We're destroying the myths that make the world go round.'

'Now you say, "And what are we putting in their place?" You're stale and stupid, Karl. You've never looked rationally at anything – including yourself.'

'What of it? You say the myth is unimportant.'

'The reality that creates it is important.'

'Jung knew that the myth can also create the reality.'

'Which shows what a muddled old fool he was.'

He stretched his legs. In doing so, he touched hers and he recoiled. He scratched his head. She still lay there smoking, but she was smiling now.

'Come on,' she said. 'Let's have some stuff about Christ.'

He said nothing.

She handed him the stub of her cigarette and he put it in the ashtray. He looked at his watch.

It was two o'clock in the morning.

'Why do we do it?' he said.

'Because we must.'

She put her hand to the back of his head and pulled it towards her breasts. 'What else can we do?'

He began to cry.

Generous in victory, she stroked his head and murmured to him.

Ten minutes later he made love to her savagely.

Then minutes after that he was crying again.

★

Betrayal.

He betrayed himself and was thus betrayed.

'I want to help people.'

'You'd better get someone to help you first.'

'Oh, Monica. Monica.'

> We Protestants must sooner or later face this question: Are we to understand the 'imitation of Christ' in the sense that we should copy his life and, if I may use the expression, ape his stigmata: or in the deeper sense that we are to live our own proper lives as truly as he lived his in all its implications? It is no easy matter to live a life that is modelled on Christ's, but it is unspeakably harder to live one's own life as truly as Christ lived his. Anyone who did this would . . . be misjudged, derided, tortured and crucified . . . A neurosis is a disassociation of personality.
>
> JUNG, *Modern Man in Search of a Soul*

Lonely . . .

I am lonely . . .

'So he's dead, is he? Never sent me a penny while he was alive. Never came to see you. Now he leaves you a business.'

'Mum – it's a bookshop. It probably doesn't do very well.'

'A bookshop! I suppose that's typical of him. A bookshop!'

'I'll sell it, if you like, Mum – give you the money.'

'Thanks very much,' she said with irony. 'No, you keep it. Maybe you'll stop borrowing from me now.'

'It's funny they didn't write earlier,' he said.

'They might have invited us to the funeral.'

'Would you have gone?'

'He was my husband, wasn't he? Your father.'

'I suppose it took them a while to find out where we lived.'

'How many Glogauers are there in London?'

'True. Come to think of it – it's odd you never heard of him.'

'Why should I? He wasn't in the phone book. What was the shop called?'

'The Mandala Bookshop. It's in Great Russell Street.'

'Mandala. What sort of a name is that?'

'It sells books about mysticism and stuff.'

'Well, you certainly take after him, don't you? I always said you took after him.'

He picked his way among his father's books. The front part of the shop was relatively tidy; the books arranged on the shelves that crowded the small space. The back of the shop, however, was filled with rocking piles of books that reached to the ceiling, surrounding the untidy desk.

In the cellar there were even more books, stacked one upon the other, with narrow passages winding like a maze between them.

He despaired of tidying the place.

In the end he just left the books as they were, made a few alterations in the main part of the shop, moved a few pieces of his own furniture into the upper part, and then felt settled. What was the point of changing anything?

He came across some privately printed poems under the name of John Fry. The strange girl who worked in the shop told him that they were his father's. He read a few. They were not very good, rather high-flown in their symbolism and imagery, but they revealed a personality so much like his own that he could not bear to read them for long.

'He was a funny old man,' said the fat customer with the drink-flushed face who came in to buy books about black-magic rites. 'A bit barmy in his way, I think. An evil old man, he struck me as. Always shouting at people. The arguments you used to hear from the back of the shop! Did you know him?'

'Not very well,' said Glogauer. 'Fuck off, will you!'

It was the first brave thing he ever remembered doing. He grinned as the man sputtered out of the shop.

His first few months as owner of the shop gave him a sense of stature. But as the bills came in and difficult customers had to be dealt with, the feeling gradually wore off.

He awoke in the cave and said aloud, 'I've no business being here. My existence here is an impossibility. There is no such thing as time travel.'

He did not succeed in convincing himself. His sleep had been disturbed, full of dreams and memories. He could not even be sure if the memories were exact. Had he really ever existed elsewhere, in another time?

He got up and wrapped his linen loincloth about his waist, going to the entrance of the cave.

The morning sky was grey and the sun had not yet risen. The earth was cold under his bare feet as he walked towards the river.

He reached the river and bent to wash his face, seeing his reflection in the dark water. His hair was long, black and matted, his beard covering the whole of his lower face, his eyes slightly mad. There was nothing at all to distinguish him from any one of the Essenes, save his thoughts. And the thoughts of many of the Essenes were strange enough. Were they any wilder than his belief that he was a visitor from a future century?

He shuddered as he splashed cold water on his face.

There was the time machine. He had seen that only yesterday. That was proof.

This sort of speculation was nonsense, anyway, he thought, straightening. It got you nowhere. It was self-indulgent.

On the other hand, what of John's belief that he was a great magus? Was it right to go along with him, let him believe he had the powers of a seer? And was it right that John should use him to restore the flagging faith of those who awaited revolution?

It didn't matter. He was here, this was happening to him, there was nothing he could do about it. He had to stay alive, if possible, so that in a year he could witness the crucifixion, if it did, indeed, take place.

Why did the crucifixion in particular obsess him? Why should that be proof of Christ's divinity? It would not be, of course, but it would enable him to get the feel of what had really happened, what the people had really felt.

Was Christ like John the Baptist? Or a subtler politician, working chiefly in the cities, making friends in the Establishment? And working secretly – for John had not heard of him and John of all people should have known, for he was supposed to be Jesus's cousin.

Perhaps, Glogauer thought, he was mixing with the wrong company.

He smiled and turned back towards the village. He felt tense suddenly. Something dramatic was going to happen today, something that was to decide his future for him. For some reason, however, he rebelled against the idea of baptizing the Baptist. It was wrong. He had no right to pose as a great prophet.

He rubbed at his head. There was a slight ache there. He hoped it would go before he saw John.

Behold the Man

Our birth is but a sleep and a forgetting . . .

WORDSWORTH

The cave was warm, and thick with his memories and thoughts. He entered it with some relief.

Later, he would leave it for the last time.

Then there would be no escape.

'All of us choose our archetypal roles quite early in life,' he told the group. 'And do not be deceived by the grand term "archetype" – for it applies as much to the bank clerk living in Shepperton as it does to the great figures of history – "archetypal" does not mean "heroic" really. That bank clerk's inner life is as rich as yours or mine, the role he sees himself as fulfilling is quite as important to him as anyone else's. Though his suburban suit may deceive you – and deceive those he lives and works with – he –'

'Nonsense, nonsense,' said Sandra Peterson, waving her heavy arms. 'They're not bloody archetypes – they're stereotypes . . .'

'There is no such thing,' Glogauer insisted. 'It's inhuman to judge people in that way . . .'

'I don't know what you call it, but I know that these people are the grey ones – the forces of mediocrity who try to drag the others down!'

Glogauer was shocked, almost in tears. 'Really, Sandra, I'm trying to explain –'

'I'm sure you're completely misinterpreting Jung,' she said firmly.

'I've studied everything he wrote!'

'I think Sandra's got a point,' said Mrs Rita Blen. 'After all – this sort of thing is what we're here to thrash out, isn't it?'

It might work.

He had timed it right.

The gas fire was on when Monica got to the flat over the book-shop. The smell of gas filled the room. He lay near the fire.

She opened a window, then crossed to where he lay.

'God, Karl, what you'll do to get attention.'

He began to laugh.

'Jesus. Am I so transparent?'

'I'm off,' she said.

She didn't call for nearly a fortnight. He knew she would. After all, she was getting on, and she wasn't that attractive. She only had him.

'I love you, Monica,' he said as he crawled into bed beside her.
She had her pride. She made no response.

John stood outside the cave now. He was calling to him.
'It is time, magus.'
Reluctantly, he left the cave. He looked appealingly at the Baptist.
'John – are you sure?'
The Baptist turned and began to march towards the river.
'Come. They are waiting.'

'My life's a mess, Monica.'
'Isn't everyone's, Karl?'

Part Two

10

And thine the Human Face, & thine
The Human Hands & Feet & Breath,
   Entering thro' the Gates of Birth
And passing thro' the Gates of Death.

        WILLIAM BLAKE, Jerusalem: To the Jews

JOHN WAS UP TO HIS WAIST in the sluggish waters of the river. All the Essenes had come to witness his baptism. They stood on the banks, making no sound.

Balanced in the sandy soil between the top of the bank and the water, Glogauer looked down at him and spoke in his odd, heavily accented Aramaic.

'John, I cannot. It is not for me to do it.'

The Baptist frowned. 'You must.'

Glogauer began to gasp, his eyes filling with tears as he gave John a look of agonized appeal.

But the Baptist showed him no mercy.

'You must. It is your duty.'

Glogauer felt light-headed as he lowered himself into the river beside the Baptist. He shivered.

He stood in the water trembling, unable to move.

His foot slipped on the rocks on the river-bottom and John reached out and gripped his arm, steadying him.

In the clear, harsh sky, the sun was a zenith, beating down on his unprotected head.

'Emmanuel!' John cried suddenly. 'The spirit of Adonai is within you!'

Glogauer was startled. 'What . . . ?' he said in English. He blinked rapidly.

'The spirit of Adonai is within you, Emmanuel!'

Glogauer still found it hard to speak. He shook his head slightly. The headache had not worn off and now the pain was growing. He could hardly see. He knew he was having his first migraine attack since he had come here.

He wanted to vomit.

John's voice sounded distorted, distant.

He swayed in the water.

As he began to fall towards the Baptist, the whole scene around him became indistinct.

He felt John catch him and heard himself say desperately: 'John –
you must baptize *me!*' And then there was water in his mouth and
throat and he was coughing.

He had not felt this kind of panic since the night he had first gone
to bed with Monica and thought he was impotent.

John's voice was crying something.

Whatever the words were, they drew a response from the people
on the banks.

The roaring in his ears increased, its quality changing. He
thrashed in the water, then felt himself lifted to his feet.

Still the pain and panic filled him. He began to vomit into the
water, stumbling as John's hands gripped his arms painfully and
guided him up the bank.

He had let John down.

'I'm sorry,' he said. 'I'm sorry. I'm sorry. I'm sorry . . .'

He had lost John his chance of victory. 'I'm sorry. I'm sorry.'

Again, he had not had the strength to do the right thing. 'I'm
sorry.'

A peculiar rhythmic humming came from the mouths of the Essenes as they swayed; it rose as they swayed to one side, fell as they
swayed to the other.

As John released him, Glogauer covered his ears. He was still
retching, but it was dry now, and worse than ever.

He staggered away, barely keeping his balance, running, with his
ears still covered; running over the rocky scrubland; running as the
sun throbbed in the sky and its heat pounded at his head; running
away.

> But John forbad him, saying, I have need to be baptized of thee,
> and comest thou to me? And Jesus answering said unto him,
> Suffer it to be so now: for thus it becometh us to fulfil all
> righteousness. Then he suffered him. And Jesus, when he was
> baptized, went up straightway out of the water: and, lo, the
> heavens were opened unto him, and he saw the Spirit of God
> descending like a dove, and lighting upon him: And lo a voice
> from heaven, saying, This is my beloved Son, in whom I am
> well pleased.
>
> MATTHEW 3: 14–17

He had been fifteen, doing quite well at the grammar school.

He had read in the newspapers about the Teddy-boy gangs

that roamed South London, but the occasional youth he had seen in pseudo-Edwardian clothes had seemed harmless and stupid enough.

He had gone to the pictures in Brixton Hill and decided to walk home to Streatham because he had spent most of the bus money on ice-cream.

They came out of the cinema at the same time. He hardly noticed them as they followed him down the hill.

Then, quite suddenly, they had surrounded him.

They were pale, mean-faced boys, most of them a year or two older than he. He realized that he knew two of them vaguely. They were at the big council school in the same street as the grammar school. They used the same football ground.

'Hello,' he said weakly.

'Hello, son,' said the oldest Teddy boy. He was chewing gum, standing with one knee bent, grinning at him. 'Where you going, then?'

'Home.'

'Heouwm,' said the biggest one, imitating his accent.

'What are you going to do when you get there?'

'Go to bed.'

Karl tried to get through the ring, but they wouldn't let him.

They pressed him back into a shop doorway. Behind them, cars droned by on the main road. The street was brightly lit, with street lamps and neon from the shops.

Several people passed, but none of them stopped. Karl began to feel panic.

'Got no homework to do, son?' said the boy next to the leader. He was red-headed and freckled and his eyes were a hard grey.

'Want to fight one of us?' another boy asked. It was one of the boys Karl had recognized.

'No. I don't fight. Let me go.'

'You scared, son?' said the leader, grinning. Ostentatiously, he pulled a streamer of gum from his mouth and then replaced it. He began chewing again, the grin still on his face.

'No. Why should I want to fight you? I don't think anyone should fight.'

'You haven't got much choice, have you, son?'

'Look, I'm late. I've got to get back.'

'You got time for a few rounds . . .'

'I told you. I don't want to fight you.'

'You reckon you're better than us, is that it, son?'

'No.' He was beginning to tremble. Tears were coming into his eyes. 'Of course not.'

''Course not, son.'

He moved forward again, but they pushed him back into the doorway.

'You're the bloke with the kraut name, ain't you?' said the other boy he knew. 'Glow-worm or somethink.'

'Glogauer. Let me go.'

'Won't your mummy like it if you're back late?'

'More a yid name than a kraut name.'

'You a yid, son?'

'He looks like a yid.'

'You a yid, son?'

'You a Jewish boy, son?'

'You a yid, son?'

'Shut up!' Karl screamed. 'Why are you picking on me?'

He pushed into them. One of them punched him in the stomach. He grunted with pain. Another pushed him and he staggered.

People were still hurrying by on the pavement. Some of them glanced at the group as they went past.

One man stopped, but his wife pulled him on. 'Just some kids larking about,' she said.

'Get his trousers down,' one of the boys suggested with a laugh. 'That'll prove it.'

Karl pushed through them and this time they didn't resist.

He began to run down the hill.

'Give him a start,' he heard one of the boys say.

He ran on.

They began to follow him, laughing and jeering.

They did not catch up with him by the time he turned into the avenue where he lived. Perhaps they hadn't intended to catch him. He blushed.

He reached the house and ran along the dark passage beside it. He opened the back door. His mother was in the kitchen.

'What's the matter with you?' she said.

She was a tall, thin woman, nervous and hysterical. Her dark hair was untidy.

He went past her into the breakfast-room.

'What's the matter, Karl?' she called. Her voice was high-pitched.

'Nothing,' he said.

He didn't want a scene.

11

IT WAS COLD WHEN HE WOKE up. The false dawn was grey and he could see nothing but barren country in all directions. He could remember very little about the previous day, except that he had let John down somehow and had run a long way.

He was dazed. His skull felt empty. The back of his neck still ached.

Dew had gathered on his loincloth. He unwrapped it and wet his lips, rubbing the material over his face.

As always after a migraine attack he felt weak and completely drained mentally and physically.

Looking down at his naked body, he noticed how skinny he had become.

'I'm like a Belsen victim,' he thought.

He wondered why he had panicked so much when John had asked him to baptize him. Was it simply honesty – something in him which resisted deceiving the Essenes at the very last minute? It was hard to know.

He wrapped the torn loincloth about his hips and tied it tightly just above his left thigh. He supposed he had better try to get back to the camp and find John and apologize, ask if he could make amends.

Then, perhaps, he would move on.

The time machine was still in the Essene village. If a good blacksmith could be found, or some other metal-worker, perhaps there was a chance that it could be repaired. It was a faint hope. Even if it could be patched together, the journey back would be dangerous.

He wondered if he ought to go back right away, or try to shift to a time nearer to the actual crucifixion. It was important that he experience the mood of Jerusalem during the Feast of the Passover, when Jesus was supposed to have entered the city.

Monica had thought Jesus had stormed the city with an armed band. She had said that all the evidence pointed to that.

All the evidence of one sort did point to it, he supposed, but he could not accept the evidence. There was more to it, he was sure.

If only he could meet Jesus.

John had apparently never heard of him, though he had mentioned that there was a prophecy that the Messiah would be a Nazarene.

But there were many prophecies and many of them conflicted.

He began to walk in what he assumed to be the general direction of the Essene village. He could not have come very far.

By noon it had become much hotter and the ground more barren. His eyes were screwed up against the glare and the air shimmered. The feeling of exhaustion with which he had awakened had increased; his skin burned, his mouth was dry and his legs would hardly hold him. He was hungry and he was thirsty and there was nothing to eat or drink. There was no sign of the range of hills where the Essenes had their village.

He was lost and he hardly cared. In his mind he had almost become one with the desert landscape. If he perished here, the transition between life and death would barely be felt. He would lie down and his body would merge with the brown ground.

Mechanically, he moved on through the desert.

Later he saw a hill about two miles away to the south. The sight brought a small return of consciousness. He decided to head for it. From there he would probably be able to get his bearings, perhaps even see a township where they would give him food and water.

He rubbed at his forehead and eyes, but the touch of his own hand was painful to him. He began to plod towards the hill.

The sandy soil turned to floating dust around him as his feet disturbed it. The few primitive shrubs clinging to the ground tore at his ankles and calves, and the jutting rocks tripped him.

He was bleeding and bruised by the time he reached the slopes of the hill.

He rested for a while, staring vaguely around him at the almost featureless landscape, then he began to clamber up the hillside.

The journey to the summit (which was much further away than he had originally judged) was difficult.

He would slide on the loose stones of the hillside, falling on his face, bracing his torn hands and feet to stop himself from sliding down to the bottom, clinging to the tufts of grass and lichen that grew here and there, embracing larger projections of rock when he could, resting frequently, his mind and body both numb with pain and weariness.

He forgot why he climbed, but he became, like some barely sentient life-form, determined to reach the summit. Like a beetle, he dragged himself up the mountain.

He sweated beneath the sun. The dust stuck to the moisture on his near-naked body, caking him from head to foot. His loincloth was in shreds.

The barren world reeled around him, sky somehow merging with land, yellow rock with white clouds. Nothing seemed still.

He fell and his body slid down the mountain. His thigh was gashed, his head badly bruised.

As soon as he stopped sliding, he began to climb again, crawling slowly up the burning rock.

Time had become meaningless, identity meaningless. Now, for the first time, he was in a position to appreciate Headington's theories, but consciousness had disappeared also. He was a thing that moved up the mountain.

He reached the summit and stopped crawling.

For a little while he lay there blinking, and then his eyes closed.

He heard Monica's voice and raised his head. For a moment he thought he glimpsed her from the corner of his eye.

Don't be melodramatic, Karl . . .

She had said that many times. His own voice replied now.

I'm born out of my time, Monica. This age of reason has no place for me. It will kill me in the end.

Her voice replied.

Guilt and fear and cowardice and your own masochism. You could have been a brilliant psychiatrist, but you've given in to all your own neuroses so completely . . .

'Shut up!'

He rolled over on his back. The sun blazed down on his tattered body.

'Shut up!'

The whole Christian syndrome, Karl. You'll become a Catholic convert next, I shouldn't doubt. Where's your strength of mind?

'Shut up! Go away, Monica!'

Fear shapes your thoughts. You're not searching for a soul or even a meaning for life. You're searching for comfort.

'Leave me alone, Monica!'

His filthy hands covered his ears. His hair and beard were matted with dust. Blood had congealed on the wounds that were now on every part of his body. Above, the sun seemed to pound in unison with his heartbeats.

You're going downhill, Karl, don't you realize that? Downhill. Pull yourself together. You're not entirely incapable of rational thought . . .

'Oh, Monica! Shut up!'

His voice was harsh and cracked.

A few ravens circled the sky above him now. He heard them calling back at him in a voice not unlike his own.

God died in 1945 . . .

'It isn't 1945 – it's AD 28. God is alive!'

How you can bother to wonder about an obvious syncretistic religion like Christianity – rabbinic Judaism, Stoic ethics, Greek mystery cults, Oriental ritual . . .

'It doesn't matter!'

Not to you in your present state of mind.

'I need God!'

That's what it boils down to, doesn't it? An inadequate human being always ends up like you. Okay, Karl, carve your own crutches. Just think what you could have been if you'd come to terms with yourself . . .

Glogauer pulled his ruined body to its feet and stood on the summit of the hill and screamed.

The ravens were startled. They wheeled in the sky and flew away.

The sky was darkening now.

> Then was Jesus led up of the Spirit into the wilderness to be tempted of the devil. And when he had fasted forty days and forty nights, he was afterward an hungred.
>
> MATTHEW 4: 1–2

12

THE MADMAN CAME STUMBLING INTO TOWN.

His head was turned upward to face the sun; his eyes rolled; his arms were limp at his sides and his lips moved wordlessly.

His feet stirred the dust and made it dance and dogs barked around him as he walked. Children laughed at him, then they threw pebbles at him, then they crept away.

The madman began to speak.

To the townspeople, the words they heard were in no familiar language; yet they were uttered with such intensity and conviction that God himself might be using this emaciated, naked creature as his spokesman.

They wondered where the madman had come from.

Once some Roman legionaries had stopped and with brusque kindness asked him if he had any relatives they could take him to. They had addressed him in pidgin-Aramaic and had been surprised when he replied in a strangely accented Latin that was purer than the language they spoke themselves.

They asked him if he was a rabbi or a scholar. He told them he was neither.

The officer of the legionaries had offered him some dried meat and wine. He had eaten the meat and asked for water. They gave it to him.

The men were part of a patrol that passed this way once a month. They were stocky, brown-faced men, with hard, clean-shaven faces. They were dressed in stained leather kilts and breastplates and sandals and had iron helmets on their heads, scabbarded short swords at their hips.

Even as they stood around him in the evening sunlight they did not seem relaxed. The officer, softer-voiced than his men but otherwise much like them save that he wore a metal breastplate and a long cloak and a plume in his helmet, asked the madman what his name was.

For a moment the madman had paused, his mouth opening and closing, as if he could not remember what he was called.

'Karl,' he said at length, doubtfully. It was more a suggestion than a statement.

'Sounds almost like a Roman name,' said one of the legionaries.

'Or Greek, maybe,' said another. 'There are a lot of Greeks round here.'

'Are you a citizen?' the officer asked.

But the madman's mind was evidently wandering. He looked away from them, muttering to himself.

All at once, he looked back at them and said: 'Nazareth. Where is Nazareth?'

'That way.' The officer pointed along the road that cut between the hills.

The madman nodded as if satisfied.

'Karl . . . Karl . . . Carlus . . . I don't know . . .' The officer reached out and took the madman's chin in his hand, looking into his eyes. 'Are you a Jew?'

This seemed to startle the madman.

He sprang to his feet and tried to push through the circle of soldiers. They let him through, laughing. He was a harmless madman.

They watched him run down the road.

'One of their prophets, perhaps,' said the officer, walking to-wards his horse. The country was full of them. Every other man you met claimed to be spreading the message of their god. They didn't make trouble and religion actually seemed to keep their minds off rebellion.

We should be grateful, thought the officer.

His men were still laughing.

They began to march down the road in the opposite direction to the one the madman had taken.

Later he fell in with a group of people as emaciated as himself. They were on an obscure pilgrimage to a town he had never heard of. Like the Essenes, their sect demanded a strict return to the Mosaic law, but they were vague on other matters, save for some idea that King David would be sent by God to them to help them drive out the Romans and conquer Egypt, a country which they somehow identified with Rome and with Babylon.

They treated him as an equal.

He travelled with them for several days. Then, one night as they camped by the side of the road, a dozen horsemen in armour and livery much more resplendent than that of the Romans, came galloping by, knocking over cooking pots and riding through the fires.

'Herod's soldiers!' one of the sect cried.

Women were screaming and men were running into the night. Soon most of them had disappeared and only two women and the madman were left.

The leader of the soldiers had a dark, handsome face and a thick, oiled beard. He pulled the madman up to his knees by his hair and spat in his face.

'Are you one of these rebels we've been hearing so much about?'

The madman muttered, but shook his head.

The soldiers cuffed him. He was so weak that he fell instantly to the ground.

The soldier shrugged. 'He's no threat. There are no arms here. We've been misled.'

He looked calculatingly at the women for a moment and then turned to his men, his eyebrows raised. 'If any of you are hard up enough – you can have them.'

The madman lay on the ground and listened to the cries of the women as they were raped. He felt he should get up and go to their assistance, but he was too weak to move, too afraid of the soldiers. He did not want to be killed. It would mean that he would never achieve his goal.

Herod's soldiers rode away eventually and the members of the sect began to creep back.

'How are the women?' asked the madman.

'They are dead,' someone told him.

Someone else began to chant from the Scriptures, verses about vengeance and righteousness and the punishments of the Lord.

Overwhelmed, the madman crawled away into the darkness.

He left the sect the next morning when he discovered that their route would not take them through Nazareth.

The madman passed through many towns – Philadelphia, Gerasa, Pella and Scythopolis – following the Roman roads.

Of every traveller he met who would stop, he would ask the same question in his outlandish accent: 'Where lies Nazareth?'

In every town he would make sure that he left on the Nazareth road.

In some towns they had given him food. In others they had pelted him with stones and driven him away. In others they had asked for his blessing and he had done what he could, for he wanted the food they would give him, laying hands on them, speaking in his strange tongue.

In Pella he cured a blind woman.

He had crossed the Jordan by the Roman viaduct and continued northwards towards Nazareth.

Although there was no difficulty in getting directions for Nazareth, it became increasingly difficult to force himself towards the town.

He had lost a great deal of blood and had eaten very little on the journey. His manner of travelling was to walk until he collapsed, then lie there until he could go on, or, as had happened increasingly, until someone found him and had given him a little sour wine or bread to revive him.

After the incident with Herod's soldiers, he became warier, and always travelled alone, never identifying himself with any particular sect or group he met.

Sometimes people would ask him, 'Are you the prophet whom we await?'

He would shake his head and say, 'Find Jesus. Find Jesus.'

The white town consisted primarily of double- and single-storeyed houses of stone and clay-brick, built around a market place that was fronted by an ancient, simple synagogue. Outside the synagogue old men, dressed in dark robes and with shawls over their heads, sat and talked.

The town was prosperous and clean, thriving on Roman commerce. Only one or two beggars were in the streets and these were well fed. The streets followed the rise and fall of the hillside on which they were built. They were winding streets, shady and peaceful: country streets.

There was a smell of newly cut timber everywhere in the air, and the sound of carpentry, for the town was chiefly famous for its skilled carpenters. It lay on the edge of the Plain of Jezreel, close to the trade route between Damascus and Egypt, and wagons were always leaving it, laden with the work of the town's craftsmen.

The town was called Nazareth.

Now the madman had found Nazareth.

The townspeople looked at him with curiosity and more than a little suspicion as he staggered into the market square. He could be a wandering prophet or he could be possessed by devils. He could be a beggar or some member of a sect like the Zealots, who were so unpopular these days for the disaster they had brought upon

Jerusalem forty years before. The people of Nazareth did not care for rebels or fanatics. They were comfortable, richer than they had ever been before the Romans came.

As the madman passed the knots of people standing by the merchants' stalls, they fell silent until he had gone by.

Women pulled their heavy woollen shawls about their well-fed bodies and men tucked in their cotton robes so that he would not touch them. Normally their instinct would have been to have taxed him with his business in the town, but there was an intensity about his gaze, a quickness and vitality about his face, in spite of his emaciated appearance, that made them treat him with some respect and they kept their distance.

When he reached the centre of the market place, he stopped and looked around him. He seemed slow to notice the people. He blinked and licked his lips.

A woman passed, eyeing him warily. He spoke to her, his voice soft, the words carefully formed.

'Is this Nazareth?'

'It is.' She nodded and increased her pace.

A man was crossing the square. He was dressed in a woollen robe of red and brown stripes. There was a red skullcap on his curly, black hair. His face was plump and cheerful.

The madman walked across the man's path and stopped him.

'I seek a carpenter.'

'There are many carpenters in Nazareth. It is a town of carpenters! I am a carpenter myself.' The man was good-humoured, patronizing. 'Can I help you?'

'Do you know a carpenter called Joseph? A descendant of David. He has a wife called Mary and several children. One is called Jesus.'

The cheerful man screwed his face into a mock frown and scratched the back of his neck. 'I know more than one Joseph. And I know many Marys . . .' His eyes became reflective then and his lips curved as if in pleasant reminiscence. 'I think I know the one you're looking for. There's a poor fellow in yonder street.' He pointed. 'He has a wife called Mary. Try there. You should soon find him, unless he's delivering his work. Look for a man who never laughs.'

The madman glanced in the direction the man had pointed. As soon as he saw the street, he seemed to forget everything else and began to move mechanically towards it.

In the narrow street the smell of cut timber was even stronger. He walked ankle-deep in wood-shavings.

In Nazareth the heat was less dry than he had become used to. It was more like a fine, English summer's day, a sweet, lazy day . . .

The madman's heart began to thump.

From every building came a thud of hammers, the scrape of saws. There were planks of all sizes resting against the pale, shaded walls of the houses and there was hardly room to pass between them.

The madman paused. Fear made him tremble.

Many of the carpenters had their benches just outside their doors. They were carving bowls, operating simple lathes, shaping wood into everything imaginable.

The madman began to move again.

The carpenters looked up as they saw the madman coming down their street. He approached one old carpenter in a leather apron who sat at his bench carving a figurine. The man had grey hair and seemed short-sighted as he peered up at the madman.

'What do you want? I have no money for beggars.'

'I am not a beggar. I am seeking someone who lives in this street.'

'What's his name?'

'Joseph. He has a wife called Mary.'

The old man gestured with his hand that held the half-completed figurine. 'Two houses along on the other side of the street.'

He began to tremble and he began to sweat.

Fool – it's only . . .

Oh, God . . .

Probably find they know nothing. This is a coincidence.

Oh, God!

The house the madman came to had very few planks leaning against it and the quality of the timber seemed poorer than the other wood he had seen. The bench near the entrance was warped on one side and the man who sat hunched over it repairing a stool seemed misshapen too.

The madman touched his shoulder and he straightened up. His face was lined and pouched with misery. The eyes were tired and his thin beard had premature streaks of grey. He coughed slightly, perhaps in surprise at being disturbed.

'Are you Joseph?' asked the madman.

'I've no money.'

'I want nothing – just to ask some questions.'

'I'm Joseph. What do you want to know?'

'Have you a son?'

'Several, and daughters, too.'

The madman paused. Joseph looked at him curiously. He seemed to be frightened. It was a new experience for Joseph to find himself the cause of another's fear.

'What's the matter?'

The madman shook his head. 'Nothing.' His voice was hoarse. 'Your wife is called Mary? You are of David's line?'

The man gestured impatiently. 'Yes, yes – for what good either have done me . . .'

'I wish to meet one of your sons. Have you one called Jesus? Can you tell me where he is?'

'That good-for-nothing. What has he done now?'

'Where is he?'

Joseph's eyes became calculating as he stared at the madman. 'Are you a seer of some kind? Have you come to help my son?'

'I am a prophet of sorts. I believe I can foretell the future.'

Joseph got up with a sigh. 'I haven't much time. I've work to deliver in Nain as soon as possible.'

'Let me see him.'

'You can see him. Come.'

Joseph led the madman through the gateway into the cramped courtyard of the house. It was crowded with pieces of wood, broken furniture and implements, rotting sacks of shavings.

They entered the darkened house.

The madman was breathing heavily.

In the first room, evidently a kitchen, a woman stood by a large clay stove. She was tall and beginning to get fat. Her long black hair was unbound and greasy, falling over large, lustrous eyes that still had the heat of sensuality. She looked the madman over.

'I see you've found another well-paying customer, Joseph,' she said sardonically.

'He's a prophet.'

'Oh, a prophet. And hungry, I suppose. Well, we've no food for beggars or prophets, whatever they choose to call themselves.' She gestured with a wooden spoon at a small figure sitting in the shadow of a corner. 'That useless thing eats enough as it is.' The figure shifted as they spoke.

'He seeks our Jesus,' said Joseph to the woman. 'Perhaps he has come to ease our burden.'

The woman gave the madman a sidelong look and shrugged. She

licked her red lips with a fat tongue. 'Maybe you're right. There's something about him . . .'

'Where is he?' said the madman hoarsely.

The woman put her hands under her large breasts and shifted their position in the rough, brown dress she wore. She rubbed her hand on her stomach and then gave the madman a hooded look. 'Jesus!' she called, not turning.

The figure in the corner stood up.

'That's him,' said the woman with a certain satisfaction.

How?
It c . . .
Jesus!
I need . . .
NO!

The madman frowned, shaking his head rapidly.

'No,' he said. 'No.'

'What do you mean, "no"?' she said querulously. 'I don't care what you do. If you can stop him stealing. He doesn't know any better, but he'll be in real trouble one day, when he steals from someone who doesn't know about him . . .'

'No . . .'

The figure was misshapen.

It had a pronounced hunched back and a cast in its left eye. The face was vacant and foolish. There was a little spittle on the lips.

'Jesus?'

It giggled as its name was repeated. It took a crooked, lurching step forward.

'Jesus,' it said. The word was slurred and thick. 'Jesus.'

'That's all he can say,' said the woman. 'He's always been like that.'

'God's judgement,' said Joseph.

'Oh, shut up!' She gave her husband a savage grin.

'What is wrong with him?'

There was a pathetic, desperate note in the madman's voice.

'He's always been like that.' The woman turned back to the stove. 'You can have him if you want him. Take him away with you. Addled inside and outside. I was carrying him when my parents married me off to that half-man . . .'

'You sow! You shameless . . .' Joseph stopped as his wife grinned again, daring him to continue. Making some attempt to save his pride, he tried to smile back. 'You had a good story for them, didn't you? The oldest excuse ever! Taken by an angel! Taken by a devil, more likely!'

'He was a devil,' she grinned. 'And he was a man . . .'

Joseph drooped for a moment, then, as if remembering the fear he had seemed to inspire in the madman earlier, turned to the man and said in a bullying tone, 'What's your business with our son?'

'I wished to talk to him. I . . .'

'He's no oracle – no seer – we used to think he might be. There are still people in Nazareth who come to him to cure them or tell their fortunes, but he only giggles at them and speaks his name over and over again . . .'

'Are you sure – there is not – something about him – something you have not noticed?'

'Sure!' Mary snorted emphatically. 'We need money badly enough. If he had any magical powers, we'd know by now.'

Jesus giggled again.

'Jesus,' he said. 'Jesus, Jesus.'

He lurched away into another room.

Joseph ran after him. 'He can't go in there! I won't have him wetting the floor again!'

While Joseph was in the other room, Mary gave the madman another appraising look. 'If you can tell fortunes, you must come and tell mine some time. He'll be leaving tonight for Nain . . .'

Joseph led the cripple back into the kitchen and made him sit on a stool in the corner. 'Stay there, bastard!'

The madman shook his head. 'It is impossible . . .'

Had history itself changed?

Was this all the story was based on?

It was impossible . . .

Joseph appeared to notice the look of agony in the madman's eyes.

'What is it?' he said. 'What do you see? You said you foretold the future. Tell us how we will fare!'

'Not *now*,' said the prophet, turning away. 'How can I? Not now.'

He ran from the dark house and into the sun. He ran down the street with its smell of planed oak, cedar and cypress.

Some of the carpenters looked up, wondering if he was a thief. But they saw he carried nothing.

He ran back to the market place and stopped, looking vacantly about him.

The madman, the prophet, Karl Glogauer, the time-traveller, the neurotic psychiatrist manqué, the searcher for meaning, the masochist, the man with a death-wish and the messiah-complex, the anachronism, made his way through the market place gasping for breath.

He had seen the man he had sought. He had seen Jesus, the son of Mary and Joseph.

He had seen a man he recognized without any doubt as a congenital imbecile.

The cheerful man with the red cap was still in the market place, buying cooking pots to give as a wedding present. As the stranger stumbled past, he nodded towards him. 'That's the one.'

'Where's he from?'

'No idea. Not these parts, judging by his accent. I gather he's some relative of old sour-faced Joseph – you know, the one with the wife . . .'

The man selling pots grinned.

They watched him sink down in the shade by the wall of the synagogue.

'What is he? A religious fanatic? A Zealot or something?' said the man selling pots.

The other shook his head. 'He's got the look of a prophet, hasn't he? But I don't know. Maybe he just fell on hard times where he comes from and decided to seek the help of his relatives . . .'

'Seek old Joseph's help!' The man laughed.

'Maybe he got driven out of wherever he lived,' said the man with the red cap. 'Who knows? He couldn't have got much joy from Joseph. He wasn't there very long.'

'There's nowhere else for him to go,' said the man selling pots firmly.

He stayed by the wall of the synagogue until nightfall. He began to feel very hungry. Also, for the first time in more than a month, he began to feel lust. It was as if the urge had come to his rescue, as if in lust he could forget the bafflement that filled his head.

He rose slowly and began to make his way back towards the street.

He walked down the street of the carpenters and it was silent now. A few voices could be heard from within the houses, and the bark of a dog.

He reached the house. The bench had gone, and the wood. The gate was barred.

He tapped on it.

There was no reply.

He tapped a little louder, hardly understanding his instinct for discretion.

The gate was opened and her face looked out at him. She gave him a fat, knowing smile.

'Come in,' she said. 'He left for Nain hours ago.'

'I'm hungry,' he said.

'I'll give you something to eat.'

In the kitchen, something stirred in the darkness, but he did not look at it. He hurried through to the next room. A lamp burned there. A ladder led up into an opening in the ceiling.

'Wait here,' she said. 'I'll get food.'

She came and went from the kitchen several times, bringing first water so that he could wash, then a dish of dried meat, bread and a jug of wine.

'It's all we've got,' she said.

She looked into his dark, moody face. He had cleaned the dust from his body and combed out his hair and beard. He looked quite presentable now. But his eyes were withdrawn as he ate the food and he would not look at her directly.

She was breathing heavily now. The lust in her big body was becoming hard to control. She hitched her skirt up to above her calves and spread her legs apart when she sat on the stool near him.

He continued to chew, but now his eyes were on her body.

'Hurry up,' she said.

He finished the food and slowly drank the last of the wine.

Then she was on him, her hands tearing off his rag of a loincloth, her fingers on his genitals, her lips on his face, her great body heaving against him.

He gasped and drew up her skirt, driving his fingers into her, rocking against her, rolling her over on to the floor, hastily pushing her legs apart.

She moaned, screamed, snarled, jerked and clawed, then lay still as he continued to thrust into her. But the lust went and he could not finish. He sighed, glancing up suddenly.

The idiot stood in the doorway looking at them, spittle hanging from his chin, a vacant grin on his face.

Part Three

13

And the Word was made flesh, and dwelt among us.

JOHN 1: 14

EVERY TUESDAY IN THE SPARE ROOM above the Mandala Book-shop, the Jungian discussion group would meet to thrash out difficult points of doctrine and for purposes of group analysis and group therapy.

Glogauer had not organized the group, but he had willingly lent his premises to it. It was a great relief to talk with like-minded people once a week.

An interest in Jung brought them together, but everyone had special interests of his own. Mrs Rita Blen charted the courses of flying saucers, though it was not clear if she actually believed in them or not. Hugh Joyce was convinced that all Jungian archetypes derived from the original race of Lemurians who had perished millennia before. Alan Cheddar, the youngest of the group, was interested in Indian mysticism, and Sandra Peterson, the organizer, was a great witchcraft specialist.

James Headington was interested in time. The group's pride, he was Sir James Headington the physicist, wartime inventor, very rich and with all sorts of decorations for his contribution to the Allied victory. He had had the reputation of being a great improviser during the war, but afterwards he had become something of an embarrassment to the War Office. He was barmy, they thought, and what was worse he aired his barminess in public.

Sir James had a thin, aristocratic face (though he had been born in Norwood of middle-class parents), a thin, slightly prissy mouth, a shock of longish white hair and heavy black eyebrows. He wore old-fashioned suits and very bright flowered-patterned shirts and ties. Every so often he would tell the other members about the progress he was making with his time machine. They humoured him. Most of them were a little inclined to exaggerate their own experiences connected with their different interests.

One Tuesday evening, after everyone else had left, Headington asked Glogauer if he would like to go down to Banbury and have a look over his laboratory.

'I'm doing all sorts of spectacular experiments at the moment. Sending rabbits through time, that sort of thing. You really must look over the lab.'

'I can't believe it,' Glogauer said. 'You're really able to send things through time?'

'Oh, yes. You're the first I've told about it.'

'I can't believe it!' And he couldn't.

'Come down and have a look for yourself.'

'Why are you telling me?'

'Oh, I don't know. I like you, I suppose.'

Glogauer smiled. 'Well, all right. I will come down. When would be best?'

'Any time you like. Why not come down Friday and stay over the week-end?'

'You're sure you don't mind?'

'Not a bit!'

'I have a girlfriend . . .'

'Mmm . . .' Headington looked doubtful. 'I'm not too keen to broadcast this everywhere at the moment . . .'

'I'll put her off.'

'Good man! Catch the six-ten from Paddington if you can. I'll meet you at the station. See you Friday.'

'See you Friday.'

Glogauer watched him leave and he began to grin. The old boy was probably mad. He probably had a whole lot of expensive electronic junk down there, but it would be fun to have a week-end away from London and see exactly what was going on at Banbury.

Headington owned a large old rectory in a village about two miles from Banbury. The laboratory buildings in the grounds were all fairly new.

Headington employed two young men as full-time assistants; they were just leaving as the physicist guided Glogauer into the main building.

As Glogauer had suspected, the place was a clutter of Heath Robinson gadgets, with wires and cables hanging everywhere.

'Here,' said Headington, drawing Glogauer by the arm to a clearer part of the laboratory. On a wide bench stood several black boxes wired together. In the centre of these was another box, of silver grey.

Headington glanced at his watch and studied the dials on the black boxes. 'Now. Let's see.' He adjusted various controls. Then he went to a bank of cages on the other side of the room and re-moved a twitching white rabbit. He placed the rabbit in the silver box, made a few more adjustments to the controls on the black boxes, then turned a switch that had been screwed to the bench. 'Power,' he said.

Glogauer blinked. The air had seemed to shake for a moment. The silver box was gone.

'Good God!'

Headington chuckled. 'See – off through time!'

'It's vanished,' Glogauer agreed. 'But that doesn't prove it's gone into the future.'

'True. In fact it's gone into the past. Can't get into the future. An impossibility at the moment.'

'Well – I meant it didn't prove that the rabbit's travelling through time.'

'Where else could it have gone? Take my word for it, Glogauer. That rabbit's gone back a hundred years.'

'How do you know?'

'Short-range tests have proved it. I can send something back to a pretty accurately worked-out date. Believe me.'

Glogauer folded his arms across his chest. 'I believe you, Sir James.'

'We're building the big job now. Be able to send a man back. Only trouble is, the trip's a bit rough at present. Look . . .' He touched a stud on the nearest black box. Immediately, the silver box was back on the bench. Glogauer touched it. It was quite hot.

'Here.' Headington reached into the box and drew out the rabbit. Its head was bloody and its bones seemed to be broken. It was alive, but evidently in dreadful pain. 'See what I mean?' said Headington. 'Poor little thing.'

Glogauer turned away.

Back in the study Headington talked about his experiments, but he assumed that Glogauer was familiar with the language of physics and Glogauer was too proud to admit he knew next to nothing about physics, so he sat in his chair for several hours, nodding intelligently while Headington went on enthusiastically.

Headington showed him to his bedroom later. It was an oak-panelled room with a wide, comfortable modern bed.

'Sleep well,' said Headington.

That night, Glogauer was awakened and saw a figure seated on the edge of his bed. It was Headington and he was completely naked. He had his hand on Karl's shoulder.

'I don't suppose . . .' began Headington.

Glogauer shook his head. 'Sorry, Sir James.'

'Ah well,' said Headington. 'Ah well.'

Immediately he had left, Glogauer began to masturbate.

Headington had telephoned him several days later to ask if he'd like to make another trip to Banbury, but Glogauer had refused politely.

'We're ironing out some of the minor problems,' Headington had told him. 'For instance, we've decided on the best way to protect the passenger. Neither of my lads will volunteer to be it, though. You're not interested, are you, Glogauer?'

'No,' Glogauer said. 'Sorry, Sir James.'

During the next few weeks, Glogauer became disturbed. Monica came less frequently to see him and, when she did, she seemed to have no enthusiasm for lovemaking of any sort.

One night he lost his temper and began raving at her.

'What's the matter with you? You're as cold as a barrel of ice-cream!'

She stood half an hour of this before she said wearily, 'Well, I had to tell you sometime. If you must know, I'm having an affair with somebody.'

'What?' He calmed immediately. 'I don't believe it.' He had always been so confident that nobody else would be attracted to her. He almost asked her who would have her, but changed his mind.

'Who is he?' he said at last.

'She,' said Monica. 'It's a girl at the hospital. It makes a change.'

'Oh, Jesus!'

Monica sighed. 'It's a relief, really. I don't get an awful lot out of it – but I've got so sick of your emotions, Karl. Sick and tired.'

'Then why don't you leave me altogether? What sort of a compromise is this?'

'I suppose I can't give up hope,' said Monica. 'I still think there's something in you worth working on. I'm a fool, I suppose.'

'What are you trying to do to me?' He had become hysterical. 'What – what's . . . ? You've betrayed me!'

'See what I mean. It's not a betrayal, Karl – it's a bloody holiday.'

'Then you'd better make it permanent,' he said wildly, going over to her clothes and throwing them at her. 'Fuck off, you bitch!'

She got up with a weary resigned expression and began to dress.

When she was ready she opened the door. He was crying on the bed.

'Cheerio, Karl.'

'Fuck off!'

The door closed.

'You bitch! Oh, you bitch!'

The next morning, he telephoned Sir James Headington.

'I've changed my mind,' he said. 'I'll do what you want me to do. I'll be your subject. There's only one condition.'

'What's that?'

'I want to choose the time and place I go to.'

'Fair enough.'

A week later they were on board a privately chartered ship bound for the Middle East. A week after that he left 1970 and arrived in AD 28.

14

THE SYNAGOGUE WAS COOL AND QUIET with a subtle scent of incense. Dressed in the clean white robe Mary had given him when he had left early that morning, he let the rabbis guide him into the courtyard. They, like the townspeople, did not know what to make of him, but they were sure that it was not a devil that possessed him.

From time to time he would look down at his body and touch it as if in surprise, or he would finger the robe, puzzled. He had almost forgotten Mary.

'All men have a messiah-complex, Karl,' Monica had said once.

The memories were less complete now – if they were memories at all. He was becoming confused.

'There were dozens of messiahs in Galilee at the time. That Jesus should have been the one to carry the myth and the philosophy was a coincidence of history . . .'

'There must have been more to it than that, Monica.'

It was the rabbis' custom to give shelter to many of the roaming prophets who were now everywhere in Galilee, as long as they were not members of the outlawed sect.

This one was stranger than the rest. His face was immobile most of the time and his body was still, but tears frequently coursed down his cheeks. They had never seen such agony in a man's eyes before.

'Science can say how, but it never asks why,' he had told Monica. 'It can't answer.'

'Who wants to know?' she replied.

'I do.'

'Well, you'll never find out, will you?'

Bitch! Betrayer! Bastard!

Why did they always let him down?

'Be seated, my son,' said the rabbi. 'What do you wish to ask of us?'

'Where is Christ?' he said.

They did not understand the language.

'Is it Greek?' asked one, but another shook his head.

★

Kyrios: The Lord.
  Adonai: The Lord.
  Where was the Lord?

He frowned, looking vaguely about him.
  'I must rest,' he said in their language.
  'Where are you from?'
  He could not think what to answer.
  'Where are you from?' a rabbi repeated.
  At length he murmured, '*Ha-Olam Hab-Bah* . . .'
  They looked at one another. '*Ha-Olam Hab-Bah*,' they said.

Ha-Olam Hab-Bah; *Ha-Olam Haz-Zeh*: The world to come and the world that is.

'Do you bring us a message?' said one of the rabbis. This prophet was so different. So strange, one could almost believe that he was a true prophet. 'A message?'
  'I do not know,' said the prophet hoarsely. 'I must rest. I am dirty. I have sinned.'
  'Come. We will give you food and a place to sleep. We will show you where to bathe and where to pray.'
  Servants brought hot water and he cleansed his body. They trimmed his beard and hair and cut his nails.
  Then, in the cell that the rabbis had set aside for their visitor, they brought rich food which he found it difficult to eat. And the bed with its straw-stuffed mattress was too soft for him. He was not used to it. But he had had no real rest at Joseph's house and he lay down on it.
  He slept badly, shouting as he dreamed, and, outside the room, the rabbis listened, but could understand little of what he said.

'Of all things you should study, Karl, I should have thought Aramaic would be the last! No wonder you . . .'

My devil, my temptress, my desire, my cross, my love, my lust, my need, my food, my anchor, my master, my slave, my flesh, my satisfaction, my destroyer.
  Ah, for all the loving days that might have been if I had been strong; for Eva and those who did not want me for my weaknesses; for all the rewards granted to the brave, for all the realities given to

the strong, I yearn. This is the final irony.

The formal irony, inevitable and just.

And I am not satisfied.

Karl Glogauer stayed in the synagogue for several weeks. He would spend most of his time reading in the library, searching through the long scrolls for some answer to his dilemma. The words of the Testaments, in many cases capable of a dozen interpretations, only confused him further. There was nothing to grasp, nothing to tell him what had gone wrong.

This is a comedy. Is this what I deserve? Is there no hope? No solution?

The rabbis kept their distance for the most part. They had accepted him as a holy man. They were proud to have him in their synagogue. They were sure that he was one of the special chosen of God and they waited patiently for him to speak to them.

But the prophet said little, muttering only to himself in snatches of their own language and snatches of the incomprehensible language he often used, even when he addressed them directly.

In Nazareth, the townsfolk talked of little else but the mysterious prophet in the synagogue. They knew he was a relative of Joseph and Joseph was now proud to acknowledge the fact. They knew that Joseph was of the line of David, whatever the sour-faced carpenter was otherwise. So therefore the prophet was of the line of David. An important sign, everyone agreed.

They would ask questions of the rabbis but the wise men would tell them nothing, save that they should go about their business, that there were things they were not yet meant to know. In this way, as priests had always done, they avoided questions they could not answer while at the same time appearing to have much more knowledge than they actually possessed.

Then, one sabbath, he appeared in the public part of the synagogue and took his place with the others who had come to worship.

The man who was reading from the scroll on his left stumbled over the words, glancing at the prophet from the corner of his eye.

The prophet sat and listened, his expression remote.

The chief rabbi looked uncertainly at him, then signed that the scroll should be passed to the prophet. This was done hesitantly by a boy who placed the scroll in the prophet's hands.

The prophet looked at the words for a long time and it seemed that he would refuse to read, for he looked startled. Then he straightened his shoulders and began to read in a clear voice, almost without trace of his usual accent. He read from the book of Esaias.

The people listened with close attention.

> The Spirit of the Lord is upon me, because he hath anointed me to preach the gospel to the poor; he hath sent me to heal the brokenhearted, to preach deliverance to the captives, and recovering of sight to the blind, to set at liberty them that are bruised, To preach the acceptable year of the Lord. And he closed the book, and gave it again to the minister, and sat down. And the eyes of all of them that were in the synagogue were fastened on him.
>
> Luke 4: 18–20

Glogauer did not thereafter resume his study of the Testaments, but took to walking about the streets and talking to the people. They would be respectful, asking his advice on all manner of things, and he would do his best to give them good advice.

Not since his first weeks with Eva had he felt like this.

He resolved not to lose it a second time.

When at first they asked him to lay hands on the sick, he was reluctant and refused, but once, with what seemed to be an obvious case of hysterical blindness, judging from what the relatives told him, he did lay his hands on the woman's eyes and her blindness left her.

In spite of himself, Glogauer returned to his cell in the synagogue excited. There were so many examples of hysterical conditions of all kinds here.

Perhaps it was the creation of the times, he could not tell. At last he dismissed the thoughts. He would worry about them later.

The next day he saw Mary crossing the market place. She led her bastard son by his coat.

Glogauer turned hurriedly and went back into the synagogue.

15

THEY FOLLOWED HIM NOW, AS HE walked away from Nazareth towards the Lake of Galilee. He was dressed in the fresh white linen robe they had given him and he moved with wonderful dignity and grace; a great leader, a great prophet; but though they thought he led them, they, in fact, drove him before them.

To those that asked on the way they said, 'He is our messiah.' And there were already rumours of many miracles.

My redemption, my role, my destiny. In overcoming one temptation I must first succumb to another; cowardice and pride. Living a lie to create the truth. I have betrayed so many who have betrayed me because I betrayed myself.

But Monica would approve of my pragmatism now . . .

When he saw the sick, he pitied them and tried to do what he could because they expected something of him. Many he could do nothing for, but others, obviously with easily remedied psychosomatic conditions, he could help. They believed in his power more strongly than they believed in their sickness. So he cured them.

When he came to Capernaum some fifty people followed him into the streets of the city. It was already known that he was in some way associated with John the Baptist, who enjoyed considerable prestige in Galilee and had been declared a true prophet by many Pharisees. Yet this man had a power greater, in some ways, than John's. He was not the orator that the Baptist was, but he had worked miracles.

Capernaum was a sprawling town beside the crystal lake of Galilee, its houses separated by large market gardens. Fishing boats were moored at the white quayside, as well as trading ships that plied the lakeside towns.

Though the green hills came down from all sides of the lake, Capernaum itself was built on flat ground, sheltered by the hills. It was a quiet town and, like most others in Galilee, had a large population of gentiles. Greek, Roman and Egyptian traders walked its streets and many had permanent homes there. There was a prosperous middle class of merchants, artisans and ship-owners as well as doctors, lawyers and scholars, for Capernaum was on the borders of the provinces of Galilee, Trachonitis and Syria and, though a comparatively small town, was a useful junction for trade and travel.

The strange, mad prophet in his swirling linen robes, followed by the heterogeneous crowd that was primarily composed of poor folk, but also could be seen to contain men of some distinction, swept into Capernaum.

The news had spread that the man really could foretell the future, that he had already predicted the arrest of John by Herod Antipas and soon after Herod had imprisoned the Baptist at Peraea.

That was what impressed them. He did not make his predictions in general terms, using vague words the way other prophets did. He spoke of things that were to happen in the near future and he spoke of them in detail.

None, at this point, knew his name. That gave him an added mystery, an added stature. He was simply the prophet from Nazareth, or the Nazarene.

Some said he was a relative, perhaps the son, of a carpenter in Nazareth but this could be because the written words for 'son of a carpenter' and 'magus' were almost the same and the confusion had come about in this way.

There was even a very faint rumour that his name was Jesus. The name had been used once or twice, but when they asked him if that was, indeed, his name, he denied it or else, in his abstracted way, refused to answer at all.

His actual preaching tended to lack the fire and point of John's and many of his references seemed particularly oblique, even to the religious men and the scholars whose curiosity brought them to listen to him.

This man spoke gently, rather vaguely, and smiled often. He spoke of God in a strange way, too, and he appeared to be connected, as John was, with the Essenes, for he preached against the accumulation of personal wealth and spoke of mankind as a brotherhood, as they did.

But it was the miracles that they watched for as he was guided to the graceful synagogue of Capernaum.

No prophet before him had healed the sick and seemed to understand the troubles that people rarely spoke of. It was his sympathy that they responded to, rather than the words he spoke.

Yet sometimes he would become withdrawn and refuse to speak, would become lost in his own thoughts, and some would notice how tortured his eyes seemed, and they would leave him, believing him to be communicating with God.

These periods grew less lengthy and he would spend more time with the sick and the miserable, doing what he could for them, and even the wise and the rich in Capernaum began to respect him.

Perhaps the greatest change in him was that for the first time in his life Karl Glogauer had forgotten about Karl Glogauer. For the first time in his life he was doing what he had always considered himself too weak to do, and at the same time fulfilling his largest ambition, to achieve what he had hoped to achieve before he gave up psychiatry.

There was something more, something that he recognized instinctively rather than intellectually. He now had the opportunity to find at the same time both redemption and confirmation for his life up to the moment he had fled from John the Baptist in the desert.

But it was not his own life he would be leading now. He was bringing a myth to life, a generation before that myth would be born. He was completing a certain kind of psychic circuit. He told himself that he was not changing history; he was merely giving history more substance.

Since he had never been able to bear to think that Jesus had been nothing more than a myth, it became a duty to himself to make Jesus a physical reality rather than the creation of a process of mythogenesis. Why did it matter? he wondered; but he would be quick to dismiss the question, for such questions confused him, seemed to offer a trap, an escape and the possibility, once again, of self-betrayal.

So he spoke in the synagogues and he spoke of a gentler God than most of them had heard of, and where he could remember them, he told them parables.

And gradually the need to justify intellectually what he was doing faded and his sense of identity grew increasingly more tenuous and was replaced by a different sense of identity, in which he would give greater and greater substance to the role he had chosen. It was an archetypal role in all senses, a role to appeal to a disciple of Jung. It was a role that went beyond mere imitation. It was a role that he must now play out to the very last detail.

Karl Glogauer had discovered the reality he had been seeking. That was not to say he did not still have doubts.

> And in the synagogue there was a man, which had a spirit of an unclean devil, and cried out with a loud voice, Saying, Let us

alone; what have we to do with thee, thou Jesus of Nazareth? art thou come to destroy us? I know thee who thou art; the Holy One of God. And Jesus rebuked him, saying, Hold thy peace, and come out of him. And when the devil had thrown him in the midst, he came out of him, and hurt him not. And they were all amazed, and spake among themselves, saying, What a word is this! for with authority and power he commandeth the unclean spirits, and they come out. And the fame of him went out into every place of the country round about.

LUKE 4: 33–7

16

I know that my redeemer liveth, and that he shall stand at the latter day upon the earth.

JOB 19: 25

O felix culpa, quae talem ac tantum meruit habere Redemptorem.

Missal – 'Exsultet' on Holy Saturday

'MASS HALLUCINATION. MIRACLES, FLYING SAUCERS, ghosts, the beast from the id, it's all the same,' Monica had said.

'Very likely,' he had replied. 'But *why* did they see them?'

'Because they wanted to.'

'Why did they want to?'

'Because they were afraid.'

'You think that's all there is to it?'

'Isn't it enough?'

When he left Capernaum for the first time, many more people accompanied him.

It had become impractical to stay in the town, for its business had been brought almost to a standstill by the crowds that sought to see him work his simple miracles.

So he spoke to them in the spaces between the towns, from hillsides and on the banks of rivers.

He talked with intelligent, literate men who appeared to have something in common with him. Among these were the owners of fishing fleets – Simon, James and John and others. Another was a doctor, another a civil servant who had first heard him speak in Capernaum.

'There must be twelve,' he said to them one day, and he smiled. 'There must be a zodiac.'

And he picked them out by their names. 'Is there a man here called Peter? Is there one called Judas?'

And when he had picked them, he asked the others to go away for a while, for he wished to talk to the twelve alone.

It must be as exact as I can remember. There will be difficulties, discrepancies, but I must at least supply the basic structure.

He was not careful in what he said, people noticed. He was even more specific in his attacks and his examples than John the Baptist. Few prophets were as brave; few offered such confidence.

Many of his ideas were strange. Many of the things he talked about were unfamiliar to them. Some Pharisees thought he blasphemed.

Occasionally someone would attempt to warn him, suggest that for the sake of his cause he modify some of his pronouncements, but he would smile and shake his head. 'No. I must say what I must say. It is already decided.'

One day he met a man he recognized as an Essene from the colony near Machaerus.

'John would speak with you,' said the Essene.

'Is John not dead yet?' he asked the man.

'He is confined at Paraea. I would think Herod is too frightened to kill him. He lets John walk about within the walls and gardens of the palace, lets him speak with his men, but John fears that Herod will find the courage soon to have him stoned or decapitated. He needs your help.'

'How can I help him? He is to die. There is no hope for him.'

The Essene looked uncomprehendingly into the mad eyes of the prophet.

'But, master, there is no one else who can help him.'

'He must not be helped. He must die.'

'He told me, if you refused at first, to say that you failed him once, do not fail him now.'

'I am not failing him. I am redeeming my failure now. I have done all that I should have done. I have healed the sick and preached to the poor.'

'I did not know he wished this. Now he needs help, master. You could save his life. You are powerful and the people listen to your words. Herod could not refuse you.'

The prophet drew the Essene away from the twelve.

'His life cannot be saved.'

'Is it God's will?'

The prophet paused and looked down at the ground.

'John must die.'

'Master – is it God's will?'

The prophet looked up and spoke solemnly. 'If I am God, then it is God's will.'

Hopelessly, the Essene turned and began to walk away from the prophet.

The prophet sighed, remembering the Baptist and how he had liked him. Doubtless John had been chiefly responsible for saving his life. But there was nothing he could do. John the Baptist was ordained to die.

He moved on, with his following, through Galilee. Apart from his twelve educated men, the rest who followed him were still primarily poor people. To them he offered their only hope of good fortune. Many were those who had been ready to follow John against the Romans. But now John was imprisoned.

Perhaps this man would lead them in revolt, to loot the riches of Jerusalem and Jericho and Caesarea?

Tired and hungry, their eyes glazed by the burning sun, they followed the man in the white robe. They needed to hope and they found reasons for their hope. They saw him work greater miracles.

Once he preached to them from a boat, as was often his custom, and as he walked back to the shore through the shallows, it seemed to them that he walked over the water.

All through Galilee in the autumn they wandered, hearing from everyone the news of John's beheading. Despair at the Baptist's death turned to renewed hope in this fresh prophet who had known him.

In Caesarea they were driven from the city by Roman guards used to the wild men with their prophecies who roamed the rural districts.

They were banned from other cities as the prophet's fame grew. Not only the Roman authorities, but the Jewish ones as well seemed unwilling to tolerate the new prophet as they had tolerated John. The political climate was changing.

It became hard to get food. They lived on what they could find, hungering like starved animals.

Karl Glogauer, witch–doctor, psychiatrist, hypnotist, messiah, taught them how to pretend to eat and take their minds off their hunger.

> The Pharisees also with the Sadducees came, and tempting desired him that he would shew them a sign from heaven. He answered and said unto them, When it is evening, ye say, It will

be fair weather: for the sky is red. And in the morning, It will be foul weather to day: for the sky is red and lowring. O ye hypocrites, ye can discern the face of the sky; but can ye not discern the signs of the times?

MATTHEW 16: 1–3

'You must be more careful. You will be stoned. They will kill you.'
  'They will not stone me.'
  'That is the law.'
  'It is not my fate.'
  'Do you not fear death?'
  'It is not the greatest of my fears.'
  I fear my own ghost. I fear that the dream will end. I fear . . .
  But I am not lonely now.

Sometimes his conviction in his chosen role wavered and those that followed him would be disturbed when he contradicted himself.
  Often now they called him the name they had heard, Jesus the Nazarene.
  Most of the time he did not stop them from using the name, but at others he became angry and cried peculiar, guttural words.
  'Karl Glogauer! Karl Glogauer!'
  And they said, Behold, he speaks with the voice of Adonai.
  'Call me not by that name!' he would shout, and they would become disturbed and leave him by himself until his anger had subsided. Usually, then, he would seek them out, as if anxious for their company.

I fear my own ghost. I fear the lonely Glogauer.

They noticed that he did not like to see his own reflection and they said that he was modest and sought to emulate him.

When the weather changed and the winter came, they went back to Capernaum, which had become a stronghold of his followers.
  In Capernaum he waited the winter through talking to all who would listen, and most of his words concerned prophecies.
  Many of these prophecies concerned himself and the fates of those that followed him.

  Then charged he his disciples that they should tell no man that he was Jesus the Christ. From that time forth began Jesus to shew unto his disciples, how that he must go unto Jerusalem and suffer many things of the elders and chief priests and scribes, and be killed, and be raised again the third day.

MATTHEW 16: 20–1

They were watching television at her flat. Monica was eating an apple. It was between six and seven on a warm Sunday evening. Monica gestured at the screen with her half-eaten apple.

'Look at that nonsense,' she said. 'You can't honestly tell me it means anything to you.'

The programme was a religious one, about a pop-opera in a Hampstead church. The opera told the story of the crucifixion.

'Pop-groups in the pulpit,' she said. 'What a comedown.'

He didn't reply. The programme seemed obscene to him, in an obscure way. He couldn't argue with her.

'God's corpse is really beginning to rot now,' she jeered. 'Whew! What a stink!'

'Turn it off, then . . .'

'What's the pop-group called? The Maggots?'

'Very funny. I'll turn it off, shall I?'

'No, I want to watch. It's amusing.'

'Oh, turn it off!'

'Imitation of Christ!' she snorted. 'It's a bloody caricature.'

A Negro singer, who was playing Christ and singing flat to a banal accompaniment, began to drone out lifeless lyrics about the brotherhood of man.

'If he sounded like that, no wonder they nailed him up,' said Monica.

He reached forward and switched the picture off.

'I was enjoying it,' she said in mock disappointment. 'It was a lovely swan-song.'

Later, she said with a trace of affection that worried him, 'You old fogey. What a pity. You could have been John Wesley or Calvin or someone. You can't be a messiah these days, not in your terms. There's nobody to listen.'

17

THE PROPHET WAS LIVING IN THE house of a man called Simon, though the prophet preferred to call him Peter. Simon was grateful to the prophet because he had cured his wife of a complaint which she had suffered from for some time. It had been a mysterious illness, but the prophet had cured her almost effortlessly.

There were a great many strangers in Capernaum at that time, many of them coming to see the prophet. Simon warned him that some were known agents of the Romans or the hostile Pharisees. Many of the Pharisees had not, on the whole, been antipathetic towards the prophet, though they distrusted the talk of miracles they had heard. However, the whole political atmosphere was disturbed and the Roman occupation force, from Pilate, through his officers, down to the troops, was tense, expecting an outbreak but unable to see any really tangible signs that one was coming.

An abnormally abstemious man, Pilate poured water into the small measure of wine at the bottom of the cup and considered his position.

He hoped for trouble on a large scale.

If some sort of rebel band, like the Zealots, attacked Jerusalem, it would prove to Tiberius that he had, against all Pilate's advice, been too lenient with the Jews over the matter of the votive shields. Pilate would be vindicated and his power over the Jews increased. Perhaps then he could start to put through some real policies. At present he was on bad terms with all the tetrarchs of the provinces – particularly with the unstable Herod Antipas who had seemed at one time his only supporter.

Aside from the political situation, his own domestic situation was upset in that his neurotic wife was having her nightmares again and was demanding far more attention than he could afford to give her.

There might be a possibility, he thought, of provoking an incident, but he would have to be careful that Tiberius never learnt of it.

He wondered if this new prophet might provide a focus. So far the man had proved a bit disappointing. He had done nothing against the laws of either the Jews or the Romans, though he had been a trifle scathing about the established priesthood. Still, nobody ever worried about that – it was common to attack the priesthood in general. The priests themselves were too complacent most of the time to pay much attention to attacks. There was no law that forbade a man to claim he was a messiah, as some said this one had done, and he was hardly, at this stage, inciting the people to revolt – rather the contrary. Also one couldn't arrest a man because some of his followers were ex-followers of John the Baptist. The whole Baptist business had been mishandled when Herod had panicked.

Looking through the window of his chamber, with a view of the minarets and spires of Jerusalem, Pilate considered the information his agents had brought him.

Soon after the festival that the Romans called Saturnalia, the prophet and his followers left Capernaum again and began to travel through the country.

There were fewer miracles now that the hot weather had passed, but his prophecies were eagerly sought. He warned them of all the mistakes that would be made in the future, and of all the crimes that would be committed in his name, and he begged them to think before they acted in the name of Christ.

Through Galilee he wandered, and through Samaria, following the good Roman roads towards Jerusalem.

The time of the Passover was coming close now.

I have done all that I could think of to do. I have worked miracles, I have preached, I have chosen my disciples. But all this had been easy, because I have been what the people demanded. I am their creation.

Have I done enough? Has the course been set irrevocably?

We shall know soon.

In Jerusalem, the Roman officials discussed the coming festival. It was always a time of the worst disturbances. There had been riots before during the Feast of the Passover, and doubtless there would be trouble of some kind this year, too.

Pilate asked the Pharisees to come to see him. When they arrived, he spoke to them as ingratiatingly as possible, asking for their co-operation.

The Pharisees said they would do what they could, but they could not help it if the people acted foolishly.

Pilate was pleased. He had been seen by the others to be trying to avert trouble. If it came now, he could not be blamed.

'You see,' he said to the other officials. 'What can you do with them?'

'We'll get as many troops as we can recalled to Jerusalem as soon as possible,' said his second-in-command. 'But we're already spread a bit thin.'

'We must do our best,' said Pilate.

When they had gone, Pilate sent for his agents. They told him that the new prophet was on his way.

Pilate rubbed his chin.

'He seems harmless enough,' said one of the men.

'He might be harmless now,' said Pilate, 'but if he reaches Jerusalem during the Passover, he might not be so harmless.'

Two weeks before the Feast of the Passover, the prophet reached the town of Bethany near Jerusalem. Some of his Galilean followers had friends in Bethany and these friends were more than willing to shelter the man they had heard of from other pilgrims on their way to Jerusalem and the Great Temple.

The reason they had come to Bethany was that the prophet had become disturbed by the number of people following him.

'There are too many,' he had said to Simon. 'Too many, Peter.'

His face was haggard now. His eyes were set deeper into their sockets and he said little.

Sometimes he would look around him vaguely, as if unsure where he was.

News came to the house in Bethany that Roman agents had been making enquiries about him. It did not disturb him. On the contrary, he nodded thoughtfully, as if satisfied.

'Pilate is said to be looking for a scapegoat,' warned John.

'Then he shall have one,' replied the prophet.

Once he walked with two of his followers across country to look at Jerusalem. The bright yellow walls of the city looked splendid in the afternoon light. The towers and tall buildings, many of them decorated in mosaic reds, blues and yellows, could be seen from several miles away.

The prophet turned back towards Bethany.

There it is and I am afraid. Afraid of death and afraid of blasphemy.

But there is no other way. There is no sure manner to accomplish this save to live it through.

'When shall we go into Jerusalem?' one of his followers asked him.

'Not yet,' said Glogauer. His shoulders were hunched and he grasped his chest with his arms and hands as if cold.

Two days before the Feast of the Passover in Jerusalem, the prophet took his men towards the Mount of Olives and a suburb of Jerusalem that was built on the slopes of the mount and called Bethphage.

'Get me a donkey,' he told them. 'A colt. I must fulfil the prophecy now.'

'Then all will know you are the messiah,' said Andrew.

'Yes.'

The prophet sighed.

This fear is not the same. It is more the fear of an actor about to play his final, most dramatic scene . . .

There was cold sweat on the prophet's lip. He wiped it off.

In the poor light he peered at the men around him. He was still uncertain of some of their faces. He had been interested only in their names and their number. There were ten here. The other two were looking for the donkey.

There was a light, warm breeze blowing. They stood on the grassy slope of the Mount of Olives, looking towards Jerusalem and the Great Temple which lay below.

'Judas?' said Glogauer hesitantly.

There was one called Judas.

'Yes, master,' he said. He was tall and good-looking with curly red hair and neurotic, intelligent eyes. Glogauer believed he was an epileptic.

Glogauer looked thoughtfully at Judas Iscariot. 'I will want you to help me later,' he said, 'when we have entered Jerusalem.'

'How, master?'

'You must take a message to the Romans.'

'The Romans?' Judas looked troubled. 'Why?'

'It must be the Romans. It can't be the Jews. They would use stones or a stake or an axe. I'll tell you more when the time comes.'

The sky was dark now, and the stars were out over the Mount of Olives. It had become cold. Glogauer shivered.

18

Rejoice greatly, O daughter of Zion; shout, O daughter of Jerusalem: behold, thy King cometh unto thee: he is just, and having salvation; lowly, and riding upon an ass, and upon a colt the foal of an ass.

ZECHARIAH 9: 9

'Osha'na! Osha'na! Osha'na!'

As Glogauer rode the donkey into the city, his followers ran ahead, throwing down palm branches. On both sides of the street were crowds, forewarned by the followers of his coming.

Now the prophet could be seen to be fulfilling the prophecies of the ancient prophets and many more believed in him, believed that he had come, in Adonai's name, to lead them against the Romans. Even now, possibly, he was on his way to Pilate's house to confront the procurator.

'Osha'na! Osha'na!'

Glogauer looked around distractedly. The back of the donkey, though softened by the coats of his followers, was uncomfortable. He swayed and clung to the beast's mane. He heard the words, but could not make them out clearly.

'Osha'na! Osha'na!'

It sounded like 'Hosanna' at first, before he realized that they were shouting the Aramaic for 'Free us'.

'Free us! Free us!'

John had planned to rise in arms against the Romans this Passover. Many had expected to take part in the rebellion.

They believed that he was taking John's place as a rebel leader.

'No,' he muttered at them as he looked around at their expectant faces. 'No. I am the messiah. I cannot free you. I can't . . .'

Their faith was unfounded, but they did not hear him above their own shouts.

Karl Glogauer entered Christ and Christ entered Jerusalem. The story was approaching its climax.

'Osha'na!'

It was not in the story. He could not help them.

It was his flesh.

It was his flesh being given away piece by piece to whoever desired it. It no longer belonged to him.

Verily, verily, I say unto you, that one of you shall betray me. Then the disciples looked one on another, doubting of whom he spake. Now there was leaning on Jesus' bosom one of his disciples, whom Jesus loved. Simon Peter therefore beckoned to him, that he should ask who it should be of whom he spake. He then lying on Jesus' breast saith unto him, Lord, who is it? Jesus answered, He it is, to whom I shall give a sop, when I have dipped it. And when he had dipped the sop, he gave it to Judas Iscariot, the son of Simon. And after the sop Satan entered into him. Then said Jesus unto him, That thou doest, do quickly.

JOHN 13: 21–7

Judas Iscariot frowned with some uncertainty as he left the room and went out into the crowded street, making his way towards the governor's palace. Doubtless he was to perform a part in a plan to deceive the Romans and have the people rise up in Jesus's defence, but he thought the scheme foolhardy. The mood amongst the jostling men, women and children in the streets was tense. Many more Roman soldiers than usual patrolled the city.

'But they have no cause to arrest you, Lord,' he had said to the prophet.

'I will give them cause,' the prophet had replied.

There had been no other way to organize it.

He did not think it would matter. The chroniclers would rearrange it.

Pilate was a stout man in spite of eating and drinking little. His mouth was self-indulgent and his eyes were large and shallow.

He looked disdainfully at the Jew.

'We do not pay informers whose information is proved to be false,' he warned.

'I do not seek money, Lord,' said Judas, feigning the ingratiating manner that the Romans seemed to expect of the Jews. 'I am a loyal subject of the Emperor.'

'Who is this rebel?'

'Jesus of Nazareth, lord. He entered the city today . . .'

'I know. I saw him. But I heard he preached of peace and obeying the law.'

'To deceive you, lord. But today he has betrayed himself, angering the Pharisees, speaking against the Romans. He has revealed his true intentions.'

Pilate frowned. It was likely. It smacked of the kind of deceit he had grown to anticipate in these soft-spoken people.

'Have you proof?'

'There are a hundred witnesses.'

'Witnesses have poor memories,' said Pilate with some feeling. 'How do we identify them?'

'Then I will testify to his guilt. I am one of his lieutenants.'

It seemed too good to be true. Pilate pursed his lips. He could not afford to offend the Pharisees at this moment. They had given him enough trouble. Caiaphas, in particular, would be quick to cry 'injustice' if he arrested the man.

'You say he has offended the priests?'

'He claims to be the rightful king of the Jews, the descendant of David,' said Judas, repeating what his master had told him to say.

'Does he?' Pilate looked thoughtfully out of the window.

'As for the Pharisees, lord . . .'

'What of them?'

'They would see him dead. I have it on good authority. Certain of the Pharisees who disagree with the majority tried to warn him to flee the city, but he refused.'

Pilate nodded. His eyes were hooded as he considered this information. The Pharisees might hate the prophet, but they would be quick to make political capital out of his arrest.

'The Pharisees want him taken into custody,' Judas continued. 'The people flock to listen to the prophet and today many of them rioted in the Temple in his name.'

'That was him, was it?' It was true that some half-a-dozen people had attacked the money-changers in the Temple and tried to rob them.

'Ask those arrested who inspired them in their crime,' said Judas. 'They were the Nazarene's men.'

Pilate chewed his lower lip.

'I could not make the arrest,' he said. The situation in Jerusalem was already dangerous, but if they were to arrest this 'king' they might precipitate a full-scale revolt that he would not be able to handle. He wanted trouble, but he did not want to seem to be the cause of it. Tiberius would blame him, not the Jews. However, if the Jews were to make the arrest, it would divert the people's anger away from the Romans sufficiently for the troops to be able to handle matters. The Pharisees must be won over. They must make the arrest. 'Wait here,' he said to Judas. 'I will send a message to Caiaphas.'

> And they came to a place which was named Gethsemane: and he saith to his disciples, Sit ye here, while I shall pray. And he taketh with him Peter and James and John, and began to be sore amazed, and to be very heavy; And saith unto them, My soul is exceeding sorrowful unto death: tarry ye here, and watch.
>
> MARK 14: 32–4

Glogauer could see the mob approaching now. For the first time since Nazareth he felt physically weak and exhausted.

They were going to kill him. He had to die; he accepted that, but he was afraid of the pain that was to come. He sat down on the ground of the hillside, watching the torches as they came closer.

'The ideal of martyrdom only ever existed in the minds of a few ascetics,' Monica had said. 'Otherwise it was morbid masochism, an easy way to forgo ordinary responsibility, a method of keeping repressed people under control . . .'

'It isn't as simple as that . . .'

. *'It is, Karl.'*

He could show Monica now.

His regret was that she was unlikely ever to know. He had meant to write everything down and put it into the time machine and hope that it would be recovered. It was strange. He was not a religious man in the usual sense. He was an agnostic. It was not conviction that had led him to defend religion against Monica's cynical contempt for it; it was rather lack of conviction in the ideal in which she had set her own faith, the ideal of science as a solver of all problems. He could not share her faith and there was nothing else but religion, though he could not believe in the kind of God of Christianity. The God seen as a mystical force of the mysteries of Christianity and other great religions had not been personal enough for him. His rational mind had told him that God did not exist in any personal form. His unconscious had told him that faith in science was not enough. He remembered the self-contempt he had once felt and wondered why he had felt it.

'Science is basically opposed to religion,' Monica had once said. 'No matter how many Jesuits get together and rationalize their views of science, the fact

remains that religion cannot accept the fundamental attitudes of science and it is implicit in science to attack the fundamental principles of religion. The only area in which there is no difference and need be no war is the ultimate assumption. One may or may not assume there is a God. But at soon as one begins to defend one's assumption, there must be strife.'

'You're talking about organized religion . . .'

'I'm talking about religion as opposed to belief. Who needs the ritual of religion when we have the far superior ritual of science to replace it? Religion is a reasonable substitute for knowledge. But there is no longer any need for substitutes, Karl. Science offers a sounder basis on which to formulate systems of thought and ethics. We don't need the carrot of heaven and the big stick of hell any more when science can show the consequences of actions and men can judge easily for themselves whether those actions are right or wrong.'

'I can't accept it.'

'That's because you're sick. I'm sick, too, but at least I can see the promise of health.'

'I can only see the threat of death . . .'

As they had agreed, Judas kissed him on the cheek and the mixed force of Temple guards and Roman soldiers surrounded him.

To the Romans he said, with some difficulty, 'I am the king of the Jews.' To the Pharisees' servants he said: 'I am the messiah who has come to destroy your masters.'

Now he was committed and the final ritual was to begin.

19

IT WAS AN UNTIDY TRIAL, an arbitrary mixture of Roman and
Jewish law which did not altogether satisfy anyone. The object was
accomplished after several conferences between Pontius Pilate and
Caiaphas and three attempts to bend and merge their separate legal
systems in order to fit the expediencies of the situation. Both needed
a scapegoat for their different purposes and so at last the result was
achieved and the madman convicted, on the one hand of rebellion
against Rome and on the other of heresy.

A peculiar feature of the trial was that the witnesses were all
followers of the man and yet seemed eager to see him convicted.

'Ah, these morbid fanatics,' said Pilate. He was content.

The Pharisees agreed that the Roman method of execution would
fit the time and the situation best in this case and it was decided to
crucify him. The man had prestige, however, so that it would be
necessary to use some of the tried Roman methods of humiliation in
order to make him into a pathetic and ludicrous figure in the eyes of
the pilgrims.

Pilate assured the Pharisees that he would see to it, but he made
sure that they signed documents that gave their approval to his
actions.

The prisoner seemed almost content, though withdrawn. He had
spoken enough during the trial to condemn himself, but had said
little in his defence.

It is done.

My life is confirmed.

> And the soldiers led him away into the hall, called Praetorium;
> and they called together the whole band. And they clothed him
> with purple, and platted a crown of thorns, and put it about his
> head, And began to salute him, Hail, King of the Jews! And
> they smote him on the head with a reed, and did spit upon
> him . . . And when they had mocked him, they took off the
> purple from him, and put his own clothes on him, and led him
> out to crucify him.
>
> MARK 15: 16-20

'Oh, Karl, you'll do anything for attention . . .'
'You're after the limelight, young man . . .'

'God, Karl, what you'll do to get attention . . .'

Not now. Not this. It's too noble.

Were the faces laughing at him through the haze of pain?

Was his own face there, a look of ludicrous self-pity in its eyes? His own ghost . . . ?

But they could not rid him of the deep feeling of satisfaction that was there. The first full experience of the kind he had ever had.

His brain was clouded now, by pain and by the ritual humiliation; by his having completely given himself up to his role.

He was too weak to bear the heavy wooden cross and he walked behind it as it was dragged towards Golgotha by a Cyrenian whom the Romans had press-ganged for the purpose.

As he staggered through the crowded, silent streets, watched by those who had thought he would lead them against the Roman overlords, his eyes would refuse to focus and he occasionally staggered off the road and was nudged back on to it by one of the Roman guards.

'You are too emotional, Karl. Why don't you use that brain of yours and pull yourself together . . . ?'

He remembered the words, but it was difficult to remember who had said them or who Karl was.

The road that led up the side of the hill was stony and he slipped sometimes, remembering another hill he had climbed. It seemed to him that he had been a child, but the memory merged with the others and it was impossible to know.

He was breathing heavily and with some difficulty. The pain of the thorns in his head was barely felt, but his whole body seemed to throb in unison with his heartbeats. It was like a drum.

It was evening. The sun was setting. He fell on his face, cutting his head on a sharp stone, just as he reached the top of the hill. He fainted.

He had been a child. Was he still a child? They would not murder a child. If he made it plain to them that he was a child . . . ?

And they bring him unto the place Golgotha, which is, being interpreted, The place of a skull, And they gave him to drink wine mingled with myrrh: but he received it not.

MARK 15: 22-3

He knocked the cup aside. The soldier shrugged and reached out for one of his arms. Another soldier already held the other arm.

As he recovered consciousness he began to tremble violently. He felt the pain intensely as the ropes bit into the flesh of his wrists and ankles. He struggled.

He felt something cold placed against his palm. Although it only covered a small area in the centre of his hand it seemed very heavy. He heard a sound that also was a rhythm with his heartbeats. He turned his head to look at the hand. It was a man's hand.

The large iron peg was being driven into the hand by a soldier swinging a mallet as he lay on a heavy wooden cross which was at this moment horizontal on the ground. He watched, wondering why there was no pain. The soldier swung the mallet higher as the peg met the resistance of the wood. Twice he missed the peg and struck the fingers.

He looked to the other side and saw that the second soldier was also hammering in a peg. Evidently he had missed a great many times because the fingers of that hand were bloody and crushed.

The first soldier finished hammering in his peg and turned his attention to the feet.

He felt the iron slide through his flesh, heard it hammering home.

Using a pulley, they began to haul the cross into the vertical position. Glogauer noticed that he was alone. No others were being crucified that day.

The little silver cross, dangling between the breasts, the rough wooden cross advancing.

His erection came and went.

He had a clear view of the lights of Jerusalem below him. There was a little light in the sky, but it was fading.

Soon it would be completely dark.

There was a small crowd looking on. One of the women seemed familiar. He called to her.

'Monica?'

But his voice was cracked and the word was a whisper. The woman did not look up.

He felt his body dragging at the nails which supported it. He thought he felt a twinge of pain in his left hand. He seemed to be bleeding heavily.

It was odd, he reflected, that it should be him hanging here. He supposed that it was the event he had originally come to witness. There was little doubt, really. Everything had gone perfectly.

The pain in his left hand increased.

He glanced down at the Roman guards who were playing dice at the foot of the cross. He smiled. They were absorbed in their game. He could not see the markings of the dice from this distance.

He sighed. The movement of his chest seemed to throw extra strain on his hands. The pain was quite bad now. He winced and tried somehow to ease himself back against the wood.

He was breathing with difficulty. The pain began to spread through his body. He gritted his teeth. It was dreadful. He gasped and shouted. He writhed.

There was no longer any light in the sky. Heavy clouds obscured stars and moon.

From below came whispered voices.

'Let me down,' he called. 'Oh, please let me down!'

I am only a little boy.

'Fuck off, you bitch!'

The pain filled him. He was gasping rapidly for air. He slumped forward, but nobody released him.

A little while later he raised his head. The movement caused a return of the agony and again he began to writhe on the cross. He was being slowly asphyxiated.

'Let me down. Please. Please stop it!'

Every part of his flesh, every muscle and tendon and bone of him, was filled with impossible pain.

He knew he would not survive until the next day as he had thought he might.

> And at the ninth hour Jesus cried with a loud voice, saying, 'Eloi, Eloi, lama sabachthani?' which is, being interpreted, My God, my God, why hast thou forsaken me?
>
> MARK 15: 34

Glogauer coughed. It was a dry, barely heard sound. The soldiers below the cross heard it because the night was now so quiet.

'It's funny,' said one. 'Yesterday they were worshipping the bastard. Today they seemed to want to kill him – even the ones who were closest to him.'

'I'll be glad when we get out of this country,' said his companion.

They shouldn't kill a child, he thought.

He heard Monica's voice again. 'It's weakness and fear, Karl, that's driven you to this. Martyrdom is a conceit.'

He coughed once more and the pain returned, but it was duller now. His breathing was becoming more shallow.

Just before he died he began to talk again, muttering the words until his breath was gone. 'It's a lie – it's a lie – it's a lie . . .'

Later, after his body was stolen by the servants of some doctors who believed it might have special properties, there were rumours that he had not died. But the corpse was already rotting in the doctors' dissecting-rooms and would soon be destroyed.

Behold the Man
and other stories

Constant Fire

A little something for Alfie Bester

Kindle me to constant fire,
Lest the nail be but a nail!
Give me wings of great desire,
Lest I look within and fail!

. . . Red of heat to white of heat,
Roll we to the Godhead's feet!
Beat, beat! white of heat,
Red of heat, beat, beat!

George Meredith,
The Song of Theodolinda

1. In Which Your Auditor Gives Credit to His Sources

THE INCIDENTS INVOLVING MR JHEREK CARNELIAN and Mrs Amelia Underwood, their adventures in time, the machinations of, among others, the Lord of Canaria, are already familiar to those of us who follow avidly any fragment of gossip coming back from the End of Time.

We know, too, why it is impossible to learn further details of how life progresses there since the inception of Lord Jagged's grand (and some think pointless) scheme, details of which have been published in the three volumes jointly entitled *The Dancers at the End of Time* and in the single volume, companion to this, called *Legends from the End of Time*.

Time travellers, of course, still visit the periods immediately preceding the inception of the scheme. They bring us back those scraps of scandal, speculation, probable fact and likely lies which form the bases for the admittedly fanciful reconstructions I choose to term my 'legends from the future' – stories which doubtless would cause much amusement if those I write about were ever to read them (happily, there is no evidence that the tales survive our present century, let alone the next few million years).

If this particular tale seems more outrageous and less likely than any of the others, it is because I was gullible enough to believe the sketch of it I had from an acquaintance who does not normally journey so far into the future. A colleague of Miss Una Persson in the Guild of Temporal Adventurers, he does not wish me to reveal his name and this, fortunately, allows me to be rather more frank about him than would have been possible.

My friend's stories are always interesting, but they are consistently highly coloured; his exploits have been bizarre and his claims incredible. If he is to be believed, he has been present at a good many of the best-known key events in history, including the crucifixion of Christ, the massacre at My Lai, the assassination of Naomi Jacobsen in Paris and so on, and has often played a major role.

From his base in West London (twentieth century, Sectors 3 and 4) my friend has ranged what he terms the 'chrono-flow', visiting periods of the past and future of this earth as well as those of other earths which, he would have us accept, co-exist with ours in a complex system of intersecting dimensions making up something called the 'multiverse'.

Of all the temporal adventurers I have known, my friend is the most ready to describe his exploits to anyone who will listen. Presumably, he is not subject to the Morphail Effect (which causes most travellers to exercise the greatest caution regarding their actions and conversations in any of the periods they visit) mainly because few but the simple-minded, and those whose logical faculties have been ruined by drink, drugs or other forms of dissipation, will take him seriously.

My friend's own explanation is that he is not affected by such details; he describes himself rather wildly as a 'chronic outlaw' (a self-view which might give the reader some insight into his character). You might think he charmed me into believing the tale he told me of Miss Mavis Ming and Mr Emmanuel Bloom, and yet there is something about the essence of the story that inclined me to believe it – for all that it is, in many ways, one of the most incredible I have heard. It cannot, of course, be verified readily (certainly so far as the final chapters are concerned) but it is supported by other rumours I have heard, as well as my own previous knowledge of Mr Bloom (whose earlier incarnation appeared in a tale, told to me by one of my friend's fellow-Guild members, published variously as *The Fireclown* and *The Winds of Limbo*, some years ago).

The events recorded here follow directly upon those recorded in *Legends from the End of Time* and in effect take up Miss Ming's story where we left it after her encounter with Dafnish Armatuce and her son Snuffles.

As usual, the basic events described are as I had them from my source. I have re-arranged certain things, to maintain narrative tensions, and added to an earlier, less complete, draft of my own which was written hastily, before all the information was known to me. The 'fleshing-out' of the narrative, the interpretations where they occur, many of the details of conversations, and so on, must be blamed entirely on your auditor.

In the previous volume to this, I have already recounted something of that peculiar relationship existing between Miss Ming and Doctor Volospion: the unbearable bore and that ostentatious misanthrope.

Why Doctor Volospion continued to take perverse pleasure in the woman's miserable company, why she allowed him to insult her in the most profound of ways – she who spent the greater part of her days avoiding any sort of pain – we cannot tell. Suffice to say that relationships of this sort exist in our own society and can be equally puzzling.

Perhaps Doctor Volospion found confirmation of all his misanthropy in her; perhaps she preferred this intense, if unpleasant, attention to no attention at all. She confirmed his view of life, while he confirmed her very existence.

But it is the purpose of a novel, not a romance, to speculate in this way and it is no part of my intention to dwell too much upon such thoughts.

Here, then, for the reader's own interpretation (if one is needed), is the tale of Miss Ming's transformation and the part which both Doctor Volospion and Emmanuel Bloom had in it.

Michael Moorcock
Ladbroke Grove
November 1975

2. In Which Miss Mavis Ming Experiences a Familiar Discomfort

THE PECULIAR EFFECT OF ONE SUN RISING JUST AS ANOTHER SET, causing shadows to waver, making objects appear to shift shape and position, went more or less entirely unobserved by the great crowd of people who stood, enjoying a party, in the foothills of a rather poorly finished range of mountains erected some little time ago by Werther de Goethe during one of his periodic phases of attempting to recreate the landscape, faithful to the last detail, of Holman Hunt, an ancient painter Werther had discovered in one of the rotting cities.

Werther, it is fair to say, had not been the first to make such an attempt. However, he held to the creed that an artist should, so far as his powers allowed, put up everything exactly as he saw it in the painting. Werther was a purist. Werther volubly denied the criticisms of those who found such literal work bereft of what they regarded as true artistic inspiration. Werther's theories of Fidelity to Art had enjoyed a short-lived vogue (for a time the Duke of Queens had been an earnest acolyte) but his fellows had soon tired of such narrow disciplines.

Werther, alone, refused to renounce them.

As the party progressed, another of the suns eventually vanished while the other rose rapidly, reached zenith and stopped. The light became golden, autumnal, misty. Of the guests but three had paused to observe the phenomenon: they were Miss Mavis Ming, plump and eager in her new dress; Li Pao, bland in puritanical denim; and Abu Thaleb, their host, svelte and opulent, splendidly overdressed.

'Whose suns?' murmured Abu Thaleb appreciatively. 'How pretty! And subtle. Rivals, perhaps . . . '

'To your own creations?' asked Li Pao.

'No, no – to one another.'

'They could be Werther's,' suggested Miss Ming, anxious to return to their interrupted topic. 'He hasn't arrived yet. Go on, Li Pao. You were saying something about Doctor Volospion.'

A fingered ear betrayed Li Pao's embarrassment. 'I spoke of no one specifically, Miss Ming.' His round Chinese face became expressionless.

'By association,' Abu Thaleb prompted, a somewhat sly smile manifesting itself within his pointed beard, 'you spoke of Volospion.'

'Ah! You would make a gossip of me. I disdain such impulses. I merely observed that only the weak hate weakness; only the wounded condemn the pain of others.' He wiped a stain of juice from his severe blouse and turned his back on the tiny sun.

Miss Ming was arch. 'But you *meant* Doctor Volospion, Li Pao. You were *suggesting* . . . '

A tide of guests flowed by, its noise drowning what remained of her remark, and when it had passed, Li Pao (perhaps piqued by an element of truth) chose to show impatience. 'I do not share your obsession with your protector, Miss Ming. I generalized. The thought can scarcely be considered a specific one, nor an original one. I regret it. If you prefer, I retract it.'

'I wasn't *criticising*, Li Pao. I was just *interested* in how you saw him. I mean, he has been very *kind* to me, and I wouldn't like anybody to think I wasn't aware of all he's *done* for me. I could still be in his menagerie couldn't I? But he showed his respect for me by letting me go – that is, asking me to be his *guest* rather than – well, whatever you'd call it.'

'He is a model of chivalry.' Abu Thaleb stroked an eyebrow and hid his face with his hand. 'Well, if you will excuse me, I must see to my monsters. To my guests.' He departed, to be swallowed by his party, while Li Pao's imploring look went unnoticed.

Miss Ming smoothed the front of Li Pao's blouse. 'So you see,' she said, 'I was only curious. It certainly wasn't *gossip* I wanted to hear. But I respect your opinions, Li Pao. We are fellow-"prisoners", after all, in this world. Both of us would probably prefer to be back in the past, where we belong – you in the twenty-seventh century, to take your rightful position as chairman or whatever of China, and me in the twenty-first, to, to . . . ' Inspiration left her momentarily. She contented herself with a coy wink. 'You mustn't pay any attention to little Mavis. There's no malice in her.'

'Aha.' Li Pao closed his eyes and drew a deep breath.

Miss Ming's sky-blue nail traced patterns on the more restrained blue of his chest. 'It's not in Mavis's nature to think naughty thoughts. Well, not that sort of naughty thought, at any rate!' She giggled.

'Yaha?' It was almost inaudible.

From somewhere overhead came the distant strains of one of Abu Thaleb's beasts. Li Pao raised his head as if to seek the source. He contemplated heaven.

Miss Ming, too, looked up. 'Nothing,' she said. 'It must have come from over there.' She pointed and, to her chagrin, her finger indicated the approaching figure of Ron Ron Ron who was, like herself and Li Pao, an expatriate (although in his case from the 140th century). 'Oh, look out, Li Pao. It's that bore Ron coming over . . .'

She was surprised when Li Pao expressed enthusiastic delight. 'My old friend!'

She was sure that Li Pao found Ron Ron Ron just as awful as everyone else but, for his sake, she smiled as sweetly as she could. 'How *nice* to see you!'

Ron Ron Ron had an expression of *hauteur* on his perfectly oval face. This was his usual expression. He, too, seemed just a little surprised by Li Pao's effusion. 'Um?'

The two men contemplated one another. Mavis plainly felt that it was up to her to break the ice. 'Li Pao was just saying – *not* about Doctor Volospion or anybody in particular – that the weak hate weakness and won't – what was it, Li Pao?'

'It was not important, Miss Ming. I must . . . ' He offered Ron Ron Ron a thin smile.

Ron Ron Ron cleared his throat. 'No, please . . . '

'It was very *profound*,' said Miss Ming. 'I thought.'

Ron Ron Ron adjusted his peculiar jerkin so that the edges were exactly in line. He fussed at a button. 'Then you must repeat it for me, Li Pao.' The shoulders of his jerkin were straight-edged and the whole garment was made to the exact proportions of a square. His trousers were identical oblongs; his shoes, too, were exactly square. The fingers of his hands were all of the same length.

'Only the weak hate weakness . . . ' murmured Miss Ming encouragingly, 'and . . . '

Li Pao's voice was almost a shriek: ' . . . only the wounded condemn the pain of others. You see, Ron Ron Ron, I was not – '

'An interesting observation.' Ron Ron Ron put his hands together under his chin. 'Yes, yes, yes. I see.'

'No!' Li Pao took a desperate step forwards, as if to leave.

'By the same argument, Li Pao,' began Ron Ron Ron, and Li Pao became passive, 'you would imply that a strong person who exercised that strength is, in fact, revealing a weakness in his character, eh?'

'No. I . . .'

'Oh, but we must have a look at this.' Ron Ron Ron became almost animated. 'It suggests, you see, that indirectly you condemn my efforts as leader of the Symmetrical Fundamentalist Movement in attempting to seize power during the Anarchist Beekeeper period.'

'I assure you, that I was not . . . ' Li Pao's voice had diminished to a whisper.

'Certainly we were strong enough,' continued Ron Ron Ron. 'If the planet had not, in the meantime, been utilized as a strike-base by some superior alien military force (whose name we never did learn), which killed virtually all opposition and enslaved the remaining third of the human race during the duration of its occupation – not much more than twenty years, admittedly – before they vanished again, either because our part of the galaxy was no longer of strategic importance to them or because their enemies had defeated them, who knows what we could have achieved.'

'Wonders,' gasped Li Pao. 'Wonders, I am sure.'

'You are kind. As it was, Earth was left in a state of semi-barbarism which had no need, I suppose, for the refinements either of Autonomous Hiveism or Symmetrical Fundamentalism, but given the chance I could have – '

'I am sure. I am sure.' Li Pao's voice had taken on the quality of a labouring steam-engine.

'Still,' Ron Ron Ron went on, 'I digress. You see, because of my efforts to parley with the aliens, my motives were misinterpreted – '

'Certainly. Certainly.'

' – and I was forced to use the experimental time craft to flee here. However, my point is this . . . '

'Quite, quite, quite . . . '

Miss Ming shook her head. 'Oh, you men and your politics. I . . . '

But she had not been forceful enough. Ron Ron Ron's (or Ron's Ron's Ron's, as he would have preferred us to write) voice droned on, punctuated by Li Pao's little gasps and sighs. She could not understand Li Pao's allowing himself to be trapped in this awful situation. She had done her best, when he seemed to want to talk to Ron Ron Ron, to begin a conversation that would interest them both, knowing that the only thing the two men had in common was a past taste for political activity and a present tendency, in their impotence, to criticize the shortcomings of their fellows here at the End of Time. But now Li Pao showed no inclination at all to take Ron Ron Ron up on any of his points, which were certainly of no interest to anyone but the Symmetrical Fundamentalist himself. She knew what it was like with some people; if a string was pulled in them, they couldn't stop themselves going on and on. A lot of those she had known, back home in twenty-first-century Iowa, had been like that.

Again, thought Mavis, it was up to her to change the subject. For Li Pao's sake as well as her own.

' . . . they never did separate properly, you see,' said Ron Ron Ron.

'Separate?' Miss Ming seized the chance given her by the pause in his monologue. She spoke brightly. 'Properly? Why, that's like my Swiss cheese plant. The one I used to have in my office? It grew so big! But the leaves wouldn't separate properly. Is that what happened to yours, Ron Ron Ron?'

'We were discussing strength,' said Ron Ron Ron in some bewilderment.

'Strength! You should have met my ex. I've mentioned him before? Donny Stevens, the heel. Now say what you like about him, but he was *strong*! Betty – you know, that's the friend I told you about? – *more* than a friend really . . . ' she winked. ' . . . Betty used to say that Donny Stevens was prouder of his pectorals than he was of his prick! Eh?' She shook with laughter.

The two men looked at her in silence.

Li Pao sucked his lower lip.

'And that was saying a lot, where Donny was concerned,' Mavis added.

'Ushshsh . . . ' said Li Pao.

'Really?' Ron Ron Ron spoke in a peculiar tone.

The silence returned at once. Dutifully, Mavis tried to fill it. She put a hand on Ron Ron Ron's tubular sleeve.

'I shouldn't tell you this, what with my convictions and all – I was polarized in '65, became an all-woman woman, if you get me, after my divorce – but I miss that bastard of a bull sometimes.'

'Well . . . ' Ron Ron Ron hesitated.

'What this world needs,' said Mavis as she got into her stride, 'if you ask me, is a few more real men. You know? Real men. The girls around here have got more balls than the guys. One real man and, boy!, you'd find my tastes changing just like that . . . ' She tried, unsuccessfully, to snap her fingers.

'Ssssss . . . ' said Li Pao.

'Anyway,' Mavis was anxious to reassure him that she had not lost track of the original topic, 'It's the same with Swiss cheese plants. They're strong. Any conditions will suit them and they'll strangle anything that gets in their way. They use – they *used* to use, I should say – the big ones to fell other trees in Paraguay. I think it's Paraguay. But when it comes to getting the leaves to separate, well, all you can say is that they're bastards to train. Like strong men, I guess. In the end you have to take 'em or leave 'em as they come.'

Mavis laughed again, waiting for their responding laughter, which did not materialize. She was valiant:

'I stayed with my house-plants, but I left that stud to play in his own stable. And how he'd been playing! Betty said if I tried to count the number of mares he'd serviced while *I* thought he was stuck late at the lab I'd need a computer!'

Li Pao and Ron Ron Ron now stood side by side, staring at her.

'*Two* computers!' She had definitely injected a bit of wit into the conversation and given Li Pao a chance to get on to a subject he preferred but evidently neither of them had much of a sense of humour. Li Pao now glanced at his feet. Ron Ron Ron had a silly fixed grin on his face and was just grunting at her, even though she had stopped speaking.

Miss Ming decided to soldier on;

'Did I tell you about the busy Lizzie that turned out to be poison ivy? We were out in the country one day, this was before my divorce – it must have been just after we got married – either '60 or '61 – no, it must have been '61 definitely because it was spring – probably May . . . '

'*Look!*'

Li Pao's voice was so loud that it startled Mavis.

'What?'

'There's Doctor Volospion.' He waved towards where the crowd was thickest. 'He was signalling to you, Miss Ming. Over there!'

The news heartened her. This would be her excuse to get away. But she could not, of course, show Li Pao how pleased she was. So she smiled indulgently. 'Oh, let him wait. Just because he's my host here doesn't mean I have to be at his beck and call the whole time!'

'Please,' said Ron Ron Ron, removing a small, pink, even-fingered hand from a perfectly square pocket. 'You must not let us, Miss Ming, monopolize your time.'

'Oh, well . . . ' She was relieved. 'I'll see you later, perhaps. Byee.' Her wink was cute; she waggled her fingers at them. But as she turned to seek out Doctor Volospion it seemed that he had disappeared. She turned back and to her surprise saw Li Pao sprinting away from Ron Ron Ron towards the foot of one of Abu Thaleb's monsters, perhaps because he had seen someone to whom he wished to speak. She avoided Ron Ron Ron's eye and set off in the general direction indicated by Li Pao, making her way between guests and wandering elephants who were here in more or less equal numbers.

'At least I did my best,' she said. 'They're very difficult men to talk to.'

She yawned. She was already beginning to be just a trifle bored with the party.

3. In Which Miss Ming Fails to Find Consolation

THE ELEPHANTS, ALTHOUGH THE MOST NUMEROUS, were not the largest beasts providing the party's entertainment; its chief feature being the seven monstrous animals who sat on green-brown haunches and raised their heavy heads in mournful song.

These beasts were the pride of Abu Thaleb's collection. They were perfect reproductions of the singing gargantua of Justine IV, a planet long since vanished in the general dissipation of the cosmos (Earth, the reader will remember, had used up a good many other star systems to rejuvenate its own energies).

Abu Thaleb's enthusiasm for elephants, and all that was elephantine, was so great that he had changed his name to that of the ancient Commissar of Bengal solely because one of that legendary dignitary's other titles had been Lord of All Elephants.

The gargantua were more in the nature of huge baboons, their heads resembling those of Airedale terriers (now, of course, long-extinct) and were so large that the guests standing closest to them could not see them as a whole at all. Moreover, so high were these shaggy heads above the party that the beautiful music of their voices was barely audible.

Elsewhere, the Commissar's guests ate from trays carried upon the backs of baby mammoths, or leaned against the leather hides of hippopotami which kneeled here and there about the grounds of Abu Thaleb's vast palace, itself fashioned in the shape of two marble elephants standing forehead to forehead, with trunks entwined.

Mavis Ming paused beside a resting oryx and pulled a tiny savoury doughnut or two from its left horn, munching absently as the beast's huge eyes regarded her. 'You look,' she remarked to it, 'as fed up as I feel.' She could find no one to keep her company in that whole cheerful throng. Almost everyone she knew had seemed to turn aside just as she had been about to greet them and Doctor Volospion himself was nowhere to be seen.

'This party,' she continued, 'is definitely tedious.'

'What a supehb fwock, Miss Ming! So fwothy! So yellah!'

Sweet Orb Mace, in flounces and folds of different shades of grey, presented himself before her, smiling and languid. His eyebrows were elaborately arched; his hair incredibly ringleted, his cheeks exquisitely rouged. He made a leg.

The short-skirted yellow dress, with its several petticoats, its baby-blue trimmings (to match her eyes, her best feature), was certainly, Mavis felt, the sexiest thing she had worn for a long while, so she was not surprised by his compliment.

She gave one of her little-girl trills of laughter and pirouetted for him.

'I thought,' she told him, 'that it was high time I felt feminine again. Do you like the bow?' The big blue bow in her honey-blonde hair was trimmed with yellow and matched the smaller bows on her yellow shoes.

'Wondahful!' pronounced Sweet Orb Mace. 'It is quite without compahe!'

She was suddenly much happier. She blew him a kiss and fluttered her lashes. She warmed to Sweet Orb Mace, who could sometimes be such good company (whether as a man or a woman, for his moods varied from day to day) and she took his arm, confiding: 'You know how to flatter a girl. I suppose you, of all people, *should* know. I'll tell you a secret. I've been a bit cunning, you see, in wearing a full skirt. It makes my waist look a little slimmer. I'm the first to admit that I'm not the thinnest girl in the world, but I'm not about to emphasize the fact, am I?'

'Wemahkable.'

Amiably, Sweet Orb Mace strolled in harness while Mavis whispered further secrets. She told him of the polka-dot elephant she had had when she was seven. She had kept it for years, she said, until it had been run over by a truck, when Donny Stevens had thrown it through the apartment window into the street, during one of their rows.

'I could have taken almost anything else,' she said.

Sweet Orb Mace nodded and murmured little exclamations, but he scarcely seemed to have heard the anecdote. If he had a drawback as a companion, it was his vagueness; his attention wavered so.

'He accused *me* of being childish,' exclaimed Mavis putting, as it were, twice the energy into the conversation, to make up for his failings. 'Ha! He had the mental age of a dirty-minded eleven-year-old! But there you go. I got more love from that elephant than I ever got from Donny Stevens. It's always the people who try to be nice who come in for the nasty treatment, isn't it?'

'Wather!'

'He blamed me for everything. Little Mavis *always* gets the blame! Ever since I was a kid. Everybody's whipping boy, that's Miss Mavis Ming! My father . . . '

'Weally?'

She abandoned this line, thinking better of it, and remained with her original sentiment. 'If you don't stand up for yourself, some-one'll always step on you. The things I've done for people in the past. And you know what almost always happens?'

'Natuwally . . . '

'They turn round and say the cruellest things to you. They always blame you when they should really be blaming themselves. That woman – Dafnish Armatuce – *well* . . . '

'Twagic.'

'Doctor Volospion said I'd been too easy-going with her. I looked after that kid of hers as if it had been my own! It makes you want to give up sometimes, Sweet Orb. But you've got to keep on trying, haven't you? Some of us are fated to suffer . . . '

Sweet Orb Mace paused beside a towering mass of ill-smelling hairy flesh which moved rhythmically and shook the surrounding ground so that little fissures appeared. It was the gently tapping toe of one of Abu Thaleb's singing gargantua. Sweet Orb Mace stared gravely up, unable to see the head of the beast. 'Oh, cehtainly,' he agreed. 'Pwetty tune, don't you think?'

She lifted an ear, but shrugged. 'No, I don't.'

He was mildly surprised.

'Too much like a dirge for my taste,' she said. 'I like something catchy.' She sighed, her mood returning to its former state. 'Oh, dear! This is a very boring party.'

He became astonished.

'This pwofusion of pachyderms bohwing? Oh, no! I find it fascinating, Miss Ming. An extwavagance of elephants, a genewosity of giants!'

She could not agree. Her eye, perhaps, was jaundiced.

Sweet Orb Mace, sensing her displeasure, became anxious. 'Still,' he added, 'evewyone knows how easily impwessed I am. Such a poah imagination of my own, you know.'

She sighed. 'I expected more.'

'Monsters?' He glanced about, as if to find her some. 'Awgonheart Po has yet to make his contwibution! He is wumouhed to be supplying the main feast.'

'I didn't know.' She sighed again. 'It's not that. I was hoping to meet some nice person. Someone – you know – I could have a real relationship with. I guess I expected too much from that Dafnish and her kid – but it's, well, turned me on to the *idea*. I'm unfulfilled as a woman, Sweet Orb Mace, if you want the raw truth of it.'

She looked expectantly at her elegantly poised escort.

'Tut,' said Sweet Orb Mace abstractedly. 'Tut, tut.' He still stared skywards.

She raised her voice. 'You're not, I guess, in the mood yourself. I'm going to go home if things don't perk up. If you feel like coming back now – or dropping round later . . . ? I'm still staying at Doctor Volospion's.'

'Weally?'

She laughed at herself. 'I should try to sound more positive, shouldn't I? Nobody's going to respond well to a faltering approach like that. Well, Sweet Orb Mace, what about it?'

'It?'

She was actually depressed now.

'I meant . . . '

'I pwomised to meet O'Kala Incarnadine heah,' said Sweet Orb Mace. 'I was suah – ah – and theah he is!' carolled her companion. 'If you will excuse me, Miss Ming . . . 'Another elaborate bending of the body, a sweep of the hand.

'Oh, sure,' she murmured.

Sweet Orb Mace rose a few feet into the air and drifted towards O'Kala Incarnadine, who had come as a rhinoceros.

'The way I'm beginning to feel,' said Miss Ming to herself, 'even O'Kala Incarnadine's looking attractive. Bye, bye, Sweet Orb. No sweat. Oh, Christ! This boredom is *killing*!'

And then she had seen her protector, her host, her mentor, her guardian angel and, with a grateful 'Hi!' she flew.

Doctor Volospion was sighted at last! He seemed at times like this her only stability. He it was who had first found her when, in her time machine, dazed and frightened, she had arrived at the End of Time. Doctor Volospion had claimed her for his menagerie, thinking from her conversation that she belonged to some religious order (she had been delirious) and had discovered only later that she was a simple historian who believed that she had returned to the past, to the Middle Ages. He had been disappointed but had treated her courteously and now allowed her the full run of his house. She did not fit into his menagerie which was religious in emphasis, consisting of nuns, prophets, gods, demons and so forth. She could have founded her own establishment, had she wished, but she preferred the security of his sometimes dolorous domicile.

She slowed her pace. Doctor Volospion was hailing the Commissar of Bengal, whose howdah-shaped golden air cab was drifting back to the ground (apparently, Abu Thaleb had been feeding his gigantic pets).

'Coo-ee!' cried Miss Ming as she approached.

But Doctor Volospion had not heard her.

'Coo-ee.'

He joined in conversation with Abu Thaleb.

'Coo-ee, Doctor!'

Now the sardonic, saturnine features turned to regard her. The sleek black head moved in a kind of bow and the corners of the thin, red mouth lifted.

She was panting as she reached them. 'It's only little me!'

Abu Thaleb was avuncular. 'Miss Ming, again we meet. Scheherazade come among us.' The dusky Commissar was one of the few regular visitors to Doctor Volospion's, perhaps the only friend of the Doctor's to treat her kindly. 'You enjoy the entertainment, I hope?'

'It's a great party if you like elephants,' she said. But the joke had misfired; Abu Thaleb was frowning. So she added with some eagerness: 'I personally *love* elephants.'

'I did not know we had that in common.'

'Oh, yes. When I was a little girl I used to go for rides at the zoo whenever I could. At least once a year, on my birthday. My daddy would try to take me, no matter what else was happening . . . '

'I must join in the compliments.' Doctor Volospion cast a glinting eye from her toes to her bow. 'You outshine us all, Miss Ming. Such taste! Such elegance! We, in our poor garb, are mere flickering candles to your super-nova!'

Her giggle of response was hesitant, as if she suspected him of satire, but then an expression almost of tranquillity passed across her features. His flattery appeared to have a euphoric effect upon her. She became a fondled cat.

'Oh, you always do it to me, Doctor Volospion. Here I am trying to be brittle and witty, cool and dignified, and you make me grin and blush like a schoolgirl.'

'Forgive me.'

She frowned, finger to lips. 'I'm trying to think of a witticism to please you.'

'Your presence is uniquely pleasing, Miss Ming.'

Doctor Volospion moved his thin arms which were hardly able to bear the weight of the sleeves of his black and gold brocade gown.

'But . . . '

Doctor Volospion turned to Abu Thaleb. 'You bring us a world of gentle monsters, exquisite Commissar. Gross of frame, mild of manner, delicate of spirit. Your paradoxical pachyderms!'

'They are very *practical* beasts, Doctor Volospion.' Abu Thaleb spoke defensively, as if he, too, suspected irony.

People would often respond in this way to Doctor Volospion's remarks which were almost always, on the surface at least, bland enough.

'Oh, indeed!' Doctor Volospion eyed a passing calf which had paused and was tentatively extending its trunk to accept a piece of fruit from the Commissar's open palm. 'Servants of man since the beginning of time.'

'Worshipped as gods in many eras and climes . . . ' added Abu Thaleb.

'Gods! True. Ganesh . . . '

Abu Thaleb had lost his reservations:

'I have recreated examples of every known species! The English, the Bulgarian, the Chinese, and of course the Indian . . . '

'You have a favourite?' Volospion heaved at a sleeve and scratched an eyebrow.

'My favourites are the Swiss Alpine elephants. There is one now. Notice its oddly shaped hooves. These were the famous white elephants of Sitting Bull, used in the liberation of Chicago in the fiftieth century.'

Miss Ming felt bound to interrupt. 'Are you absolutely certain of that, Commissar? The story sounds a bit familiar, but isn't quite right. I am an historian, after all, if not a very good one. You're not thinking of Carthage . . . ?' She became confused, apparently afraid that she had offended him again. 'I'm sorry. I shouldn't have butted in. You know what a silly little ignoramus I am . . . '

'I am absolutely certain, my dear,' said Abu Thaleb kindly. 'I had most of the information from an old tape which Jherek Carnelian found for me in one of the rotting cities. The translation might not have been perfect, but . . . '

'Ah, so Carthage could have sounded like Chicago, particularly after it has been through a number of transcriptions. You see *Sitting Bull* could have been –'

Doctor Volospion broke in on her speculations. 'What romantic times those must have been! Your own stories, Miss Ming, are redolent with the atmosphere of our glorious and vanished past!' He looked at Abu Thaleb as he spoke. Abu Thaleb moved uncomfortably.

Mavis Ming laughed. 'Well, it wasn't all fun, you know.' She sighed with pleasure, addressing Abu Thaleb. 'The thing I like about Doctor Volospion is the way he always lets me talk. He's always *interested* . . . '

Abu Thaleb avoided both their eyes.

'Say what you like about him,' she continued, 'Doctor Volospion's a gentleman!' She became serious. 'No, in a lot of ways the past was hell, though I must say there were satisfactions I never realized I'd miss till now. Sex, for instance.'

'You mean sexual pleasure?' The Commissar of Bengal drew a banana from his quilted cuff and began to peel it.

Miss Ming appeared to be taken aback by this gesture. Her voice was distant. 'I certainly do mean that.'

'Oh, surely . . . ' murmured Doctor Volospion.

Miss Ming found her old voice. 'Nobody around here ever seems to be interested. I mean, really interested. If that's what's meant by an ancient race, give me what you call the Dawn Ages – my time – any day of the week! Well, not that you have days or weeks, but you know what I mean. Real sex!'

She seemed to realize that she was in danger of becoming intense and she tried to lighten the effect of her speech by breaking into what, in the Dawn Age, might have been a musical laugh.

When her laughter had died away, Doctor Volospion touched his right index finger to his left eyelid. 'Can this be true, Miss Ming?'

'Oh, you're a sweetie, Doctor Volospion. You make a girl feel really foolish sometimes. It's not your fault. You've got what we used to call an "unfortunate tone" – it seems to make a mockery of everything. I know what it is. You don't have to tell me. You're really quite shy, like me. I've lived with you long enough to know . . . '

'I am honoured, as always, by your interpretation of my character. But I am genuinely curious. I can think of so many who concern themselves with little else but sexual gratification. My Lady Charlotina, O'Kala Incarnadine, Gaf the Horse in Tears and, of course, Mistress Christia, the Everlasting Concubine.' He cast an eye over the surrounding guests. 'Jherek Carnelian *crucifies* himself in pursuit of his sexual object . . . '

'It's not what I meant,' she explained. 'You see, they only *play* at it. They're not really *motivated* by it. It's hard to explain.' She became coy. 'Anyway, I don't think any of those are my types, actually.'

The Commissar of Bengal finished feeding his banana to a passing pachyderm. 'I seem to recall that you were quite struck by My Lady Charlotina at one time, Miss Ming.' he said.

'Oh, that was –'

Miss Ming studied something beyond her left shoulder. 'And then there was that other lady. The time-traveller, who I rather took to, myself. Why, we were almost rivals for a while. *You* were in love, you said, Miss Ming.'

'Oh, now you're being cruel! I'd rather you didn't mention . . . '

'Of course.' Now he looked beyond her right shoulder. 'A tragedy.'

'It's not that I – I mean, I don't like to think. I was badly let down by Dafnish – and by Snuffles, in particular. How was I to know that . . . Well, if you hadn't consoled me then, I don't know what I'd have done. But I wish you wouldn't bring it up. Not here, at least. Oh, people can be so *baffling* sometimes. I'm not perfect, I know, but I do my best to be tactful. To look on the bright side. To help others. Betty used to say that I ought to think more of my *own* interests. She said I wasn't selfish enough. Oh, dear – people must think me a terrible fool. When they think of me at *all!*' She sniffed. 'I'm sorry . . . '

She craned to look back, following Doctor Volospion's gaze.

Li Pao was near by, bowing briefly to Doctor Volospion, making as if to pass on, for he was apparently in some haste, but Doctor Volospion smilingly called him over.

'I was complimenting our host on his collection,' he explained to Li Pao.

Abu Thaleb made a modest gesture.

Miss Ming bit her lip.

Li Pao cleared his throat.

'Aren't they fine?' said Doctor Volospion.

'It is pleasant to see the beasts working,' Li Pao said pointedly, 'if only for the delight of these drones.'

Doctor Volospion's smile broadened. 'Ah, Li Pao, as usual you refuse amusement! Still, that's your recreation, I suppose, or you would not attend so many of our parties.'

Li Pao bridled. 'I come, Doctor Volospion, on principle. Occasionally, there is one who will listen to me for a few moments. My conscience drives me here. One day perhaps I will begin to convince you of the value of moral struggle.'

An affectionate trunk nuzzled his oriental ear. He moved his head.

Doctor Volospion was placatory. 'I *am* convinced, Li Pao, my dear friend. Its value to the twenty-seventh century is immeasurable. But here we are at the End of Time and we have quite different needs. Our future is uncertain, to say the least. The cosmos contracts and perishes and soon we must perish with it. Will industry put a stop to the dissolution of the universe? I think not.'

Miss Ming patted at a blonde curl.

'Then you fear the end?' Li Pao said with some satisfaction.

Doctor Volospion affected a yawn. 'Fear? What is that?'

Li Pao's chuckle was grim. 'Oh, it's rare enough here, but I think you reveal at least a touch of it, Doctor Volospion.'

'Fear!' Doctor Volospion's nostrils developed a contemptuous flare. 'You suggest that I –? But this is such a baseless observation. An accusation, even!'

'I do not accuse, Doctor Volospion. I do not denigrate. Fear, where real danger threatens, is surely a sane enough response? A healthy one? Is it insane to ignore the knife which strikes for the heart?'

'Knife? Heart?' Abu Thaleb lured the persistent elephant towards him, holding a bunch of grapes. 'Do forgive me, Li Pao . . . '

Doctor Volospion said softly: 'I think, Li Pao, that you will have to consider me insane.'

Li Pao would not relent. 'No! You are afraid. Your denials display it, your posture pronounces it!'

Doctor Volospion moved an overloaded shoulder. 'Such instincts, you see, have atrophied at the End of Time. You credit your own feelings to me, I think.'

Li Pao's gaze was steady. 'I am not deceived, Doctor Volospion. What are you? Time-traveller or space-traveller? You are no more born of this age than am I, or Miss Ming, here.'

'What –?' Doctor Volospion was alerted.

'You say that you do not fear,' continued the Chinese. 'Yet you hate well enough, that's plain. Your hatred of Lord Jagged, for instance, is patent. And you exhibit jealousies and vanities that are unknown, say, to the Duke of Queens. If these are innocent of true guile, you are not. It is why I know there is a point in my talking to you.'

'I will not be condescended to!' Doctor Volospion glared.

'I repeat – I praise these emotions. In their place –'

'Praise?' Doctor Volospion raised both his hands, palms outward, to bring a pause. His voice, almost a whisper, threatened. 'Strange flattery, indeed! You go too far, Li Pao. The manners of your own time would never allow such insults.'

'I do think you've gone just a teeny bit too far, Li Pao.' Mavis Ming was anxious to reduce the tension. 'Why are you so bent on baiting Doctor Volospion? He's done nothing to you.'

'You refuse to admit it,' Li Pao continued relentlessly, 'but we face the death of everything. Thus I justify my directness.'

'Shall we die gracelessly, then? Pining for hope when there is none? Whining for salvation when we are beyond help? You are offensive at every level, Li Pao.'

Miss Ming was desperate to destroy this atmosphere. 'Oh, look over there!' she cried. 'Can it be Argonheart Po arrived at last, with the food?'

'He *is* late,' said Abu Thaleb, looking up from his elephant.

Li Pao and Doctor Volospion both ignored this side-tracking.

'There *is* hope, if we work,' said Li Pao.

'What? This is unbelievable.' Doctor Volospion sought an ally but found only the anxious eyes of Mavis Ming. He avoided them. 'The end looms – the inevitable beckons. Death comes stalking over the horizon. Mortality returns to the Earth after an absence of millennia. And you speak of what? Of work? Work!' Doctor Volospion's laugh was harsh. 'Work? For what? This age is called the End of Time for good reason, Li Pao! We have run our race. Soon we shall all be ash on the cosmic wind.'

'But if a few of us were to consider . . . '

'Forgive me, Li Pao, but you bore me. I have had my fill of bores today.'

'You boys should really stop squabbling like this.' Determinedly, Mavis Ming adopted a matronly role. 'Silly, gloomy talk. You're making me feel quite depressed. What possible good can it do for anyone? Let's have a bit more cheerfulness, eh? Did I ever tell you about the time I – well, I was about fourteen, and I'd done it for a dare – we got caught in the church by the Reverend Kovac – I'd told Sandy, that was my friend –'

Doctor Volospion's temper was not improved. An expression of pure horror bloomed on her round face as she realized that she had made another misjudgement and caused her protector to turn on her.

He was vicious. 'The role of diplomat, Miss Ming, does not

greatly suit you.'

'Oh!'

Abu Thaleb became aware, at last, of the ambience. 'Come now . . . '

'You will be kind enough not to interfere, not to interject your absurd and pointless anecdotes into the conversation, Miss Ming!'

'Doctor Volospion!' It was a shriek of betrayal. Miss Ming took a step backwards. She became afraid.

'Oh, she meant no harm . . . ' Li Pao was in no position to mediate.

'How,' enquired Doctor Volospion of the shaking creature, 'would you suggest we settle our dispute, Miss Ming? With swords, like Lord Shark and the Duke of Queens? With pistols? Reverb-guns? Flame-lances?'

Her throat quivered. 'I didn't mean . . . '

'Well? Hm?' His long chin pointed at her throat. 'Speak up, my portly referee. Tell us!'

She had become very pale and yet her cheeks flamed with humiliation and she did not dare look at any of them. 'I was only trying to help. You were so angry, both of you, and there's no need to lose your tempers . . . '

'Angry? You are witless, madam. Could you not see that we jested?'

There was no evidence. Miss Ming became confused.

Li Pao's lips were pursed, his cheeks were as pale as hers were red. Doctor Volospion's eyes were hard and fiery. Abu Thaleb gave vent to a troubled muttering.

Miss Ming seemed fixed in her position by a terrible fascination. Mindlessly, she stared at the eyes of her accuser. It seemed that her urge to flee was balanced by her compulsion to stay, to fan these flames, to produce the holocaust that would consume her, and her mouth opened and words fled out of it, high and frightened:

'Not a very funny joke, I must say, calling someone fat and stupid. Make up your mind, Doctor Volospion. Only a minute or two ago you said how nice I looked. Don't pick on little Mavis, just because you're losing your argument!' She panted. 'Oh!'

She cast about for friends, but all eyes were averted, save Volospion's, and those pierced.

'Oh!' she said again.

Doctor Volospion parted his teeth a fraction, to hiss:

'I should be more than grateful, Miss Ming, if you would be

silent. For once in your life I suggest that you reflect on your own singular lack of sensitivity –'

'Oh!'

'– on your inability to interpret the slightest nuance of social intercourse save in your own unsavoury terms.'

'O-oh!'

'A psychic cripple, Miss Ming, has no business swimming in the fast-running rivers of philosophical discussion.'

'Volospion!' Li Pao made a hesitant movement.

Perhaps Miss Ming did not hear his words at all, perhaps she only experienced his tone, his vicious stance. 'You *are* in a bad mood today . . . ' she began, and then words gave way to her strangled, half-checked sobs.

'Volospion! Volospion! You round on that wretch because you cannot answer me!'

'Ha!' Doctor Volospion turned slowly, hampered by his robes.

Abu Thaleb had been observing Miss Ming. He spoke conversationally, leaning forward to stare at her face, his huge, feathered turban nodding. 'Are those tears, my dear?'

She snorted.

'I had heard of elephants weeping,' said Abu Thaleb with some animation. 'Or was it giraffes? – but I never thought to have the chance to witness . . . '

His tone produced a partial recovery in her. She lifted a wounded face. 'Oh, be quiet! You and your stupid elephants.'

'So, all our time-travellers are blessed with the same brand of good manners, it seems.' Volospion had become cool. 'I fear we have yet to grasp the essence of your social customs, madam.'

She trembled.

'Childish irony . . . ' said Li Pao.

'Oh, stop it, Li Pao!' Mavis flinched away from him. 'You started all this.'

'Well, perhaps . . . '

Abu Thaleb put a puzzled tongue to his lower lip. 'If . . . '

'Oh,' she sobbed, 'I'm so *sorry*, Commissar. I'm sorry, Doctor Volospion. I didn't mean to . . . '

'It is we who are in the wrong,' Li Pao told her. 'I should have known better. You are a troubled young girl at heart . . . '

Her weeping grew mightier.

Doctor Volospion, Abu Thaleb and Li Pao now stood around her, looking down at her.

'Come, come,' said Abu Thaleb. He patted the crown of her head.

'Oh, I'm sorry. I was only trying to help . . . Why does it always have to be me . . . ?'

Doctor Volospion at last placed a hand on her arm. 'Perhaps I had best escort you home?' He was magnanimous. 'You should rest.'

'Oh!' She moved to him, as if to be comforted, and then withdrew. 'Oh, you're right! You're right! I'm fat. I'm stupid. I'm ugly.' She pulled away from him.

'No, no . . .' murmured Abu Thaleb. 'I think that you are immensely attractive . . .'

She raised a trembling chin. 'It's all right.' She swallowed. 'I'm fine now.'

Abu Thaleb gave a sigh of relief. The other two, however, continued to watch her.

She sniffed. 'I just didn't want to see anyone having a bad time, hurting one another. Yes, you're right, Doctor Volospion. I shouldn't have come. I'll go home.'

Doctor Volospion replaced his hand, to steady her. His voice was low and calming. 'Good. I will take you in my air car.'

'No. You stay and enjoy yourself. It's my fault. I'm very sorry.'

'You are too distraught.'

'Perhaps I should take her,' said Li Pao. 'After all, I introduced the original argument.'

'We all relieve the boredom in one way or another,' said Doctor Volospion quietly. 'I should not have responded as I did.'

'Nonsense. You had every reason . . .'

'Boo-hoo,' said Miss Ming. She had broken down again.

Abu Thaleb said coaxingly: 'Would you like one of my little flying elephants, my dear, for your very own? You could take it with you.'

'Oh-ah-ha-ha . . .'

'Poor thing,' said Abu Thaleb. 'I think she would have been better off in a menagerie, Doctor Volospion. Some of them feel much safer there, you know. Our world is too difficult for them to grasp. Now, if I were you . . .'

Doctor Volospion tightened his grip.

'Oh!'

'You are too sensitive, Miss Ming,' said Li Pao. 'You must not take us seriously.'

Doctor Volospion laughed. 'Is that so, Li Pao?'

'I meant . . . '

'Ah, look!' Doctor Volospion raised a hand to point. 'Here's your friend, Miss Ming.'

'Friend?' Red eyes were raised. Another sniff.

'Your friend, the cook.'

It was Argonheart Po, in smock and cap of dark brown and scarlet, so corpulent as to make Miss Ming look slim. He advanced towards them with monumental dignity, pushing small elephants from his path. With a brief bow he acknowledged the company and then addressed Abu Thaleb.

'I have come to apologize, epicurean Commissar, for the lateness of my contribution.'

'No, no . . . ' Abu Thaleb seemed weary of what appeared to be a welter of regrets.

'There is an internal fault in my recipe,' explained the master chef, 'which I am loath to disguise by any artifice . . . '

The Commissar of Bengal waved a white-gloved hand. 'You are too modest, kaiser of kitchens. You are too much a perfectionist. I am certain that none of us would detect any discrepancy . . . '

Argonheart Po acknowledged the compliment with a smile. 'Possibly. But *I* would know.' He confided to the others: 'The cry of the artist, I fear, down the ages. I hope, Abu Thaleb, that things will right themselves before long. If not, I shall bring you those confections which have been successful, but I will abandon the rest.'

'Drastic . . . ' Abu Thaleb lowered his eyes and shook his head. 'Can we not help in some way?'

'The very reason I came. I hoped to gain an opinion. If there is someone who could find it within themselves to leave the party for a short while, to return with me and sample my creations, not so much for their flavour as for their consistency. It would not require much time, nor would it require a particularly sophisticated palate, but . . . '

'Miss Ming!' said Doctor Volospion.

'Me,' she said.

'Here is your chance to be of service.'

'Well,' she began, 'as everyone knows, I'm no gourmet. Not that I don't enjoy my chow, and, of course, Argonheart's is always excellent, but I'd like to help out, if I can.' She was twice the woman.

'It is not a gourmet's opinion I seek,' Argonheart Po told her. 'You will do excellently, Miss Ming, if you can spare a little time.'

'You would be delighted, wouldn't you, Miss Ming?' said Abu Thaleb sympathetically.

'Delighted,' she confirmed. She cast a wary glance at Doctor Volospion. 'You wouldn't mind?'

'Certainly not!' He was almost effusive.

'A splendid idea,' said Li Pao, blatantly relieved.

'Well, then, I shall be your taster, Argonheart.' She linked her arm in the cook's. 'And I really am sorry for that silly fuss, everybody.'

They shook their heads. They waved their fingers.

She smiled. 'It did clear the air, anyway, didn't it? You're all friends again now.'

'Absolutely,' said Li Pao.

'Well, that's fine.'

'And you won't be wanting the little elephant?' Abu Thaleb asked. 'I can always create another.'

'I'd *love* one, Abu. Another time, perhaps when I have a menagerie of my own. And power rings of my own and everything. I've nowhere to keep it while I stay with Doctor Volospion.'

'Ah, well.' Abu Thaleb also seemed relieved.

'I think,' said Argonheart Po, 'that we should go as quickly as possible.'

'Of course,' she said, 'You really must take me in hand, Argonheart, and tell me exactly what you expect me to do.'

'An opinion, I assure you, is all I seek.'

They made their adieux.

'*Well,*' she confided to Argonheart as they left, 'I must say you turned up at just the right moment. Honestly, I've never *seen* such a display of temper! You're so calm, Argonheart. So unshakably dignified, you know? I did my best, of course, to calm everyone down, but they were just *determined* to have a row! Of course, I do blame Li Pao. Doctor Volospion had a perfectly understandable point of view, but would Li Pao listen to him? Not a bit of it. I suspect that Li Pao never listens to anyone but himself. He can be so thoughtless sometimes, don't you find that?'

The master chef smacked his lips.

4. In Which Mavis Ming Is Once Again Disappointed in Her Ambitions

Argonheart Po dipped his fingers into his rainbow plesiosaurus (sixty distinct flavours of gelatine) and withdrew it as the beast turned its long neck round to investigate, mildly, the source of the irritation.

The great cook put a hand to mouth, sucked, and sighed.

'What a shame! such an excellent taste.'

His creature, lumbering on massive legs that were still somewhat wobbly, having failed to set at the same time as the rest of its bulk, moved to rejoin the herd grazing some distance away on the especially prepared trees of pastry and angelica Argonheart Po had designed to occupy them until it was time to drive them to the party which was only a mile or two off (the gargantua were plainly visible on the horizon).

'You agree, then, Miss Ming? The legs lack coherence.' He licked a disappointed mouth.

'Isn't there something you could add?' she suggested. 'Those flippers were really meant for the sea, you know . . . '

'Mm?'

'It's not your fault, not strictly speaking. The design of the creature itself is wrong. You must be able to do *something*, Argonheart, dear.'

'Oh, indeed. A twist of a power ring and all would be well, but I should continue to be haunted by the mystery. Was the temperature too high, for instance? You see, I allow for all the possibilities. My researches show that the animal could move on land. I wonder if the weight of the beast alters the atomic structure of the gelatine. If so, I should have prepared for it in my original recipe. There is no time to begin again.'

'But Argonheart . . . '

He shook his huge head. 'I must cull the herd of the failures and present, I am afraid, only a partial spectacle.'

'Abu Thaleb will still be pleased, I'm sure.'

'I hope so.' He voiced a stupendous and sultry sigh.

'It *is* nice to be out of the hurly-burly for a bit,' she told him, her mind moving on to other topics.

'If you would care to rejoin the party now?'

'No. I want to be here with you. That is, if you have no objection to little Mavis watching a real artist at work.'

'Of course.'

She smiled at him. 'It's such a relief, you see, to be out here alone with a real man. With someone who *does* something.'

She simpered. 'What I mean is, Argonheart, is that I've always wanted . . . '

She gasped as he jumped, his hands flailing, to taste a passing pterodactyl. He missed it by several inches, staggered and fell to one knee.

'Cunning beasts, those.' He picked himself up. 'My fault. I should have made them easier to catch. Too much sherry and not enough blancmange.'

She sidled up to him again. 'My husband, Donny Stevens, was a real man, for all his faults.'

Argonheart returned suddenly to his knees. He cupped his hands around something which wobbled, glinting green and yellow in the pale sunshine. 'Oh, this makes up for everything. See what it is, Miss Ming?'

'A dollop of jello?'

'Dollop? *Dollop!*' He breathed upon it. He fondled the rounded, quivering surface. He spoke reverently. 'This is an egg, Miss Ming. One of my creations has actually laid an egg. Good heavens! I could breed them. What an achievement!' His expression became seraphic.

'A man like you is capable of anything, Argonheart. I often felt Donny was like that. I never thought I'd miss the bastard.'

He was searching the ground for more eggs.

'You remind me of him a little,' she said softly. 'You are *real*, Argonheart.'

Argonheart Po's only weakness was for metaphysical speculation. Miss Ming had captured his attention. Stroking his egg, he looked round. 'Mm?'

Her breast rose and fell rapidly. 'A real man.'

He was curious. 'You believe everyone else imaginary, then? But why should I be real when the others are not? Why should *you* be real? Reality, after all, can be the syllabub that melts upon the tongue, leaving not even a flavour of memory . . . '

Her breathing became calmer. She turned to contemplate the half-melted remains of a completely unsuccessful stegosaurus.

'I meant,' she said, 'that Danny was a manly man. Stupid and vain, of course. But that's all part of it. And obsessed with his work

– well, when he wasn't screwing his assistants.' She laid her hand upon his trembling egg. 'I like you, Argonheart. Have you ever thought . . . ?'

But the chef's attention was wavering again as he bent to scoop up a little iguanadon. He placed his egg carefully upon a slab of marzipan rock and held the iguanadon out to her for her inspection.

With a frustrated sigh she licked the beast's slippery neck. 'Too much lime for my taste.'

She gave a theatrical shudder and laughed. 'Far too bitter for me, Argonheart, dear.'

'But the texture? It was the texture, alone, I needed to know about.'

The iguanadon struggled, squawking rather like a chicken, and was released. It ran, glistening, semi-transparent, green and orange, in a crazy path towards the nearby cola lake.

'Perfect,' she said. 'Firm and juicy.'

He nodded sadly. 'The small ones are by far the most successful. But that will scarcely satisfy Abu Thaleb. I meant the monsters for him. The little beasts were only to set off the large ones – to set the scale, do you see. I was too ambitious, Miss Ming. I tried to produce too much and too many.' His fat brow wrinkled.

'You haven't been listening, Argonheart, dear,' she chided. 'Argonheart?'

Reluctantly he withdrew from his regrets. 'We were discussing the nature of reality.'

'No.'

'You were discussing what? Men?'

She patted at the yellow flounces of her frock. 'Or their absence?' She chuckled. 'I could do with one . . . '

He had picked up a ladle in his plump, gloved hand. She followed him as he approached his lake, bent on a final taste.

'A man? What could you do with one?' He sipped.

'I need one.'

'A special kind?'

'A real one.'

'Couldn't you make something – someone, I mean – to suit you? Doctor Volospion would help.' He looked across the tranquil surface, like molten amber. 'Delicious!'

She seemed pained. 'There's no need, dear, to throw that particular episode in my face.'

'Um. Yet, I'm indulging myself, I fear.' He stooped, dipped his ladle, drew it to his red lips, sampled self-critically and nodded his head. 'Yes. The conception was too grandiose. Given another day I could put everything to rights, but poor Abu Thaleb expects . . . Ah, well!'

'Forget all about that for a moment.' Lust was mounting in her. She slipped a hand along his massive thigh. 'Make love to me, Argonheart. I've been so unhappy.'

He rubbed his several chins. 'Oh, I see.'

'You knew all along, didn't you? What I wanted?'

'Um.'

'You're so proud, Argonheart. So masculine. A lot of girls don't like fat men, but I do.' She giggled. 'It's what they used to say about me. All the more to get hold of. Please, Argonheart, please!'

'My confections,' he murmured lamely.

'You can spare a few minutes, surely?' She dug her nails into his chest. 'Argonheart!'

'They could –'

'You must relax sometime. You have to relax. It gives you a new perspective.'

'Well, yes, that's true.'

'Argonheart!' She moved against him.

'I certainly cannot improve anything now. Perhaps you are right. Yes . . . '

'Yes! You'll feel so much better. And I will, too.'

'Possibly . . . '

'Definitely!'

She pulled him towards a pile of discarded dark brown straw. 'Here's a good place.' She sank into it, tugging at his gloved hand.

'What?' he murmured. 'In the vermicelli?'

It was already beginning to stick to her sweating arms, but it was plain that such considerations were no longer important. 'Why not? Why not? Oh, my darling. Oh, Argonheart!'

He drew off his gloves. He reached down and removed a strand or two of the vermicelli from her elbow and placed it neatly on her neck. He stood back.

She writhed in the chocolate.

'Argonheart!' She mewed.

With a shrug, he fell beside her in the chocolate.

It was at the point where she had helped him to drag the tight scarlet smock up to his navel while wriggling her own blue lace knickers to just below her knees that they heard a shriek that filled the sky and saw the crimson spaceship falling through the dark blue heavens in an aura of multi-coloured flame.

Argonheart's belly quivered against her as he paused.

'Golly!' said Mavis Ming.

Argonheart licked her shoulder, but his attention was no longer with her. He glanced back. The spaceship was still falling. The noise was immense.

'Don't stop,' she said. 'There's still time. It won't take long.'

But Argonheart was already rolling over in the vermicelli, pulling his smock back into position. He stood up. Shreds of half-melted confectionery dropped from his legs.

A dreadful wail escaped Miss Ming. It was drowned by the roar of the ship.

With her fist she pounded at the vermicelli. It flew in all directions. She appeared to be swearing. And then, when the ship's noise had dropped momentarily to a muted howl, and as Mavis Ming drew up her underwear, her voice, disappointed, despairing, could be heard again.

'What a moment to pick! Poor old Mavis. Isn't it just your luck.'

5. In Which Certain Denizens at the End of Time Indulge themselves in Speculation as to the Nature of the Visitor from Space

IT WAS A SPACESHIP FROM SOME MYTHICAL ANTIQUITY, all fins and flutes and glittering bubbles, tapering at the nose, bulbous at the base, where its rockets roared. It slowed as they watched, falling with a peculiar swaying motion, as if its engines malfunctioned, the vents first on one side and then on the other sputtering, gouting, sputtering again until, just before the ship reached the ground, the rockets flared in unison, bouncing the machine like a ball on a water jet, gradually subsiding until it had settled to earth.

Miss Ming, observing it from her nest of chocolate worms, tightened her lips.

Even after the ship had landed, flame still rolled around its hull, sensuous flame caressing the scarlet metal.

The surrounding terrain sent up heavy black smoke, crackling as if to protest. The smoke curled close to the ground, moving towards the ship: eels attracted to wreckage.

Miss Ming was in no temper to admire the machine; she glared at it.

'It has a certain authority, the ship,' murmured Argonheart Po.

'A fine sense of timing, I must say! A little lovemaking would have improved my spirits no end and taken away the nasty taste of Doctor Volospion's tantrum. It isn't as if I get the chance every day and I haven't had a man for ages. I don't even know if one can still give me what I need! Even you, Argonheart . . . '

She pouted, brushing at the nasty sticky stuff clinging to her petticoats. 'I'm too furious to speak!'

Argonheart Po helped her from the pile and, perhaps moved by unconscious chivalry, pecked her upon the cheek. The smell of burning filled the air.

'Ugh,' she said. 'What a *stink*, too!'

'It is the least attractive of odours,' Argonheart said.

'It's horrible. Surely it can't just be coming from that ship?'

The heat from the vessel was heavy on their skins. Argonheart Po, had his body been so fashioned, would have been sweating quite as much as Miss Ming. His sensitive nose twitched.

'There is something familiar about it,' he agreed, 'which I would not normally identify with hot metal.' He perused the landscape. His cry of horror echoed over it.

'Ah! Look what it has done! Look! Oh, it is too bad!'

Miss Ming looked and saw nothing. 'What?'

Argonheart was in anguish. His hands clenched, his eyes blazed.

'It has melted half my dinosaurs. That is what is making the smoke!'

Argonheart Po began to roll rapidly in the direction of the ship, Mavis Ming forgotten.

'Hey!' she cried. 'What if there's danger?'

He had not heard her.

With a whimper, she followed him.

'Murderer!' cried the distressed chef. 'Philistine!' He shook his fist at the ship. He danced about it, forced back by its heat. He attempted to kick it and failed.

'Locust!' he raved. 'Ravager! Insensitive despoiler!'

His energy dissipated, he fell to his knees in the glutinous mess. He wept. 'Oh, my monsters! My jellies!'

Mavis Ming hovered a short distance away. She wore the pout of someone who considered themselves abandoned in their hour of need.

'Argonheart!' she called.

'Burned! All burned!'

'Argonheart, we don't know what sort of creatures are *in* that spaceship. They could mean us harm!'

'Ruin, ruin, ruin . . . '

'Argonheart. I think we should go and warn someone, don't you?' She discovered that her lovely shoes were stuck. As she lifted her feet, long strands of toffee-like stuff came with them. She waded back to a patch of dust still free of melted dinosaur.

Her attention focused upon the ship as curiosity conquered caution. 'I've seen alien spacecraft before,' she said. 'Lots of them. But this doesn't look alien at all. It's got a distinctly human look to it, in fact.'

Argonheart Po raised his mighty body to its feet and, with shoulders bowed, mourned his dead creations.

'Argonheart, don't you think it's got a rather *romantic* appearance, really?'

Argonheart Po turned his back on the source of his anger and folded his arms across his chest. He wore a martyred air, yet his dignity increased.

Mavis Ming continued to inspect the spaceship. A strange smile had replaced the expression of anxiety she had worn earlier. 'Come to think of it, it's just the sort of ship I used to read about when I was a little girl. All the space-heroes had ships like that.' She became fey. 'Perhaps at long last my prayers have been answered, Argonheart.'

The master chef grunted. He was lost in profundity.

Miss Ming uttered her trilling laugh. 'Has my handsome space-knight arrived to carry me off, do you think? To the wonderful planet of Paradise V?'

From Argonheart there issued a deep, violent rumbling, as of an angry volcano. 'Villain! Villain!'

She put a hand to her mouth. 'You could be right. It could easily carry a villain. Some pirate captain and his cut-throat crew.' She became reminiscent. 'My two favourite authors, you know, when I was young – well, I'd still read them now, if I could – were J. R. R. Tolkien and A. A. Milne. Well, this is more like the *movie* versions, of course, but still . . . Oooh! Could they be *rapists* and *slavers*, Argonheart?'

She took his silence for disapproval. 'Not that I really want anything nasty to happen to us. Not really. But it's *thrilling*, isn't it, wondering?'

'I –,' said Argonheart Po. 'I –'

Miss Ming, as she anticipated the occupants of the ship, seemed torn between poles represented in her fantasies by the evil, fascinating Sauron and the soft, jolly Winnie-the-Pooh.

'Will they be fierce, do you think, Argonheart? Or cuddly?' She bit her lower lip. 'Better still, they might be fierce *and* cuddly!'

'Aaaaaah,' breathed Argonheart.

She looked at him in surprise. She appeared to make an effort to retrieve herself from sentiment which, she had doubtless learned, was not always socially acceptable in this world. She achieved the retrieval by a return to her previous alternative, her vein of heavy cynicism. 'I was only joking,' she said.

'Sadist,' hissed Argonheart. 'This might have been deliberately engineered.'

'Well,' she said having determined her new attitude, 'at least it might be someone to relieve the awful *boredom* of this bloody planet!'

Still bowed, her baffled and grieving escort turned from the blackened fragments of his culinary dreams to stare wistfully after his surviving stegosauri and tyrannosauri which, startled by the ship, were in rapid and uncertain flight in all directions.

His self-control returned. He became a fatalist. His little shrug went virtually unnoticed by her.

'It is fate,' declared the master chef. 'At least I am no longer in a dilemma. The decision has been taken from me.'

He began to wade, as best the sticky glue would allow him, towards her.

'Couldn't you round them up?' she asked. 'The ones who survived?'

'And make only a paltry contribution? No. I shall find Abu Thaleb and tell him he must create something for himself. A few turns of a power ring, of course, and he will have a feast of sorts, though it will lack the inspiration of anything I could have prepared for him.' A certain guilt, it seemed, inspired him to resent the object of his guilt and therefore made him feel somewhat aggressive towards Abu Thaleb.

He reached Miss Ming's side. 'Shall we return to the party together?'

'But what of the ship?'

'It has done its terrible work.'

'But the people who came in it?'

'I forgive them,' said Argonheart with grandiose magnanimity.

'I mean – don't you want to see what they look like?'

'I bear them no ill-will. They were not aware of the horror they brought. It is ever thus.'

'They might be interesting.'

'*Interesting?*' Argonheart Po was incredulous.

'They might have some news, or something.'

Argonheart Po looked again upon the spaceship. 'They are scarcely likely to be anything but crude, ill-mannered rogues, Miss Ming. Surely, they must have seen, by means of their instruments, my herds?'

'It could be a crash-landing.'

'Perhaps.' Argonheart Po was a fair-minded chef. He did his best to see her point. 'Perhaps.'

'They might need help.'

He cast one final glance about the smoking detritus and said, with not a little violence, 'Well, I hope that they find it.'

'Shouldn't we . . . ?'

'I return to find Abu Thaleb and tell him of the disaster.'

'Oh, very well, I suppose I shall have to come with you. But, really, Argonheart, you're looking at this in a rather selfish way, aren't you? This could be a great event. Remember those other aliens who turned up recently? They were trying to help us, too, weren't they? It would be lovely to have some *nice* news for a change . . .'

She reached for his arm, so that he might escort her through the glutinous pools.

At that moment there came a grinding noise from the vessel. Both looked back.

A circular section in the hull was turning.

'The airlock,' she gasped. 'It's opening.'

The door of the airlock swung back, apparently on old-fashioned hinges, to reveal a dark hole from which, for a few seconds, flames poured.

'They can't be human,' she said. 'Not if they live in fire.'

No further flames issued from within the ship but from the darkness of the interior there came at intervals tiny flashes of light.

'Like fireflies,' whispered Mavis Ming.

'Or eyes,' said Argonheart, his attention held for the moment.

'The feral eyes of wild invaders.' Miss Ming seemed to be quoting from one of her girlhood texts.

An engine murmured and the ship shivered. Then, from somewhere inside the airlock, a wide band of metal began to emerge.

'A ramp,' said Mavis Ming. 'They're letting down a ramp.'

The ramp slid slowly to the ground, making a bridge between airlock and earth, but still no occupant emerged.

Mavis cupped her hands around her mouth. 'Greetings!' she cried. 'The peaceful people of Earth welcome you!'

There was still no acknowledgement from the ship. Grainy dust drifted past. There was silence.

'They might be afraid of us,' suggested Mavis.

'Most probably they are ashamed,' said Argonheart Po. 'Too abashed to display themselves.'

'Oh, Argonheart! They probably didn't even see your dinosaurs!'

'Is that an excuse?'

'Well . . .'

Now a muffled, querulous voice sounded from within the airlock, but the language it used was unintelligible.

'We have no translators.' Argonheart Po consulted his power rings. 'I have no means of making him speak any sort of tongue I'll understand. Neither have I the means to understand him. We must go. Lord Jagged of Canaria usually has a translation ring. Or the Duke of Queens. Or Doctor Volospion. Anyone who keeps a menagerie will . . . '

'Ssh,' she said. 'The odd thing is, Argonheart, that while I can't actually understand the words, the language *does* seem familiar. It's like – well, it's like English – the language I used to speak before I came here.'

'You cannot speak it now?'

'Obviously not. I'm speaking this one, whatever it is, aren't I?'

The voice came again. It was high-pitched. It tended to trill, like birdsong, and yet it was human.

'It's not unpleasant,' she said, 'but it's not what I would have called *manly*.' She was kind: 'Still, the pitch might be affected by a change in the atmosphere, mightn't it?'

'Possibly.' Argonheart peered. 'Hm. One of them seems to be coming out.'

At last a space-traveller emerged at the top of the ramp.

'Oh, dear,' murmured Miss Ming. 'What a disappointment! I hope they're not all like him.'

Although undoubtedly humanoid, the stranger had a distinctly bird-like air to him. There was a wild crest of bright auburn hair, which rose all around his head and created a kind of ruff about his neck; there was a sharp pointed nose; there were vivid blue eyes which bulged and blinked in the light; there was a head which craned forward on an elongated neck and which would sometimes jerk back a little, like a chicken's as it searched for grain amid the farmyard's dust; there was a tiny body which also moved in rapid, poorly-coordinated jerks and twitches; there were two arms, held stiffly at the sides of the body, like clipped wings. And then there was the plaintive, questioning cry, like a puzzled gull's:

'Eh? Eh? Eh?'

The eyes darted this way and that and then fixed suddenly upon Mavis Ming and Argonheart Po. They received the creature's whole attention.

'Eh?'

He blinked imperiously at them. He trilled a few words.

Argonheart Po waited until the newcomer had finished before announcing gravely:

'You have ruined the Commissar of Bengal's dinner, sir.'

'Eh?'

'You have reduced a carefully planned feast to a rabble of side-dishes!'

'Fallerunnerstanja,' said the visitor from space. He reached back into the airlock and produced a black frock coat dating from a period at least 150 years before Mavis Ming's own. He drew the coat over his shirt and buttoned it all the way down. 'Eh?'

'It's not very clean,' said Mavis, 'that coat. Is it?'

Argonheart had not noticed the stranger's clothes. He was regretting his outburst and trying to recover his composure, his normal amiability.

'Welcome,' he said, 'to the End of Time.'

'Eh?'

The space-traveller frowned and consulted a bulky instrument in his right hand. He tapped it, shook it and held it up to his ear.

'Well,' said Mavis with a sniff. '*He* isn't much, is he? I wonder if they're all like him.'

'He could be the only one,' suggested Argonheart Po.

'Like that?'

'The only one at all.'

'I hope not!'

As if in response to her criticism the creature waved both his arms in a sort of windmilling motion. It seemed for a moment as if he were trying to fly. Then, with stiff movements, reminiscent of a poorly-controlled marionette, the creature retreated back into his ship.

'Did we frighten him, do you think?' asked Argonheart Po in some concern.

'Quite likely. What a weedy little creep!'

'Mm?'

'What a rotten specimen! He doesn't go with the ship at all. I was expecting someone tanned, brawny, handsome . . . '

'Why so? You know these ships? You have met those who normally use them?'

'Only in my dreams,' she said.

Argonheart made no further effort to follow her. 'He is humanoid, at least. It makes a change, don't you think, Miss Ming, from all those others?'

'Not much of one though.' She shifted a gluey foot. 'Ah, well! Shall we return, as you suggested?'

'You don't think we should remain?'

'There's no point, is there? Let someone else deal with him. Some-one who wants a curiosity for their menagerie.'

Argonheart Po offered his arm again. They began to wade to-wards the dusty shore.

As they reached the higher ground they heard a familiar voice from overhead. They looked up.

Abu Thaleb's howdah hovered there.

'Aha!' said the Commissar of Bengal. His face, with its beard carefully curled and divided into two parts, set with pearls and rubies, after the original, peered over the edge of the air car. 'I thought so.' He addressed another occupant, invisible to their eyes. 'You see, Volospion, I was right.'

'Oh, dear.' Mavis tried to re-arrange her disordered dress. 'Doctor Volospion, too . . . '

Volospion's tired tones issued from the howdah. 'Yes, indeed. You were quite right, Abu Thaleb. I apologise. It is a spaceship. Well, if you feel you would like to descend, I shall not object.'

The howdah came down to earth beside Argonheart Po and Miss Ming. Within, it was lined with dark green and blue plush.

Doctor Volospion lay among cushions, still in black and gold, his tight hood covering his skull and framing his pale face. He made no attempt to move. He scarcely acknowledged Miss Ming's presence as he addressed Argonheart Po:

'Forgive this intrusion, great prince of pies. The Commissar of Bengal is bent on satisfying his curiosity.'

Argonheart Po made to speak but Abu Thaleb had already begun again:

'What a peculiar odour it has – sweet, yet bitter . . . '

'My creations . . . ' said Argonheart.

'Like death,' pronounced Doctor Volospion.

'The smell is all that is left,' insisted Argonheart now, 'of the dinner I was preparing for your party, Abu Thaleb. The ship's landing destroyed almost all of it.'

Climbing from his howdah the slender Commissar clapped the chef upon his broad back. 'Dear Argonheart, how sad! But another time, I hope, you will be able to recreate all that you have lost today.'

'It is true that there were imperfections,' Argonheart told him, 'and I would relish the opportunity to begin afresh.'

'Soon, soon, soon. What a lovely little ship it is!' Abu Thaleb's plumes bounced upon his turban. 'I had yearnings, you see, to embellish my menagerie, but I fear the ship is too small to accommodate the kind of prize I seek.'

Mavis Ming said: 'You'd be even more disappointed than me, Abu Thaleb. You should see the little squirt we saw just before you turned up. He –'

Doctor Volospion, so it seemed, had not heard her begin to speak. He called from his cushions:

'Your menagerie is already a marvel, belle of Bengal. The most refined collection in the world. Splendid, specialized, so much more sophisticated than the scrambled skelter of species scraped together by certain so-called connoisseurs whose zoos surpass yours only in size but never in superiority of sensitive selection!'

Mavis Ming displayed confusion. Although Doctor Volospion appeared to address Abu Thaleb he seemed to be speaking for her benefit. She looked from one to the other, wondering if she should form a smile.

Doctor Volospion winked at her.

Mavis grinned. She had been forgiven for her outburst. The joke was at Abu Thaleb's expense.

She began to giggle.

'Go on, Doctor Volospion. I'm sure Abu Thaleb enjoys your flattery,' she said.

'In taste, salutory Commissar, you are assured of supremacy, until our planet passes at last into that limbo of silence and non-existence which must soon, we are told, be its fate.'

Abu Thaleb's back was to Miss Ming and she seemed glad of this. She held her breath. She went deep red. She made a muted, spluttering noise.

But now the Commissar of Bengal was looking back at Doctor Volospion. 'Oh, really, my friend!' He was good-natured. 'You are capable of subtler mockery than this!'

'But I am a true showman, Abu Thaleb. I relate properly to my audience.'

'Can that be so?' Abu Thaleb turned to Mavis. 'You have seen the visitors, then, Miss Ming?'

'Briefly,' she said. 'Actually, there only seems to be one.'

Abu Thaleb stroked his beard, his pearls and rubies. 'He is not in any way, I suppose, um – elephantoid?'

She was prepared to allow herself a giggle now. She glanced sidelong towards the lounging Volospion.

'Not a trace of a trunk, I'm afraid.' She looked for approval from her protector. 'Not even a touch of a tusk. He couldn't be less like a jumbo, although his nose is long enough, I suppose. He's more like one of those little birds, Abu Thaleb, who pick stuff out of elephant's teeth.'

'Excellent!' applauded Doctor Volospion. 'Ha, ha, ha!'

Abu Thaleb turned and regarded her with mysterious gravity. 'Teeth?'

She giggled again. 'Don't they have teeth, then, any more?'

Argonheart Po seemed much embarrassed. His glance at Doctor Volospion was almost disapproving. 'I must away to my thoughts,' he said. 'I shall leave this sad scene. There is nothing I can save. Not now. So I'll wish you all farewell.'

'Are we to be denied even a taste of your palatable treasure, Argonheart?' Doctor Volospion used much the same voice as the one he had used to speak to Abu Thaleb. 'Hm?'

Argonheart Po cleared his throat. He shook his head. He glanced at the ground. 'I think so.'

'Oh, but Argonheart, you still have a few dinosaurs left. Can't I see one now? On the horizon.' Miss Ming clutched at his hand but failed to engage.

'No more, no more,' said the master chef.

Doctor Volospion spoke again. 'Ah, mighty lord of the larder, how haughty you can sometimes be! Just a morsel of mastodon, perhaps, to whet our appetites?'

'I made no mastodons!' bellowed Argonheart Po, and now he was striding away. 'Goodbye to you!'

Doctor Volospion stirred in his cushion. 'Well, well. Obsessive people can be very boorish sometimes, I think.'

Mavis Ming said: 'He was more interested in his confectionery than any opportunity for contact with another intelligence. Still, he *was* upset.'

'Then you are the only one of us to have tasted his preparations.' Abu Thaleb looked doubtfully at the congealing lake between him and the spaceship.

'How were his dishes, by the by, Miss Ming?' Doctor Volospion wished to know. 'You sampled them, eh?'

Miss Ming adopted something of a worldly air for Doctor Volospion's approval. She uttered a light, amused laugh. 'Oh, a bit over-flavoured, really, if the truth be told.'

His thin tongue ran the line of his lips. 'Too strong, the taste?'

'He's not as good as they say he is, if you ask me. All this' – she rotated a wrist – 'all these big ideas.'

Abu Thaleb would not allow such malice. 'Argonheart Po is the greatest culinary genius in the history of the world!'

'Perhaps our world has not been well favoured with cooks . . . ' suggested Doctor Volospion slyly.

'And he is the most good-hearted of fellows! The *time* he must have spent preparing the feast for today!'

'Time?' inquired Volospion in some disbelief. 'Time? Time?'

'His presents are famous. Not long since, he made me a savoury mammoth that was the most delicious thing I have ever eaten. An arrangement of flavours defeating description, and yet possessing a unity of taste that was inevitable!' Abu Thaleb was displaying unusual vivacity.

Doctor Volospion was incapable of diplomacy now. He was as one who has hooked his shark and refuses to cut the line, no matter what damage may ensue to both boat and man.

'Perhaps you confuse the subject-matter with the art, admirable Abu?'

Mavis Ming would also take hold of the rod, secure in the approval of her protector, inspired by his wit. 'One man's elephant steak, after all, is another man's bicarbonate of soda!'

And now it was as if rod and line snapped over the side to be borne to the depths.

Abu Thaleb stared at her in frank bewilderment.

Doctor Volospion turned from his prey, his grey face controlled. There was a pause. His expression changed. A secretive smile, for himself more than for her.

The Commissar of Bengal had been saved from conflict and as a result became confused. 'Well,' he said weakly, 'I for one am always astonished by his invention.'

Miss Ming became aware of the atmosphere. Such an atmosphere often followed her funniest observations. 'I'm being too subtle and obscure. I'm sorry. No – Argonheart can be very clever. Very clever indeed. He's very nice. He's always made me feel very much at home. Oh, dear! Do I always manage to spoil things? It can't be me, can it?'

Doctor Volospion, for reasons of his own, had cast a fresh line. 'My dear Miss Ming, you are being too kind again!'

He raised a long hand, the fingers curled forwards to form a claw. 'Do not let this clever commissar confuse you into compromising your opinions. Be true to your own convictions. If you find Argonheart's work unsatisfactory, not up to the demands of your palate, then say so.'

Abu Thaleb this time ignored the bait. 'Volospion, you mock us both too much,' he protested. 'Leave Miss Ming, at least, alone!'

'Oh, he's not mocking *me*,' Miss Ming observed.

'I?' Doctor Volospion moved his brows in apparent astonishment. 'Mock?'

'Yes. Mock.' Abu Thaleb studied the spaceship.

'You do me too much credit, my friend.'

'Hum,' said Abu Thaleb.

Mavis Ming laughed amiably. 'You never know when he's being serious or when he's joking, do you, Commissar?'

Abu Thaleb was brief. 'Well, Miss Ming, if you are not discomforted, then –'

He was interrupted by Doctor Volospion, who pointed to the ship.

'Ha! Our guest emerges!'

6. In Which Mr Emmanuel Bloom Lays Claim to His Kingdom

ONCE MORE HE STOOD BEFORE THEM, HIS HEAD BENT FORWARDS, his bright blue eyes glittering, his stiff arms at his sides, his red hair flaring to frame his face. He remained for some while at the top of the ramp. He watched them, not with caution but with dispassionate curiosity.

He had changed his clothes.

Now he had on a suit of crumpled black velvet, a shirt whose stiff, high collar rose as if to support his chin, whose cuffs covered his clenched hands to the knuckles. His feet were small and there were tiny, shining pumps on them. He leaned so far over the ramp that he threatened to topple straight down it.

'What an altogether ridiculous figure,' hissed Miss Ming to Doctor Volospion. 'Don't you think?'

She would have said more but, for the moment, she evidently felt the compelling authority of those bulging blue eyes.

'Not from space at all,' complained the Commissar of Bengal. 'He's a time-traveller. His clothes . . . '

'Oh, no.' Miss Ming was adamant. 'We saw him arrive. The ship came from space.'

'From the *sky*, perhaps, but not from space.' Abu Thaleb pushed pearls away from his mouth. 'Now –'

But the newcomer had struck a strange pose, arms stiffly extended before him, little mouth smiling, head held up. He spoke in fluting musical tones that were this time completely comprehensible to them all.

'I welcome you, people of Earth, to my presence. I cannot say how moved I am to be among you again and I appreciate your own feelings on this wonderful day. For the Hero of your greatest legends returns to you. Ah, but how you must have yearned for me. How you must have prayed for me to come back to you! To bring you Life. To bring you Reassurance. To bring you that Tranquillity that can only be achieved by Pain! Well, dear people of Earth, I am back. At long last I am back!'

'Back . . . ?' grunted Abu Thaleb.

'Oh, the journey has demented him,' suggested Mavis Ming.

Abu Thaleb cleared his throat. 'I believe you have the advantage, sir . . . '

'We missed the name,' explained Doctor Volospion, his voice a fraction animated.

A sweet smile appeared upon the creature's ruby lips. 'But you *must* recognize me!'

'Not a stirring of memory, for my part,' said Doctor Volospion.

'A picture, perhaps, in the old cities. But no . . . ' said Abu Thaleb.

'You *do* look like someone. Some old writer or other,' said Miss Ming. 'I never did literature.'

He frowned. He turned his palms inwards. He looked down at his strange body. His voice trilled on. 'Yes. Yes. I suppose it is possible that you do not recognize this particular manifestation.'

'Perhaps you could offer a clue.' Doctor Volospion sat up in his cushions for the first time.

He was ignored. The newcomer was patting at his chest. 'I have changed my physical appearance so many times that I have forgotten how I looked at first. The body has probably diminished quite a lot. The hands are certainly of a different shape. Once, as I recall, I was fat. As fat as your friend – ah, he's gone! – the one who was here when I first emerged and whose language I couldn't understand – the translator is working fine now, eh? Good, good. Oh, yes! Quite as fat as him. Fatter. And tall, I think, too. Much taller than any of you. But I leant towards economy. I had the opportunity to change. To be more comfortable in the confines of my ship. I caused my physique to be altered. Irreversibly. This form was modelled after a hero of my own whose name and achievements I forget.' He drew a deep breath. 'Still, the form is immaterial. I am here, as I say, to bring you Fulfilment.'

'I am sure that we are all grateful,' said Doctor Volospion.

'But your name, sir?' Abu Thaleb reminded him.

'Name? Names! Names! Names! I have so many!' He flung back his head and gave forth a warbling laugh. 'Names!'

'Just one would help . . . ' said Abu Thaleb without irony.

'Names?' His blue eyes fixed them. He gestured. 'Names? How would you have me called? For I am the Phoenix! I am the Sun's Eagle! I am the Sun's Revenge!' He strutted to the very edge of the ramp but still did not descend. He leaned against the airlock opening. 'You shall know me. You shall! For I am the claws, come to take back the heart you stole from the centre of that great furnace that is my Lord and my Slave. Eh? Do you recall me now, as I remind you of your crimes?'

'Quite mad,' said Miss Ming in a low, tense voice. 'I think we'd better . . . ' But her companions were fascinated.

'Here I am!' He spread his legs and arms, to fill the airlock: X. 'Magus, clown and prophet, I – Master of the World! Witness!'

Mavis Ming gasped as flames shot from his fingertips. Flames danced in his hair. Flames flickered from his nostrils. 'Clownly, kingly, priestly eater and disgorger of fire! Ha!'

He laughed and gestured and balls of flame surrounded him.

'I have no ambiguities, no ambitions – I *am* all things! Man and woman, god and beast, child and ancient – all are compatible and all co-exist in me.'

A huge sheet of fire seemed to engulf the whole ship and then vanish, leaving the newcomer standing there at the airlock, his high voice piping, his blue eyes full of pride.

'I am Mankind! I am the Multiverse! I am Life and Death and Limbo, too. I am Peace, Strife and Equilibrium. I am Damnation and Salvation. I am all that exists. And I am *you!*'

He threw back his little head and began to laugh while the three people stared at him in silent astonishment. For the first time he walked a little way down the ramp, balancing on the balls of his feet, extending his arms at his sides. And he began to sing:

> 'For I am GOD – and SATAN, too!
> 'PHOENIX, FAUST and FOOL!
> 'My MADNESS is DIVINE, and COOL my SENSE!
> 'I am your DOOM, your PROVIDENCE!'

'We are still, I fear, at a loss . . . ' murmured Doctor Volospion, but he could not be heard by that singing creature whose attention was suddenly, as if for the first time, on Mavis Ming.

Miss Ming retreated a step or two. 'Oo! What do you think you're looking at, chum!'

He stopped his singing. His features became eager. He bent to regard her.

'Ah! What a *splendid* woman!'

He moved still further down the ramp and he was sighing with pleasure.

'Oh, Madonna of Lust. Ah, my Tigress, my Temptation. Mm! Never have I seen such beauty! But this is Ultimate Femininity!'

'I've had enough,' said Miss Ming severely, and she began to edge away.

He did not follow, but his eyes enchained her. His high, singsong voice became ecstatic.

'What Beauty! Ah – I will bring great wings to beat upon your breast.' His hands clenched at air. 'Tearing talons your talents shall grasp! Claws of blood and sinew shall catch the silver strings of your cool harp! Ha! I'll have you, madam, never fear! Ho! I'll bring your blood to the surface of your skin! Hei! It shall pulse there – in service to my sin!'

'I'm not hanging around,' she said, but she did not move.

The other two watched, forgotten by both, as the strange, mad figure pranced upon his ramp, paying court to the fat, bewildered lady in blue and yellow below.

'You shall be mine, madam. You shall be mine! This is worth all those millennia when I was denied any form of consolation, any sort of human company. I have crossed galaxies and dimensions to find my reward! Now I know my two-fold mission. To save this world and to win this woman!'

'No chance,' she breathed. 'Ugh!' She panted but could not flee.

He ignored her, or else had not heard her, his attention drawn back to Doctor Volospion. 'You asked my name. Now do you recognize me?'

'Not specifically.' Even Doctor Volospion was impressed by the intensity of the newcomer's speech. 'Um – perhaps another clue?'

Bang! A stream of flame had shot from the man's hand and destroyed one of Werther's unfinished mountains.

Boom! The sky darkened and thunder shook the landscape while lightning struck all about them. Chaos swirled around the ship and out of it stared the newcomer's face shouting:

'There! Is that enough to tell you?'

Abu Thaleb demurred. 'That was one of a set of mountains manufactured by someone who was hoping . . . '

'Manufactured?'

The thunder stopped. The lightning ceased. The sky became clear again.

'Manufactured? You *make* these pathetic landscapes? From *choice*? Pah!'

'There are other things we make . . . '

'And what puny conceits! Paint! I use all that is real for *my* canvases. Fire, water, earth and air – and human souls!'

'We can sometimes achieve quite interesting effects,' continued Abu Thaleb manfully, 'by . . . '

'Nonsense! Know you this – that I am the Controller of your Destinies! Re-born, I come among you to give you New Life! I offer the Universe!'

'We have had the universe,' said Doctor Volospion. 'That is partly why we are in our current predicament. It is all used up.'

'Bah! Well, well, well. So I must take it upon myself again to rescue the race. I shall not betray you – as you have betrayed me in the past. Again I give you the opportunity. Follow me!'

The Commissar of Bengal passed a hand over the gleaming cork-screw curls of his blue-black beard; he tugged at the red Star of India decorating his left ear-lobe; he fingered a feather of his turban.

'Follow you? By Allah, sir, I'm confounded! Follow you? Not a word, I fear. Not a syllable.'

'That is not what I meant.'

'I think,' interposed Doctor Volospion, 'that our visitor regards himself as a prophet – a chosen spokesman for some religion or other. The phrase he uses is more than familiar to me. Doubtless he wishes to convert us to the worship of his god.'

'God? God! God! I am no servant of a Higher Power!' The visitor's neck flashed back in shock. 'Unless, as can fairly be said, I serve myself – and Mankind, of course . . . '

Doctor Volospion casually changed the colour of his robes to dark green and silver, then to crimson and black. He sighed. He became all black.

The visitor watched this process with some contempt. 'What have we here? A jester to my clown?'

Doctor Volospion glanced up. 'Forgive me if I seem unmannerly. I was seeking an appropriate colour for my mood.'

Abu Thaleb was dogged. 'Sir, if you could introduce yourself, perhaps a little more formally . . . ?'

The stranger regarded him through a milder eye, as if giving the Commissar's remark weighty consideration.

'A name? Just one,' coaxed the Lord of All Elephants. 'It might jog our memories, d'you see?'

'I am your Messiah.'

'There!' cried Doctor Volospion, pleased with his earlier inter-pretation.

The messiah raised inflexible arms towards the skies. 'I am the Prophet of the Sun! Flamebringer, call me!'

Still more animated, even amused, Doctor Volospion turned his attention away from his cuffs (now of purple lace) to remark: 'The name is not familiar, sir. Where are you from?'

'Earth! I am from Earth!' The prophet gripped the lapels of his velvet coat. 'You must know me. I have given you every hint.'

'But when did you *leave* Earth?' Abu Thaleb put in, intending help. 'Perhaps we are further in your future than you realize. This planet, you see, is millions, billions, of years old. Why, there is every evidence that it would have perished a long time ago – so far as supporting human life was concerned, at any rate – if we had not, with the aid of our great, old cities, maintained it. You could be from a past so distant that no memory remains of you. The cities, of course, do remember a great deal, and it is possible that one of *them* might know you. Or there are time-travellers here, like Miss Ming, with better memories of earlier times than even the cities possess. What I am trying to say, sir, is that we are not being deliberately obtuse. We should be only too willing to show you proper respect if we knew who you were and how we should show it. It is on you, the onus, I regret.'

The head jerked from side to side; a curious cockatoo. 'Eh?'

'Name, rank and serial number!' Miss Ming guffawed.

'Eh?'

'We are an ancient and ignorant people,' Abu Thaleb apologized. 'Well, at least, I speak for myself. I am very ancient and extremely ignorant. Except, I should explain, in the matter of elephants, where I am something of an expert.'

'Elephants?'

The stranger's blue eyes glittered. 'So this is what you have become? Dilettantes! Fops! Dandies! Cynics! Quasi-realists!'

'We have become all things at the End of Time,' said Doctor Volospion. 'Variety flourishes, if originality does not.'

'Pah! I call you lifeless bones. But fear not. I am returned to resurrect you. I am Power. I am the forgotten Spirit of Mankind. I am Possibility.'

'Quite so,' said Doctor Volospion agreeably. 'But I think, sir, that you underestimate the degree of our sophistication.'

'We have really considered the matter quite closely, some of us,' Abu Thaleb wished the stranger to know. 'We are definitely, it seems, doomed.'

'Not now! Not now!' The little man jerked his hand and fire began to roar upon Argonheart Po's cola lake. It was a bright, unlikely red. There was heat.

'Delightful,' murmured Doctor Volospion. 'But if I may demonstrate . . . ' He turned a sapphire ring on his right finger. Pale blue
clouds formed over the lake. A light rain fell. The fire guttered. It
died. 'You will see,' added Doctor Volospion quickly, noting the
stranger's expression, 'that we enjoy a certain amount of control
over the elements.' He turned another ring. The fire returned.

'I am not here to match conjuring tricks with you, my jackal-eyed
friend!' The stranger gestured and a halo of bright flame appeared
around his head. He swept his arms about and black clouds filled the
sky once more and thunder boomed again; lightning crashed. 'I use
my mastery merely to demonstrate my moral purpose.'

Doctor Volospion raised a delighted hand to his mouth. 'I did not
realize . . . '

'Well, you shall! You shall know me! I shall awaken the memory
dreaming in the forgotten places of your minds. Then, how gladly
you will welcome me! For I am Salvation.' He struck a pose and his
high, musical voice very nearly sang his next speech:

'Oh, call me Satan, for I am cast down from Heaven! The
teeming worlds of the Multiverse have been my domicile till now;
but here I am, come back to you, at long last. You do not know me
now – but you shall know me soon. I am He for whom you have
been waiting. I am the Sun Eagle. Ah, now shall this old world
blossom with my fire. For I shall be triumphant, the terrible, in-
tolerant Master of your Globe.'

He paused only for a second to review his audience, his head on
one side. Then he filled his lungs and continued with his litany:

'This is my birthright, my duty, my desire. I claim the World. I
claim all its denizens as my subjects. I shall instruct you in the
glories of the Spirit. You sleep now. You have forgotten how to fly
on the wild winds that blow from Heaven and from Hell, for now
you cower beneath a mere breeze that is the cold Wind of Limbo. It
flattens you, deadens you, and you abase yourselves passively before
it, because you know no other wind.'

His hands settled upon his hips. 'But I am the wind. I am the air
and the fire to resurrect your Spirit. You two, you bewildered men,
shall be my first disciples. And you, woman, shall be my glorious
consort.'

Mavis Ming gave a little shudder and confided to Abu Thaleb: 'I
couldn't think of anything worse. What a bombastic little idiot! Isn't
one of you going to put him in his place?'

'Oh, he is entertaining, you know,' said Abu Thaleb tolerantly.

'Charming,' agreed Doctor Volospion. 'You should be flattered, Miss Ming.'

'What? Because he hasn't seen another woman in a thousand years?'

Doctor Volospion smiled. 'You do yourself discredit.'

The stranger did not seem upset by the lack of immediate effect he had on them. He turned grave, intense eyes upon her. Mavis Ming might have blushed. He spoke with thrilling authority, for all his pre-pubescent pitch:

'Beautiful and proud you may be, woman, yet you shall bend to me when the time comes. You shall not then react with callow cynicism.'

'I think you've got rather old-fashioned ideas about women, my friend,' said Miss Ming staunchly.

'Your true soul is buried now. But I shall reveal it to you.'

The sky began to clear. A flock of transparent pteranodons sailed unsteadily overhead, fleeing the sun. Miss Ming pretended an interest in the flying creatures. But it was plain that the stranger had her attention.

'I am Life,' he said, 'and you are Death.'

'Well . . . ' she began, offended.

He explained: 'At this moment everything is Death that is not me.'

'I'm beginning to pity you,' said Mavis Ming in an artificial voice. 'It's obvious that you've been so long in space, whatever your name is, that you've gone completely mad!' She made nervous tuggings and pullings at her costume. 'And if you're trying to scare me, or turn my stomach, or make fun of me, I can assure you that I've dealt with much tougher customers than you in my time. All right?'

'So,' he said, in tones meant only for her, 'your mind resists me. Your training resists me. Your mother and your father and your society resist me. Perhaps even your body resists me. But your soul does not. Your soul listens. Your soul pines for me. How many years have you refused to listen to its promptings? How many years of discomfort, of sorrow, of depravity and degradation? How many nights have you battled against your dreams and your true desires? Soon you shall kneel before me and know your own power, your own strength.'

Miss Ming took a deep breath. She looked to Doctor Volospion for help, but his expression was bland, mildly curious. Abu Thaleb seemed only embarrassed.

'Listen, you,' she said. 'Where I come from women have had the vote for a hundred and fifty years. They've had equal rights for almost a hundred. There are probably more women in administrative jobs than there are men and more than fifty per cent of all leading politicians are women and when I left we hadn't had a big war for ten years, and we know all about dictators, sexual chauvinists and old-fashioned seducers. I did a History of Sexism course as part of my post-graduate studies, so I know what I'm talking about.'

He listened attentively enough to all this before replying. 'You speak of Rights and Precedents, woman. You refer to Choice and Education. But what if these are the very chains which enslave the spirit? I offer you neither security nor responsibility – save the security of knowing your own identity and the responsibility of maintaining it. I offer you Dignity.'

Miss Ming opened her mouth.

'I note that you are a romantic, sir,' said Doctor Volospion with some relish.

The stranger no longer seemed aware of his presence, but continued to stare at Mavis Ming who frowned and cast about in her troubled skull for appropriate defence. She failed and instead sought the aid of her protector.

'Can we go now?' she whispered to Doctor Volospion. 'He might do something dangerous.'

Doctor Volospion lowered his voice only a trifle. 'If my reading of our friend's character is correct, he shares a preference with all those of his type for words and dramatic but unspecific actions. I find him quite stimulating. You know my interests'. . . . '

'Do not reject my gifts, woman,' warned the stranger. 'Others have offered you Liberty (if that is what it is) but I offer you nothing less than yourself – your whole self.'

Miss Ming tried to bridle, and unsuccessful, turned away. 'Really, Doctor Volospion,' she began urgently, 'I've had enough . . . . '

Abu Thaleb attempted intercession. 'Sir, we have few established customs, though we have enjoyed and continue to enjoy many fashions in manners, but it would seem to me that, since you are a guest in our age . . . '

'Guest!' The little man was astonished. 'I am not your guest, sir, I am your Saviour.'

'Be that as it may . . . '

'There is no more to be said. There is no question of my calling!'

'Be that as it may, you are disturbing this lady, who is not of our time and is therefore perhaps more sensitive to your remarks than if she were, um, indigenous to the age. I think "stress" is the word I seek, though I am not too certain of how "stress" manifests itself. Miss Ming?' He begged for illumination.

'He's a pain in the neck, if that's what you mean,' said Miss Ming boldly. 'But you get used to that here.' She drew herself up.

'As a gentleman, sir – ' continued Abu Thaleb.

'Gentleman? I have never claimed to be a "gentleman". Unless by that you mean I am a man – a throbbing, ardent, lover of women – of one woman, now – of *that* woman!' His quivering finger pointed.

Miss Ming turned her back full on him and clambered into Abu Thaleb's howdah. She sat, stiff-necked, upon the cushions, her arms folded in front of her.

The stranger smiled almost tenderly. 'Ah, she is so beautiful! So feminine! Ah!'

'Doctor Volospion,' Miss Ming's voice was flat and cold. 'I should like to go home now.'

Doctor Volospion laughed.

'Nonsense, my dear Miss Ming.' He bowed a fraction to the stranger, as if to apologize. 'It has been an eternity since we entertained such a glorious guest. I am eager to hear his views. You know my interest in ancient religion – my collection, my menagerie, my investigations – well, here we have a genuine prophet.' A deeper bow to the stranger. 'A preacher who shows Li Pao up for the parsimonious hair-splitter that he is. If we are to be berated for our sins, then let it be full-bloodedly, with threats of fire and brimstone!'

'I said nothing of brimstone,' said the stranger.

'Forgive me.'

Miss Ming leaned from the howdah to put her lips to Doctor Volospion's ear. 'You think he's genuine, then?'

He stroked his chin. 'Your meaning is misty, Miss Ming.'

'Oh, I give up,' she said. 'It's all right for everybody else, but that madman's more or less announced his firm decision to rape me at the earliest opportunity.'

'Nonsense,' objected Doctor Volospion. 'He has been nothing but chivalrous.'

'It would be like being raped by a pigeon,' she added. She withdrew into herself.

Doctor Volospion's last glance in her direction was calculating but when he next addressed the stranger he was all hospitality. 'Your own introduction, sir, has been perhaps a mite vague. May I be more specific in my presentation of myself and my friends. This lovely lady, whose beauty has understandably made such an impression upon you, is Miss Mavis Ming. This gentleman is Abu Thaleb, Commissar of Bengal –'

'– and Lord of All Elephants,' modestly appended the Commissar.

'– while I, your humble servant, am called Doctor Volospion. I think we share similar tastes, for I have long studied the religions and the faiths of the past and judge myself something of a connoisseur of belief. You would be interested, I think, in my collection, and I would greatly value your inspection of it for, in truth, there are few fellow-spirits in this world–weary age of ours.'

The stranger's red lips formed a haughty smile. 'I am no theologian, Doctor Volospion. At least, only in the sense that I am, of course, All Things . . . '

'Of course, of course, but –'

'And I see you for a trickster, a poseur.'

'I assure you –'

'I know you for a poor ghost of a creature, seeking in bad casuistry, to give a dead mind some semblance of life. You are cold, sir, and the cruelties by means of which you attempt to warm your own blood are petty things, the products of a niggardly imagination and some small, but ill-trained, intelligence. Only the generous can be truly cruel, for they know also what it is to be truly charitable.'

'You object to casuistry, and yet you do not disdain the use of empty paradox, I note.' Doctor Volospion remained, so it appeared, in good humour. 'I am sure, sir, when we are better acquainted, you will not be so wary of me.'

'Wary? I should be wary? Ha! If that is how you would misrepresent my nature, to comfort yourself, then I give you full permission. But know this – in giving that permission I am allowing you to remain in the grave when it might have been that you could have known true life again.'

'I am impressed . . . '

'No more! I am your Master, whether you acknowledge it or no, whether I care or no, and that is unquestionable. I'll waste no more energy in debate with you, manikin.'

'Manikin!' Miss Ming snorted. 'That's a good one.'

Doctor Volospion put a finger on his lips. 'Please, Miss Ming. I would continue this conversation.'

'After he's insulted you –'

'He speaks his mind, that is all. He does not know our preferences for euphemism and ornament, and so –'

'Exactly,' said Abu Thaleb, relieved. 'He will come to understand our ways soon.'

'Be certain,' fluted the stranger, 'that it is you who will come to understand my ways. I have no respect for customs, manners, fashions, for I am Bloom the Eternal. I am Bloom, who has experienced all. I am Emmanuel Bloom, whom Time cannot touch, whom space cannot suppress!'

'A name at last,' said Doctor Volospion in apparent delight. 'We greet you, Mr Bloom.'

'That's funny,' said Miss Ming, 'you don't look Jewish.'

7. In Which Doctor Volospion Becomes Eager to Offer Mr Bloom His Hospitality

MR EMMANUEL BLOOM SEEMED FOR THE MOMENT TO have lost interest in them. He stood upon the ramp of his spaceship and stared beyond Argonheart Po's cola lake (still bearing a whisp or two of flame) towards the barren horizon. He shook his head in some despair. 'My poor, poor planet. What have they made of it in my absence?'

'Do you think we could go now?' complained Miss Ming to Doctor Volospion and Abu Thaleb. 'If you really want to see him again you could tell him where to find you.' She had an inspiration. 'Or invite him to your party, Abu Thaleb, to make up for what he did to Argonheart's feast!'

'He would be welcome, of course,' said the Commissar doubtfully.

'His conversation would be refreshing, I think,' said Doctor Volospion. He plucked at his ruff and then, with a motion of a ring, disposed of it altogether. He was once again in green and silver, his cap tight about his head, emphasizing the angularity of his white features. 'There are many there who would respond rather better than can I to the tone of his pronouncements. Werther de Goethe, for instance, with his special yearning for sin? Or even Jherek Carnelian, if he is still with us, with his pursuit of the meaning of morality. Or Mongrove, who shares something of his monumental millennianism. Mongrove is back from space, is he not?'

'With his aliens,' Abu Thaleb confirmed.

'Well, then, perhaps you should invite him now, courteous Commissar?'

'We could tell him that the party was in his honour,' suggested Abu Thaleb. 'That would please him, don't you think? If we humour him . . . '

'Can't he hear us?' hissed Miss Ming.

'I think he only listens to us when it interests him to do so,' guessed Doctor Volospion. 'His mind appears on other things at present.'

'This is all very uncomfortable for me,' said Mavis Ming, 'though I suppose I shouldn't complain. Not that there's a lot of point, because nobody ever listens to little Mavis. It's too much to expect, isn't it? But, mark my words, he's going to make trouble for all of us, and especially for me. We shouldn't be wondering about inviting him to parties. We should tell him he's not welcome. We should give him his marching orders. Tell him to leave!'

'It is traditional to welcome all visitors to our world, Miss Ming,' said Abu Thaleb. 'Even the dullest has something to offer and we, in turn, can often offer sanctuary. This Mr Bloom, while I agree with you he seems a little deluded as to his importance to us, must have had many experiences of interest. He has travelled, he tells us, through time and through space. He has knowledge of numerous different societies. There will be many here who will be glad to meet him. Lord Jagged of Canaria, I am sure –'

'Jagged is gone from us again,' said Volospion somewhat sharply. 'Fled, some say, back into time – to avoid disaster.'

'Well, there are women, too, who would delight in meeting one so passionate. My Lady Charlotina, Mistress Christia, the Iron Orchid . . . '

'They're welcome,' said Mavis Ming. 'More than welcome. Though what any woman would see in the little creep, I don't know.'

'Once he meets other ladies, doubtless his own infatuation for you will subside,' said Abu Thaleb encouragingly. 'As you say, you are probably the first woman he has seen for many a long year and he has had no opportunity to select from all our many, wonderful women one who pleases him even more than you do at present. He is evidently a man of great passion. One might almost call it elephantine in its grandeur.'

Miss Ming put her chin on her fist.

There was a bang. Pensively, Mr Bloom had blown up the rest of Werther's mountains. He continued to remain with his hands on his hips, contemplating the distance.

'Miss Ming. As a student of history have you any knowledge of Mr Bloom?' Doctor Volospion came and sat next to her in the howdah.

'None,' she said. 'Not even a legend. He must be after my time.'

'A near-contemporary, I would have thought, judging by his dress.'

'He said himself he'd taken on someone else's appearance. Someone he'd admired.'

'Ah, yes. Another prophet, do you think?'

'From the nineteenth century? Who was there? Karl Marx?

Nietzsche? Wagner? Maybe he looks a bit like Wagner. No. Someone like that, though. English? It's just not my period, Doctor Volospion. And religion was never my strong subject. The Middle Ages were my own favourite, because people lived such simpler lives, then. I could get quite nostalgic about the Middle Ages, even now. That's probably why I originally started doing history. When I was a little girl you couldn't get me away from all those stories of brave knights and fair ladies. I guess I was like a lot of kids, but I just hung on to that interest, until I went to university, where I got more interested in the politics, well, that was Betty, really, who was the political nut, you know. But she really had some strong ideas about politics – good ideas. She –'

'But you do not recognize Mr Bloom?'

'You couldn't fail to, could you, once you'd seen him? No. Doctor Volospion, can't you send me home on my own?' pleaded Miss Ming. 'If I had a power ring, even a little one, I could . . . '

She had hinted to him before that if she were equipped with a power ring or two she would be less of a nuisance to him. Few time-travellers, however, were given the rings which tapped the energy of the old cities, certainly not when, like Miss Ming, they were comparative newcomers to the End of Time. As Doctor Volospion had explained to her before, there was a certain discipline of mind – or at least a habit of mind – which had to be learned before they could be used. Also they were not one of the artifacts which could be reproduced at will. There was a relatively limited number of them. Miss Ming had never been quite convinced by Doctor Volospion's arguments against her having her own power ring, but there was little she could do save hope that one day he would relent.

'Regretfully . . . ' He gestured. 'Not yet, Miss Ming.' It was not clear to which of her suggestions he was referring. She allowed her disappointment to show on her plump face.

'Hm,' said Mr Bloom from above, 'it is evident that the entire planet will have to be consumed so that, from the ashes, a purer place may prosper.'

'Mr Bloom!' cried Abu Thaleb. 'I would remind you, sir, that while you are a most honoured guest to our world, you will inconvenience a great many people if you burn them up.'

Bloom blinked as he looked down at Abu Thaleb. 'Oh, they will not die. I shall resurrect them.'

'They are perfectly capable of resurrecting one another, Mr Bloom. That is not my point. You see, many of us have embarked on schemes – oh, menageries, collections, creations of various kinds – and if you were to destroy them they would be seriously disappointed. It would be the height of bad manners, don't you think?'

'You have already heard my opinion of manners.'

'But –'

'It is for your own good,' Bloom told him.

'Aha! The authentic voice of the prophet!' cried Doctor Volospion. 'Sir, you must be my guest!'

'You begin to irritate me, Doctor Volospion,' piped Emmanuel Bloom, 'with your constant references to me as a guest. I am not a guest. I am the rightful inheritor of this world, controller of the destinies of all who dwell in it, sole Saviour of your souls.'

'Quite,' apologized Doctor Volospion. 'I should imagine, however, that your spaceship, however grandly furnished and with whatever fine amenities, palls on you as a domicile after so many centuries. Perhaps if you would allow me to put my own humble house at your disposal until a suitable palace – or temple, perhaps – can be built for you, I should be greatly flattered.'

'Your feeble attempts at guile begin to irritate me, Doctor Volospion. I am Emmanuel Bloom.'

'So you have told us . . . '

'I am Emmanuel Bloom and I can see into every soul.'

'Naturally. I merely . . . '

'And this priestly fawning only makes me despair of you still further. If you would defy me, defy me with some dignity.'

'Mr Bloom, I am simply attempting to make you welcome. Your ideas, your language, your attitudes, they are all decidedly unfashionable now. It was my intention to offer you a dwelling from which you may observe the age at the End of Time, and make plans for its specific salvation – at your leisure.'

'My plans are simple enough. They can apply to any age. I shall destroy everything. Then I shall create it afresh. Your identity will not only be preserved, it will be fully alive, perhaps for the first time since you were born.'

'Most of us,' Abu Thaleb wished to point out, 'were not actually born at all, Mr Bloom . . . '

'That is immaterial. You exist now. I shall help you find yourselves.'

'Most of us are content . . . '

'You think you are content. Are you never restless? Do you never wake from slumber recalling a dream of something lost, something finer than anything you have ever experienced before?'

'As a matter of fact I have not slept for many a long year. The fashion died, with most people, even before I became interested in elephants.'

'Do not seek to confuse the issue, Abu Thaleb.'

'Mr Bloom, I *am* confused. I have no wish to have my precious pachyderms destroyed by you. My enthusiasm is at its height. I am sure the same can be said for at least half the population, small though it is, of this planet.'

'I cannot heed you,' said Emmanuel Bloom, feeling in the pockets of his velvet suit. 'You will be grateful when it is done.'

'At least you might canvas the opinion of a few more people, Mr Bloom.' Abu Thaleb begged. 'I mean to say, for all I know, most people might think the idea a splendid one! It would make a dramatic change, at least . . . '

'And besides,' said Doctor Volospion, 'we certainly have the means to resist you, Mr Bloom, should you begin seriously to discommode us.'

Emmanuel Bloom began to stride up the ramp of his spaceship. 'I am weary of all this. Woman, do you come with me now?'

Miss Ming maintained silence.

'Please reconsider, Mr Bloom,' Doctor Volospion said spiritedly, 'as my guest you would share the roof with many great philosophers and prophets, with messiahs and reformers of every description.'

'It sounds,' piped Mr Bloom, 'like Hell.'

'And there are things you should see. Souvenirs of a million faiths. Miraculous artifacts of every kind.'

Emmanuel Bloom seemed mildly interested. 'Eh?'

'Magical swords, relics, supernatural stones – my collection is justly famous.'

Emmanuel Bloom continued on his way.

'You would, as well as enjoying this fabulous company, be sharing the same roof as Miss Ming, who is another guest of mine,' said Doctor Volospion.

'Miss Ming comes with me. Now.'

'Oh, no I don't,' exclaimed Miss Ming.

'What?' Emmanuel Bloom paused again.

'Miss Ming stays with me,' said Doctor Volospion. 'If you wish to visit her, you may visit her at my dwelling.'

'Oh, don't bother with him!' said Mavis Ming.

'You will come to me, in Time, Mavis Ming,' said Emmanuel Bloom.

'That's the funniest thing I've ever heard,' she told him. She said to Doctor Volospion: 'It's a bit insensitive of you, isn't it, Doctor Volospion, to use me as bait? Why do you want him so badly?'

Doctor Volospion ignored the question.

'You would be very comfortable at Castle Volospion,' he told Mr Bloom. 'Everything you could desire – food, wine, luxurious furniture, women, boys, any animal of your taste . . . '

'I need no luxuries and I desire only one woman. She shall be mine soon enough.'

'It would make Miss Ming happy, I am sure, if you became my g— if you used my house.'

'You are determined, I think, to misunderstand my mission upon this world. I have come to re-fire the Earth, as its Leader and its Hero. To restore Love and Madness and Idealism to their proper eminence. To infuse your blood with the stuff that makes it race, that makes the heart beat and the head swim! Look about you, manikin, and tell me if you see any heroes. You no longer have heroes – and you have such paltry villains!'

'It does not seem reasonable of you to judge by we three alone,' said Abu Thaleb.

'Three's enough. Enough to tell the general condition of the whole. Your society is revealed in your language, your gestures, your costumes, your landscapes! Oh, how sad, how ruined, how unfulfilled you are! Ah, how you must have longed, in your secret thoughts, those thoughts hidden even from yourselves, for me to return. And look now – you still do not realize it.'

He smiled benevolently down on them standing near the entrance to his ship.

'But that realization shall dawn anon, be sure of that. You ask me to live in one of your houses – in a tomb, I say. And could I bear to leave my ship behind? My much-named ship, the *Golden Hind*? Or *Firedrake* call her, or *Virgin Flame* – *Pi-meson* or the *Magdalaine* – sailing out of Carthage, Tyre, Old Bristol or Bombay: Captain Emmanuel Bloom, late of Jerusalem, founder of the Mayan faith, builder of pyramids, called Ra or Raleigh, dependent on your taste – Kubla Khan or Prester John, Baldur, Mithras, Zoroaster – the Sun's Fool, for I bring you Flame in which to drown! I am blooming Bloom, blunderer through the million planes – I am Bloom, the booming drum of destiny. I am Bloom – the Fireclown! Aha! Now you know me!'

The three faces stared blankly up.

He leaned with his hand against the entrance to the airlock, his head on his shoulder, his eye beady and intelligent. 'Eh?'

Doctor Volospion remained uncharacteristically placatory. 'Perhaps you could enlighten us over a meal? You must be hungry. We can offer the choicest foods, to suit the most demanding of tastes. Please, Mr Bloom, I ask again that you reconsider . . . '

'No.'

'You feel I have misinterpreted you, I know. But I am an earnest student. I remain a mite confused. Your penchant for metaphor . . .'

The Fireclown clapped a tiny hand to a tiny knee. He frowned at Doctor Volospion. 'One metaphor is worth a million of your euphemisms, Doctor Volospion. I have problems to consider and must seek solitude. I have poetry to write – or to recall – I forget which – and need time for meditation. I should accept your invitation for it is my duty to broaden your mind – but that duty can wait.'

He turned again to regard the woman.

'You'll join me now, Miss Ming?'

His huge blue eyes flashed suddenly with an intelligence, a humour, which shocked her completely from her hard-won composure.

'What?' The response was mindless.

He stretched out a hand. 'Come with me now. I offer you pain and knowledge, lust and freedom. Hm?'

She began to rise, as if mesmerized. She seemed to be shivering. Then she sat down. 'Certainly not!'

Emmanuel Bloom laughed. 'You'll come.' He returned his attention to Doctor Volospion. 'And I would advise you, sir, to save your breath in this meaningless and puny Temptation. Your hatred of me is patent, whether you admit it to yourself or not. I would warn you to cease your irritation.'

'You still refuse to believe my good faith, Mr Bloom. So be it.' Doctor Volospion bowed low.

The ramp was withdrawn. The airlock shut.

No further sound escaped the ship.

8. In Which Miss Ming Begins to Feel a Certain Curiosity concerning the Intentions of Emmanuel Bloom

IF ANYONE AT THE END OF TIME EXPECTED MR BLOOM to begin immediately to exercise his particular plans for bringing Salvation to the planet they were to be disappointed, for his extravagant space-ship (which the fashion of the moment declared to be in hideous taste) remained where it landed and Emmanuel Bloom, the Fireclown, did not re-emerge. A few sightseers came to view the ship – the usual sensation-seekers like the Duke of Queens (who wanted to put the ship at once into his collection of ancient flying machines), My Lady Charlotina of Below the Lake, O'Kala Incarnadine, Sweet Orb Mace, the Iron Orchid, Bishop Castle and their various followers, imitators and hangers-on – but in spite of all sorts of hallooings, bangings, catcalls, lettings-off of fireworks, obscene displays (on the part of the ladies who were curious to see what Miss Ming's most ardent suitor really looked like) and the rest, the great Saviour of Mankind refused to reveal himself; nothing occurred which could be interpreted as action on the Fireclown's part. No fires swept the Earth, no thunders or lightnings broke the calm of the skies, there was no destruction of artifacts nor any further demolition of landscapes. Indeed, it was singularly peaceful, even for the End of Time, and certain people became almost resentful of Mr Bloom's refusal to attempt, at least, a miracle or two.

'Doctor Volospion exaggerated!' pronounced My Lady Charlotina, all in blue and sage, the colours of dreams, as she lunched on a green and recently constructed hillside overloooking the ship (it now stood in clouds of daisies, a memento of the Duke of Queens' pastoral phase which had lasted scarcely the equivalent of an ancient Earth summer) and raised a turnip (another memento) to her ethereal lips. 'You know his obsessions, my dear O'Kala. His taste for monks and gurus and the like.'

O'Kala Incarnadine, currently a gigantic fieldmouse, nibbled at the lemon he held in both front paws. 'I am not familiar with the creatures,' he said.

'They are not creatures, exactly. They are a kind of person. Lord Jagged was good enough to inform me about them, although, of course, I have forgotten most of what he said. My point is, O'Kala, that Doctor Volospion *wished* this Mr Bloom to be like a guru and so interpreted his words accordingly.'

'But Miss Ming confirmed . . . '

'Miss Ming!'

O'Kala shrugged his mousy shoulders in assent.

'Miss Ming's bias was blatant. Who could express such excessive ardour of anyone, let alone Miss Ming?' My Lady Charlotina wiped the white juice of the turnip from her chin.

'Jherek – he pursues his Amelia with much the same enthusiasm.'

'Amelia is an ideal – she is slender, beautiful, unattainable – everything an ideal should be. There is nothing unseemly in Jherek's passion for such a woman.' My Lady Charlotina was unaware of anything contradictory in her remarks. After her brief experience in the Dawn Age she had developed a taste for propriety which had not yet altogether vanished.

'In certain guises,' timidly offered O'Kala, 'I have lusted for Miss Ming myself, so . . . '

'That is quite different. But this Mr Bloom is a *man*.'

'Abu Thaleb's tale was not dissimilar to Doctor Volospion's.'

'Abu Thaleb is impressionable. On elephants he is unequalled, but he is no expert on prophets.'

'Is anyone?'

'Lord Jagged. That is why Doctor Volospion apes him. You know of the great rivalry Volospion feels for Lord Jagged, surely? For some reason, he identifies with Jagged. Once he used to emulate him in everything, or sought to. Jagged showed no interest. Gave no praise. Since then – oh, so long ago my memory barely grants me the bones of it – Doctor Volospion has set himself up as a sort of contra-Jagged. There are rumours – no more than that, for you know how secretive Jagged can be – rumours of a sexual desire which flourished between them for a while, until Jagged tired of it. Now that Lord Jagged has disappeared, I suspect that Doctor Volospion would take his place in our society, for Jagged has the knack of making us all curious about his activities. You have my opinion in a nutshell – Volospion makes much of this Bloom in an effort to pique our interest, to gossip about him in lieu of Jagged.'

O'Kala Incarnadine wiped his whiskers. 'Then he has succeeded.'

'For the moment, I grant you, but unsubtly. It will not last.'

My Lady Charlotina sighed and sucked at a celery stalk, letting her gaze wander to the scarlet spaceship. 'Our curiosity is still with

Jagged. Where can he be? This,' she indicated the vessel with her vegetable, 'is no more than a diversion.'

'It would be amusing, though, if Mr Bloom did begin to lay waste the world.'

'There is no logic to it. The world will be finished soon enough, as everyone knows. The very Universe in which our planet hangs is on the point of vanishing for ever. Mr Bloom has brought his salvation at altogether the wrong moment and at a time when salvation itself is unfashionable, even as a topic of conversation.'

'The reasons are obvious . . . ' began O'Kala, in a rare and philosophical mood, ' . . . for who would wish to discuss such matters, now that we know –?'

'Quite.' My Lady Charlotina waved. An air car was approaching. It was the shape of a great winged man, its bronze head flashing in the red light of the sun, its blind eyes glaring, its twisted mouth roaring as if in agony. The Duke of Queens had modelled his latest car after some image recently discovered by him in one of the rotting cities.

The car landed near by and from it trooped many of My Lady Charlotina's most intimate friends. From his saddle behind the head of the winged man the Duke of Queens raised his hand in a salute. He had on an ancient astronaut's jacket, in silver-tipped black fur, puffed pantaloons of mauve and ivory stripes, knee-boots of orange lurex hide, a broad-brimmed hat of panda ears, all sewn together in the most fanciful way.

'My Lady Charlotina! We saw you and had to greet you. We are on our way to enjoy the new boys Florence Fawkes had made for her latest entertainment. Will you come with us?'

'Perhaps, but boys . . . ' She lifted a corner of her mouth.

My Lady Charlotina noted that Doctor Volospion and Mavis Ming were among those pouring from the body of the winged man. She greeted Sweet Orb Mace with a small kiss, laid a sincere hand upon the arm of Bishop Castle, winked at Mistress Christia and smiled charmingly at Miss Ming.

'Aha! The beauty for whom Mr Bloom crossed the galaxies. Miss Ming, you are the focus of all our envy!'

'Have you seen Mr Bloom?' asked Miss Ming.

'Not yet, not yet.'

'Then wait before you envy me,' she said.

Doctor Volospion's cunning eye glittered. 'There is nothing more certain to attract the attention of a lady to a gentleman, even in these weary times of ours, than the passion of that gentleman for another lady.'

'How perceptive you are, dear Doctor Volospion! It must be admitted. In fact, I believe I already admitted it, when I first greeted you.'

Doctor Volospion bowed his head.

'You are looking at your best,' she continued, for it was true. 'You are always elegant, Doctor Volospion.' He had on a long, full-sleeved robe of bottle-green, trimmed with mellow gold, the neck high, to frame his sharp face, a matching tight-fitting cap upon his head, buttoned beneath the pointed chin.

'You are kind, My Lady Charlotina.'

'Ever truthful, Doctor Volospion.' She gave her attention to Miss Ming's white frills. 'And this dress. You must feel so much younger in it.'

'Much,' agreed Miss Ming. 'How clever of you to understand what it was to be like me! How many hundreds of years can it have been?'

'More than that, Miss Ming. Thousands, almost certainly. I see, at any rate, that your would-be ravisher has yet to come out of his little lair again.'

'He can stay there for ever as far as I'm concerned.'

'I have made one or two attempts to rouse him,' said Doctor Volospion. 'I sought to shift the ship, too, but it is protected now by a singularly intractable force-field. Nothing I possess can dissipate that field.'

'So he does have the power he boasted of, eh?' Bishop Castle in his familiar tall *tête* which cast a shadow over half the company, looked without much interest at the spaceship.

'Apparently,' said Doctor Volospion.

'But why doesn't he *use* it?' The Duke of Queens joined them. 'Has he perished in there, do you think. In his own mad flames?'

'We should have smelled something, at least,' said O'Kala Incarnadine.

'Well,' Sweet Orb Mace was now a pretty blonde in a black sari, '*you* would have smelled something, O'Kala, with your nose.'

O'Kala wrinkled his current one.

'He's playing cat and mouse with me, that's what I think,' said Mavis Ming with a nervous glance at the vessel. 'Oh, I'm sorry, O'Kala, I didn't mean to suggest . . . '

O'Kala Incarnadine made a toothy grin. 'I pity any ordinary cat who met a mouse like me!'

'He's hoping I'll give in and go to him. That's typical of some men, isn't it? Well, I had enough of crawling with Donny Stevens. Never again, I told my friend Betty. And never again it was!'

'But you have been tempted, eh?' My Lady Charlotina became intimate.

'Not once.'

My Lady Charlotina let disappointment show.

'I wish,' said Mavis Ming, 'that he'd either start something or else just go away. It must have been weeks and weeks he's been waiting there! It's getting on my nerves, you know.'

'Of course, it must be, my dear,' said Sweet Orb Mace.

'Well,' the Duke of Queens reminded them all, 'Florence Fawkes awaits us. Will you come, My Lady Charlotina? O'Kala?'

'I have a project,' said My Lady Charlotina, by way of an excuse, 'to finish. Of course, it is very hard to tell if it is properly finished or not. An invisible city populated with invisible androids. You must come and feel it soon.'

'A lovely notion,' said Bishop Castle. 'Are the androids of all sexes?'

'All.'

'And it is possible to –?'

'Absolutely possible.'

'It would be interesting –'

'It is.'

'Aha!' Bishop Castle tilted his *tête*. 'Then I look forward to visiting you at the earliest chance, My Lady Charlotina. What entertainments you do invent for us!' He bowed, almost toppled by his headgear.

The Duke of Queens had resumed his saddle. 'All aboard!' he cried enthusiastically.

It was then that there came a squeak from the space vessel below. The airlock opened. All heads turned.

Emmanuel Bloom's bright-blue eyes regarded them. His high-pitched voice drifted up to them.

'So you have come to me,' he said.

'I?' said the Duke of Queens in astonishment.

'I have waited,' Emmanuel Bloom said, 'for you, Miss Ming. So that you may share my joy.'

Miss Ming drew back into the main part of the gathering. 'I was only passing . . . ' she began.

'Come.' He extended a stiff hand from the interior of the ship. 'Come.'

'Certainly not!' She hid behind Doctor Volospion.

'So, the one with the jackal eyes holds you still. And against your will, I am sure.'

'Nothing of the sort! Doctor Volospion is my host, that is all.'

'You are too afraid to tell me the truth.'

'She speaks the truth, sir,' said Volospion in an off-hand tone. 'She is free to come and go from my house as she pleases.'

'Some pathetic enchantment, no doubt, keeps her there. Well, woman, never fear. The moment I know that you need me I shall rescue you, wherever you may be hidden.'

'I don't *need* rescuing,' declared Miss Ming.

'Oh, but you do. So badly do you need it that you dare not tell yourself!'

My Lady Charlotina cried: 'Excuse me, sir, for intruding, but we were wondering if your plans for the destruction of the world were completely formulated. I, for one, would appreciate a little notice.'

'My meditations are not yet completed,' he told her. He still stared at Miss Ming. 'Will you come to me now?'

'Never!'

'Remember my oath.'

Doctor Volospion stepped forward. 'I would remind you, sir, that this lady is under my protection. Should you make any further attempt to annoy her then I must warn you that I shall defend her to the death!'

Miss Ming was taken aback by this sudden about-face. 'Oh, Doctor Volospion! How *noble!*'

'What's this?' said Bloom, blinking rapidly. 'More posturing?'

'I give fair warning, that is all.'

Doctor Volospion folded his arms across his chest and stared full into the eyes of Emmanuel Bloom.

Bloom remained unimpressed. 'So you do keep her prisoner, as I suspected. She believes she has her liberty, but you know better!'

'I shall accept no more insults.' Doctor Volospion lifted his chin in defiance.

'This is not mere braggadocio, I can tell. It is calculated. But what do you plan?'

'Any more of this, sir,' said Doctor Volospion in ringing tones, 'and I shall have to demand satisfaction of you.'

The Fireclown laughed. 'I shall free the woman soon.'

The airlock shut with a click.

'How extraordinary!' murmured My Lady Charlotina. 'How exceptional of you, Doctor Volospion! Miss Ming must feel quite moved by your defence of her.'

'I am, I am.' Miss Ming's small eyes were shining. 'Doctor Volospion. I never *knew* . . . '

Doctor Volospion strode for the air car. 'Let us leave this wretched place.'

Miss Ming tripped behind him. It was as if she had found her true knight at last.

9. In Which the Fireclown Brings Some Small Salvation to the End of Time

IT WAS, AS IT HAPPENED, MY LADY CHARLOTINA who first experienced the fiery wrath of Emmanuel Bloom.

Tiring (for reasons described elsewhere) of her apartments under Lake Billy the Kid, she had begun a new palace which was to be constructed in an arrangement of clouds above the site of the lake, so that it hovered over the water, reflecting both this and the sun. It was to be primarily white but with some other pale colours here and there, perhaps for flanking towers. She had spent considerable thought upon the palace and it was still by no means complete, for My Lady Charlotina was not one of those who could create a complete conception with the mere twist of a power ring; she must consider, she must alter, she must build piece by piece. Thus, in the clouds over Lake Billy the Kid, there were half-raised towers, towers without tops, domes with spires and domes that were turreted; there were gaps where halls had been, there were whole patches of space representing apartments which, at a whim, she had returned to their original particles.

After resting, My Lady Charlotina emerged from Lake Billy the Kid and stood upon the shore, surrounded by comfortable oaks and cypresses. She arranged the mist upon the water into more satisfactory configurations, making it drift so high that it mingled with the clouds on which her new palace was settled, and she was about to eradicate a tower which offended, now, her sense of symmetry, when there came a loud roaring sound and the whole edifice burst into flame.

My Lady Charlotina gasped with indignation. Her first thought was that one of her friends had misjudged an experiment and accidentally set fire to her palace, but she soon guessed the true cause of the blaze.

'The lunatic incendiary!' she cried, and she flung herself into the sky, not to go to her crackling palace (which was beyond salvaging) but to look down upon the world and discover the whereabouts of the Fireclown.

He was not a mile from the conflagration, standing on top of a great plinth meant to support a statue of himself which the Duke of Queens had never bothered to complete. He wore his black velvet, his bow tie, his shirt with its ruffles. He rested upon the plinth like a parrot upon its pedestal, shifting from side to side and flapping his arms at his sides as he studied his handiwork. He did not see My Lady Charlotina as, in golden gauze, she fluttered down towards him.

She paused, to hover a few feet above his head; she waited, watching him, until he became aware of her presence. She listened to him as he spoke to himself.

'Quite good. A fitting symbol. It will look well in any legends, I think. It is best for the first few miracles to be spectacular and not directed at individuals. I should not leave it too late, however, before rescuing the remains of any residents and resurrecting them.'

She could not contain herself.

'I, sir, might have been the only resident of that castle in the clouds. Happily, I had not arrived at it before you began your fire-raising!'

His little head jerked here and there. At last he looked up. 'So!'

'The palace was to be my new home, Mr Bloom. It was impolite of you to destroy it.'

'There were no inhabitants?'

'Not yet.'

'Well, then, I shall be on my way.'

'You make no attempt to apologize?'

Mr Bloom was amused. 'I can scarcely apologize for something so calculating. You ask me to lie? I am the Fireclown. Why should I lie?'

She was speechless. Mr Bloom began to climb down a ladder he had placed against the plinth. 'I bid you good-morning, madam.'

'Good-*morning*?'

'Or good-afternoon – you keep no proper hours on this planet at all. It is hard to know. That will be changed,' he smiled, 'in Time.'

'Mr Bloom, your purposes here are quite without point. Are we to be impressed by such displays?' She waved her hand towards the blazing palace. Her clouds had turned brown at the edges. 'Time, Mr Bloom is not what it was. Times, Mr Bloom, have changed since those primitive Dawn Ages when such "miracles" might have provoked interest, even surprise, in the inhabitants of this world. Watch!' She turned a power ring. The fire vanished. An entire, if uninspired, fairy palace glittered again in pristine clouds.

'Hum,' said Mr Bloom, still on his ladder. He began to climb back to the top of the plinth. 'I see. So Volospion is not the only conjurer here.'

'We all have that power. Or most of us. It is our birthright.'

'Birthright? What of my birthright?'

'You have one?'

'It is the world. I explained to Doctor Volospion, madam . . . '
He was aggrieved. 'Did he speak to no one of my mission here?'

'He told us what you had said, yes.'

'And you are not yet spiritually prepared, it seems. I left you
plenty of time for contemplation of your fate. It is the accepted
method, where Salvation is to be achieved.'

'We have no need of Salvation, Mr Bloom. We are immortal, we
control the Universe – what's left of it – we are, most of us, without
fear (if I understand the term properly).' My Lady Charlotina was
making an untypical effort to meet Emmanuel Bloom half-way. It
was probably because she had no strong wish to be at odds with
him, since she was curious to know better the man who courted
Miss Ming with such determination. 'Really, Mr Bloom, you have
arrived too late. Even a few hundred years ago, before we heard of
the dissolution of the Universe, there might have been some enjoyment for all, but not now. Not now, Mr Bloom.'

'Hum.' He frowned. He lifted a hand to his face and appeared to
peck at his cuff. 'But I have no other role, you see. I am a Saviour.
It is all I can do.'

'Must you save a whole world? Aren't there a few individuals you
could concentrate on?'

'It hardly seems worth while. I am, to be more specific, a World
Saviour – a Saver of Worlds. I have ranged the Multiverse saving
them. From all sorts of things, physical and spiritual. And I always
leave the places that I have saved spiritually regenerated. Ask any of
them. They will all tell you the same. I am loved throughout the
teeming dimensions.'

'Then perhaps you could find another world . . . '

'No, this is the last. I left it long ago, promising that I would
return and save it, as my final action.'

'Well, you are too late.'

'Really, madam, I cannot take your word for it. I am the greatest
authority on such matters in the Universe, to say the least. I am the
Champion Eternal, Hero of a million legends. When Law battles
Chaos, I am always called. When civilizations are threatened with
total extermination, it is to me that they turn for rescue. And when
decadence and despair rule an otherwise secure and prosperous

world, it is for Emmanuel Bloom, the Fireclown, Time's Jester, that they yearn. And I come.'

'But we did not call you, we require no rescuing. We are not yearning, I assure you, even a fraction.'

'Miss Ming is yearning.'

'Miss Ming's yearning is hardly spiritual.'

'So you think. I know better.'

'Well, then, I'll grant you that Miss Ming is yearning. But I am not yearning. Doctor Volospion is incapable, I am sure, of yearning. Yearning, all in all, Mr Bloom, is extinct in this age.'

'Forgotten, hidden, unheeded, but I know it is there. I know. A deep, unadmitted sadness. A demand for Romance. A pining for Ideals.'

'We take up Romance from time to time, and we have an interest, on occasion, in Ideals — but these are passing enthusiasms, Mr Bloom. Even those of us most obsessed with such things show no particular misery when circumstances or changing fashion require that they be dropped.'

'How shallow are those who dwell here now! All, that is, save Miss Ming.'

'Some think her the shallowest of us all.' My Lady Charlotina regretted her spite, for she did not wish to seem malicious in Mr Bloom's eyes.

'It is often the case,' he said, 'with those who cannot see beyond flesh and into the soul.'

'I doubt if there are many souls remaining among us,' said My Lady Charlotina. 'Since we are almost every one of us self-made creatures. There is even some speculation that we are not human at all, but sophisticated androids.'

'It could be the explanation,' he mused.

'I hope you will not be wholly frustrated,' she said sympathetically, watching him climb down his ladder. 'I can imagine what it is like to possess only one role.'

She settled, like a butterfly, upon the vacated plinth.

He reached the ground and peered up at her, arms held stiffly, as usual, by his side, red hair flaring. 'I assure you, madam,' he piped, 'that I am not in the least impressed by what you have told me.'

'But I speak the truth.'

'Unlike Volospion, who lies, lies, lies. I agree that you believe, as does Miss Ming, that you speak the truth. But I see decadence. And where there is decadence, there is misery. And where there is misery, then must come the Fireclown, to bring laughter, joy, terror, to banish all anxieties.'

'Your logic is, I fear obsolete, Mr Bloom. There is no misery here, to speak of. And,' she added, 'there is no joy. Instead, we have a comfortable balance. It enables us to contemplate our own end with a certain grace.'

'Hum.'

'Surely, this equilibrium is what all human morality and philosophy has striven for over the millennia?' she said, seating herself on the edge of the plinth and arranging her gold gauze about her legs. 'Would you set the see-saw swinging again?'

He frowned. 'No heights or depths here, eh?'

'For most of us, no.'

'No Heaven and Hell?'

'Only those we create for our own amusement.'

'No terror and no ecstasy?'

'Scarcely a scrap.'

'How can you bear it?'

'It is the ultimate achievement of our race. We enjoy it.'

'Are there none who –?'

'Those time-travellers, space-travellers, a few who have induced special anachronistic tendencies in themselves. Yes, there are some who might respond to you. A good few of them are not with us at present, however. The Iron Orchid's little son, Jherek Carnelian, his great love Amelia Underwood, his mentor Lord Jagged of Canaria and perhaps a few others, one loses track. Doctor Volospion? Perhaps, for it is rumoured that he is not of this age at all. Li Pao and various aliens who have visited us and stayed . . . Yes, from these you could derive a certain satisfaction. Some would undoubtedly welcome you, for one reason or another . . . '

'It is usually for one reason or another,' said the Fireclown frankly. 'Men see me as many things. It is because I *am* many things.'

'And all of them excellent, I am sure.'

'But I must do what I must do,' he said. 'It is all I know. For I am Bloom the Destroyer, Bloom the Builder, Bloom the Bringer of Brightness, Bloom who Blooms for Ever! And my mission is to save you all.'

'I thought we had at least removed ourselves from generalities, Mr Bloom,' she said, a little chidingly.

He turned away disconsolately, so My Lady Charlotina thought.

'Generalities, madam, are all I deal in. They are my stock-in-trade. It is the gift I bring – to remove petty anxieties, momentary considerations, and to replace them with grandeur, with huge, simple, glorious Ideals.'

'It is not a simple problem,' she said. 'I can see that.'

'It must be a *simple* problem!' he complained. 'All problems are simple. All!'

He disappeared into the soft trees surrounding the plinth. She heard his voice muttering for some while, but he made no formal farewell, for he was too much lost in his own concerns. A short time later she saw a distant tree burst into flame and subside almost at once. She saw a rather feeble bolt of lightning crash and split a trunk. Then he was gone away.

My Lady Charlotina remained on the plinth, for she was enjoying a rare sense of melancholy and was reluctant to let the mood pass.

10. In Which the Fireclown Attempts to Deny Any Suggestion So Far Made that He Is an Anachronism

MY LADY CHARLOTINA'S WORDS HAD FAILED, AS WAS SOON to be shown, to convince Mr Bloom. Yet there was something pathetic in his acts of destruction, something almost sad about the way he demolished the Duke of Queens' *City of Tulips* (each dwelling a separate flower) or laid waste Florence Fawkes' delightful little *Sodom* with all its inhabitants, including Florence Fawkes who was never, due to an oversight, resurrected. It was in a half-abstracted mood that he brought a rain of molten lava to disrupt the party which Bishop Castle was giving for moody Werther de Goethe (and which, as it happened, was received with approval by all concerned, since Werther was one of the few to appreciate the Fireclown's point of view and died screaming of repentance and the like. Though when he was resurrected, almost immediately, he did complain that the consistency of the lava was not all that it might have been – too lumpy, he thought). The Fireclown rarely appeared personally on any of these occasions. He seemed to have lost the will to enjoy intercourse with his fellows. Moreover, there was scarcely anyone who found him very entertaining, after the first demolition or two, largely because his wrath always took exactly the same form. Werther de Goethe sought him out and enthused. He found, he said, Mr Bloom deeply refreshing, and he offered himself as an acolyte. Mr Bloom had informed him that he would let Werther know when acolytes were needed, if at all. Lord Mongrove also visited the Fireclown, hoping for conversation, but the Fireclown told him frankly that his talk was depressing. My Lady Charlotina visited him, too, and came away refusing to tell anyone what had passed between herself and Mr Bloom, though she seemed upset. And when Mistress Christia followed close in the footsteps of her friend and was also rebuffed, Mr Bloom told her sombrely that he waited for one woman and one alone – the beautiful Mavis Ming.

Upon hearing this, Miss Ming shuddered and suggested that someone destroy the Fireclown before he did any more damage to the world.

If it had not been for the immense and unshakeable force-field around the Fireclown's ship, there is no doubt that some of the denizens at the End of Time would have at least made an attempt to halt the Fireclown's inconveniencing activities. It was of a type unfamiliar even to the rotting cities, who did their best to analyse it and produce a formula for coping with it, but failed, forgetting the purpose of half their experiments before they were completed and drawing no conclusions from those they did complete, for the same reason. In most cases they took a childish delight in the more spectacular effects of their experiments and would play with the energies they had created until, growing tired and petty, they refused to help any further.

The Fireclown had been unable to bring quite the holocaust he had promised, for things were rebuilt as soon as he had destroyed them, but he had at least become a large flea upon the flanks of society, wrecking carefully planned picnics, entertainments, artistic creations and games, so that precautions had to be taken against him which spoiled the general effect intended. Force-fields had to be produced to protect property for the first time in untold thousands of years and even the Duke of Queens, that most charitable of immortals, agreed that his ordinary enjoyment of life was being detrimentally influenced by Mr Bloom, particularly since the destruction of his menagerie, the resurrection of which had greatly discommoded him.

There came such a twittering of protest as had never been heard at the End of Time and plans were discussed interminably for ridding the world of this pest. Deputations were sent to his ship and were ignored, polite notes left at his airlock's entrance were either burned on the spot or allowed to drift away on the wind.

'It is quite ridiculous,' said My Lady Charlotina, 'that this puny prophet should be allowed to figure so largely in our lives. If only Lord Jagged were here, he would surely find a solution.'

She spoke spitefully, for she knew that Doctor Volospion was in earshot. They were both attending the same reception, given on Sweet Orb Mace's new lawns which surrounded his mansion, modelled on one of the baroque juvenile slaughterhouses of the late 200,006th century. From within sounded the most authentic screams, causing all to compliment Sweet Orb Mace on an unprecedented, for her, effort of imagination.

'Lord Jagged has undoubtedly found that his interests are not best served by remaining at the End of Time,' said Doctor Volospion from behind her.

She pretended surprise, 'How do you do, Doctor Volospion?' She inspected his costume – another long-sleeved robe, this one of maroon and white. 'Hm.'

'I am well, My Lady Charlotina.'

'The Fireclown has made no attack upon you, yet? That is strange. Of all of us, it is you whom he actually appears to dislike.'

Doctor Volospion lowered his eyes and smiled. 'He would not harm Miss Ming, my guest.'

'Of course!'

She swept silky skirts of brown and blue about her and made to move on, but Volospion stayed her. 'I gather there has been much debate about this Fireclown.'

'Far too much.'

'He would be a marvellous prize for my menagerie.'

'So that is why he mistrusts you!'

'I think not. It is because my logic defeats him.'

'I did not know.'

'Yes. I have probably had the longest debate of anyone at the End of Time with Bloom. He found that he could not best me in argument. It is sheer revenge, the rest. Or so I suspect.'

'Aha?' My Lady Charlotina turned her fine and scented head so that she could smile pleasantly upon the Duke of Queens, strutting past in living koalas. 'Then surely you can conceive a means of halting his activities, Doctor Volospion?'

'I believe that I have done so, madam.'

She laughed, almost rudely. 'But you decide to keep it to yourself.'

'The Fireclown has a certain sensitivity. For all I know he has the means to overhear us.'

'I should not have thought that, temperamentally, he was an ordinary eavesdropper.'

'But I feel, none the less, that I should be cautious.'

'So you'll not illuminate me?'

'To my regret.'

'Well, I wish you luck with your plan, Doctor Volospion.' She looked here and there. 'Where is your guest, the Fireclown's quarry? Where is Miss Ming?'

He expressed secret glee. 'Not here.'

'Not here? She travels to meet her suitor at last?'

'No. On the contrary . . . '

'Then what?' My Lady Charlotina expressed cool impatience.

'Wait,' said Doctor Volospion. 'I protect her, as I promised. I am her true knight. You heard me called that. Well, I am doing my duty, My Lady Charlotina.'

'You are vague, Doctor Volospion.'

'Oh, madam, recall that encounter when we stood upon the cliff above Mr Bloom's ship!'

She drew her beautiful brows together. 'You acted uncharacteristically, as I remember.'

'You thought so.'

'Oh,' she was again impatient. 'Yes, yes . . . '

'Mr Bloom noticed, do you think?'

'He remarked on it, did he not?'

Doctor Volospion brought his hands together at his groin, his maroon and white sleeves swirling. He had an expression upon his pale, ascetic features of extreme self-satisfaction. 'Miss Ming,' he said, 'is safe in my castle. A force-field, quite as strong as the Fireclown's, surrounds it. For her own good, she cannot leave its confines.'

'You have locked her up?'

'For her own good. She agreed, for she fears the Fireclown greatly. I merely pointed out to her that it was the best way of ensuring that she would never encounter him.'

'In your menagerie?'

'She is comfortable, secure and, doubtless, happy,' said Doctor Volospion.

'True knight, say you? Sorcerer, more accurately!' My Lady Charlotina for the first time showed admiration of Doctor Volospion's cunning. 'I see! Excellent!'

Doctor Volospion's thin smile was almost joyous. His cold eyes sparkled. 'I shall show you, I think, that I am no mere shadow of Jagged.'

'Did anyone suggest . . . ?'

'If anyone did suggest such a thing, they shall be proved in error.'

She pursed her lips and looked first at one of her feet and then the other. 'If the plan works . . . '

'It will work. The art of conflict is to turn the antagonist's own strengths against him and to draw out his weaknesses.'

'It is one interpretation of the art. There have been so many, down all these millions of days.'

'You shall see, madam.'

'The Fireclown knows what you have done?'

'He has already accused me of it.'

'Well, you shall have the gratitude of each of us if you succeed, Doctor Volospion.'

'It is all I wish.'

The ground shook. They both turned, to see a magnificent pink pachyderm lumbering towards them. The beast bore a swaying howdah in which were seated both Abu Thaleb and Argonheart Po.

Abu Thaleb, in quilted silks of rose and sable, leaned down to greet them. 'My Lady Charlotina! I see music! And my old friend, Volospion. It has been so long . . . '

'I will leave you to this reunion,' murmured My Lady Charlotina, and with a curtsy to the Commissar of Bengal she departed.

'Have you been all this time in your castle, Volospion?' asked Abu Thaleb. 'We have not met since that time when we were all three together, Argonheart, you and I, when Mr Bloom's ship had first landed. I have looked for you at many a gathering.'

'My attention, for my sins, has been much taken up with our current problem,' said Doctor Volospion.

'Ah, if only there were a solution,' rumbled Argonheart Po. 'We should have realized, when my dinosaurs were incinerated . . . '

'It was the moment to act, of course,' agreed Doctor Volospion. His neck grew stiff with craning and he lowered his head.

'It needs only Miss Ming,' said Abu Thaleb, lowering himself over the side of the howdah and beginning to descend by means of a golden rope-ladder the side of his great beast, 'to complete the original quartet.'

'She cannot be with us. She remains in safety in my castle.'

'Probably wise.' Abu Thaleb reached the ground. He signed for Argonheart Po that his way was now clear. The monstrous chef heaved his bulk gingerly to the edge and put a tentative foot upon a golden rung. Doctor Volospion watched with some fascination as the corpulent figure, swathed in white, came down the pink expanse.

'It is my duty to protect the lady from any danger,' Doctor Volospion said with a certain semblance of piety.

'She must be very much pleased by your thoughtfulness. She is so lacking in inner tranquillity that the trappings of security, physical and tactile, must mean much to her.'

'I think so.'

'Of course,' said Abu Thaleb doubtfully, 'this will confirm Mr Bloom's suspicions of you. Are you sure –?'

'I shall have to bear those suspicions, as a gentleman. I do my duty. If my actions are misinterpreted, particularly by Mr Bloom, that is no fault of mine.'

'Naturally.' Abu Thaleb dismissed his elephant. 'But if Mr Bloom were to take it into his head to – um – rescue Miss Ming?'

'I am prepared.'

Argonheart Po grunted. 'You are looking paler than ever, Doctor Volospion. You should eat more.'

'More? I do not eat at all.'

'There is more to eating than merely sustaining the flesh,' said Argonheart Po pointedly. 'If it comes to that, none of us *needs* to eat, there are so many quicker ways of absorbing energy, but there is a certain instinctive relish to such old-fashioned activities which it is as well to enjoy. After all, we are all human. Well, most of us.'

Abu Thaleb was upset by what seemed to him to be one friend's criticism of another. 'Argonheart, my dear, we all have preferences. Doctor Volospion enjoys rather more intellectual pastimes than do we. We must respect his tastes.'

Argonheart Po was quick to apologize. 'I did not mean to infer . . . '

'I detected no inference,' said Doctor Volospion with an extravagant wave of his hand. 'My interests, as you must know, are specialized. I study ancient faiths and have little time for anything else. It is perhaps because I would wish to believe in something supernatural. However, in all my studies I have yet to find something which cannot be explained or dismissed either as natural or as delusion. I do, admittedly, possess one or two miraculous artifacts which would *seem* to possess qualities not easily defined by science, but I fear it is only lack of knowledge on my part, and that these, too, will be shown to be the products of man's ingenuity.'

Argonheart Po smiled. 'If, one day, you will let me, I shall produce a culinary miracle for you and defy you to detect all the flavours and textures I shall put into it.'

'One day, perhaps, I should be honoured, mighty king of the kitchen.'

And to Abu Thaleb's relief, the two parted amicably.

Doctor Volospion, alone for the moment, glanced about him. He seemed unusually content. A little sigh of pleasure passed between his normally tight-pressed lips. He could, upon occasions, produce in himself a semblance of gaiety and now there was a lightness to his step as he moved to greet Mistress Christia, the Everlasting Concubine, changing his costume as he went, to brilliant damson doublet and hose, curling shoes, a hat with a high crown and an elongated peak which could be doffed to brush the turf with a flourish as he bowed low. 'Beautiful Christia, queen of my heart, how I have longed for this opportunity to see you alone!'

Mistress Christia wore ringlets today of light red-gold, a translucent gown of sea-green antique rayon, bracelets of live lizards, their tails held between their tiny forepaws.

'Oh, Doctor Volospion, how you flatter me! I have heard that you keep the most sought-after beauty in the world imprisoned in one of your gloomy towers!'

'You have heard? Already? It is true.' He pretended shame. 'I cannot help it. I am sworn to do so.'

'It is fitting, then, that you dally with me – for my reputation –'

'Is enviable,' he said.

She kissed his chilly cheek. 'But I know you to be heartless.'

'It is you, Mistress Christia, who gives me a heart.'

'But you will lay it at another's feet, I know. It is my fate, always.'

His attention was distracted, all at once. Sweet Orb Mace's juvenile slaughterhouse was blazing. And a look of joy crossed Doctor Volospion's face.

Mistress Christia was bemused. 'You seem pleased at this? Poor Sweet Orb Mace and his lovely little house.'

'Oh, no, no, that is not it, at all.' He moved like a moth for the flames, his face lit by them. And then fire licked his body again and he was naked. There came a chorus from all around. Everyone was likewise unclad.

From out of the inferno stepped Emmanuel Bloom. He wore a black and white pierrot costume.

'I have come,' he trilled amiably, 'to be worshipped. I strip you naked. Thus I will strip your souls.' He looked at their bare bodies and seemed rather confounded by some of the sights.

Fussing, a number of the guests were already replenishing themselves. Costumes blossomed on flesh again.

'No matter,' said the Fireclown, 'I have made my moral point.'

With a caress Doctor Volospion brought rippling velvet to his body, dark reds and greens glowed upon him. 'Shall you never tire of these demonstrations?' he asked.

Emmanuel Bloom shrugged. 'Why should I? It is my way of preaching to you. There are many excellent precedents for the method. A miracle and a parable or two work, as it were, wonders.'

'You have converted no one, sir,' said My Lady Charlotina, in a huge china bell, decorated with little flowers. Her voice tended to echo.

The Fireclown agreed with her. 'It is taking longer than I expected, madam. But I am persistent, by nature. And patient, in my way.'

'Well, sir, we lose patience,' said Abu Thaleb. 'I regret to say it, but it is true.' He turned for confirmation to his friends. All nodded. 'You see?'

'Is consensus truth?' the Fireclown wished to know. 'Agree what you like between yourselves, for it will not alter what is so.'

'It could be said that that which all are agreed upon is truth,' mildly proposed Argonheart Po, who saw the chance of a metaphysical spat. 'Do we not make the truth from the stuff of chaos?'

'If the will is strong enough, perhaps,' said Emmanuel Bloom. 'But your wills are nothing. Mine is immeasurably powerful. You use gadgetry for your miracles. Do you see me using anything else but the power of my mind?'

'Your ship's force-field . . . ' suggested Doctor Volospion.

'That, too, is controlled by my mind.'

Doctor Volospion seemed unhappy with this information.

'And where is my soulmate?' inquired Mr Bloom. 'Where is my consort? Where are you hiding her, Volospion? Eh, manikin? Speak!' He glared up at his smiling adversary.

'She is protected,' said Volospion, 'from you.'

'Protected? She needs no protection from Emmanuel Bloom. So, you imprison her.'

'For her own safety,' said My Lady Charlotina. 'It is what Miss Ming wants.'

'She is deluded.' The Fireclown displayed irritation. 'Deluded by this conjuror and his jesuitry. Give her up to me. I demand it. If I can save no other soul in this whole world, I shall save hers, I swear!'

'Never,' said Doctor Volospion, 'would I give another human creature into your keeping. How could I justify my conscience?'

'Conscience! Pah!'

'She is secure,' My Lady Charlotina glanced once at Doctor Volospion, 'is she not? Locked in your deepest dungeon?'

'Well . . . ' Doctor Volospion's shrug was modest.

'Ah, I cannot bear it! Know this, creeping jackal, sniggering quasi-priest, that I shall release her. I shall rescue her from any prison you may conceive. Why do you do this? Do you bargain with me?'

'Bargain?' said Doctor Volospion. 'What have you that I should wish to bargain?'

'What do you wish from me?' The Fireclown had become agitated. 'Tell me!'

'Nothing. You have heard my reasons for keeping Miss Ming safe from your threats . . . '

'Threats? When did I threaten?'

'You have frightened the poor woman. She is not very intelligent. She has scant self-confidence . . . '

'I offer her all of that and more. It is promises, not threats, I make! Bah!' The Fireclown set the lawn to smouldering and, as a consequence, many of the guests to dancing. At length everyone withdrew a few feet into the air, though still disturbed by rich smoke. Only the Fireclown remained on the ground, careless of the heat. 'I can give that woman everything. You take from her what little pride she still has. I can give her beauty and love and eternal life . . . '

'The secret of eternal life, Mr Bloom, is already known to us,' said My Lady Charlotina from above. She had some difficulty in seeing him through the smoke, which grew steadily thicker.

'This? It is a state of eternal death. You have no true enthusiasms any longer. The secret of eternal life, madam, is enthusiasm, nothing more or less.'

'Enough?' said a distant Argonheart Po. 'To sustain us physically?'

'To relish everything to the full, for its own sake, that's the answer.' Mr Bloom's black and white pierrot costume was almost invisible now in the boiling smoke. 'Away with your charms and potions, your Shangri-Las, your planets of youth, of frozen cells and brain transfers! – many's the entity I've seen last little more than a thousand years before boredom shrivels up his soul and kills him.'

'Kills him?' Argonheart's voice was even fainter.

'Oh, his body may live. But one way or another, boredom kills him!'

'Your ideas remain somewhat out of date,' said My Lady Charlotina. 'Immortality is no longer a matter of potions, enchantments or surgery . . . '

'I speak of the soul, madam.'

'Then you speak of nothing at all,' said Doctor Volospion.

There was no reply.

The Fireclown was gone.

11. In Which Doctor Volospion Is Subjected to a Siege and Attempts to Parley

MISS MING WAS NEITHER CHAINED NOR BOUND, neither did she languish in a dungeon, but she did confine herself, at Doctor Volospion's request, to her own apartments, furnished by him to her exact requirements, and at first she was content to accept this security. But as time passed she came to pine for human company, for even Doctor Volospion hardly ever visited her, and her only exchanges were with mechanical servants. When she did encounter her dark-minded host she would beg for news of Bloom, praying that by now he would have abandoned his plans and left the planet.

She saw Doctor Volospion soon after the party at Sweet Orb Mace's, where the house and lawn had been burned.

'He is still, I fear, here,' Volospion informed her, seating himself on a pink, quilted pouf. 'His determination to save the world has weakened just a little, I would say.'

'So he will go soon?'

'His determination to win your hand, Miss Ming, is if anything stronger than ever.'

'So he remains . . . ' She sank upon a satin cushion.

'Everyone shares your dismay. Indeed, I have been deputized to rid the world of the madman, in an informal way, and I have racked my brains to conceive a plan, but none comes. Can you think of anything?'

'Me? Little Mavis? I am very honoured, Doctor Volospion, but . . . ' She played with the neck of her blue lace negligée. 'If you have failed, how can *I* help?'

'I thought you might have a better understanding of your suitor's mentality. He loves you very much. He told me so again, at the party. He accused me of keeping you here against your will.'

She uttered her familiar tinkling laugh. 'Against my will? What does he intend to do, but carry me off!' She shuddered.

'Quite.'

'I still can't believe he was serious,' she said. 'Can you?'

'He is deeply serious. He is a man of much experience. That we know. He has considerable learning and his powers are impressive. As a lover, you could know worse, Miss Ming.'

'He's repulsive.'

Doctor Volospion rose from the pouf. 'As you say. Well – why, what is that beyond the window?'

The window to which he pointed was large but filled with small panels of thick glass, obscured, moreover, by the frothy blue curtains on either side of it, reminiscent of the ornament on a baby's cradle, the ribbons being pink and yellow.

It seemed that a small nova flared above the dour landscape of brooding trees and rocks surrounding Castle Volospion. The light approached them and then began to fall, just short of the force-field which protected the whole vast building (or series of buildings, as they actually were). Its colour changed from white to glowing red and it became identifiable as Emmanuel Bloom's baroque spacecraft.

'Oh, no!' wailed Miss Ming.

'Rest assured,' said Doctor Volospion. 'My force-field, like his own, is impregnable. He cannot enter.'

The vessel landed, destroying a tree or two as it did so and turning rocks to a pool of black glass.

Miss Ming fled hastily to the window and drew the curtains. 'There! This is torment, Doctor Volospion. I'm so unhappy!' She began to weep.

'I will do what I can,' he said, 'to dissuade him, but I can make no promises. He is so dedicated.'

'You'll go to see him?' She snuffled. Her blue eyes begged. 'You'll make him go away?'

'As I said –'

'Oh! Can't you kill him? Can't you?'

'Kill? What a waste that would be of such an authentic messiah . . . '

'You're still thinking of yourself. What about me?'

'Of course, I know that you are feeling some stress but, perhaps with your help, I could solve our problem.'

'You could?' She dried her eyes upon her lacy sleeve.

'It would demand from you, Miss Ming, considerable courage, but the end would, I assure you, be worthwhile to us all.'

'What?'

'I shall tell you if and when the opportunity arises.'

'Not now?'

'Not yet.'

'I'll do anything,' she said, 'to be rid of him.'

'Good,' he said. He left her apartments.

Doctor Volospion strode, in ornamental green and black, through

: 214 :

the candle-light of his corridors, climbing stairs of grey-brown stone until he had reached a roof. Into the late evening air, which he favoured, he stepped, upon his battlements, to peruse the Fireclown's ship.

Doctor Volospion laughed and his joy was mysterious. 'So, sir, you lay siege to my castle!'

His voice echoed from many parts of his stronghold, from massive towers, from steeples and from eaves. A cool breeze blew at his robes as he stood there in his pride and his mockery. Behind him stretched bridges without function, buttresses which gave support to nothing, domes which sheltered only empty air. Above were dark masses of cloud in a sky the colour of steel. Below, lurid and out of key with all these surroundings, stood the spaceship.

'I warn you, sir, you shall be resisted!' continued Doctor Volospion.

But there was still no reply.

'Miss Ming is in my charge. I have sworn an oath to protect her!'

The air lock hatch swung back. Little tongues of flame came forth and dissipated in the dank air. The ramp licked out and touched the glassy rock and the Fireclown made his appearance. He wore a scarlet cap and a jerkin of red and yellow stripes. One leg was amber and the other orange, one foot, with bell-toed shoes, matched the red of his jerkin and the other matched the yellow. He had painted his face so that it was now the ridiculous mask of a traditional clown of antiquity and yet, withal, Doctor Volospion received the impression that Emmanuel Bloom was dressed for battle. Doctor Volospion smiled.

The thin, bird-like voice rose to the battlements. 'Let the woman go free!'

'She fears you, sir,' said Doctor Volospion equably. 'She begs me to slay you.'

'Of course, of course. It is because, like so many mortals, she is terror-struck by some hint of what I can release in her. But that is of no consequence, at this moment. You must remove yourself from the position you have taken between us.'

Emmanuel Bloom walked in poorly coordinated strides down his ramp, crossed the grass and was halted by the force-field. 'Remove this,' he commanded.

'I cannot,' Doctor Volospion told him.

'You must!'

'My pledge to Miss Ming . . . '

'Is meaningless, as well you know. You serve only yourself. It is your doom ever to serve yourself and thus never to know true life!'

'You invent a role for me as you invent one for Miss Ming. Even your own role is invented. Your imagination, sir, is disordered. I advise you, with all courtesy, to leave, or change your ways, or alter your ambitions. This masquerade of yours will bring you only misery.' Doctor Volospion adopted the voice of sympathy.

'Must I suffer further examples of your hypocrisy, manikin? Let down this screen and show me to my soulmate.' Emmanuel Bloom banged a small fist upon the field, causing it to shimmer somewhat. His mad blue eyes were fierce and paradoxical in their setting of paint.

'Your "soulmate" sir, reviles you.'

'Your interpretations are of no interest to me. Let me see her!'

'If you saw her, she would confirm my words.'

'Her voice, perhaps, but not her soul.'

'I'll indulge you no further, sir.' Doctor Volospion turned from the battlements.

Behind him there came a most terrible tumult. He felt heat upon his back. He whirled. The Fireclown could not be seen, for now a wall of flame reared in place of the force-field. And the wall screamed.

Doctor Volospion touched a power ring and the flames became transparent ice through which he could just make out the silhouette of the Fireclown.

'Mr Bloom!' he called. 'We can play thus for many a century and consume all our energies. If I admitted you, would you give me your word that you would use no violence against either myself or Miss Ming, that you would not attempt to achieve your ends with force?'

'I never use force. I use my power to produce living parables, that is all, and so convince those who would oppose me.'

'But you would give your word?'

'If you require it, you have it.' And then the Fireclown raised his shadowy fist again and struck at the ice which shattered. He strode through the hole he had made. 'But you see how easily I can dispose of your protection!'

Doctor Volospion hid his mouth behind his hand. 'Ah, I had not realized . . . ' He lowered his lids so that his eyes might not be seen yet it might have been that a cunning humour glittered there for a moment.

'Will you admit me to your castle, Doctor Volospion, so that I may see Miss Ming for myself?'

'Give me a little while so that I may prepare the lady for your visit. You will dine with me?'

'I will undergo any ritual you wish, but when I leave, it shall be with Mavis Ming, my love.'

'You gave your word . . . '

'I gave my word and I shall keep it.'

Doctor Volospion quit his battlements.

12. In Which Doctor Volospion Gives a Tour of His Museum and His Menagerie of Forgotten Faiths

MAVIS MING WAS DESOLATE.

'Oh, you have betrayed me!'

'Betrayed?' Doctor Volospion laid a hand upon her trembling shoulder. 'Nothing of the sort. This is all part of my plan. I beg you to become an actress, Miss Ming. Show, as best you can, some little sympathy for your suitor. It will benefit you in the end.'

'You're laying a trap for him, aren't you?'

'I can only say, now, that you will soon be free of him.'

'You're certain.'

'Certain.'

'I'm not sure I could keep it up.'

'Trust me. I have so far proved myself your loyal protector, have I not?'

'Of course. I didn't mean to imply . . . ' She was hasty to give him reassurance.

'Then dress yourself and join us, as soon as you can, for dinner.'

'You'll be eating? You never –'

'It is the ceremony which is important.'

She nodded. 'All right.'

He crossed to the door. She said: 'He's not really very intelligent, is he?'

'I think not.'

'And you're very clever indeed.'

'You are kind.'

'What I mean is, I'm sure you *can* trick him, Doctor Volospion, if that's what you mean to do.'

'I appreciate your encouragement, Miss Ming.' He went out.

Mavis looked to her wardrobe. She dragged from it an evening dress of green and purple silk. She passed to her mirror and looked with displeasure upon her red-rimmed eyes, her bedraggled hair. 'Chin up, Mavis,' she said, 'it'll all be over soon. And it means you can go visiting again. What a relief that'll be! And if I play my part right, they'll have me to thank, as well as Doctor Volospion. I'll get a bit of respect.' She settled to her toilet.

It was to her credit that she made the most of herself, in her own eyes. She curled her hair so that it hung in blonde waves upon her shoulders. She applied plenty of mascara, to make her eyes look larger. She was relatively subtle with her rouge and she touched her best perfumed deodorant to all those parts of her body which, in her opinion, might require it (her cosmetics were largely twentieth-century, created for her by Doctor Volospion at her own request, for she considered the cosmetics of her own time to be crude and synthetic by comparison). She arranged an everlasting orchid upon her dress; she donned diamond earrings, a matching necklace, bracelets. 'Good enough to dine with the Emperor of Africa,' she said of herself, when she was ready.

She left her apartments and began her journey through passages which, in her opinion, Doctor Volospion kept unnecessarily dark, although, as she knew, it was done for the artistic effect he favoured.

At last she reached the great, gloomy hall where Doctor Volospion normally entertained his guests. Hard-faced metal servants already waited on the long table at one end of which sat dignified Doctor Volospion, and the pipsqueak Bloom, dressed in the silliest outfit Mavis Ming had ever seen. Strips of ancient neon, blue–white, illuminated this particular part of the castle, though they had been designed to malfunction and so flickered on and off, creating sudden shadows and brilliances which always disturbed Miss Ming. The walls were of undressed stone and bore no decoration save the tall portrait of Doctor Volospion over the massive fireplace in which a small electric fire had been positioned. The fire was also an antique, designed to simulate burning coal.

Becoming aware of her entrance, both men rose from their seats.

'My madonna!' breathed Bloom.

'Good evening, Miss Ming.' Doctor Volospion bowed.

Emmanuel Bloom seemed to be making an effort to contain himself. He sat down again.

'Good evening, gentlemen.' She responded to this effort with one of her own. 'How nice to see you again, Mr Bloom!'

'Oh!' He lifted a chop to his grease-painted mouth.

Simple food was placed by servants before her. She sat at Doctor Volospion's left. She had no appetite, but she made some show of eating, noting that Doctor Volospion did the same. She hoped that Bloom would not subject them to any more of his megalomaniacal monologues. It was still difficult to understand why a man of

Doctor Volospion's intelligence indulged Bloom at all, and yet they seemed to converse readily enough.

'You deal, sir, in ideals,' Doctor Volospion was saying, 'I, in realities: though I remain fascinated by the trappings by means of which men seek to give credence to their dreamings.'

'The trappings are all you can ever know,' said the Fireclown, 'for you can never experience the ecstasy of Faith. You are too empty.'

'You continue to be hard on me, sir, while I try –'

'I speak the truth.'

'Ah, well. I suppose you do read me aright, Mr Bloom.'

'Of course, I do. I gave my word only that I should not take Miss Ming from here by force. I did not agree to join in your courtesies, your hypocrisies. What are your manners when seen in the light of the great unchangeable realities of the Multiverse?'

'Your belief in the permanence of anything, Mr Bloom, is incredible to me. Everything is transitory. Can the experience of a billion years have taught you nothing?'

'On the contrary, Doctor Volospion.' He did not amplify. He chewed at his chop.

'Has experience left you untouched? Were you ever the same?'

'I suppose my character has changed little. I have known the punishments of Prometheus, but I have been that god's persecutor, too – for Bloom has bloomed everywhere, in every guise . . . '

'More peas?' interrupted Miss Ming.

Emmanuel Bloom shook his head.

'But creed has followed creed, movement followed movement, down all the centuries,' continued Doctor Volospion, 'and not one important change in any of them, though millions have lost their lives over some slight interpretation. Are men not fools to destroy themselves thus? Questing after impossibilities, golden dreams, romantic fancies, perfect . . . '

'Oh, certainly. Clowns, all of them. Like me.'

Doctor Volospion did not know what to make of this.

'You agree?'

'The clown weeps, laughs, knows joy and sorrow. It is not enough to look at his costume and laugh and say – here is mankind revealed. Irony is nothing by itself. Irony is a modifier, not a protection. We live our lives because we have only our lives to live.'

'Um,' said Doctor Volospion. 'I think I should show you my collection. I possess mementoes of a million creeds.' He pointed with his thumb at the floor. 'Down there.'

'I doubt that they will be unfamiliar to me,' said Bloom. 'What do you hope to prove?'

'That you are not original, I suppose.'

'And by this means you think you will encourage me to leave your planet without a single pledge fulfilled?'

Doctor Volospion made a gesture. 'You read me so well, Mr Bloom.'

'I'll inspect this stuff, if you wish. I am curious. I am respectful, too, of all prophets and all objects of devotion, but as to my originality . . . '

'Well,' said Doctor Volospion, 'we shall see. If you will allow me to conduct you upon a brief tour of my collection, I shall hope to convince you.'

'Miss Ming will accompany us?'

'Oh, I'd love to,' said Miss Ming courageously. She hated Doctor Volospion's treasures.

'I think my collection is the greatest in the Universe,' continued Doctor Volospion. 'No better has existed, certainly in Earth's history. Many missionaries have come this way. Most have made attempts to – um – save us. As you have. They have not been, in the main, as spectacular, I will admit, nor have they claimed as much as you claim. However . . . ' He took a pea upon his fork. There was something in the gesture to make Miss Ming suspect that he planned something more than a mere tour of his treasures. ' . . . you would agree that your arguments are scarcely subtle. They allow for no nuance.'

Now nothing would stop the Fireclown. He rose from the table, his bird-like movements even more exaggerated than usual. He strutted the length of the table. He strutted back again. 'A pox on nuance! Seize the substance, beak and claws, and leave the chitterlings for the carrion! Let crows and storks squabble over the scraps, these subtleties – the eagle takes the main carcass, as much or as little as he needs!' He fixed his gaze upon Miss Ming. 'Forget your quibbling scruples, madonna! Come with me now. Together we'll leave the planet to its fate. Their souls gutter like dying candles. The whole world reeks of inertia. If they will not have my Ideals, then I shall bestow *all* my gifts on you!'

Mavis Ming said in strangled tones: 'You are very kind, Mr Bloom, but . . . '

'Perhaps that particular matter can be discussed later,' proposed Doctor Volospion, tightening his cap about his head and face.

'Now, sir, if you will come?'

'Miss Ming, too?'

'Miss Ming.'

The trio left the hall, with Miss Ming reluctantly trailing behind. She desperately hoped that Doctor Volospion was not playing one of his games at her expense. He had been so nice to her lately, she thought, that he was evidently mellowing her, yet she hated in herself that slight lingering suspicion of him, that voice which had told her, on more than one occasion, that if someone liked her, then that someone could have no taste at all and was therefore not worth knowing.

They descended and they descended, for it was Doctor Volospion's pleasure to bury his collection in the bowels of his castle. Murky corridor followed murky corridor, lit by flambeaux, candles, rush torches, oil-lamps, anything that would give the minimum of light and cast the maximum number of shadows.

'You have,' said Mr Bloom after some while of this trampling, 'an unexceptional imagination, Doctor Volospion.'

'I do not concern myself with the lust for variation enjoyed by most of my fellows at the End of Time,' remarked the lean man. 'I follow but a few simple obsessions. And in that, I think, we share something, Mr Bloom.'

'Well –' began the Fireclown.

But then Doctor Volospion had stopped at an ironbound door. 'Here we are!' He flung the door wide. The light from within seemed intense.

The Fireclown strutted, stiff-limbed as ever, into the high vaulted hall. He blinked in the light. He sniffed the warm, heavy air. For almost as far as the eye could see there were rows and rows of cabinets, pedestals, display domes; Doctor Volospion's museum.

'What's this?' inquired Mr Bloom.

'My collection of devotional objects, culled from all ages. From all the planets of the universe.' Doctor Volospion was proud.

It was difficult to see if Mr Bloom was impressed, for his clown's paint hid most expression.

Doctor Volospion paused beside a little table. 'Only the best have been preserved. I have discarded or destroyed the rest. Here is a history of folly!' He looked down at the table. On it lay a dusty scrap of skin to which clung a few faded feathers. Doctor Volospion plucked it up. 'Do you recognize that, Mr Bloom, with all your experience of time and space?'

The long neck came forwards to inspect the thing. 'The remains of a fowl?' suggested Mr Bloom. 'A chicken, perhaps?'

Miss Ming wrinkled her nose and backed away from them. 'I never liked this part of the castle. It's creepy. I don't know how –' She pulled herself together.

'Eh?' said Mr Bloom.

Doctor Volospion permitted a dark smile. 'It is all that remains of Yawk, Saviour of Shakah, founder of a religion which spread through fourteen star-systems and eighty planets and lasted some seven thousand years until it became the subject of a jehad.'

'Hm,' said Mr Bloom non-committally.

'I had this,' confided Doctor Volospion, 'from the last living being to retain his faith in Yawk. He regarded himself as the only guardian of the relic, carried it across countless light-years, preaching the gospel of Yawk (and a fine, poetic tale it is), until he reached Earth.'

'And then?' Bloom reverently replaced the piece of skin.

'He is now a guest of mine. You will meet him later.'

A smile appeared momentarily on Miss Ming's lips. She believed that she had guessed what her host had in mind.

'Aha,' murmured the Fireclown. 'And what would this be?' He moved on through the hall, pausing beside a cabinet containing an oddly wrought artifact made of something resembling green marble.

'A weapon,' said Volospion. 'The very gun which slew Marchbanks, the Martyr of Mars, during the revival, in the twenty-fifth century (AD, of course), of the famous Kangaroo Cult which had swept the solar system about a hundred years previously, before it was superseded by some atheistic political doctrine. You know how one is prone to follow the other. Nothing, Mr Bloom, changes very much, either in the fundamentals or the rhetoric of religions and political creeds. I hope I am not depressing you?'

Bloom snorted. 'How could you? None of these others has experienced what I have experienced. None has had the knowledge I have gained and, admittedly, half-forgotten. Do not confuse me with these, I warn you, Doctor Volospion, if you wish to continue to converse with me. I could destroy all this in a moment, if I wished, and it would make no difference . . . '

'You threaten?'

'What?' The little man removed his clown's cap and ran his fingers through the tangles of his auburn hair. 'Eh? Threaten? Don't be foolish. I gave my word. I was merely lending emphasis to my statement.'

'Besides,' said Doctor Volospion smoothly. 'You could do little now, I suspect, for there are several force-fields lying between you and your ship now – they protect my museum – and I suspect that your ship is the main source of your power, for all you claim it derives entirely from your mind.'

Emmanuel Bloom chuckled. 'You have found me out, Doctor Volospion, I see.' He seemed undisturbed. 'Now, then, what other pathetic monuments to the nobility of the human spirit have you locked up here?'

Doctor Volospion extended his arms. 'What would you see?' He pointed in one direction. 'A wheel from Krishna's chariot?' He pointed in another. 'A tooth said to belong to the Buddha? One of the original Tablets of Moses? Bunter's bottle? The sacred crown of the Kennedys? Hitler's nail? There,' he tapped a dome, 'you'll find them all in that case. Or over here,' a sweep of a green and black arm, 'the finger-bones of Karl Marx, the knee-cap of Mao Tse-tung, a mummified testicle belonging to Heffner, the skeleton of Maluk Khan, the tongue of Suhulu. Or what of these? Filp's loin-cloth, Xiombarg's napkin, Teglardin's peach rag. Then there are the coins of Bibb–Nardrop, the silver wands of Er and Er, the towels of Ich – all the way from a world within the Crab Nebula. And most of these, in this section here, are only from the Dawn Age. Farther along are relics from all other ages of this world and the Universe. Rags and bones, Mr Bloom. Rags and bones.'

'I am moved,' said Emmanuel Bloom.

'All that is left,' said Doctor Volospion, 'of a million mighty causes. And all, at core, that those causes ever were!'

The clown's face was grave as he moved among the cases.

Mavis Ming was shivering. 'This place really *does* depress me,' she whispered to her guardian. 'I know it's my fault, but I've always hated places like this. They seem ghoulish. Not that I'm criticizing, Doctor Volospion, but I've never been able to understand why a man like you could indulge in such a strange hobby. It's all research material, of course. We have to do research, don't we? Well, at least, you do. It's nice that someone does. I mean this is your area of research, isn't it, this particular aspect of the galaxy's past? It's why I'll never make a first-rank historian, I suppose. It's the same, you know, when I lived with Donny Stevens. It was the cold-blooded killing of those sweet little rabbits and monkeys at the lab. I simply refused, you know, to let him or anyone else talk about it when I was around. And with the time machine, too, they sent so many to God knows where before they'd got it working properly. When can I stop this charade, Doctor . . . ?'

Volospion raised a finger to his lips. Bloom was some distance away but had turned, detecting the voice, no doubt, of his loved one.

'Rags and bones,' said Doctor Volospion, as if he had been reiterating his opinions to Miss Ming.

'No,' called Bloom from where he stood beside a case containing many slightly differently shaped strips of metal, 'these were merely the instruments used to focus faith. Witness their variety. Anything would do as a lens to harness the soul's fire. A bit of wood. A stone. A cup. A custard pie. Nothing here means anything without the presence of the beings who believed in their validity. Whether that piece of worm-eaten wood really did come from Christ's cross or not is immaterial. As a symbol . . . '

'You question the authenticity of my prizes?'

'It is not important . . . '

Doctor Volospion betrayed agitation. It was genuine. 'It is to me, Mr Bloom. I will have nothing in my museum that is not authentic!'

'So you have a faith of your own, after all.' Bloom's painted lips formed a smile.

He leaned, a tiny jester, a cockerel, against a force dome.

Doctor Volospion lost none of his composure. 'If you mean that I pride myself on my ability to sniff out any fakes, any piece of doubtful origin, then you speak rightly. I have faith in my own taste and judgement. But come, let us move on. It is not the museum that I wish you to inspect, but the menagerie, which is of greater interest, for there . . . '

'Show me this cup you have. This Holy Grail. I was looking for it.'

'Well, if you feel you have the leisure. Certainly. There it is. In the cabinet with Jissard's space-helmet and Panjit's belt.'

Emmanuel Bloom trotted rapidly in the direction indicated by Doctor Volospion, weaving his way among the various displays, until he came to the far wall where, behind a slightly quivering energy screen, between the helmet and the belt, stood a pulsing, golden cup, semi-transparent, in which a red liquid swirled.

Bloom's glance at the cup was casual. He made no serious

attempt to inspect it. He turned back to Doctor Volospion, who had followed behind.

'Well?' said Volospion.

Bloom laughed. 'Your taste and judgement fail you, Doctor Volospion. It is a fake, that Grail.'

'How could you know?'

'I assure you that I am right.'

Bloom began to leave the case, but Doctor Volospion tugged at his arm. 'You would argue that it is merely mythical, wouldn't you? That it never existed. Yet there is proof that it did.'

'Oh, I need no proof of the Grail's existence. But if it were the true Grail how could you, of all people, keep it?'

Doctor Volospion frowned. 'You are vaguer than usual, Mr Bloom. I keep the cup because it is mine.'

'Yours?'

'I had it from a time-traveller who had spent his entire life searching for it and who, as it happens, found it in one of our own cities. Unfortunately, the traveller destroyed himself soon after coming to stay with me. They are all mad, such people. But the thing itself is authentic. He had found many fakes before he found the true Grail. He vouched for this one. And he should have known, a man who had dedicated himself to his quest and who was willing to kill himself once that quest was over.'

'He probably thought it would bring him back to life,' mused the Fireclown. 'That is part of the legend, you know. One of the real Grail's minor properties.'

'Real? This man's opinion was irrefutable.'

'Well, I am glad that he is dead,' said Bloom, and then he laughed a strange, deep-throated laugh which had no business coming from that puny frame, 'for I should not have liked to have disappointed him.'

'Disappointed?' Volospion flushed. 'Now –'

'That cup is not even a very good copy of the original, Doctor Volospion.'

Doctor Volospion drew himself up and arranged the folds of his robe carefully in front of him. His voice was calm when he next spoke. 'How would you know such a thing, Mr Bloom? You claim great knowledge, yet you exhibit no signs of it in your rather foolish behaviour, your pointless pursuits. You dress a fool and you are a fool, say I.'

'Possibly. None the less, that Grail is a fake.'

'Why do you know?' Doctor Volospion's gaze was not quite as steady as it might have been.

'Because,' explained Bloom amicably, 'I am, among many other things, the Guardian of the Grail. That is to say, specifically, that I am graced by the presence of the Holy Grail.'

'What!' Doctor Volospion was openly contemptuous.

'You probably do not know,' Mr Bloom went on, 'that only those who are absolutely pure in spirit, who never commit the sin of accidie (moral torpor, if you prefer) may ever see the Grail and only one such as myself may ever receive the sacred trust of Joseph of Arimathaea, the Good Soldier, who carried the Grail to Glastonbury. I have had this trust for several centuries, at least. I am probably the only mortal being left alive who deserves the honour (though, of course, I am not so proud as to be certain of it). My ship is full of such things – relics to rival any of these here – collected in an eternity of wandering the many dimensions of the Universe, tumbling through Time, companion to chronons . . . '

Doctor Volospion's face wore an expression quite different from anything Miss Ming had ever seen. He was deeply serious. His voice contained an unusual vibrancy.

'Oh, don't be taken in by him, Doctor Volospion,' she said, giving up any idea of trying to placate the Fireclown. 'He's an obvious charlatan.'

Bloom bowed. Doctor Volospion did not even hear her.

'How can you prove that your Grail is the original, Mr Bloom?'

'I do not have to *prove* such a thing. The Grail chooses its own guardian. The Grail will only appear to one whose Faith is Absolute. My Faith is Absolute.'

Bloom began to stride towards Mavis Ming. Volospion followed thoughtfully in his wake.

'Oo!' squeaked Miss Ming, seeing her protector distracted and fearing a sudden leap. 'Get off!'

'I am not, Miss Ming, on. I promise you no violence, not yet, not until you come to me.'

'Oh! You think that I'd –?' She struggled with her own revulsion and the remembrance of her promise to Doctor Volospion.

'You still make a pretence at resistance, I see.' Bloom beamed. 'Such is female pride. I came here to claim a world and now I willingly renounce that claim if it means that I can possess you, woman, body and soul. You are the most beautiful creature I have ever seen in all the aeons of my wandering. Mavis! Mavis! Music floods my being at the murmur of your exquisite name. Queen Mavis – Maeve, Sorceress Queen, Destroyer of Cachuain, Beloved of the Sun – ah, you have the power to do it – but you shall not destroy me again, Beautiful Maeve. You shall find me in Fire and in Fire shall we be united!'

It was true that, for the first time, Miss Ming's expression began to soften, but Doctor Volospion came to her aid.

'I am sure Miss Ming is duly flattered,' he said. It was evident, with his next statement, that he merely resented the interruption to his line of thought. 'But as for the Holy Grail, you do not, I suppose, have it about you?'

'Of course not. It appears only at my prayer.'

'You can summon it to you?'

'No. It appears. During my meditations.'

'You would not care to meditate now? To prove that yours is the true one.'

'I have no urge to meditate.' Mr Bloom dismissed the Doctor from his attention and, hands outstretched in that stiff, awkward way of his, moved to embrace Miss Ming, only to pause as he felt Volospion's touch on his arm.

'It is in your ship, then?'

'It visits my ship, yes.'

'Visits?'

'Doctor Volospion. I have tried to explain to you clearly enough. The grail you have is not a mystical artifact, no matter how miraculous it seems to be. The true Holy Grail *is* a mystical artifact and therefore it comes and goes, according to the spiritual ambience. That is why your so-called Grail is plainly a fake. It if were real, it would not be here!'

'This is mere obfuscation . . . '

'Doctor Volospion, you are a most obtuse creature.'

Miss Ming began to move slowly backwards.

'Mr Bloom, I ask only for illumination . . . '

'I try to bring it. But I have failed with you, as I have failed with everyone but Miss Ming. That is only to be expected of one who is not really alive at all. Can one hold an intelligent conversation with a corpse?'

'You are crudely insulting, Mr Bloom. There is no call . . . ' Doctor Volospion had lost most of his usual self-control.

Mavis Ming, terrified of further conflict in which, somehow, she knew she would be the worst sufferer, if her experience were anything to go by, broke in with a nervous yelp:

'Show Mr Bloom your menagerie, Doctor Volospion! The menagerie! The menagerie!'

Doctor Volospion turned glazed and dreaming eyes upon her. 'What?'

'The menagerie. There are many entities there that Mr Bloom might wish to converse with.'

The Fireclown bent to straighten one of his long shoes and Mavis Ming seized the chance to wink broadly at Doctor Volospion.

'Ah, yes, the menagerie. Mr Bloom?'

'You wish to show me the menagerie?'

'Yes.'

'Then lead me to it,' said Bloom generously.

Doctor Volospion continued to brood as he advanced before them, through another series of gloomy passages whose gently sloping floors took them still deeper underground. Doctor Volospion had a tendency to favour the subterranean in almost everything.

By the time, however, that they had reached the series of chambers Doctor Volospion chose to call his 'crypts', their guide had resumed his normal manner of poised irony.

These halls were far larger than the museum. On either side were reproduced many different environments, in the manner of zoological gardens, in which were incarcerated his collection of creatures culled from countless cultures, some indigenous and others alien to Earth.

Enthusiasm returned to Volospion's voice as he pointed out his prizes while they progressed slowly down the central aisle.

'My Christians and my Hare Krishnans,' declaimed the doctor, 'my Moslems and my Marxists, my Jews and my Joy-pushers, my Dervishes, Buddhists, Hindus, Nature-worshippers, Confucians, Leavisites, Sufis, Shintoists, New Shintoists, Reformed Shintoists, Shinto-Scientologists, Mansonite Water-sharers, Anthroposophists, Flumers, Haythornthwaitists, Fundamentalist Ouspenskyians, Sperm Worshippers, followers of the Five Larger Moon Devils, followers of the Stone that Cannot Be Weighed, followers of the Sword and the Stallion, Awaiters of the Epoch, Mensans, Doo-en Skin Slicers, Crab-bellied Milestriders, Poobem Wrigglers, Tribunites, Calligraphic Diviners, Betelgeusian Grass Sniffers, Aldebaranian Grass Sniffers, Terran Grass Sniffers and Frexian Anti-Grass Sniffers. There are the Racists (Various) − I mix them

together in the one environment because it makes for greater interest. The River of Blood was my own idea. It blends very well, I
think, into the general landscape.' Doctor Volospion was evidently
extremely proud of his collection. 'They are all, of course, in their
normal environments. Every care is taken to see that they are preserved in the best of health and happiness. You will note, Mr
Bloom, that the majority are content, so long as they are allowed to
speak or perform the occasional small miracle.'

The Fireclown's attention seemed elsewhere.

'The sound,' said Doctor Volospion, and he touched a power
ring, whereupon the air was filled with a babble of voices as
prophets prophesied, preachers preached, messiahs announced various millennia, saviours summoned disciples, archbishops
proclaimed Armageddon, fakirs mourned materialism, priests
prayed, imams intoned, rabbis railed and druids droned. 'Enough?'

The Fireclown raised a hand in assent and Doctor Volospion
touched the ring again so that much of the noise died away.

'Well, Mr Bloom, do you find these pronouncements essentially
distinguishable from your own?'

But the Fireclown was again studying Mavis Ming who was, in
turn, looking extremely self-conscious. She was blushing through
her rouge. She pretended to take an interest in the sermon being
delivered by a snail-like being from some remote world near the
galaxy's centre.

'What?'

Bloom cocked an ear in Volospion's direction. 'Distinguishable?
Oh, of course. Of course. I respect all the views being expressed.
They are, I would agree, a little familiar, some of them. But these
poor creatures lack either my power or my experience. I would
guess, too, that they lack my courage. Or my purity of purpose.
Why do you keep them locked up here?'

Doctor Volospion ignored the final sentence. 'Many would differ
with you, I think.'

'Quite so. But you cease to entertain me, Doctor Volospion. I
have decided to take Miss Ming, my madonna, back to my ship
now. The visit has been fairly interesting. More interesting than I
believed it would be. Are you coming, Miss Ming?'

Miss Ming hesitated. She glanced at Doctor Volospion. 'Well, I –'

'Do not consult this corpse,' Mr Bloom told her. 'I shall be your
mentor. It is my duty and destiny to remove you from this environment at once, to bring you to the knowledge of your own divinity!'

Mavis Ming breathed heavily, still flushed. Her eyes darted from Bloom to Volospion. 'I don't think you'll be removing either me *or* yourself from this castle, Mr Bloom.' She smiled openly now at Doctor Volospion and her eyes were full of hope and terror. They asked a hundred questions. She seemed close to panic and was poised to flee.

Emmanuel Bloom gave a snort of impatience. 'Miss Ming, my love, you are mine.' His high, fluting voice continued to trill, but it was plain that she no longer heard his words. His bird-like hands touched hers. She screamed.

'Doctor Volospion!'

Doctor Volospion was fully himself. 'It is hardly gentlemanly, as I have pointed out, to force your attentions upon a lady, Mr Bloom. I would remind you of your word.'

'I keep it. I use no violence.'

Doctor Volospion now appeared to be relishing the drama. The fingers of his left hand hovered over the fingers of his right, on which were most of his power rings.

The Fireclown's hands remained on Miss Ming's. 'He's really strong!' she cried. 'I can't get free, Doctor Volospion. Oo . . . ' It seemed that an almost euphoric weakness suffused her body now. She was panting, incapable of thought; her lips were dry, her tongue was dry, and the only word she could form was a whispered 'No'.

Doctor Volospion seemed ignorant of the degree of tension in the menagerie. Many of the prophets, both human and alien, had stopped their monologues and now pressed forward to watch the struggle.

Doctor Volospion said firmly: 'Mr Bloom, since you remain here as my guest, I would ask you to recall . . . '

The blue eyes became shrewd even as they stared into Mavis Ming's. 'Your guest? No longer. We leave. Do you come, Mavis mine?'

'I – I–' It was as if she wished to say yes to him, yet she continued to pull back as best she could.

'Mr Bloom, you have had your opportunity to leave this planet. You refused to take it. Well, now you have no choice. You shall stay for ever (which is not, we think, that long).'

Mr Bloom raised a knowing head. 'What?'

'You have told us, yourself, that you are unique, sir.' Doctor Volospion was triumphant. 'You prize yourself so highly, I must accept your valuation.'

'Eh?'

'From henceforth, sir prophet, you will grace my menagerie. Here you will stay – my finest acquisition.'

'What? My power!' Did Mr Bloom show genuine surprise? His gestures became melodramatic to a degree.

Doctor Volospion was too full of victory to detect play-acting, if play-acting there was. 'Here you may preach to your heart's content. You will find the competition stimulating, I am certain.'

Bloom received this intelligence calmly. 'My power is greater than yours,' he said.

'I led you to think that it was, so that you would feel confident when I suggested a tour of my collection. Twelve force-screens of unimaginable strength now lie between you and your ship, cutting you off from the source of your energy. Do you think you could have shattered my first force-field if I had not allowed it?'

'It seemed singularly easy,' agreed the Fireclown. 'But you seem still unclear as to the nature of my own power. It does not derive from a physical source, as yours does, though you are right in assuming it comes from my ship. It is spiritual inspiration which allows me to work my miracles. The source of that inspiration lies in the ship.'

'This so-called Grail of yours?'

Bloom fell silent.

'Well, call on it, then,' said Doctor Volospion.

Every scrap of bombast had disappeared from Bloom. It was as if he discarded a useless weapon, or rather a piece of armour which had proved defective. 'There is no entity more free in all the teeming Multiverse than the Fireclown.' His unblinking eyes stared into Miss Ming's again. 'You cannot imprison me, sir.'

'Imprison?' Doctor Volospion derided the idea with a gesture. 'You shall have everything you desire. Your favourite environment shall be recreated for you. If necessary, it is possible to supply the impression of distance, movement. Regard the state as well earned retirement, Mr Bloom.'

The avian head turned on the long neck, the paint around the mouth formed an expression of some gravity (albeit exaggerated). Mr Bloom did not relax his grip upon Miss Ming's hands.

'Your satire palls, Doctor Volospion. It is the sort that easily grows stale, for it lacks love; it is inspired by self-hatred. You are typical of those faithless priests of the fifth millennium who were once your comrades in vice.'

Doctor Volospion showed shock. 'How could you possibly know my origins? The secret . . . '

'There are no secrets from the Sun,' said the Fireclown. 'The Sun knows All. Old He may be, but His memory is clearer than those of your poor, senescent cities.'

'Do not seek to confound me, sir, with airy generalities of that sort. How do you know?'

'I have eyes,' said Bloom, 'which have seen all things. One gesture reveals a society to me – two words reveal an individual. A conversation betrays every origin.'

'This Grail of yours? It helps you?'

The Fireclown ignored him. 'The eagle floats on currents of light, high above the world, and the light is recollection, the light is history. I know you, Doctor Volospion, and I know you for a villain, just as I know Mavis Ming as a goddess – chained and gagged, perverted and alone, but still a goddess.'

Doctor Volospion's laugh was cruel. 'All you do, Mr Bloom, is to reveal yourself as a buffoon! Not even your insane faith can make an angel of Miss Ming!'

Mavis Ming was not resentful. 'I've got my good points,' she said, 'but I'm no Gloria Gutzmann. And I try too hard, I guess, and people don't like that. I can be neurotic, probably. After all, that affair with Snuffles didn't do anyone any good in the end though I was trying to do Dafnish Armatuce a favour.'

She babbled on, scarcely conscious of her words, while the adversaries, pausing in their conflict, watched her.

'But then, maybe I *was* acting selfishly, after all. Well, it's all water under the bridge, isn't it? What's done is done. Who can blame anybody, at the end of the day?'

Mr Bloom's voice became a caressing murmur. He stroked her hands. 'Fear not, Miss Ming. I am the Flame of Life. I carry a torch that will resurrect the spirit, and I carry a source to drive out devils. I need no armour, save my faith, my knowledge, my understanding. I am the Sun's soldier, keeper of His mysteries. Give yourself to me and become fully yourself, alive and free.'

Mavis Ming began to cry. The Fireclown's vivid mask smiled in a grotesque of sympathy.

'Come with me now,' said Bloom.

'I would remind you that you are powerless to leave,' said Doctor Volospion.

The Fireclown dropped her hands and turned so that his back was to her. His little frame twitched and trembled, his red-gold mass of hair might have been the bristling crest of some exotic fowl, his little hands clenched and unclenched at his sides, like claws, as his beautiful musical voice filled that dreadful menagerie.

'Ah, Volospion, I should destroy you – but one cannot destroy the dead!'

Doctor Volospion was apparently unmoved. 'Possibly, Mr Bloom, but the dead can imprison the living, can they not? If that is so, I possess the advantage which men like myself have always possessed over men such as you.'

The Fireclown wheeled to grasp Miss Ming. She cried out:

'Stop him, Doctor Volospion, for Christ's sake!'

And at last Doctor Volospion's long hand touched a power ring and the Fireclown was surrounded by bars of blue, pulsing energy.

'Ha!' The clown capered this way and that, trying to free himself and then, as if reconciled, sat down on the floor, crossing his little legs, his blue eyes blinking up at them as if in sudden bewilderment.

Doctor Volospion smiled.

'Eagle, is it? Phoenix? I must admit that I see only a caged sparrow.'

Emmanuel Bloom paid him no heed. He addressed Mavis Ming.

'Free me,' he said. 'It will mean your own freedom.'

Mavis Ming giggled.

13. In Which Doctor Volospion Asks Mavis Ming to Make a Sacrifice

SHE AWOKE FROM ANOTHER NIGHTMARE.

Mavis Ming was filled with a sense of desolation worse than she had experienced in the past.

'Oh dear,' she murmured through her night-mask.

An impression of her dream was all that was left to her, but she seemed to recall that it involved Mr Bloom.

'What a wicked little creature! He's frightened me more than anything's ever frightened me before. Even Donny's tantrums weren't as bad. He deserves to be locked up. He deserves it. In any other world it would be his just punishment for doing what he has done. If Doctor Volospion hadn't stopped him, he would have raped me, for sure. Oh, why can't I stop thinking about what he said to me? It's all nonsense. I wish I was braver. I can't believe he's safely out of the way. I wish I had the nerve to go and see for myself. It would make me feel so much better.'

She sank into her many pillows, pulling the sheets over her eyes. 'I know what those energy cages are like. It's the same sort I was in when I first arrived. He'll never get out. And I can't go to see him. That ridiculous flattery. And Doctor Volospion doesn't help by telling me all the time that he thinks Bloom's love is "genuine", whatever *that* means. Oh, it's worse now. It is. Why couldn't Doctor Volospion have made him go away? Keeping him here is *torture!*'

Doctor Volospion had even suggested, earlier, that it would be charitable if she went to his cage to 'comfort' him.

'Repulsive little runt!' She pushed her pink silky sheets and turned up the lamp (already fairly bright) whose stand was in the shape of a flesh-coloured nymph rising naked from the powder-blue petals of an open rose. 'I do wish Doctor Volospion would let me have a power ring of my own. It would make everything much easier. Everyone else has them. Lots of time-travellers do.' She crossed the soft pale yellow carpet to her gilded Empire-style dressing-table to look at her face in the mirror.

'Oh, I look *awful!* That dreadful creature.'

She sighed. She often had trouble sleeping, for she was very highly strung, but this was much worse. For all their extravagant

: 235 :

entertainments, their parties where the world was moulded to their whims, what they really needed, thought Mavis, was a decent TV network. TV would be just the answer to her problems right now.

'Perhaps Doctor Volospion could find something for me in one of those old cities,' she mused. 'I'll ask him. Not that he seems to be doing me many favours, these days. How long's he had the Fireclown now? A couple of weeks? And spending all his time down there. Maybe he loves Bloom and that's what it's all about.' She laughed, but immediately became miserable again.

'Oh, Mavis. Why is it always you? The world just isn't on your side.' She gave one of her funny little crooked smiles, very similar to those she had seen Barbara Stanwyck giving in those beautiful old movies.

'If only I could have gone *back* in time, to the twentieth century, even, where the sort of clothes and lifestyle they had were so *graceful*. They had simpler lives, then. Oh, I know they must have had their problems, but how I wish I could be there now! It's what I was looking forward to, when they elected me to be the first person to try out the time machine. Of course, it was proof of how popular I was with the other guys at the department. Everyone agreed unanimously that I should be the first to go. It was a great honour.'

Apparently, this thought did not succeed in lifting her spirits. She raised a hand to her head.

'Oh, oh – here comes the headache! Poor old Mavis!'

She began to pad back towards the big circular bed. But the thought of a continuance of those dreams, even though she had pushed them right out of her mind, stopped her. It had been Doctor Volospion's suggestion that she continue to lead the sort of life she had been used to – with regular periods of darkness and daylight and a corresponding need to sleep and eat, even though he could easily have changed all that for her.

To be fair to him, she thought, he tended to follow a similar routine himself, ever since he had heard that Lord Jagged of Canaria had adopted this ancient affectation. If she had had a power ring or an air car at her disposal (again she was completely reliant on Volospion's good graces) she would have left the palace and gone to find some fun, something to take her mind off things. She looked at her Winnie-the-Pooh clock – another three hours before the palace would be properly activated. Until then she would not even be able to get a snack with which to console herself.

'I'm not much better off than that little creep down there,' she said. 'Oh, Mavis, what sort of a state have they got you into!'

A tap, now, at the door.

Grateful for the interruption, Mavis pulled on her fluffy blue dressing-robe. 'Come in!'

Doctor Volospion, a satanic Hamlet in black and white doublet and hose, entered her room. 'You are not sleeping, Miss Ming? I heard your voice as I passed . . . '

Hope revealed itself in her eyes. 'I've got a bit of a headache, Doctor.' He could normally cure her headaches. Her mood improved. She became eager, anxious to win his approval. 'Silly little Mavis is having nightmares again.'

'You are unhappy?'

'Oh, no! In this lovely room? In your lovely palace? It's everything a little girl dreams about. It's just that awful Mr Bloom. Ever since . . . '

'I see.' The saturnine features showed enlightenment. 'You are still afraid. He can never escape, Miss Ming. He has tried, but I assure you my powers are far greater than his. He becomes tiresome, but he is no threat.'

'You'll let him go, then?'

'If I could be sure that he would leave the planet, for he fails to be as entertaining as I had hoped. And if he would give me that Grail of his, from which his power, I am now certain, derives. But he refuses.'

'You could take it now, couldn't you?'

'Not from him. Not from his ship. The screen is still impenetrable. No, you are our only hope.'

'Me?'

'He would not have allowed himself to be trapped at all, if it had not been for you.' Doctor Volospion sighed deeply. 'Well, I have just returned from visiting him again. I have offered him his liberty in return for that one piece of property, but he fobs me off with arguments that are typically specious, with vague talk of faith and trust – you have heard his babble.'

Mavis murmured sympathetically. 'I've never seen you so cast down, Doctor Volospion. You never know with some people, do you? He's best locked up for his own good. He's a sort of cripple, isn't he? You know what some cripples are like. You can't blame them. It's the frustration. It's all bottled up in them. It turns them into sex maniacs.'

'To do him justice, Miss Ming, his interest seems only in you. I have offered him many women, both real and artificial, from the menageries. Many of them are very beautiful, but he insists that none of them has your "soul", your – um – true beauty.'

'Really?' She was sceptical, still. 'He's insane. A lot of men are like that. That's one of the reasons I gave them up. At least with a lady you know where you are on that score. And Mr Bloom has got about as much sex-appeal as a seagull – less! Did you ever hear of a really sweet old book called *Jonathan* . . . '

'Your headache is better, Miss Ming?'

'Why, yes.' She touched her hair. 'It's almost gone. Did you . . .?'

Doctor Volospion drew his own brows together and traced be-ringed fingers across the creases. 'You do not give yourself enough credit, Miss Ming . . . '

She smiled. 'That's what Betty was always telling me when I used to feel low. But poor old Mavis . . . '

'He demands that you see him. He speaks of nothing else.'

'Oh!' She paused. She shook her head. 'No, I couldn't, really. As it is, I haven't had a good night's sleep since the day he arrived.'

'Of course, I understand.'

Miss Ming was touched by Doctor Volospion's uncharacteristic sadness. He seemed to have none of his usual confidence. She moved closer to him.

'Don't worry, Doctor Volospion. Maybe it would be best if you tried to forget about him.'

'I need the Grail. I am obsessed with it. And I cannot rid myself of the notion that, somehow, *he* is tricking *me*.'

'Impossible. You're far too clever. Why is this Grail so important to you?'

Doctor Volospion withdrew from her.

'I'm sorry,' she said. 'I didn't mean to pry.'

'Only you can help me, Miss Ming.'

The apparent pleading in his voice moved her to heights of sympathy. 'Oh . . . '

'You could convince him, I think, where I could not.'

She was relenting, against all her instincts. 'Well, if I saw him for a few moments . . . And it might help me, too – to lay the ghost, if you know what I mean.'

His voice was low. 'I should be very grateful to you, Miss Ming. Perhaps we should go immediately.'

She hesitated. Then she patted his arm. 'Oh, all right. Give me a few minutes to get dressed.'

With a deep bow, Doctor Volospion left the room.

Miss Ming began to consider her clothes. On the one hand, she thought, some sort of sexless boiler suit would be best, to dampen Mr Bloom's ardour as much as possible. Another impulse was to put on her very sexiest clothes, to feed her vanity. In the end she compromised, donning a flowery mou-mou which, she thought, disguised her plumpness. Courageously, she went to join Doctor Volospion, who awaited her in the corridor. Together they made their way to the menagerie.

As they descended flights of stone stairs she observed: 'Surprisingly, I'm feeling quite light-headed. Almost gay!'

They passed through the tiered rows of his many devotional trophies, past the bones and the sticks and the bits of cloth, the cauldrons, idols, masks and weapons, the crowns and the boxes, the scrolls, tablets and books, the prayer-wheels and crystals and ju-jus, until they reached the door of the first section of the menagerie, the Jewish House.

'I had thought of putting him in here,' Doctor Volospion told her as they passed by the inmates, who ranted, wailed, chanted, tore their clothing or merely turned aside as they passed, 'but finally I decided on the Non-Sectarian Prophet House.'

'I hadn't realized your collection was so big. I've never seen it all, as you know.' Miss Ming made conversation as best she could. Evidently, the place still disturbed her.

'It grows almost without one realizing it,' said Doctor Volospion. 'I suppose, because so many people of a messianic disposition take an interest in the future, we are bound to get more than our fair share of prophets, anxious to discover if their particular version of the millennium has come about. Because they are frequently disappointed, many are glad of the refuge I offer.'

They went through another door.

'Martyrdom, it would seem, is the next best thing to affirmation,' he said.

They passed through a score of different Houses until, finally, they came to the Fireclown's habitat. It was designed to resemble a desert, scorched by a permanently blazing sun.

'He refused,' whispered Doctor Volospion, as they approached, 'to tell me what sort of environment he favoured, so I chose this one. It is the most popular with my prophets, as you'll have noted.'

Emmanuel Bloom, in his clown's costume, sat on a rock in the centre of his energy cage. His greasepaint seemed to have run a little, as if he had been weeping, but he did not seem in particularly low spirits now. He had not, it appeared, noticed them. He was reciting poetry to himself.

> ' . . . *Took shape and were unfolded like as flowers.*
>   *And I beheld the hours*
> '*As maidens, and the days as labouring men,*
>   *And the soft nights again*
> '*As wearied women to their own souls wed,*
>   *And eyes as the dead.*
> '*And over these living, and them that died,*
>   *From one to the other side*
> '*A lordlier light than comes of earth or air*
>   *Made the world's future fair.*
> '*A woman like to love in face, but not*
>   *A thing of transient lot –*
> '*And like to hope, but having hold on truth –*
>   *And like to joy or youth,*
> '*Save that upon the rock her feet were set –*
>   *And like what men forget,*
> '*Faith, innocence, high thought, laborious peace –*'

He had seen her. His great blue eyes blinked. His stiff little body began to rise. His bird-like, fluting voice took on a different tone.

'And yet like none of these . . . ' He put an awkward finger to his small mouth. He put his painted head on one side.

Mavis Ming cleared her throat. Doctor Volospion's hand forced her further towards the cage.

The Fireclown spoke first. 'So Guinevere comes at last to her Lancelot – or is it Kundry, come to call me Parsifal? Sorceress, you have incarcerated me. Tell your servant to release me so that, in turn, I may free you from the evil that holds you with stronger bonds than any that chain me!'

Miss Ming's smile was insincere. 'Why don't you talk properly, Mr Bloom? This is childish. Anyway, you know he's not my servant.' She was very pale.

Mr Bloom crossed the stretch of sand until he was as close to her as the cage permitted. 'He is not your master, you may be sure of that, this imitation Klingsor!'

'I haven't the faintest idea what you're talking about.' Her voice was shaking.

He pressed his tiny body against the energy screen. 'I must be free,' he said. 'There is no mission for me here, now, at the End of Time. I must continue my quest, perhaps into another Universe where Faith may yet flourish.'

Doctor Volospion came forward. 'I have brought Miss Ming, as you have so constantly demanded. You have talked to her. Now, if you will give up the Grail to me . . . '

Mr Bloom's manner became agitated. 'I have explained to you, demi-demon, that you could not keep it, even if, by some means, I *could* transfer it to you. Only the pure in spirit are entitled to its trust. If I agreed to your bargain I should lose the Grail myself, for ever. Neither would gain!'

'I find your objections without foundation.' Doctor Volospion was unruffled by the Fireclown's anger. 'What you believe, Mr Bloom, is one thing. The truth, however, is quite another! Faith dies, but the objects of faith do not, as you saw in my museum.'

'These things have no value without Faith!'

'They are valuable to me. 'That is why I collect them. I desire this Grail of yours so that I may, at least, compare it with my own.'

'You know yours to be false,' said the Fireclown. 'I can tell.'

'I shall decide which is false and which is not when I have both in my possession. I know it is on your ship, for all that you deny it.'

'It is not. It manifests itself at certain times.'

Doctor Volospion allowed his own ill-temper to show. 'Miss Ming . . . '

'Please let him have it, Mr Bloom,' said Mavis Ming in her best wheedling voice. 'He'll let you go if you do.'

The Fireclown was amused. 'I can leave whenever I please. But I gave my word on two matters. I said that I would not take you by force and that I would take you with me when I left.'

'Your boasts are shown to be empty, sir,' said Doctor Volospion. He laid the flat of his hand against the energy screen. 'There.'

Mr Bloom ran his hand through his auburn mop, continuing to speak to Miss Ming. 'You demean yourself, woman, when you aid this wretch, when you adopt that idiotic tone of voice.'

'Well!' It was possible to observe that Miss Ming's legs were shaking. 'I'm not staying here, not even for you, Doctor Volospion! It's too much. I can stand a lot of things, but not this.'

'Be silent!' The Fireclown's voice was low and firm. 'Listen to your soul. It will tell you what I tell you.'

'Miss Ming!' Seeing that she prepared to flee, Doctor Volospion seized her arm. 'For my sake do not give up. If I have that Grail . . .'

'You may see the Grail, beautiful Mavis, when I have redeemed you,' murmured the Fireclown. 'But it shall always be denied to such as he! Come with me and I shall let you witness more than Mystery.'

She panicked. 'Oh, Christ!' She was unable to control herself as she sensed the terrible pressure coming from both sides. She tried to free herself from Doctor Volospion's restraining hand. 'I can't take any more. I can't!'

'Miss Ming!' fiercely croaked a desperate Volospion. 'You promised to help.'

'Come with me!' cried the Fireclown.

She still struggled, trying to prise his grip away from the sleeve of her mou-mou. 'You can both do what you like. I don't want any part of it.'

Hysteria ruled now. She scratched Doctor Volospion's hand so that at last he released her. She ran away from them. She ran crazily between the cages of roaring, screaming, moaning prophets. 'Leave me alone! Leave me alone!'

And then, just before a door shut her from their view:

'I'm sorry! I'm sorry!'

14. In Which Miss Mavis Ming Is Given an Opportunity to Win the Forgiveness of Her Protector

WHEN MAVIS MING NEXT AWOKE, fINDING HERSELF in the soft pink security of her own bed, whence she had fled in terror after scratching Doctor Volospion, she was surprised by how refreshed she felt, how confident. Even the threat of Doctor Volospion's anger, which she feared almost as much as the Fireclown's love, failed to thrill her.

'What can he do, after all?' she asked herself. She still wore the mou-mou. She looked at the ripped sleeve, and she inspected the bruise on her arm. She doubted if the scratch she had given Doctor Volospion was any worse than the bruise he had given her, but she also recalled that, in her experience, men had a different way of looking at these things.

'Why do I feel so good? Because of a fight?' She was almost buoyant. 'Maybe because it's over. I tried to please him. I really tried. But he's got a way of double-binding a girl like nobody else. I guess little Mavis will have to find a new berth.'

She removed the mou-mou and went to take a shower. 'Well, it was high time for a change. And I'm not much gone on sharing the same roof with that mad midget downstairs.'

The shower was refreshing.

'I'm going to go out. I'm going to visit a few people. Now,' elbow on palm of hand, fingertip to chin, 'who shall I visit first?'

She reviewed her acquaintances, wondering who would be most sympathetic. Who would welcome her.

And then, of a sudden, depression swept back. It caught her so unexpectedly that she had to sit down on the edge of the unmade bed, dropping her towel to the floor. 'Oh, Christ! Oh, Christ! What in hell's wrong with you, Mavis?'

A knock on her door interrupted the catharsis before it had properly got under way.

'Yes?'

'Miss Ming?' It was, of course, Doctor Volospion.

'This is it, Mavis.' She pulled herself together. She put on a robe. 'Time for the tongue-lashing. Well. I'll tell him I'm leaving. He'll be glad of that.' She raised her voice. 'Come in!'

But he was smiling when he entered.

She looked at him in nervous astonishment.

He was dressed in robes of scarlet and green. There was a tight-fitting dark green hood on his head, emphasizing the sharpness of his features.

'You are well, Miss Ming?' As he spoke he drew on dark green gloves.

'Better than I thought. I wanted to . . . '

'I came to apologize,' he said.

She had glanced at his hand before the glove went on. There was, of course, no sign of her scratch.

'Oh,' she said. She was taken aback.

'If I had realized exactly how badly that Mr Bloom affected you, I would never have subjected you to the ordeal,' he said.

'Well, you weren't to know.' She bit her lip, as if she sensed her determination dissipating already.

'The fault was wholly mine.' He had all his old authority. It comforted her.

'I lost my cool, I guess.' Her voice shook. 'I'm sorry about your hand.'

'I deserved worse.'

His voice was warm and, as always, it caused her to purr. It would not have been surprising if she had arched her back and rubbed her body against him. 'That Mr Bloom, he just freaks me, Doctor Volospion. I don't know what it is. I suppose I've completely blown it for you, haven't I?'

'No, no,' he reassured her.

'You talked? After I'd gone?'

'Somewhat. He remains quite adamant.'

'He won't give you the Grail?'

'Unfortunately not . . . '

'It *was* my fault. I'm *really* sorry.' She responded almost without any sort of consciousness, mesmerized by him.

'It grieves me. I can think of no way of obtaining it without your help.'

'You know I'd like to.' The words emerged as if another spoke them for her. 'I mean, if there's anything I can do to make up for what happened last night . . . '

'I would not put you to further embarrassment.' He turned to leave.

'Oh, no!' She paused, making an effort of will. 'I mean, I couldn't face actually seeing him again, but if there's anything else . . . '

'I can think of nothing. Good-bye, Miss Ming.'

'There must be something?'

He paused by the door, frowning. 'Well, I suppose it is possible for you to get the Grail for me.'

'How?'

'He said that he would allow you to see it, you recall?'

'I can't really remember the details of what he said. I was too frightened.'

'Quite. You see, somehow he controls his ship's protective devices from where he is. After you had gone he told me again that he would let you see the Grail, but not me. I think he believes that if you see it you will realize that he is this spiritual saviour he sets himself up to be.'

'You mean I could get into the ship and find the Grail?'

'Exactly. Once I had it in my possession, I would let him go. You would be free of him.'

'But he'd suspect.'

'His infatuation blinds him.'

'I wouldn't have to see him again?' She spoke as firmly as she could. 'I won't do that, whatever else.'

'You will never be asked to go to the menagerie and, in a while, he will have left this planet.'

'It's stealing, of course,' she said.

'Call it recompense for all the damage he has done while here. Call it justice.'

'Yes. That's fair enough.'

'But no,' he looked kindly down on her. 'I ask too much of you.'

'You don't, really.' He had inspired in her a kind of eager courage. 'Let me help.'

'He has assured me that he will lower the barriers of his ship for you alone.'

'Then it's up to Mavis, isn't it?'

'If you feel you can do it, Miss Ming, I would show my gratitude to you in many ways when you returned with the cup.'

'It's enough to help out.' But she glanced at the power rings on his gloved fingers. 'When shall I go?' She paused. 'There won't be any danger, I suppose . . . ?'

'None at all. He genuinely loves you, Miss Ming. Of course, if you consider this action a betrayal of Mr Bloom . . . '

'Betrayal? I didn't make any deals with him.'

His voice was rich with gratification. 'It would mean much to me, as you know. My collection is important to my happiness. If I thought that I possessed an artifact that was not authentic, well, I should never be content.'

'Rely on Mavis.' Her eyes began to shine.

'You are possessed of a great and admirable generosity,' he said.

His praise sent a pulse of well-being through her whole body.

15. In Which Mavis Sets Off in Search of the Holy Grail

DOCTOR VOLOSPION HAD MADE NO ALTERATIONS TO HIS force-screen since the Fireclown had passed beyond it. Mavis Ming moved through the eternal twilight of the castle's grounds, towards the dark and ragged hole in the wall of ice. On the other side of the hole she could see the brilliant scarlet of Emmanuel Bloom's ship.

Gingerly, she stepped through the gap, sensitive to the stillness and silence of her surroundings. She wished that Doctor Volospion had been able to accompany her, at least this far, but he was wary, he had told her, of the Fireclown suspecting treachery. If Bloom detected another presence, it was likely that he would immediately restore his ship's defences.

The teardrop-shaped ship was a red silhouette against a background of dark trees. Its airlock remained open, its ramp was down. She paused as she looked up at it.

It was impossible from where she stood to see anything of the ship's interior, but she could smell a warm mustiness coming from the entrance, together with a suggestion of pale smoke. If she had not known otherwise, she might have suspected the Fireclown to be still inside. The ship was redolent of his presence.

She spoke aloud, to dispel the silence. 'Here goes, Mavis.'

She was wearing her blue and orange kimono over her bikini, for Doctor Volospion had warned her that it might be uncomfortably warm within the Fireclown's ship. She struggled up the pebbled surface of the ramp and hesitated again outside the entrance, peering in. It seemed to her that points of fire still flickered on the other side of the airlock's open door.

'Coo-ee!' she said.

She wet her lips. 'What manner of creature is lord of this fair castle?' She reassured herself with the language of her favourite books. 'Shall I find my handsome prince within? Or an ugly ogre . . . ?' She shuddered. She looked back at the battlements and towers of gloomy Castle Volospion, hoping perhaps to see her protector, but the castle seemed entirely deserted. She drew a breath and entered the airlock. It was not quite as warm as she had been led to believe.

She moved from the airlock into the true interior of the ship. She found herself pleasantly surprised by its ordinariness. It was as if firelight illuminated the large chamber, although the source of that light was mysterious.

The rosy, flickering light cast her shadow, enlarged and distorted, upon the far wall. The chamber was in disorder, as if the shock of landing had dislodged everything from its place. Boxes, parchments, books and pictures were scattered everywhere; figurines lay dented or broken upon the carpeted floor; drapes, once used to cover portholes, hung lopsidedly upon the walls, which curved inwards.

'What a lot of junk!' Her voice held more confidence. Apparently, the place had been Mr Bloom's store-room, for there was no sign of furniture.

She stumbled over crates and bales of cloth until she reached a companionway leading up to the next chamber. Doctor Volospion had told her that she would probably find the cup in the control room, which must be above. She climbed, pushed open a hatch, and found herself in a circular room which was lit very similarly to the storage chamber, but so realistically that she found herself searching for the open fireplace which seemed to be the source of the light.

Save for a faint smell of burning timber, there was no sign of a fire.

'Mavis,' she said determinedly, 'keep that imagination of yours well under control!'

This room, as she had suspected, was the Fireclown's living quarters. It contained a good-sized bed, shelves, storage lockers, a desk, a chair and a screen whereby the occupant could check the ship's functions.

She wiped sweat from her forehead, glancing around her.

Against one wall, at the end of the bed, was a large metal ziggurat which looked as if it had once been the base for something else. Would this be where the cup was normally kept? If so, Emmanuel Bloom had hidden it and her job was going to be harder. On the wall were various pictures: some were paintings, others photographs and holographs, primarily of men in the costumes of many periods. On the wall, too, was a narrow shelf, about two feet long, apparently empty. She reached to touch it and felt something there. It was thin, like a long pencil. Curiously, she rolled the object towards her until it fell into her hand. She was surprised.

It was an old-fashioned riding crop, its tip frayed and dividing at one end; a silver head at the other. The head was beautifully made –

a woman's face in what the Italians called the 'stile Liberty'. Mavis was impressed most by the look of ineffable tranquillity upon the features. The contrast between the woman's expression and the function of the whip itself disturbed Mavis so much that she replaced it hastily.

Wishing that the light were stronger, she began to search for the cup or goblet (Doctor Volospion's description had been vague). First, she looked under the bed, finding only a collection of books and manuscripts, many of them dusty.

'This whole ship could do with a good spring-clean!' She searched through the wardrobe and drawers, finding a collection of clothes to match those worn by the men whose pictures decorated the wall. This sudden intimacy with Mr Bloom's personal possessions had not only whetted her curiosity about him – his clothes, to her, were much more interesting than anything he had said – but had somehow given her a greater sympathy for him.

She began to feel unhappy about rummaging through his things; her search for the goblet became increasingly to seem like simple thievery.

Her search became more rapid as she sought to find the Grail and leave as soon as she could. If she had not made a promise to Doctor Volospion, she would have left the ship there and then.

'You're a fool, Mavis. Everyone's told you. And do you ever listen?'

As she opened a mahogany trunk, inlaid with silver and mother-of-pearl, the lid squeaked and, at the same time, she thought she heard a faint noise from below. She paused and listened, but there was no further sound. She saw at once that the trunk contained only faded manuscripts.

Miss Ming decided to return to the store-room. The curiosity which had at first directed her energy was now disssipating, to be replaced by a familiar sense of panic.

She felt her heart-rate increase and the ship seemed to give a series of little tremors, in sympathy. She returned to the companionway and lifted the hatch. She was half-way down when the whole ship shook itself like an animal, roared, as if sentient, and she was pressed back against the steps, clinging to the rail as, swaying from side to side, the ship took off.

Sweating, Miss Ming turned herself round with difficulty and began to climb back towards the living quarters where she felt she would be safer. If her throat had been less constricted, she would have screamed. The ship, she knew, was taking off under its own power. It was quite possible that she had activated it herself. Unless she could work out how to control it she would soon be adrift in the cosmos, floating through space until she died.

And she would be all alone.

It was this latter thought which terrified her most. She reached the cabin and crawled across the dusty carpet as the pressure increased, climbing on to the bed in the hope that it would cushion the acceleration effects.

The sensations she was experiencing were not dissimilar to those she had experienced on her trip through time and, as such, did not alarm her. It was the prospect of what would become of her when the ship was beyond Earth's gravity which she could not bear to consider.

It was not, she thought, as if there were many planets left in the Universe. Earth might now be the only one.

The pressure began to lift, but she remained face-down upon the bed ('these sheets could do with a wash', she was thinking) even when it was obvious that the ship was travelling at last through free space.

'Oh, you've let yourself in for it this time, Mavis,' she told herself. 'You've been conned properly, my girl.'

She wondered if, for reasons of his own, Doctor Volospion had deliberately sent her into space. She knew his capacity for revenge. Had that silly tiff meant so much to him? He had beguiled her into suggesting her own trap, her own punishment, just because of a silly scratch on the hand!

'What a bastard! What bastards they all are!' And what an idiot she had made of herself! It taught you never to be sympathetic to a man. They always used it against you. 'That's Mavis all over,' she continued, 'trusting the world. And this is how the world repays you!' But there was little conviction in her tone; her self-pity was half-hearted. Actually, she realized, she was not feeling particularly bad now that there was a genuine threat to her life. All the little anxieties fled away.

Miss Ming began to roll over on the bed. At least the ship itself was comfortable enough.

'It's cosy, really.' She smiled. 'A sort of den. Just like when I was a little girl, with my own little room, and my books and dolls.' She laughed. 'I'm actually safer here than anywhere I've been since I grew up. It shouldn't be difficult to work out a way of getting back to Earth – *if* I want to go back. What's Earth got to offer, anyway, except deceit, hypocrisy and treachery?'

She swung her legs over the edge of the bed. She looked at her new home, all her new toys.

'I think it's really what I've always wanted,' she declared.

'Now you realize that I spoke the truth!' said the triumphant voice of Emmanuel Bloom from the shadows overhead.

'My God!' said Miss Ming as she realized the full extent of Doctor Volospion's deception.

16. In Which Doctor Volospion Receives the Congratulations of His Peers and Celebrates the Acquisition of His New Treasure

MY LADY CHARLOTINA ROSE FROM DOCTOR VOLOSPION'S BED and swiftly demolished her double (Doctor Volospion would only make love to pairs of women) before touching a power ring to adorn herself in white and cerise poppies. In the shadows of the four-poster Doctor Volospion lay relishing his several victories, a beautiful cup held in his hands. He turned the cup round and round, running his fingers over an inscription which he could not read, for it was in ancient English.

'You doubt none of my powers now, I hope, My Lady Charlotina,' he said.

Her smile was slow. She knew he would have her speak of Jagged, perhaps make a comparison, but she did not have it in her to satisfy Volospion's curiosity. Lord Jagged was Lord Jagged, she thought.

'I was privileged,' she said, 'to know your plan from the start and to see it work so smoothly. I am most impressed. First, you incarcerated Miss Ming, then you lured Mr Bloom to your castle, then you pretended that his power was great enough to destroy your force-field, then you captured him, knowing that he would give anything to escape. You originally meant to hold him, of course, as one of your collection, but then you learned of the Grail . . . '

'So I offered Miss Ming in exchange for the Grail. Thus he thought he took her from me without force and that she went willingly to him – for I did not, of course, explain to Mr Bloom that I had deceived Miss Ming.'

'So much deception! It is quite hard for me to follow!' She laughed. 'What a match! The greatest cynic of our world (with the exception of Lord Shark who does not really count) pitted against the greatest idealist in the Universe!'

'And the cynic won,' said Doctor Volospion. 'As they always do.'

'Well, a cynic *would* draw that conclusion,' she pointed out. 'I had a liking for Mr Bloom, though he was a bore.'

'As was Miss Ming.'

'Great bores, both.'

'And by one stroke I rid the world of its two most awful bores,' said Doctor Volospion, in case she had not considered this achievement with the rest.

'Exactly.'

Yawning, My Lady Charlotina drifted towards a dark window. 'You have your cup. He has his queen.'

'Exactly.'

My Lady Charlotina looked up at the featureless heavens. No stars gleamed here. Perhaps they were all extinguished. She sighed.

'My only regret,' said Doctor Volospion as he carefully laid the cup upon his pillow and straightened his body, 'is that I was not able to ask Mr Bloom the meaning of this inscription.'

'Doubtless a warning to the curious,' she said 'or an offer of eternal salvation. You know more about these things, Doctor Volospion.'

A cap appeared on his head. Robes formed. Black velvet and mink. 'Oh, yes, they are always very similar. And often disappointingly ordinary.'

'It does seem a very ordinary cup.'

'The faithful would see that as a sign of its true holiness,' he told her knowledgeably.

From outside they detected a halloo.

'It is Abu Thaleb,' she said in some animation. 'And Argonheart Po and others. Li Pao, I think, is with them. Shall you admit them?'

'Of course. They will want to see my cup.'

My Lady Charlotina and Doctor Volospion left his bedroom and went down to the hall to greet their guests.

Doctor Volospion placed the cup upon the table. The ill-functioning neon played across its bright silver.

'Beautiful!' said Abu Thaleb, without as much enthusiasm as perhaps Doctor Volospion would have wished. The Commissar of Bengal brushed feathers from his eyes. 'A fitting reward for your services to us all, Doctor Volospion.'

Argonheart Po bore a tray in his great hands. He set this, now, beside the cup. 'I am always thorough in my research,' he said, 'and hope you find this small offering appropriate.' He removed the cloth to reveal his savouries. 'That is a pemmican spear. This cross is primarily the flavour of sole *à la créme*. The taste of the wafers and the blood is rather more difficult to describe.'

'What an elegant notion!' Doctor Volospion took one of the

savouries between finger and thumb and nibbled politely.

Li Pao asked: 'May I inspect the cup?'

'Of course.' Doctor Volospion waved a generous hand. 'You do not, by any chance, read, do you, Li Pao? Specifically, Dawn Age English.'

'Once,' said Li Pao. He studied the inscription. He shook his head. 'I am baffled.'

'A great shame.'

'Does it *do* anything,' wondered Sweet Orb Mace, moving from the shadows where he had been studying Doctor Volospion's portrait.

'I think not,' said My Lady Charlotina. 'It has done nothing yet, at any rate.'

Doctor Volospion stared at his cup somewhat wistfully. 'Ah, well,' he said, 'I fear I shall grow tired of it soon enough.'

My Lady Charlotina came to stand beside him. 'Perhaps it will fill the room with light or something,' she said encouragingly.

'We can always hope,' he said.

17. In Which Miss Mavis Ming At Last Attains a State of Grace

EMMANUEL BLOOM SWUNG HIMSELF FROM THE CEILING, an awkward macaw. He no longer wore his paint and motley but was again dressed in his black velvet suit.

Mavis Ming saw that he had entered by means of a hatch. Doubtless, the control cabin of the ship was above.

'My Goddess,' said the Fireclown.

She still sat on the edge of the bed. Her voice was without emotion. 'You traded me for the cup. That's what it was all about. What a fool I am!'

'No, not you. Doctor Volospion proposed the bargain and so enabled me to keep my word to him. He demanded the cup which I kept in my ship. I gave it to him.' He strutted across the cabin and manipulated a dial. Red–gold light began to fill his living quarters. Now everything glowed and each piece of fabric, wood or metal seemed to have a life of its own.

Mavis Ming stood up, and edged away from the bed. She drew her kimono about her, over her pendulous breasts, her fat stomach, her wide thighs.

'Listen,' she began. She was breathing rapidly once more. 'You can't really want me, Mr Bloom. I'm fat old Mavis. I'm ugly. I'm stupid. I'm selfish. I should be left on my own. I'm better off on my own. I know I'm always looking for company, but really it's just because I never realized . . . '

He raised a stiff right arm in a gesture of impatience. 'What has any of that to do with my love for you? What does it matter if foolish Volospion thought he was killing two birds with one stone when he was actually freeing two eagles?'

'Look,' she said, 'if . . . '

'I am the Fireclown! I am Bloom, the Fireclown! I have lived the span of Man's existence. I have made Time and Space my toys. I have juggled with chronons and made the Multiverse laugh. I have mocked Reality and Reality has shrivelled to be re-born. My eyes have stared unblinking into the hearts of stars, and I have stood at the very core of the Sun and feasted on freshly created photons. I am Bloom, Eternally Blooming Bloom. Bloom the Phoenix. Bloom, the Destroyer of Darkness. These eyes, these large bulging eyes of mine, do you think they cannot see into souls as easily as they see into suns? Can they not detect an aura of pain that disguises the true centre of a being as smoke hides fire? That is why I choose to make you wise, to enslave you so that you may know true freedom.'

Miss Ming forced herself to speak. 'This is kidnapping and kidnapping is kidnapping whatever you prefer to call it . . . '

He ignored her.

'Of all the beings on that wasteland planet, you were one of the few who still lived. Oh, you lived as a frightened rodent lives, your spirit perverted, your mind enshelled with cynicism, refusing for a moment to look upon Reality for fear that it would detect you and devour you, like a wakened lion. Yet when Reality occasionally impinged and could not be escaped, how did you respond?'

'Look,' she said, 'you've got no right . . . '

'Right? I have every right! I am Bloom! You are my Bride, my Consort, my Queen, my Goddess. There is no woman deserves the honour more!'

'Oh, Christ!' she said. 'Please let me go. Please, I can't give you anything. I can't understand you. I can't love you.' She began to cry. 'I've never loved anyone! No one but myself.'

His voice was gentle. He took a few jerky steps closer to her. 'You lie, Mavis Ming. You do not love yourself.'

'Donny said I did. They all said I did, sooner or later.'

'If you loved yourself,' he told her, 'you would love me.'

Her voice shook. 'That's good . . . '

To Mavis Ming's own ears her words were without resonance of any kind. The collection of platitudes with which she had always responded to pain; the borrowed ironies, the barren tropes with which, instinctively, she had encumbered herself in order to placate a world she had seen as essentially malevolent, all were at once revealed as the meaningless things they were, with the result that an appalling self-consciousness, worse than anything she had suffered in the past, swept over her and every phrase she had ever uttered seemed to ring in her ears for what it had been: a mew of pain, a whimper of frustration, a cry for attention, a groan of hunger.

'Oh . . . '

She became incapable of speech. She could only stare at him, backing around the wall as he came, half-strutting, half-hopping, towards her, his head on one side, an appalling amusement in his unwinking, protuberant eyes, until her escape was blocked by a heavy wardrobe.

She became incapable of movement. She watched as he reached a twitching hand towards her face; the hand was firm and gentle as it touched her and its warmth made her realize how cold, how clammy, her own skin felt. She was close to collapse, only supported by the wall of the ship.

'The Earth is far behind us now,' he said. 'We shall never return. It does not deserve us.' He pointed to the bed. 'Go there. Remove your clothes.'

She gasped at him, trying to make him understand that she could not walk. She did not care, now, what his intentions were, but she was too exhausted to obey him.

'Tired . . . ' she said at last.

He shook his head. 'No. You shall not escape by that route, madam.' He spoke kindly. 'Come.'

The high-pitched ridiculous voice carried greater authority than any she had heard before. She began to walk towards the bed. She stood looking down at the sheets; the light made these, too, seem vibrant with life of their own. She felt his little claw-like hands pull the kimono from her shoulders, undo the tie, removing the garment entirely.

She felt him break the fastening on her bikini top so that her breasts hung even lower on her body. She felt no revulsion, nothing sexual at all, as his fingers pushed the bikini bottom over her hips and down her legs. And yet she was more aware of her nakedness than she had ever been, seeing the fatness, the pale flesh, without any emotion at all, remarking its poor condition as if it did not belong to her.

'Fat . . . ' she murmured.

His voice was distant. 'It is of no importance, this body. Besides, it shall not be fat for very long.

She began to anticipate his rape of her, wondering if, when he began, she would feel anything. He ordered her to lie face-down upon the bed. She obeyed. She heard him move away, then. Perhaps he was undressing. She turned to look, but he was still in his tattered velvet suit, taking something from a shelf. He poured sweet-smelling liquid into his palms.

She tried to feel afraid, because she knew that she should feel fear, but fear would not come. She continued to look up at him, over her shoulder, as he returned. Still her body made no response. This was quite unlike her sexual fantasies. What happened now neither excited her imagination nor her body. She wished that she could feel something, even terror. Instead she was possessed by a calmness, a sense of inevitability, unlike anything she had known.

'Now,' she heard him say, 'I shall bring your blood into the light. And with it shall come the devils that inhabit it, to be withered as weeds in the sun. And when I have finished you will know Rebirth, Freedom, Dominion over the Multiverse, and more. For I am the Fireclown and my very touch is fire.'

Was it a mark of her own insanity that she could detect no insanity in his words?

His touch fell upon her flesh. He stroked her buttocks and the pain stole her breath. She did not scream, but she gasped.

He stroked again, just below the first place, and she thought his flames lashed her. Her whole body jerked, trying to escape, but a firm hand held her down again, and again he touched her.

She did not scream, but she groaned as she drew in her breath. Next he stroked her thighs; next behind her knees, and his hands were firm now as she struggled. He held her by the back of the neck; he gripped her by the shoulder, by the loose flesh of her waist, and each time he gripped her she knew fresh pain.

Mavis Ming believed at last that it was Emmanuel Bloom's intention to tear every piece of skin from her body. He held her lips, her ears, her breasts, her vagina, the tender parts of her inner thighs, and every touch was fire.

She screamed, she blubbered for him to stop, she could not believe that he, any more than she, was any longer in control of what was happening. And yet he stroked her with a regularity which denied her even this consolation, until, at length, her whole body burned and she lay still, consumed.

Slowly, the fire faded from this peak of intensity and it seemed to her that, again, her body and mind were united; this unity was new.

Emmanuel Bloom said nothing. She heard him cross the chamber to replace the bottle. She began to breathe with deep regularity, as if she slept. Her consciousness of her body produced an indefinable emotion in her. She moved her head to look at him and the movement was painful.

'I feel . . . ' Her voice was soft.

He stood with his arms stiffly at his sides. His head was cocked, his expression was tender and expectant.

She could find no word.

'It is your pride,' he said.

He reached to caress her face.

'I love you,' he said.

'I love you.' She began to weep.

He made her rise and look at her body in the oval mirror he revealed. It seemed that her skin was a lattice of long, red bruises; she could see where he had gripped her shoulders and her breasts. The pain was hard to tolerate without making at least a whisper of sound, but she controlled herself.

'Will you do this again?' she asked.

He shook his little head.

She walked back to the bed. Her back, though lacerated, was straight. She had never walked in that way before, with dignity. She sat down. 'Why did you do it?'

'In this manner? Perhaps because I lack patience. It is one of my characteristics. It was quick.' He laughed. 'Why do it to you, at all? Because I love you. Because I wished to reveal to you the woman that you are, the individual that you are. I had to destroy the shell.'

'It won't fade, this feeling?'

'Only the marks will go. It is within you to retain the rest. Will you be my wife?'

She smiled. 'Yes.'

'Well, then, this has been a satisfactory expedition, after all. Better, really, than I expected. Oh, what leaping delights we shall share, what wonders I can show you! No woman could desire more than to be the consort of Bloom, the Good Soldier, the Champion Eternal, the Master of the Multiverse! As you are my mistress, Mavis Ming.' He fell with a peculiar, spastic jerk, on his knees beside her. 'For Eternity. Will you stay? I can return you within an hour or two.'

'I will stay,' she said. 'Yet you gave up so much for me. That cup. It was your honour?'

He looked shamefaced. 'He asked for the cup I kept in my ship. I could not give him the Holy Grail, for it is not mine to give. I gave him something almost as dear to me, however. If Doctor Volospion ever deciphers the inscription on the cup, he will discover that it was awarded, in 1980, to Leonard Bloom, by the union of Master Bakers, for the best chollah of the Annual Bakery Show, White-chapel, London. He was a very good baker, my father. I loved him. I had kept his cup in all my journeys back and forth through the time-streams and it was the most valuable thing I possessed.'

'So you do not have the Grail.' She smiled. 'It was all part of your plan – pretending to own it, pretending to be powerless – you tricked Doctor Volospion completely.'

'And he tricked me. Both are satisfied, for it is unlikely he shall ever know the extent of my trickery and doubtless considers himself a fine fellow! All are satisfied!'

'And now . . . ?' she began.

'And now,' he said, 'I'll leave you. I must set my controls. You shall see all that is left of this Universe and then, through the centre of the brightest star, into the greater vastness of the Multiverse beyond! There we shall find others to inspire and if we find no life at all, upon our wanderings, it is within our power to create it, for I am the Fireclown. I am the Voice of the Sun! Aha! Look! It has come to you, too. This, my love, is Grace. This is our reward!'

The cabin was filled suddenly by brilliant golden light, apparently having as its source a beam which entered through the very shell of the spaceship, falling directly upon the ziggurat at the end of the bed.

A smell, like sweet spring flowers after the rain, filled the cabin, and then a crystal cup, brimming with scarlet liquid, appeared at the top of the ziggurat.

Scarlet rays spread from a hundred points in the crystal, almost blinding her, and, although Mavis Ming could hear nothing, she received an impression of sonorous, delicate music. She could not help herself as she lifted her aching body from the bed to the floor and knelt, staring into the goblet in awe.

From behind her the Fireclown chuckled and he knelt beside her, taking her hand.

'We are married now,' he said, 'before the Holy Grail. Married individually and together. And this is our Trust which shall be taken from us should we ever commit the sin of accidie. Here is proof of all my claims. Here is Hope. And should we ever cease to forget our purpose, should we ever fall into that sin of inertia, should we lose, for more than a moment, our Faith in our high resolve, the Grail will leave us and shall vanish for ever from the sight of Man, for I am Bloom, the Last Pure Knight, and you are the Pure Lady, chastized and chaste, who shall share these Mysteries with me.'

She began: 'It is too much. I am not capable . . . ' But then she lifted her head and she smiled, staring into the very heart of the goblet. 'Very well.'

'Look,' he said, as the vision began to fade, 'your wounds have vanished.'

Behold the Man
and other stories

Breakfast in the Ruins

For Angus Wilson with great respect

Contents

Contents

Introduction

'Michael Moorcock' died of lung cancer, aged 31, in Birmingham last year. The whereabouts of Karl Glogauer are presently unknown.

James Colvin
Three Chimneys
Raddon, Yorkshire
February 1971

1. In the Roof Garden: 1971: Scarlet Sin

Commonwealth immigrants to Britain were 22 per cent down in April. There were 1,991 compared with 2,560 in April last year.

Guardian, 25 June 1971

When in doubt, Karl Glogauer would always return to Derry and Tom's. He would walk down Kensington Church Street in the summer sunshine, ignoring the boutiques and coffee shops, until he reached the High Street. He would pass the first of the three great department stores which stood side by side, stern and eternal and bountiful, blotting out the sky, and would go through the tall glass doors of the second store, Derry's. The strongest of the citadels.

Weaving his way between the bright counters, piled with hats and silks and paper flowers, he would reach the lifts with their late art-nouveau brasswork and he would take one of them up to the third floor – a little journey through time, for here it was all art deco and Cunard style pastel plastics which he could admire for their own sake as he waited for the special lift which would come and bear him up into the paradise of the roof garden.

The gate would open to reveal something like a small conservatory in which two pleasant middle-aged ladies stood to greet the new arrivals and sell them, if required, tea-towels, postcards and guide books. To one of these ladies Karl would hand his shilling and stroll through into the Spanish Garden where fountains splashed and well tended exotic plants and flowers grew. Karl had a bench near the central fountain. If it was occupied when he arrived, he would stroll around for a while until it was free, then he would sit down, open his book and pretend to read. The wall behind him was lined with deep, airy cages. Sometimes these cages were completely deserted but at other times they would contain a few parrots, parakeets, canaries, cockatoos, or a mynah bird. Occasionally pink flamingoes were present, parading awkwardly about the garden, wading through the tiny artificial streams. All these birds were, on the whole, decently silent, almost gloomy, offering hardly any reaction to the middle-aged ladies who liked to approach them and coo at them in pathetic, sometimes desperate, tones.

If the sunshine were warm and the number of visitors small Karl would sit in his seat for the best part of a morning or an afternoon before taking his lunch or tea in the roof-garden restaurant. All the waitresses knew him well enough to offer a tight smile of recognition while continuing to wonder what a slightly seedy-looking young man in an old tweed jacket and rumpled flannels found to attract him in the roof garden. Karl recognized their puzzlement and took pleasure in it.

Karl knew why he liked to come here. In the whole of London this was the only place where he could find the peace he identified with the peace of his early childhood, the peace of ignorance (or 'innocence' as he preferred to call it). He had been born at the outbreak of the war, but he thought of his childhood as having existed a few years earlier, in the mid-thirties. Only lately had he come to understand that this peace was not really peace, but rather a sense of cosiness, the unique creation of a dying middle class. Vulgarity given a gloss of 'good taste'. Outside London there were a few other spots like it. He had found the right atmosphere in the tea-gardens of Surrey and Sussex, the parks in the richer suburbs of Dorking, Hove and Haywards Heath, all created during the twenties and thirties when, to that same middle class, comfiness had been a synonym for beauty. For all he knew too well that the urge which took him so frequently to the roof garden was both infantile and escapist, he tolerated it in himself. He would console himself sardonically that, of all his other infantile and escapist pursuits – his collection of children's books, his model soldiers – this was the cheapest. He no longer made any serious attempts to rid himself of these unmanly habits. He was their slave, just as much as he was the slave of his mother's childhood terrors; of the rich variety of horrors she had managed to introduce into his own childhood.

Thinking about his childhood as he sat in his usual place on a soft summer's day in June 1971, Karl wondered if his somewhat small creative gift was not, as most people would nowadays think, the result of his unstable upbringing at all. Perhaps, by virtue of his sensitivity, he had been unduly prone to his mother's influence. Such an influence could actually stunt talent, maybe. He did not like the drift of his thoughts. To follow their implications would be to offset the effects of the garden. He smiled to himself and leaned back, breathing in the heavy scent of snapdragons and tulips, believing, as he always did, that it was enough to admit a self-deception. It was what he called self-knowledge. He peered up at the blue uncluttered afternoon sky. The hum of the traffic in the street far below could almost be the sound of summer insects in a country garden. A country garden, long ago . . .

He leaned back on the bench a fraction more. He did not want to think about his mother, his childhood as it actually was, the failure of his ambitions. He became a handsome young aristocrat. He was a Regency buck relaxing from the wild London round of politics, gambling, duelling and women. He had just come down to his Somerset estate and had been greeted by his delightful young wife. He had married a sweet girl from these parts, the daughter of an old-fashioned squire, and she was ecstatic that he had returned home, for she doted on him. It did not occur to her to criticize the way he chose to live. As far as she was concerned, she existed entirely for his pleasure. What was her name? Emma? Sophy? Or something a little more Greek, perhaps?

The reverie was just beginning to develop into a full-scale fantasy when it was interrupted.

'Good afternoon.' The voice was deep, slightly hesitant, husky. It shocked him and he opened his eyes.

The face was quite close to his. Its owner was leaning down and its expression was amused. The face was as dark and shining as ancient mahogany; almost black.

'Do you mind if I join you on this bench?' The tall black man sat down firmly.

Frustrated by the interruption Karl pretended an interest in a paving stone at his feet. He hated people who tried to talk to him here, particularly when they broke into his daydreams.

'Not at all,' he said, 'I was just leaving.' It was his usual reply. He adjusted the frayed cuff of his jacket.

'I'm visiting London,' said the black man. His own light suit was elegantly cut, a subtle silvery grey. Silk, Karl supposed. All the man's clothes and jewellery were evidently expensive. A rich American tourist, thought Karl (who had no ear for accents). 'I hadn't expected to find a place like this in the middle of your city,' the man continued. 'I saw a sign and followed it. Do you like it here?'

Karl shrugged.

The man laughed, removing the cover from his Rolleiflex. 'Can I take a picture of you here?'

And now Karl was flattered. Nobody had ever volunteered to take his picture before. His anger began to dissipate.

'It gives life to a photograph. It shows that I took it myself.

Otherwise I might just as well buy the postcards, eh?'

Karl rose to go. But it seemed that the black man had misinterpreted the movement. 'You are a Londoner, aren't you?' He smiled,
his deep-set eyes looking searchingly into Karl's face, Karl wondered for a moment if the question had some additional meaning he
hadn't divined.

'Yes, I am.' He frowned.

Only now did the elegant negro seem to realize Karl's displeasure.
'I'm sorry if I'm imposing . . .' he said.

Again, Karl shrugged.

'It would not take a moment. I only asked if you were a
Londoner because I don't wish to make the mistake of taking a
picture of a typical Englishman and then you tell me you are French
or something!' He laughed heartily. 'You see?'

Karl didn't much care for the 'typical', but he was disarmed by
the man's charm. He smiled. The black man got up, put a hand on
Karl's shoulder and guided him gently to the fountain. 'If you could
sit on the rim for a moment . . .' He backed away and peered into
his viewfinder, standing with his legs spread wide and his heels on
the very edge of the flower bed, taking, from slightly different
angles, a whole series of photographs. Karl was embarrassed. He
felt that the situation was odd, but he could not define why it
should seem so. It was as if the ritual of photography was a hint at a
much more profound ritual going on at the same time. He must
leave. Even the click and the whirr of the camera seemed to have a
significant meaning.

'That's fine.' The photographer looked up. He narrowed his eyes
against the sunlight. 'Just one more. I'm over here from Nigeria for
a few days. Unfortunately it's more of a business visit than a
pleasure trip: trying to get your government to pay a better price for
our copper. What do you do?'

Karl waved a hand. 'Oh, nothing much. Look here, I must . . .'

'Come now! With a face as interesting as yours, you must do
something equally interesting!'

'I'm a painter. An illustrator, really.' Again Karl was flattered by
the attention. He had an impulse to tell the man anything he wanted
to know – to tell him far more, probably, than he was prepared to
listen to. Karl felt he was making a fool of himself.

'An artist! Very good. What sort of things do you paint?'

'I make my living doing military uniforms, mainly. People collect
that sort of thing. It's a specialized craft. Sometimes I do work for

the odd regiment which wants a picture to hang in the mess. Famous battles and stuff. You know . . .'

'So you're not a disciple of the avant-garde. I might have guessed. Your hair's too short! Ha ha! No cubism or action painting, eh?' The Nigerian snapped the case back on his camera. 'None of your "Which way up should I stand to look at it?"'

Karl laughed outright for the first time in ages. He was amused partly by the man's somewhat old-fashioned idea of the avant-garde, partly because he actually did paint stuff in his spare time which would fit the Nigerian's general description. All the same, he was pleased to have won the black man's approval.

'Not a revolutionary,' said the man, stepping closer. 'You're conventional, are you, in every respect?'

'Oh, hardly! Who is?'

'Who indeed? Have you had tea?' The black man took his arm, looking around him vaguely. 'I understand there's a café here.'

'A restaurant. On the other side.'

'Shall we cross?'

'I don't know . . .' Karl shivered. He didn't much care for people holding him like that, particularly when they were strangers, but a touch shouldn't make him shiver. 'I'm not sure . . .' Normally he could have walked away easily. Why should he mind being rude to a man who had so forcefully intruded on his privacy?

'You must have tea with me.' The grip tightened just a little. 'You have a bit of time to spare, surely? I rarely get the chance to make friends in London.'

Now Karl felt guilty. He remembered his mother's advice. Good advice, for a change. 'Never have anything to do with people who make you feel guilty.' She should have known! But it was no good. He did not want to disappoint the Nigerian. He felt rather faint suddenly. There was a sensation in the pit of his stomach which was not entirely unpleasurable.

They walked together through part of the Tudor Garden and through an archway which led into the Woodland Garden and there was the restaurant with its white wrought-iron tables and chairs on the veranda, its curve of glass through which the interior could be seen. The restaurant was quite busy today and was serving cucumber sandwiches and Danish pastries to little parties of women in jersey suits and silk frocks who were relaxing after their shopping. The only men present were one or two elderly husbands or fathers: tolerated because of their cheque-books. Karl and his new friend entered the restaurant and walked to the far end to a table by the window which looked out on to the lawns and willow trees skirting the miniature stream and its miniature wooden bridge. 'You had better order, I think,' said the Nigerian. 'I'm not much used to this sort of thing.' Again he smiled warmly. Karl picked up the menu.

'We might as well stick to the set tea,' said Karl. 'Sandwiches and cakes.'

'Very well.' The man's reply was vague, insouciant. He gave Karl the impression that, for all his politeness, he had weightier matters on his mind than the choice of food.

For a few moments Karl tried to signal a waitress. He felt embarrassed and avoided looking at his companion. He glanced about the crowded restaurant, at the pastel mauves and pinks and blues of the ladies' suits, the fluffy hats built up layer on layer of artificial petals, the Jaeger scarves. At last the waitress arrived. He didn't know her. She was new. But she looked like the rest. A tired woman of about thirty-five. Her thin face was yellow beneath the powder, the rouge and the lipstick. She had bags under her eyes and the deep crow's feet emphasized the bleakness of her expression. The skin on the bridge of her nose was peeling. She had the hands of a hag twice her age. One of them plucked the order pad from where it hung by a string against her dowdy black skirt and she settled her pencil heavily against the paper. It seemed that she lacked even the strength to hold the stub with only one hand.

'Two set teas, please,' said Karl. He tried to sound pleasant and sympathetic. But she paid attention neither to his face nor his tone.

'Thank you, sir.' She let the pad fall back without using it. She began to trudge towards the kitchen, pushing open the door as if gratefully entering the gates of hell.

Karl felt the pressure of his companion's long legs against his own. He tried, politely, to move, but could not; not without a violent tug. The black man seemed unaware of Karl's discomfort and leaned forward over the little table, putting his two elbows on the dainty white cloth and looking directly into Karl's eyes. 'I hope you don't think I've been rude, old chap,' he said.

'Rude?' Karl was trapped by the eyes.

'It occurred to me you might have better things to do than keep a bored tourist entertained.'

'Of course not,' Karl heard himself say. 'I'm afraid I don't know much about Nigeria. I'd like to know more. Of course, I followed the Biafran thing in the papers.' Had that been the wrong remark?

'Your Alfred had similar trouble with his "break-away" states, you know.'

'I suppose he did.' Karl wasn't sure who Alfred had been or what he had done.

The waitress came back with a mock-silver tray on which stood a teapot, a milk jug and a hot-water jug, also of mock silver, together with cups and saucers and plates. She began to set her load down between the two men. The Nigerian leaned back but continued to smile into Karl's eyes while Karl murmured 'Thank you' every time the waitress placed something in front of him. These ingratiating noises were his usual response to most minor forms of human misery, as they had been to his mother when she had made it evident what it had cost her to prepare a meal for him.

'Shall I be mother?' said Karl and again the not unpleasant sensation of weakness swept through him. The Nigerian was looking away, vague once again, his handsome profile in silhouette as he took an interest in the garden. Karl repeated eagerly: 'Shall I –?' The Nigerian said: 'Fine.' And Karl realized that he was now desperate to please his companion, that he needed the man's whole attention, that he would do anything to ensure that he got it. He poured the tea. He handed a cup to his friend, who accepted it absently.

'We haven't introduced ourselves,' Karl said. He cleared his throat. 'I'm Karl Glogauer.'

The attention was regained. The eyes looked directly into Karl's, the pressure of the leg was deliberate. The Nigerian picked up the bowl nearest him and offered it to Karl.

'Sugar?'

'Thanks.' Karl took the bowl.

'You've got nice hands,' said the Nigerian. 'An artist's hands, of course.' Briefly, he touched Karl's fingers.

Karl giggled. 'Do you think so?' The sensation came again, but this time it was a wave and there was no doubt about its origin. 'Thank you.' He smiled suddenly because to remark on their hands and to pretend to read their palms was one of his standard ways of trying to pick up girls. 'Are you going to read my palm?'

The Nigerian's brows came together in a deep frown. 'Why should I?'

Karl's breathing was heavier. At last he understood the nature of the trap. And there was nothing he wished to do about it.

In silence, they ate their sandwiches. Karl was no longer irritated by the pressure of the man's leg on his.

A little later the Nigerian said: 'Will you come back with me?'

'Yes,' whispered Karl.

He began to shake.

What would you do? (1)

You are a passenger on a plane which is about to crash. The plane is not a jet and so you have a chance to parachute to safety. With the other passengers, you stand in line and take one of the parachutes which the crew hands out to you. There is one problem. The people ahead of you on the line are already jumping out. But you have a four-month-old baby with you and it is too large to button into your clothing. Yet you must have both hands free in order to (a) pull the emergency ripcord in the event of the parachute failing to open, (b) guide the chute to safety if you see danger below. The baby is crying. The people behind you are pressing forward. Someone helps you struggle into the harness and hands you back your baby. Even if you did hold the baby in both hands and pray that you had an easy descent, there is every possibility he could be yanked from your grip as you jumped.

There are a few more seconds to go before you miss your chance to get out of the plane.

2. In the Commune: 1871: A Smile

Not only France, but the whole civilised world, was startled and dismayed by the sudden success of the Red Republicans of Paris. The most extraordinary, and perhaps
the most alarming, feature of the movement, was the fact
that it had been brought about by men nearly all of whom
were totally unknown to society at large. It was not, therefore, the influence, whether for good or evil, of a few great
names which might be supposed to exercise a species of
enchantment on the uneducated classes, and to be capable
of moving them, almost without thought, towards the
execution of any design which the master-minds might
have determined on – it was not this which had caused the
convulsion. The outbreak was clearly due less to individual
persuasion, which in the nature of things is evanescent,
than to the operation of deep-rooted principles such as
survive when men depart. The ideas which gave rise to the
Commune were within the cognisance of the middle and
upper classes of society; but it was not supposed that they
had attained such power, or were capable of such organ-
ised action. A frightful apparition of the Red Republic had
been momentarily visible in June, 1848; but it was at once
exorcized by the cannon and bayonets of Cavaignac. It was
again apprehended towards the close of 1851, and would
probably have made itself once more manifest, had not the
coup d'etat of Louis Napoleon prevented any such movement, not only at that time, but for several years to come.
Every now and then during the period of the Second
Empire, threatenings of this vague yet appalling danger
came and went, but the admirable organisation of the Imperial Government kept the enemies of social order in sub-
jection, though only by a resort to means regrettable in
themselves, against which the Moderate Republicans were
perpetually directing their most bitter attacks, little thinking that they would soon be obliged to use the same
weapons with still greater severity. Nevertheless, although
the Emperor Napoleon held the Red Republic firmly down
throughout his term of power, the principles of the
extreme faction were working beneath the surface; and
they only awaited the advent of a weaker Government,

and of a period of social disruption, to glare upon the world with stormy menace.

Anonymous, *History of the War between France and Germany*, Cassell, Petter & Galpin, 1872

– There you are, Karl.

The black man strokes his head.

Karl has removed his clothes and lies naked on the double bed in the hotel suite. The silk counterpane is cool.

– Do you feel any better now?

– I'm not sure.

Karl's mouth is dry. The man's hands move down from his head to touch his shoulders. Karl gasps. He shuts his eyes.

Karl is seven years old. He and his mother have fled from their house as the Versailles troops storm Paris in their successful effort to destroy the Commune established a few months earlier. It is civil war and it is savage. The more so, perhaps, because the French have received such an ignominious defeat at the hands of Bismarck's Prussians.

He is seven years old. It is the spring of 1871. He is on the move.

– Do you like this? asks the black man.

Karl was seven. His mother was twenty-five. His father was thirty-one, but had probably been killed fighting the Prussians at St Quentin. Karl's father had been so eager to join the National Guard and prove that he was a true Frenchman.

'Now, Karl.' His mother put him down and he felt the hard cobble of the street beneath his thin shoes. 'You must walk a little. Mother is tired, too.'

It was true. When she was tired, her Alsatian accent always became thicker and now it was very thick. Karl felt ashamed for her.

He was not sure what was happening. The previous night he had heard loud noises and the sounds of running feet. There had been shots and explosions, but such things were familiar enough since the siege of Paris. Then his mother had appeared in her street clothes and made him put on his coat and shoes, hurrying him from the room and down the stairs and into the street. He wondered what had happened to their maid. When they got into the street he saw that a fire had broken out some distance away and that there were many National Guardsmen about. Some of them were running towards the fires and others, who were wounded, were staggering in the other direction. Some bad soldiers were attacking them, he gathered, and his mother was afraid that the house would be burned down. 'Starvation – bombardment – and now fire,' she had muttered bitterly. 'I hope all the wretched Communards are shot!' Her heavy black skirts hissed as she led him through the night, away from the fighting.

By dawn, more of the city was burning and all was confusion. Ragged members of the National Guard in their stained uniforms rallied the citizens to pile furniture and bedding on to the carts which had been overturned to block the streets. Sometimes Karl and his mother were stopped and told to help the other women and children, but she gave excuses and hurried on. Karl was dazed. He had no idea where they were going. He was vaguely aware that his mother knew no better than he. When he gasped that he could walk no further, she picked him up and continued her flight, her sharp face expressing her disapproval at his weakness. She was a small, wiry woman who would have been reasonably pretty had her features not been set so solidly in a mask of tension and anxiety. Karl had never known her face to soften, either to him or to his father. Her eyes had always seemed fixed on some distant objective which, secretly and grimly, she had determined to reach. That same look was in her eyes now, though much more emphatic, and the little boy had the impression that his mother's flight through the city was the natural climax to her life.

Karl tried not to cry out as he trotted behind his mother's dusty black skirts. His whole body was aching and his feet were blistered and once he fell on the cobbles and had to scramble up swiftly in order to catch her as she turned a corner.

They were now in a narrow sidestreet not far from the rue du Bac on the Left Bank. Twice Karl had caught a glimpse of the nearby Seine. It was a beautiful spring morning, but the sky was slowly being obscured by thick smoke from the many burning buildings on both sides of the river. Noticing this, his mother hesitated.

'Oh, the animals!' Her tone was a mixture of disgust and despair. 'They are setting fire to their own city!'

'May we rest now, Mother?' asked Karl.

'Rest?' She laughed bitterly. But she made no effort to continue on her way, though she cast about her in every direction, trying to decide where she could best expect to find safety.

Suddenly, from a couple of streets away, there came a series of explosions which shook the houses. There were shots and then a great angry cry, followed by individual screams and shouts. In the guise of addressing her son, she muttered to herself.

'The streets are not safe. The dogs are everywhere. We must try to find some government soldiers and ask their protection.'

'Are those the bad soldiers, Mother?'

'No, Karl, they are the good soldiers. They are freeing Paris of those who have brought the city to ruin.'

'The Prussians?'

'The Communists. We all knew it would come to this. What a fool your father was.'

Karl was surprised to hear the contempt in her voice. She had previously always told him to look up to his father. He began to cry. For the first time since leaving the house, he felt deeply miserable, rather than merely uncomfortable.

'Oh, my God!' His mother reached out and shook him. 'We don't need your weeping on top of everything else. Be quiet, Karl.'

He bit his lip, but he was still shaken by sobs.

She stroked his head. 'Your mother is tired,' she said. 'She has always done her duty.' A sigh. 'But what's the point?' Karl realized that she was not trying to comfort him at all, but herself. Even the automatic stroking of his hair was done in an effort to calm herself. There was no real sympathy in the gesture. For some reason this knowledge made him feel deep sympathy for her. It had not been easy, even when his father was alive, with no one coming to buy clothes in the shop just because they had a German-sounding name. And she had protected him from the worst of the insults and beaten the boys who threw stones at him.

He hugged her waist. 'Have courage, Mother,' he whispered awkwardly.

She looked at him in astonishment. 'Courage? What does it gain us?' She took his hand. 'Come. We'll find the soldiers.'

Trotting beside her, Karl felt closer to her than he had ever felt, not because she had shown affection for him but because he had been able to show affection for her. Of late, he had begun to feel guilty, believing he might not love his mother as much as a good son should.

The two of them entered the somewhat broader street that was the rue du Bac and here was the source of the sounds they had heard. The Communards were being beaten back by the well-trained Versailles troops. The Versaillese, having been so roundly defeated

Michael Moorcock

by the Prussians, were avenging themselves on their recalcitrant countrymen. Most of the Communards were armed with rifles on which were fixed bayonets. They had run out of ammunition and were using the rifles as spears. Most of them were dressed in ordinary clothes, but there was a handful of National Guardsmen among them, in soiled pale blue uniforms. Karl saw a torn red flag still flying somewhere. Many women were taking part in the fighting. Karl saw one woman bayonet a wounded Versaillese who lay on the ground. His mother pulled him away. She was trembling now. As they rounded a bend in the rue du Bac, they saw another barricade. Then there was an eruption and a roar and the barricades flew apart. Through the dust and debris Karl saw bodies flung in every direction. Some of the dead were children of his own age. A terrifying wailing filled the street, a wailing which turned into a growl of anger. The remaining Communards began to fire at the unseen enemy. Another eruption and another roar and the remains of the barricade went down. For a second there was silence. Then a woman rushed from a nearby house and screamed something, hurling a burning bottle through an open window in her own cellar. Karl saw that a house on the opposite side of the street was beginning to burn. Why were the people setting fire to their own houses?

Now through the smoke and the ruins came the Versaillese in their smart dark blue and red uniforms. Their eyes were red and glaring, reflecting the flames. They frightened Karl far more than the National Guardsmen. Behind them galloped an officer on a black horse. He was screaming in the same high-pitched tone as the woman. He was waving a sabre. Karl's mother took a step towards the troops and then hesitated. She turned and began to run in the other direction, Karl running with her.

There were several shots and Karl noticed that bullets were striking the walls of the houses. He knew at once that he and his mother were being fired at. He grinned with excitement.

They dashed down the next sidestreet and had to wade through piles of garbage to enter a ruined building, an earlier victim of the first Siege. His mother hid behind a quaking wall as the soldiers ran past. When they had gone she sat down on a slab of broken stone and began to cry. Karl stroked her hair, wishing that he could share her grief.

'Your father should not have deserted us,' she said.

'He had to fight, Mother,' said Karl. It was what she had said to him when his father joined the guard. 'For France.'

'For the Reds. For the fools who brought all this upon us!'

Karl did not understand.

Soon his mother was sleeping in the ruins. He curled up beside her and slept, too.

When they awakened that afternoon there was much more smoke. It drifted everywhere. On all sides buildings burned. Karl's mother staggered up. Without looking at him or speaking to him, she seized his hand in a grip which made him wince. Her boots slipping on the stones, her skirts all filthy and ragged at the hem, she dragged him with her to the street. A young girl stood there, her face grave. 'Good-day,' she said.

'Are they still fighting?'

The girl could hardly understand his mother's accent, it had become so thick. The girl frowned.

'Are they still fighting?' his mother asked again, speaking in a peculiar, slow voice.

'Yes.' The girl shrugged. 'They are killing everyone. Anyone.'

'That way?' Karl's mother pointed towards the Seine. 'That way?'

'Yes. Everywhere. But more that way.' She pointed in the general direction of the boulevard du Montparnasse. 'Are you a petrol-woman?'

'Certainly not!' Madame Glogauer glared at the girl. 'Are you?'

'I wasn't allowed,' said the girl regretfully. 'There isn't much petrol left.'

Karl's mother took him back the way they had come. The fires which had been started earlier were now out. It appeared that they had done little damage. Not enough petrol, thought Karl.

With her sleeves over her mouth, his mother picked her way through the corpses and crossed the ruins of the barricade. The other men and women who were searching for dead friends or relatives ignored them as they went by.

Karl thought there were more dead people than living people in the world now.

They reached the boulevard St-Germaine, hurrying towards the quai d'Orsay. On the far side of the river monstrous sheets of flame sprang from a dozen buildings and smoke boiled into the clear May sky.

'I am so thirsty, Mother,' murmured Karl. The smoke and the dust filled his mouth. She ignored him.

Here again the barricades were deserted, save for the dead, the victors and the sightseers. Groups of Versaillese stood about, leaning on their rifles smoking and watching the fires, or chatting to the innocent citizens who were so anxious to establish their hatred of the Communards. Karl saw a group of prisoners, their hands bound with rope, sitting miserably in the road, guarded by the regular soldiers. Whenever a Communard moved, he would receive a harsh blow from a rifle butt or would be threatened by the bayonet. The red flag flew nowhere. In the distance came the sound of cannon fire and rifle fire.

'At last!' Madame Glogauer began to move towards the troops. 'We shall go home soon, Karl. If they have not burned our house down.'

Karl saw an empty wine bottle in the gutter. Perhaps they could fill it with water from the river. He picked it up even as his mother dragged him forward.

'Mother – we could . . .'

She stopped. 'What have you got there? Put the filthy thing down!'

'We could fill it with water.'

'We'll drink soon enough. And eat.'

She grabbed the bottle from his hand. 'If we are to remain respectable, Karl . . .'

She turned her head at a shout. A group of citizens were pointing at her. Soldiers began to run towards them. Karl heard the word 'pétroleuse' repeated several times. Madam Glogauer shook her head and threw the bottle down. 'It is empty,' she said quietly. They could not hear her. The soldiers stopped and raised their rifles. She stretched her hands towards them. 'It was an empty bottle!' she cried.

Karl tugged at her. 'Mother!' He tried to take her hand, but it was still stretched towards the soldiers. 'They cannot understand you, Mother.'

She began to back away and then she ran. He tried to follow, but fell down. She disappeared into a little alley. The soldiers ran past Karl and followed her into the alley. The citizens ran after the soldiers. They were shrieking with hysteria and bloodlust. Karl got up and ran behind them. There were some shots and some screams. By the time Karl had entered the little street the soldiers were coming back again, the citizens still standing looking at something on the ground. Karl pushed his way through them. They cuffed him and snarled at him and then they, too, turned away.

'The pigs use women and children to fight their battles,' said one man. He glared at Karl. 'The sooner Paris is cleansed of such scum the better.'

His mother lay sprawled on her face in the filth of the street. There was a dark, wet patch on her back. Karl went up to her and, as he had suspected, found that the patch was blood. She was still bleeding. He had never seen his mother's blood before. He tried hard to turn her over, but he was too weak. 'Mother?' Suddenly her whole body heaved and she drew in a great dry breath. Then she moaned.

The smoke drifted across the sky and evening came and the city burned. Red flames stained the night on every side. Shots boomed. But there were no more voices. Even the people who passed and whom Karl begged to help his wounded mother did not speak. One or two laughed harshly. With his help, his mother managed to turn herself over and sat with her back propped against the wall. She breathed with great difficulty and did not seem to know him, staring as fixedly and as determinedly into the middle distance as she had always done. Her hair was loose and it clung to her tight, anxious face. Karl wanted to find her some water, but he did not want to leave her.

At last he got up and blocked the path of a man who came walking towards the boulevard St-Germaine. 'Please help my mother, sir,' he said.

'Help her? Yes, of course. Then they will shoot me, too. That will be good, eh?' The man threw back his head and laughed heartily as he continued on his way.

'She did nothing wrong!' Karl shouted.

The man stopped just before he turned the corner. 'It depends how you look at it, doesn't it, young man?' He gestured into the boulevard. 'Here's what you need! Hey, there! Stop! I've got another passenger for you.' Karl heard the sound of something squeaking. The squeaking stopped and the man exchanged a few words with someone else. Then he disappeared. Instinctively Karl backed away with some idea of defending his mother. A filthy old man appeared next. 'I've just about got room,' he explained. He brushed Karl aside, heaved Madame Glogauer on to his shoulder and turned, staggering back down the street. Karl followed. Was the man going to help his mother? Take her to the hospital?

A cart stood in the street. There were no cart-horses, for they had all been eaten during the Siege as Karl knew. Instead, between the shafts stood several ragged men and women. They began to move

forward when they saw the old man appear again, dragging the
squeaking cart behind them. Karl saw that there were people of all
ages and sexes lying on top of one another in the cart. Most of them
were dead, many with gaping wounds and parts of their faces or
bodies missing. 'Give us a hand here,' said the old man and one of
the younger men left his place at the front and helped heave
Madame Glogauger on to the top of the pile. She groaned.

'Where are you taking her?' asked Karl.

They continued to ignore him. The cart squeaked on through the
night. Karl followed it. From time to time he heard his mother
moan.

He became very tired and could hardly see, for his eyes kept
closing, but he followed the cart by its sound, hearing the sharp
clack of clogs and the slap of bare feet on the road, the squeal of the
wheels, the occasional cries and moans of the living passengers. By
midnight they had reached one of the outlying districts of the city
and entered a square. There were Versaillese soldiers here, standing
about on the remains of a green. In the middle of the green was a
dark area. The old man said something to the soldiers and then he
and his companions began unloading the cart. Karl tried to see
which one of the people was his mother. The ragged men and
women carried their burdens to the dark area and dropped them
into it. Karl could now see that it was a freshly dug pit. He peered
in, certain that he had heard his mother's voice among the moans of
the wounded as, indiscriminately, they were buried with the dead.
All around the square shutters were closing and lights were being
extinguished. A soldier came up and dragged Karl away from the
graveside. 'Get back,' he said, 'or you'll go in with them.'

Soon the cart went away. The soldiers sat down by the graveside
and lit their pipes, complaining about the smell, which had become
almost overpowering, and passing a bottle of wine back and forth.
'I'll be glad when this is over,' said one.

Karl squatted against the wall of the house, trying to distinguish
his mother's voice amongst those which groaned or cried out from
the pit. He was sure he could hear her pleading to be let out.

By dawn, her voice had stopped and the cart came back with a
fresh load. These were dumped into the pit and the soldiers got up
reluctantly at the command of their officer, putting down their rifles
and picking up shovels. They began to throw earth on to the
bodies.

When the grave was covered, Karl got up and began to walk

away.

The guards put down their shovels. They seemed more cheerful now and they opened another bottle of wine. One of them saw Karl. 'Hello, young man. You're up early.' He ruffled the boy's hair. 'Hoping for some more excitement, eh?' He took a pull on the bottle and then offered it to Karl. 'Like a drink?' He laughed.

Karl smiled at him.

Karl gasps and he writhes on the bed.
  – What are you doing? he says.
  – Don't you like it? You don't have to like it. Not everyone does.
  – Oh, God, says Karl.
  The black man gets up. His body gleams in the faint light from the window. He moves gracefully back, out of range of Karl's vision.
  – Perhaps you had better sleep. There is lots of time.
  – No . . .
  – You want to go on?
A pause.
  – Yes . . .

What would you do? (2)

You have been brought to a room by the secret police.

They say that you can save the lives of your whole family if you will only assist them in one way.

You agree to help.

There is a table covered by a cloth. They remove the cloth and reveal a profusion of objects. There is a children's comforter, a Smith and Wesson .45, an umbrella, a big volume of *Don Quixote*, illustrated by Doré, two blankets, a jar of honey, four bottles of drugs, a bicycle pump, some blank envelopes, a carton of Sullivan's cigarettes, an enamelled pin with the word 1900 on it (blue on gold), a wrist-watch, a Japanese fan.

They tell you that all you have to do is choose the correct object and you and your family will be released.

You have never seen any of the objects before. You tell them this. They nod. That is all right. They know. Now choose.

You stare at the objects, trying to divine their significance.

3. Kaffee Klatsch in Brunswick: 1883: The Lowdown

Bismarck was very fond of enlarging on his favourite theory of the male and female European nations. The Germans themselves, the three Scandinavian peoples, the Dutch, the English proper, the Scotch, the Hungarians and the Turks, he declared to be essentially male races. The Russians, the Poles, the Bohemians, and indeed every Slavonic people, and all Celts, he maintained, just as emphatically, to be female races. A female race he un-gallantly defined as one given to immense verbosity, to fickleness, and to lack of tenacity. He conceded to these feminine races some of the advantages of their sex, and acknowledged that they had great powers of attraction and charm, when they chose to exert them, and also a fluency of speech denied to the more virile nations. He maintained stoutly that it was quite useless to expect efficiency in any form from one of the female races, and he was full of contempt for the Celt and the Slav. He contended that the most interesting nations were the epicene ones, partaking, that is, of the characteristics of both sexes, and he instanced France and Italy, intensely virile in the North, absolutely female in the South; maintaining that the Northern French had saved their country times out of number from the follies of the 'Meridionaux'. He attributed the efficiency of the Frenchmen of the North to the fact that they had so large a proportion of Frankish and Norman blood in their veins, the Franks being a Germanic tribe, and the Normans, as their name implied, Northmen of Scandinav-ian, therefore also of Teutonic, origin. He declared that the fair-haired Piedmontese were the driving power of Italy, and that they owed their initiative to their descent from the Germanic hordes who invaded Italy under Alaric in the fifth century. Bismarck stoutly maintained that efficiency, wherever it was found, was due to Teutonic blood; a state-ment with which I will not quarrel.

As the inventor of 'Practical Politics' (*Real-Politik*), Bismarck had a supreme contempt for fluent talkers and for words, saying that only fools could imagine that facts could be talked away. He cynically added that words were sometimes useful for 'papering over structural cracks' when they had to be concealed for a time.

With his intensely overbearing disposition, Bismarck could not brook the smallest contradiction, or any criticism whatever. I have often watched him in the Reichstag – then housed in a very modest building – whilst being attacked, especially by Liebknecht the Socialist. He made no effort to conceal his anger, and would stab the blotting-pad before him viciously with a metal paper-cutter, his face purple with rage.

Bismarck himself was a very clear and forcible speaker, with a happy knack of coining felicitous phrases.

Lord Frederick Hamilton, *The Vanished Pomps of Yesterday*,
Hodder & Stoughton, 1920

There is a big colour TV in the suite.

The Nigerian walks up to it. His penis is still slightly stiff. – Do you want this on?

Karl is eight. It is 1883. Brunswick. He has a very respectable mother and father. They are kind but firm. It is very comfortable.

He shakes his head.

– Well, do you mind if I watch the news?

Karl is eight. It is 1948. There is a man in pyjamas in his mother's room.

It is 1883 . . .

Karl was eight. His mother was thirty-five. His father was forty. They had a large, modern house in the best part of Brunswick. His father's business was in the centre of town. Trade was good in Germany and particularly good in Brunswick. The Glogauers were part of the best society in Brunswick. Frau Glogauer belonged to the coffee circle which once a week met, in rotation, at the house of one of the members. This week the ladies were meeting at Frau Glogauer's.

Karl, of course, was not allowed into the big drawing-room where his mother entertained. His nurse watched over him while he played in the garden in the hot summer sunshine. Through the french windows, which were open, he could just see his mother and her friends. They balanced the delicate china cups so elegantly and

: 289 :

they leaned their heads so close together when they talked. They were not bored. Karl was bored.

He swung back and forth on his swing. Up and down and back and forward and up and down and back. He was dressed in his best velvet suit and he was hot and uncomfortable. But he always dressed in this way when it was his mother's turn to entertain the kaffee klatsch, even though he wasn't invited to join them. Usually he was asked to come in just before the ladies left. They would ask him the same questions they asked every time and they would compliment his mother on his looks and his size and his health and they would give him a little piece of gâteau. He was looking forward to the gâteau.

'Karl, you must wear your hat,' said Miss Henshaw. Miss Henshaw was English and her German was rather unfortunate in that she had learned it in a village. It was Low German and it made her sound like a yokel. Karl's parents and their friends spoke nothing but the more sophisticated High German. Low German sounded just like English, anyway. He didn't know why she'd bothered to learn it. 'Your hat, Karl. The sun is too hot.'

In her garishly striped blouse and her silly stiff grey skirt and her own floppy white hat, Miss Henshaw looked awful. How dowdy and decrepit she was compared to Mother who, corseted and bustled and covered in pretty silk ribbons and buttons and lace and brocade, moved with the dignity of a six-masted clipper. Miss Henshaw was evidently only a servant, for all her pretence at authority.

She stretched out her freckled arm, offering him the little sun hat. He ignored her, making the swing go higher and higher.

'You will get sunstroke, Karl. Your mother will be very angry with me.'

Karl shrugged and kicked his feet out straight, enjoying Miss Henshaw's helplessness.

'Karl! Karl!'

Miss Henshaw's voice was almost a screech.

Karl grinned. He saw that the ladies were looking out at him through the open window. He waved to his mother. The ladies smiled and returned to their gossip.

He knew it was gossip, about everyone in Brunswick, because once he had lain beside the window in the shrubs and listened before he had been caught by Miss Henshaw. He wished that he had understood more of the references, but at least he had got one useful tip – that Fritz Vieweg's father had been born 'the wrong side of the blanket'. He hadn't been sure of the meaning, but when he had confronted Fritz Vieweg with it, it had stopped Vieweg calling him a 'Jew-pig' all right.

Gossip like that was worth a lot.

'Karl! Karl!'

'Oh, go away, Fräulein Henshaw. I am not in need of my hat at present.' He chuckled to himself. When he talked like his father, she always disapproved.

His mother appeared in the doorway of the french window.

'Karl, dear. There is someone who would like to meet you. May we have Karl in with us for a moment, Miss Henshaw?'

'Of course, Frau Glogauer.' Miss Henshaw darted him a look of stern triumph. Reluctantly, he let the swing slow down and then jumped off.

Miss Henshaw took his hand and they walked across the ornamental pavement to the french windows. His mother smiled fondly and patted his head.

'Frau Spiegelberg is here and wants to meet you.'

He supposed, from his mother's tone, that he should know who Frau Spiegelberg was, that she must be an important visitor, not one of Frau Glogauer's regulars. A woman dressed in purple and white silk was towering behind his mother. She gave him quite a friendly smile. He bowed twice very deeply. 'Good afternoon, Frau Spiegelberg.'

'Good afternoon, Karl,' said Frau Spiegelberg.

'Frau Spiegelberg is from Berlin, Karl,' said his mother. 'She has met the great Chancellor Bismarck himself!'

Again Karl bowed.

The ladies laughed. Frau Spiegelberg said with charming, almost coquettish modesty, 'I must emphasize I am not on intimate terms with Prinz Bismarck!' and she gave a trilling laugh. Karl knew that all the ladies would be practising that laugh after she had gone back to Berlin.

'I would like to go to Berlin,' said Karl.

'It is a very fine city,' said Frau Spiegelberg complacently. 'But your Brunswick is very pretty.'

Karl was at a loss for something to say. He frowned and then brightened. 'Frau Spiegelberg –' he gave another little bow – 'Have you met Chancellor Bismarck's son?'

'I have met both. Do you mean Herbert or William or –' Frau

Spiegelberg glanced modestly at her companions again – 'Bill as he likes to be called.'

'Bill,' said Karl.

'I have attended several balls at which he has been present, yes.'

'So you – have touched him, Frau Spiegelberg?'

And again the trilling laugh. 'Why do you ask?'

'Well, Father met him once I believe when on business in Berlin . . .'

'So your father and I have an acquaintance in common. That is splendid, Karl.' Frau Spiegelberg made to turn away. 'A handsome boy, Frau –'

'And Father shook hands with him,' said Karl.

'Really? Well . . .'

'And Father said he drank so much beer that his hands were always wet and clammy and he could not possibly live for long if he continued to drink that much. Father is, himself, not averse to a few tots of beer or glasses of punch, but he swears he has never seen anyone drink so much in all his life. Is Bill Bismarck dead yet, Frau Spiegelberg?'

His mother had been listening to him in cold horror, her mouth open. Frau Spiegelberg raised her eyebrows. The other ladies glanced at each other. Miss Henshaw took his hand and began to pull him away, apologizing to his mother.

Karl bowed again. 'I am honoured to have met you, Frau Spiegelberg,' he said in his father's voice. 'I am afraid I have embarrassed you and so I will take my leave now.' Miss Henshaw's tugging became more insistent. 'I hope we shall meet again before you return to Berlin, Frau Spiegelberg . . .'

'It is time I left,' icily said Frau Spiegelberg to his mother.

His mother came out for a moment and hissed:

'You disgusting child. You will be punished for this. Your father shall do it.'

'But, Mother . . .'

'In the meantime, Miss Henshaw,' said Frau Glogauer in a terrible murmur, 'you have my permission to beat the boy.'

Karl shuddered as he caught a glint of hidden malice in Miss Henshaw's pale, grey eyes.

'Very well, madame,' said Miss Henshaw. As she led him away he heard her sigh a deep sigh of pleasure.

Already, he was plotting his own revenge.

★

– *You'll like it better when you get used to it. It's a question of your frame of mind.*

Karl sighs. – *Maybe.*

– *It's a matter of time, that's all.*

– *I believe you.*

– *You've got to let yourself go . . .*

They sip the dry, chilled champagne the black man has ordered. Outside, people are going into the theatres.

– *After all*, says the black man, *we are many people. There are a lot of different sides to one's personality. You mustn't feel that you've lost something. You have gained something. Another aspect is flowering.*

– *I feel terrible.*

– *It won't last. Your moment will come.*

Karl smiles. The black man's English is not always perfect.

– *There, you see, you are feeling more relaxed already.*

The black man reaches out and touches his arm. – *How smooth your flesh is. What are you thinking? . . .*

– *I was remembering the time I found the air-raid warden in bed with my mother. I remember her explaining it to my father. My father was a patient man.*

– *Is your father still alive?*

– *I don't know.*

– *You have a great deal to learn, yet.*

What would you do? (3)

You are returning from the theatre after a pleasant evening with your sweetheart. You are in the centre of the city and you want a taxi. You decide to go to the main railway station and find a taxi there. As you come into a side-entrance and approach a flight of steps you see an old man trying to ascend. He is evidently incapably drunk. Normally you would help him up the steps, but in this case there is a problem. His trousers have fallen down to his ankles, revealing his filthy legs. From his bottom protrude several pieces of newspaper covered in excrement. To help him would be a messy task, to say the least, and you are reluctant to spoil the previously pleasant mood of the evening. There is a second or two before you pass him and continue on your journey.

4. Capetown Party: 1892: Butterflies

In the meantime let us not forget that if errors of judgement have been committed, they have been committed by
men whose zeal and patriotism has never been doubted.
We cannot refrain, however, from alluding here to the
greatest of all lessons which this war has taught, not us
alone, but all the world – the solidarity of the Empire. And
for that great demonstration what sacrifice was not worth
making.

H. W. Wilson, *With the Flag to Pretoria*, Harmsworth
Brothers, 1900

*Karl emerges from the deep bath. Liquid drips from him. He stares in
bewilderment at himself in the wall mirror opposite.*
  – Why did you make me do that?
  – I thought you'd like it. You said how much you admired my body.
  – I meant your physique.
  – Oh, I see.
  – I look like something out of a minstrel show. Al Jolson . . .
  *– Yes, you do rather. But you could pass for what? An Eurasian? The
black man begins to laugh.*
  Karl laughs, too.
  They fall into each other's arms.
  – It shouldn't take long to dry, says the black man.
  Karl is nine. It is 1892. He is at work now.
  *– I think I like you better like that, says the black man. He puts a palm
on Karl's damp thigh. – It's your colour . . .*
  Karl giggles.
  – There, you see, it has made you feel better.

Karl was nine. His mother did not know her age. He did not know
his father. He was a servant in a house with a huge garden. A white
house. He was the punkah-wallah, the boy who operated the giant
fan which swept back and forth over the white people while they
were eating. When he was not doing this, he helped the cook in the
kitchen. Whenever he could, however, he was out in the grounds
with his net. He had a passion for butterflies. He had a large collection in the room he shared with the two other little houseboys and
his companions were very envious. If he saw a specimen he did not

own, he would forget everything else until he had caught it. Everyone knew about his hobby and that was why he was known as 'Butterfly' by everyone, from the master and mistress down. It was a kind house and they tolerated his passion. It was not everyone, even, who would employ a Cape Coloured boy, because most thought that half-breeds were less trustworthy than pure-blooded natives. The master had presented him with a proper killing jar and an old velvet-lined case in which to mount his specimens. Karl was very lucky.

Whenever the master saw him, he would say: 'And how's the young entomologist, today?' and Karl would flash him a smile. When Karl was older it was almost certain that he would be given a position as a footman. He would be the very first Cape Coloured footman in this district.

This evening it was very hot and the master and mistress were entertaining a large party of guests to dinner. Karl sat behind a screen and pulled on the string which made the fan work. He was good at his job and the motion of the fan was as regular as the swinging of a pendulum.

When his right arm became tired, Karl would use his left arm, and when his left arm was tired, he would transfer the string to the big toe of his right foot. When his right foot ached, he would use his left and by that time his right arm would be rested and he could begin again. In the meantime, he daydreamed, thinking of his lovely butterflies and of the specimens he had yet to collect. There was a very large one he wanted particularly. It had blue and yellow wings and a complicated pattern of zigzags on its body. He did not know its name. He knew few of the names because nobody could tell them to him. Someone had once shown him a book with some pictures of butterflies and the names underneath, but since he could not read he could not discover what the names were.

Laughter came from the other side of the screen. A deep voice said: 'Somebody will teach the Boers a lesson soon, mark my words. Those damned farmers can't go on treating British subjects in that high-handed fashion for ever. We've made their country rich and they treat us like natives!'

Another voice murmured a reply and the deep voice said loudly: 'If that's the sort of life they want to preserve, why don't they go somewhere else? They've got to move with the times.'

Karl lost interest in the conversation. He didn't understand it, anyway. Besides, he was more interested in butterflies. He transferred the string to his left toe.

When all the guests had withdrawn, a footman came to tell Karl that he might go to his supper. Stiffly Karl walked round the screen and hobbled towards the door. The dinner had been a long one.

In the kitchen the cook put a large plate of succulent scraps before him and said: 'Hurry up now, young man, I've had a long day and I want to get to my bed.'

He ate the food and washed it down with the half a glass of beer the cook gave him. It was a treat. She knew he had been working hard, too. As she let him out of the kitchen, she rumpled his hair and said: 'Poor little chap. How's your butterflies?'

'Very well, thank you, cook.' Karl was always polite.

'You must show them to me sometime.'

'I'll show them to you tomorrow, if you like.'

She nodded. 'Well, sometime . . . Good-night, Butterfly.'

'Good-night, cook.'

He climbed the back stairs high up to his room in the roof. The two houseboys were already asleep. Quietly, he lit his lamp and got out his case of butterflies. He would be needing another case soon.

Smiling tenderly, he delicately stroked their wings with the tip of his little finger.

For over an hour he looked at his butterflies and then he got into his bed and pulled the sheet over him. He lay staring at the eaves and thinking about the blue and yellow butterfly he would try to catch tomorrow.

There was a sound outside. He ignored it. It was a familiar sound. Feet creeping along the passage. Either one of the housemaids was on her way out to keep an assignation with her follower, or her follower had boldly entered the house. Karl turned over and tried to go to sleep.

The door of his room opened.

He turned on to his back again and peered through the gloom. A white figure was standing there, panting. It was a man in pyjamas and a dressing-gown. The man paused for a moment and then crept towards Karl's bed.

'There you are, you little beauty,' whispered the man. Karl recognized the voice as the one he had heard earlier talking about the Boers.

'What do you want, sir?' Karl sat up in bed.

'Eh? Damn! Who the devil are you?'

'The punkah-boy, sir.'

'I thought this was where that little fat maid slept. What the devil!'

There was a crunch and the man grunted in pain, hopping about the room. 'Oh, I've had enough of this!'

Now the other two boys were awake. Their eyes stared in horror at the hopping figure. Perhaps they thought it was a ghost.

The white man blundered back out of the room, leaving the door swinging on its hinges. Karl heard him go down the passage and descend the stairs.

Karl got up and lit the lamp.

He saw his butterfly case where he had left it beside the bed. The white man had stepped on it and broken the glass. All the butterflies were broken, too.

– Won't it wash off? asks Karl.
  – Do you want it to come off? Don't you feel more free?
  – Free?

What would you do? (4)

You are escaping from an enemy. You have climbed along the top of a sloping slate roof, several storeys up. It is raining. You slip and manage to hang on to the top of the roof. You try to get back, but your feet slip on the wet tiles. Below you, you can see a lead gutter. Will you risk sliding down the roof while there is still some strength left in your fingers and hope that you can catch the gutter as you go down and thus work your way to safety? Or will you continue to try to pull yourself back to the top of the roof? There is also the chance that the gutter will break under your weight when you grab it. Perhaps, also, your enemy has discovered where you are and is coming along the roof towards you.

5. Liberation in Havana: 1898: Hooks

'You may fire when ready, Gridley.'

Commodore Dewey, 1 May 1898

– There, it's dried nicely. The black man runs his nail down Karl's chest.
– Are you religious, Karl?

– Not really.

– Do you believe in incarnation? Or what you might call 'transincarnation', I suppose.

– I don't know what you're talking about.

The nail traces a line across his stomach. He gasps.

The black man bares his teeth in a sudden smile.

– Oh, you do really. What's this? Wilful ignorance? How many people today suffer from that malaise!

– Leave me alone.

– Alone?

Karl is ten, the son of a small manufacturer of cigars in Havana, Cuba. His grandfather had the cigar factory before his father. He will inherit the factory from his father.

– Yes – alone . . . .Oh, God!

. . . The black man's tone becomes warmly sympathetic. What's up?

Karl looks at him in surprise, hearing him speak English slang easily for the first time. The black man is changing.

Karl shudders. – You've – you've – made me cold . . .

– Then we'd better tuck you into bed, old chap.

– You've corrupted me.

– Corrupted? Is that what you think turns me on? The Corruption of Ignorance! The black man throws back his handsome head and laughs heartily.

Karl is ten . . .

The black man leans down and kisses Karl ferociously on the lips.

Karl was ten. His mother was dead. His father was fifty-one. His brother Willi was nineteen and, when last heard of, had joined the insurgents to fight against the Spaniards.

Karl's father had not approved of Willi's decision and had disowned his eldest son; that was why Karl was now the heir to the cigar factory. One day he would be master of nearly a hundred women and children who worked in the factory rolling the good cigars which were prized all over the world.

Not that business could be said to be good at present, with the American ships blockading the port. 'But the war is virtually over,' said Señor Glogauer, 'and things will be returning to normal soon enough.'

It was Sunday and the bells were ringing all over Havana. Big bells and little bells. It was almost impossible to hear anything else.

After church, Señor Glogauer walked with his son down the Prado towards Parque Central. Since the war, the beggars seemed to have multiplied to four or five times their previous number. Disdaining a carriage, Señor Glogauer led his son through the ragged clamourers, tapping a way through with his cane. Sometimes a particularly sluggish beggar would receive a heavy thwack for his pains and Señor Glogauer would smile to himself and put a little extra tilt on his beautifully white panama hat. His suit was white, too. Karl wore a coffee-coloured sailor suit and sweater. His father made a point of making this journey on foot every Sunday because he said Karl must learn to know the people and not fear them; they were all wretched cowards, even when you had to deal with a whole pack of them, as now.

This morning a brigade of volunteers had been lined up for inspection in the Prado. Their uniforms were ill-fitting and not all of them had rifles of the same make, but a little Spanish lieutenant strutted up and down in front of them as proudly as if he were Napoleon inspecting the Grand Army. And behind the marshalled volunteers a military band played rousing marches and patriotic tunes. The bells and the beggars and the band created such a cacophony that Karl felt his ears would close up against the noise. It echoed through the faded white grandeur of the street, from the elaborate stucco walls of the hotels and official buildings on both sides of the avenue, from the black and shining windows of the shops with their ornate gold, silver and scarlet lettering. And mingled with this noise were the smells – smells from sewers and beggars and sweating soldiers threatening to drown the more savoury smells of coffee and candy and cooking food.

Karl was glad when they entered the babble of the Café Inglaterra on the west side of the Parque Central. This was the fashionable place to come and, as always, it was crowded with the representatives of all nations, professions and trades. There were Spanish officers, businessmen, lawyers, priests. There were a number of ladies in colours as rich as the feathers of the jungle birds (from whom they had borrowed at least part of their finery), there were merchants from all the countries of Europe. There were English planters and even a few American journalists or tobacco-buyers. They sat at the tables, crowded tightly together, and drank beer or punch or whisky, talking, laughing, quarrelling. Some stood at the counters while upstairs others ate late breakfasts or early luncheons or merely drank coffee.

Señor Glogauer guided Karl into the café, nodding to acquaintances, smiling at friends, and found a seat for himself. 'You had better stand, Karl, until a seat becomes free,' he said. 'Your usual lemonade?'

'Thank you, Papa.' Karl wished he could be at home reading his book in the cool semi-darkness of the nursery.

Señor Glogauer studied the menu. 'The cost!' he exclaimed. 'I'll swear it has doubled since last week.'

The man sitting opposite spoke good Spanish but was evidently English or American. He smiled at Señor Glogauer. 'It's true what you people say – you're not being blockaded by the warships. You're being blockaded by the grocers!'

Señor Glogauer pursed his lips in a cautious smile. 'Our own people are ruining us, señor. You are quite right. The tradesmen are soaking the life out of us. They blame the Americans, but I know they had prepared for this – salting away their food knowing that if the blockade took effect they could charge anything they liked. It is hard for us at the moment, señor.'

'So I see,' said the stranger wryly. 'When the Americans get here things will be better, eh?'

Señor Glogauer shrugged. 'Not if *La Lucha* is correct. I was reading yesterday of the atrocities the American Rough Riders are committing in Santiago. They are drunk all the time. They steal. They shoot honest citizens at will – and worse.' Señor Glogauer glanced significantly at Karl. The waiter came up. He ordered a coffee for himself and a lemonade for Karl. Karl wondered if they ate children.

'I'm sure the reports are exaggerated,' said the stranger. 'A few isolated cases.'

'Perhaps.' Señor Glogauer put both his hands over the nob of his cane. 'But I fear that if they come here I – or my son – might be one of those "isolated cases". We should be just as dead, I think.'

The stranger laughed. 'I take your point, señor.' He turned in his chair and looked out at the life of the Parque. 'But at least Cuba will be master of her own fate when this is over.'

'Possibly.' Señor Glogauer watched the waiter setting down his coffee.

'You have no sympathy with the insurgents?'

'None. Why should I? They have disrupted my business.'

'Your view is understandable, señor. Well, I have work to do.' The stranger rose. Karl thought how ill and tired the man looked. He put on his own, slightly grubby, Panama. 'It has been pleasant talking with you, señor. Good-day.'

'Good-day, señor.' Señor Glogauer pointed to the vacant chair and gratefully Karl went to it, sitting down. The lemonade was warm. It tasted of flies, thought Karl. He looked up at the huge electric fans rattling round and round on the ceiling. They had only been installed last year, but already there were specks of rust on their blades.

A little later, when they were leaving the Café Inglaterra, on their way across the Parque to where Señor Glogauer's carriage waited, a Spanish officer halted in front of them and saluted. He had four soldiers with him. They looked bored. 'Señor Glogauer?' The Spaniard gave a slight bow and brought his heels together.

'Yes.' Señor Glogauer frowned. 'What is it, captain?'

'We would like you to accompany us, if you please.'

'To where? For what?'

'A security matter. I do apologize. You are the father of Wilhelm Glogauer, are you not?'

'I have disowned my son,' said Karl Glogauer's father grimly. 'I do not support his opinions.'

'You know what his opinions are?'

'Vaguely. I understand he is in favour of a break with Spain.'

'I think he is rather more active a supporter of the insurgent cause than that, señor.' The captain glanced at Karl as if sharing a joke with him. 'Well, if you will now come with us to our headquarters, we can sort this whole thing out quickly.'

'Must I come? Can't you ask me your questions here?'

'No. What about the boy?'

'He will come with his father.' For a moment Karl thought that his father needed Karl's moral support. But that was silly, for his father was such a proud, self-reliant man.

With the soldiers behind them, they walked out of the Parque Central and up Obispo Street until they reached a gateway guarded by more soldiers. They went through the gate and into a courtyard. Here the captain dismissed the soldiers and gestured for Señor

Glogauer to precede him into the building. Slowly, with dignity, Señor Glogauer ascended the steps and entered the foyer, one hand on his cane, the other grasping Karl's hand.

'And now this way, señor.' The captain indicated a dark passage with many doors leading off it on both sides. They walked down this. 'And down these steps, señor.' Down a curving flight of steps into the basement of the building. The lower passage was lit by oil-lamps.

And another flight of steps.

'Down, please.'

And now the smell was worse even than the smell of the Prado. Señor Glogauer took out a pure white linen handkerchief and fastidiously wiped his lips. 'Where are we, señor captain?'

'The cells, Señor Glogauer. This is where we question prisoners and so on.'

'You are not – I am not –?'

'Of course not. You are a private citizen. We only seek your help, I assure you. Your own loyalty is not in question.'

Into one of the cells. There was a table in it. On the table was a flickering oil-lamp. The lamp cast shadows which danced sluggishly. There was a strong smell of damp, of sweat, of urine. One of the shadows groaned. Señor Glogauer started and peered at it. 'Mother of God!'

'I am afraid it is your son, señor. As you see. He was captured only about twenty miles from the city. He claimed that he was a small planter from the other side of the island. But we found his name in his wallet and someone had heard of you – your cigars, you know, which are so good. We put two and two together and then you – thank you very much – confirmed that your son was an insurgent. But we wanted to be sure this was your son, naturally, and not someone who had managed merely to get hold of his papers. And again, we thank you.'

'Karl. Leave,' said Señor Glogauer, remembering his other son. His voice was shaking. 'At once.'

'The sergeant at the door,' said the officer, 'perhaps he will give you a drink.'

But Karl had already seen the dirty steel butcher's hooks on which Willi's wrists had been impaled, had seen the blue and yellow flesh around the wounds, the drying blood. He had seen Willi's poor, beaten face, his scarred body, his beast's eyes. Calmly, he came to a decision. He looked up the corridor. It was deserted.

When his father eventually came out of the cell, weeping and asking to be pardoned and justifying himself and calling upon God and cursing his son all at the same time, Karl had gone. He was walking steadily, walking on his little legs towards the outskirts of the city, on his way to find the insurgents still at liberty.

He intended to offer them his services.

– And why do you dislike Americans?

  – I don't like the way some of them think they own the world.

  – But didn't your people think that for centuries? Don't they still?

  – It's different.

  – And why do you collect model soldiers?

  – I just do. It's relaxing. A hobby.

  – Because you can't manipulate real people so easily?

  – Think what you like. Karl turns over on the bed and immediately regrets it. But he lies there.

  He feels the expected touch on his spine. Now you are feeling altogether more yourself, aren't you, Karl?

  Karl's face is pressed into the pillow. He cannot speak.

  The man's body presses down on his and for a moment he smiles. Is this what they mean by the White Man's Burden?

  – Sssssshhhhh, says the black man.

What would you do? (5)

You have three children.

  One is eight years old. A girl.

  One is six years old. A girl.

  One is a few months old. A boy.

  You are told that you can save any two of them from death, but not all three. You are given five minutes to choose.

  Which one would you sacrifice?

---

6. London Sewing Circle: 1905: A Message

One would have thought that the meaning of the word 'sweating' as applied to work was sufficiently obvious. But when 'the Sweating System' was inquired into by the Committee of the House of Lords, the meaning became suddenly involved. As a matter of fact the sweater was originally a man who kept his people at work for long hours. A schoolboy who 'sweats' for his examination studies for many hours beyond his usual working day. The schoolboy meaning of the word was originally the trade meaning.

But of late years the sweating system has come to mean an unhappy combination of long hours and low pay. 'The sweater's den' is a workshop – often a dwelling room as well – in which, under the most unhealthy conditions, men and women toil for from sixteen to eighteen hours a day for a wage barely sufficient to keep body and soul together.

The sweating system, as far as London is concerned, exists chiefly at the East End, but it flourishes also in the West, notably in Soho, where the principal 'sweating trade', tailoring, is now largely carried on. Let us visit the East End first, for here we can see the class which has largely contributed to the evil – the destitute foreign Jew – place his alien foot for the first time upon the free soil of England.

George R. Sims, *Living London*, Cassell & Co. Ltd, 1902

Karl turns on to his side. He is aching. He is weeping.
– Did I promise you pleasure? asks the tall, black man as he wipes his hands on a hotel towel and then stretches and then yawns. – Did I?
– No. Karl's voice is muffled and small.
– You can leave whenever you wish.
– Like this?
– You'll get used to it. After all, millions of others have . . .
– Have you known them all?
The black man parts the curtain. It is now pitch dark outside and it is silent. – Now that's a leading question, he says. – The fact is, Karl, you are intrigued by all these new experiences. You welcome them. Why be a

hypocrite?

– I'm not the hypocrite.

The black man grins and wags a chiding finger. Don't take it out on me, man. That wouldn't be very liberal, would it?

– I never was very liberal.

– You've been very liberal to me. The black man rolls his eyes in a comic grimace. Karl has seen the expression earlier. He begins to tremble again. He looks at his own brown hands and he tries to make his brain see all this in a proper, normal light.

He is eleven. A dark, filthy room. Many little sounds.

The black man says from beside the window: Come here, Karl.

Automatically Karl hauls himself from the bed and begins to make his way across the floor.

He remembers his mother and the tin of paint she threw at him which missed and ruined her wallpaper. You don't love me, she had said. Why should I? he had replied. He had been fourteen, perhaps, and ashamed of the question once he had asked it.

He is eleven. Many little regular sounds.

He approaches the black man. – That will do, Karl, says the black man. Karl stops.

The black man approaches him. Under his breath he is humming 'Old Folks at Home'. Kneeling on the carpet, Karl begins to sing the words in an exaggerated minstrel accent.

Karl was eleven. His mother was thirty. His father was thirty-five. They lived in London. They had come to London from Poland three years earlier. They had been escaping a pogrom. On their way, they had been robbed of most of their money by their countrymen. When they had arrived at the dockside, they had been met by a Jew who said he was from the same district as Karl's father and would help them. He had taken them to lodgings which had proved poor and expensive. When Karl's father ran out of money the man had loaned him a few shillings on his luggage and, when Karl's father could not pay him back, had kept the luggage and turned them out on to the street. Since then, Karl's father had found work. Now they all worked, Karl, his mother and his father. They worked for a tailor. Karl's father had been a printer in Poland, an educated man. But there was not enough work for Polish printers in London. One day Karl's father hoped that a job would become vacant on a Polish or Russian newspaper. Then they would become respectable again, as they had been in Poland.

At present, Karl, his mother and his father all looked rather older than their respective ages. They sat together at one corner of the long table. Karl's mother worked a sewing machine. Karl's father sewed the lapel of a jacket. Around the table sat other groups – a man and a wife, three sisters, a mother and daughter, a father and son, two brothers. They all had the same appearance, were dressed in threadbare clothes of black and brown. The women's mouths were tight shut. The men mostly had thin, straggly beards. They were not all Polish. Some were from other countries: Russia, Bohemia, Germany and elsewhere. Some could not even speak Yiddish and were therefore incapable of conversing with anyone not from their own country.

The room in which they worked was lit by a single gas jet in the centre of the low ceiling. There was a small window, but it had been nailed up. The walls were of naked plaster through which could be seen patches of damp brick. Although it was winter, there was no fire in the room and the only heat came from the bodies of the workers. There was a fireplace in the room, but this was used to store the scraps of discarded material which could be re-used for padding. The smell of the people was very strong, but now few of them really noticed it, unless they left the room and came back in again, which was rarely. Some people would stay there for days at a time, sleeping in a corner and eating a bowl of soup someone would bring them, before starting work again.

A week ago, Karl had been there when they had discovered that the man whose coughing they had all complained about had not woken up for seven hours. Another man had knelt down and listened at the sleeping man's chest. He had nodded to the sleeping man's wife and sister-in-law and together they had carried him from the room. Neither the wife nor the sister-in-law came back for the rest of the day and it seemed to Karl that when they did return the wife's whole soul had not been in her work and her eyes were redder than usual, but the sister-in-law seemed much the same. The coughing man had not returned at all and, of course, Karl reasoned, it was because he was dead.

Karl's father laid down the coat. It was time to eat. He left the room and returned shortly with a small bundle wrapped in newspaper, a single large jug of hot tea. Karl's mother left her sewing machine and signed to Karl. The three of them sat in the corner of the room near the window while Karl's father unwrapped the newspaper and produced three cooked herrings. He handed one to each of them. They took turns to sip from the tea-jug. The meal lasted ten minutes and was eaten in silence. Then they went back to their place at the table, having carefully cleaned their fingers on the newspaper, for Mr Armfelt would fine them if he discovered any grease spots on the clothes they were making.

Karl looked at his mother's thin, red fingers, at his father's lined face. They were no worse off than the rest.

That was the phrase his father always used when he and his mother crawled into their end of the bed. Once he had prayed every night. Now that phrase was the nearest he came to a prayer.

The door opened and the room became a little more chill. The door closed. A short young man wearing a black bowler hat and a long overcoat stood there, blowing on his fingers. He spoke in Russian, his eyes wandering from face to face. Few looked up. Only Karl stared at him.

'Any lad like to do a job for me?' said the young man. 'Urgent. Good money.'

Several of the workers had his attention now, but Karl had already raised his hand. His father looked concerned, but said nothing.

'You'll do fine,' said the young man. 'Five shillings. And it won't take you long, probably. A message.'

'A message where?' Like Karl, Karl's father spoke Russian as well as he spoke Polish.

'Just down to the docks. Not far. I'm busy, or I'd go myself. But I need someone who knows a bit of English, as well as Russian.'

'I speak English,' said Karl in English.

'Then you're definitely the lad I need. Is that all right?' glancing at Karl's father. 'You've no objection?'

'I suppose not. Come back as soon as you can, Karl. And don't let anybody take your money from you.' Karl's father began to sew again. His mother turned the handle of the sewing machine a trifle faster, but that was all.

'Come on, then,' said the young man.

Karl got up.

'It's pelting down out there,' said the young man.

'Take the blanket, Karl,' said his father.

Karl went to the corner and picked up the thin scrap of blanket. He draped it round his shoulders. The young man was already clumping down the stairs. Karl followed.

★

Outside in the alley it was almost as dark as night. Heavy rain swished down and filled the broken street with black pools in which it seemed you could fall and drown. A dog leaned in a doorway, shivering. At the far end of the alley were the lights of the pub. Blinds were drawn in half the windows of the buildings lining both sides of the street. In some of the remaining windows could be seen faint, ghostly lights. A voice was shouting, but whether it was in this alley or the next one, Karl couldn't tell. The shouting stopped. He huddled deeper into the blanket.

'You know Irongate Stairs?' The young man looked rapidly up and down the alley.

'Where the boats come ashore?' said Karl.

'That's right. Well, I want you to take this envelope to someone who's landing from the *Solchester* in an hour or so. Tell no one you have the envelope, save this man. And mention the man's name as little as you can. He may want your help. Do whatever he asks.'

'And when will you pay me?'

'When you have done the work.'

'How will I find you?'

'I'll come back here. Don't worry, I'm not like your damned masters! I won't go back on my word.' The young man lifted his head almost proudly. 'This day's work could see an end to what you people have to suffer.'

He handed Karl the envelope. On it, in Russian, was written a single word, a name: KOVRIN.

'Kovrin,' said Karl, rolling his r. 'This is the man?'

'He's very tall and thin,' said his new employer. 'Probably wearing a Russian cap. You know the sort of thing people wear when they first come over. A very striking face I'm told.'

'You've not met him?'

'A relative, come to look for work,' said the young man somewhat hastily. 'That's enough. Go, before you're too late. And tell no one save him that you have met me, or there'll be no money for you. Get it?'

Karl nodded. The rain was already soaking through his blanket. He tucked the envelope into his shirt and began to trot along the alley, avoiding the worst of the puddles. As he passed the pub, a piano began to play and he heard a cracked voice singing:

Don't stop me 'arf a pint o' beer,
It's the only fing what's keepin' me alive.

: 309 :

Breakfast in the Ruins

I don't mind yer stoppin' of me corfee and me tea,
But 'arf a pint o' beer a day is medicine to me.
I don't want no bloomin' milk or eggs,
And to buy them I'll find it very dear.
If you want to see me 'appy and contented all me life,
Don't stop me 'arf a pint o' beer!

Now I'm a chap what's moderate in all I 'ave to drink,
And if that's wrong, then tell me what is right . . .

Karl did not hear all the words properly. Besides, such songs all sounded the same to him, with virtually the same tunes and the same sentiments. He found the English rather crude and stupid, particularly in their musical tastes. He wished he were somewhere else. Whenever he wasn't working, when he could daydream quite cheerfully as he sewed pads into jackets, this feeling overwhelmed him. He longed for the little town in Poland he could barely remember, for the sun and the cornfields, the snows and the pines. He had never been clear about why they had had to leave so hastily.

Water filled his ruined shoes and made the cloth of his trousers stick to his thin legs. He crossed another alley. There were two or three English boys there. They were scuffing about on the wet cobbles. He hoped they wouldn't see him. There was nothing that cheered bored English boys up so much as the prospect of baiting Karl Glogauer. And it was important that he shouldn't lose the letter, or fail to deliver it. Five shillings was worth nearly two days' work. In an hour he would make as much as he would normally make in thirty-six. They hadn't seen him. He reached the broader streets and entered Commercial Street which was crowded with slow-moving traffic. Everything, even the cabs, seemed beaten down by the grey rain. The world was a place of blacks and dirty whites, spattered with the yellow of gas-lamps in the windows of the pie-and-mash shops, the second-hand clothes shops, the pubs and the pawnshops. Plodding dray-horses threatened to smash their heads against the curved green fronts of the trams or the omnibuses; carters swore at their beasts, their rivals and themselves. Swathed in rubber, or canvas, or gaberdine, crouching beneath umbrellas, men and women stumbled into each other or stepped aside just in time. Through all these dodged Karl with his message in his shirt, crossing Aldgate and running down the dismal length of Leman Street, past more pubs, a few dismal shops, crumbling houses, brick walls which seemed to have no function but to block light from the street, a police station with a blue lamp gleaming over its door, another wall plastered with advertisements for meat-drinks, soaps, bicycles, nerve tonics, beers, money-lenders, political parties, newspapers, music-halls, jobs (No Irish or Aliens Need Apply), furniture on easy terms, the Army. The rain washed them down and made some of them look fresh again. Across Cable Street, down Dock Street, through another maze of alleys, even darker than the others, to Wapping Lane.

When he reached the river, Karl had to ask his way, for, in fact, he had lied when he had told the man he knew Irongate Stairs. People found his guttural accent hard to understand and lost patience with him quickly, but one old man gave him the direction. It was still some distance off. He broke into a trot again, the blanket drawn up over his head, so that he looked like some supernatural creature, a body without a skull, running mindlessly through the cold streets.

When he reached Irongate Stairs, the first boats were already bringing the immigrants ashore, for the ship itself could not tie up at the wharf. He saw that it was the right ship, a mass of red and black, belching oily smoke over the oily river, smoke which also seemed pressed down by the rain and which would not rise. The *Solchester* was a regular caller at Irongate Stairs, sailing twice a week from Hamburg with its cargo of Jews and political exiles. Karl had seen many identical people in his three years in Whitechapel. They were thin and there was hunger in their eyes; bewildered, bare-headed women, with shawls round their shoulders more threadbare than Karl's blanket, dragged their bundles from the boats to the wharf, trying at the same time to keep control of their scrawny children. A number of the men were quarrelling with the boatman, refusing to pay the sixpence which was his standard charge. They had been cheated so often on their journey that they were certain they were being cheated yet again. Others were staring in miserable astonishment at the blurred and blotted line of wharves and grim buildings which seemed to make up the entire city, hesitating before entering the dark archway which protected this particular wharf. The archway was crowded with loafers and touts, all busily trying to confuse them, to seize their luggage, almost fighting to get possession of it.

Two policemen stood near the exit to Irongate Stairs, refusing to take part in any of the many arguments which broke out, unable to understand the many questions which the refugees put to them, simply smiling patronizingly and shaking their heads, pointing to the reasonably well-dressed man who moved anxiously amongst the people and asking questions in Yiddish or Lettish. Chiefly he wanted to know if the people had an address to go to. Karl recognized him. This was Mr Somper, the Superintendent of the Poor Jews' Temporary Shelter. Mr Somper had met them three years before. At that time Karl's father had been confident that he needed no such assistance. Karl saw that many of the newcomers were as confident as his father had been. Mr Somper did his best to listen sympathetically to all the tales they told him – of robbery at the frontier, of the travel agent who told them they would easily find a good job in England, of the oppression they had suffered in their own countries. Many waved pieces of crumpled paper on which addresses were written in English – the names of friends or relatives who had already settled in London. Mr Somper, his dark face clouded with care, saw to it that their baggage was loaded on to the waiting carts, assured those who tried to hang on to their bundles that they would not be stolen, united mothers with stray children and husbands with wives. Some of the people did not need his help and they looked as relieved as he did. These were going on to America and were merely transferring from one boat to another.

Karl could see no one of Kovrin's description. He was jostled back and forth as the Germans and the Romanians and the Russians, many of them still wearing the embroidered smocks of their homeland, crowded around him, shrieking at each other, at the loafers and the officials, terrified by the oppressive skies and the gloomy darkness of the archway.

Another boat pulled in and a tall man stepped from it. He carried only a small bundle and was somewhat better dressed than those around him. He wore a long overcoat which was buttoned to the neck, a peaked Russian cap and there were high boots on his feet. Karl knew immediately that this was Kovrin. As the man moved through the crowd, making for the exit where the officials were checking the few papers the immigrants had, Karl ran up to him and tugged at his sleeve.

'Mr Kovrin?'

The man looked surprised and hesitated before answering. He had pale blue eyes and high cheekbones. There was a redness on his cheekbones which contrasted rather strangely with his pale skin. He nodded. 'Kovrin – yes.'

'I have a letter for you, sir.'

Karl drew the sodden envelope from his shirt. The ink had run, but Kovrin's name was still there in faint outline. Kovrin frowned and glanced about him before opening the envelope and reading the message inside. His lips moved slightly as he read. When he had finished, he looked down at Karl.

'Who sent you? Pesotsky?'

'A short man. He did not tell me his name.'

'You know where he lives?'

'No.'

'You know where this address is?' The Russian pointed at the letter.

'What is the address?'

Kovrin scowled at the letter and said slowly: 'Trinity Street and Falmouth Road. A doctor's surgery. Southwark, is it?'

'That's on the other side of the river,' said Karl. 'A long walk. Or you could get a cab.'

'A cab, yes. You speak English?'

'Yes, sir.'

'You will tell the driver where we wish to go?'

There were fewer of the immigrants on Irongate Stairs now. Kovrin must have realized that he was beginning to look conspicuous. He seized Karl's shoulder and guided him up to the exit, showing a piece of paper to the official there. The man seemed satisfied. There was one cab standing outside. It was old and the horse and driver seemed even older. 'There,' murmured Kovrin in Russian, 'that will do, eh?'

'It is a long way to Southwark, sir. I was not told . . .' Karl tried to break free of the man's grip. Kovrin hissed through his teeth and felt in the pocket of his greatcoat. He drew out half a sovereign and pushed it at Karl. 'Will that do? Will that pay for your valuable time, you urchin?'

Karl accepted the money, trying to disguise the light of elation which had fired his eyes. This was twice what the young man had offered him – and he would get that as well if he helped the Russian, Kovrin.

He shouted up to the cabby. 'Hey – this gentleman and I wish to go to Southwark. To Trinity Street. Get a move on, there!'

'Ye can pay, can ye?' said the old man, spitting. 'I've 'ad trouble wi' you lot afore.' He looked meaningfully around him at no one. The rain fell on the sheds, on the patches of dirt, on the brick walls erected for no apparent purpose. Along the lane could just be seen the last of the immigrants, shuffling behind the carts which carried their baggage and their children. 'I'll want 'arf in advance.'

'How much?' Karl asked.

'Call it three bob – eighteenpence now – eighteenpence when we get there.'

'That's too much.'

'Take it or leave it.'

'He wants three shillings for the fare,' Karl told the Russian. 'Half now. Have you got it?'

Wearily and disdainfully Kovrin displayed a handful of change. Karl took three sixpences and gave them to the driver.

'All right – 'op in,' said the driver. He now spoke patronizingly, which was the nearest his tone could get to being actually friendly.

The hansom creaked and groaned as the cabby whipped his horse up. The springs in the seats squeaked and then the whole rickety contrivance was off, making quite rapid progress out of the dock area and heading for Tower Bridge, the nearest point of crossing into Southwark.

A boat was passing under the bridge, which was up. A line of traffic waited for it to be lowered again. While he waited Karl looked towards the West. The sky seemed lighter over that part of the city and the buildings seemed paler, purer, to him. He had only been to the West once and had seen the buildings of Parliament and Westminster Abbey in the sunshine. They were tall and spacious and he had imagined them to be the palaces of very great men. The cab jerked forward and began to move across the river, passing through a pall of smoke left behind by the funnel of the boat.

Doubtless the Russian, sitting in silence and glaring moodily out of the window, noticed no great difference between the streets on either side of the river, but Karl saw prosperity here. There were more food shops and there was more food sold in them. They went through a market where stalls sold shellfish, fried cod and potatoes, meat of almost every variety, as well as clothing, toys, vegetables, cutlery – everything one could possibly desire. With a fortune in his pocket, Karl's daydreams took a different turn as he thought of the luxuries they might buy; perhaps on Saturday after they had been to the synagogue. Certainly, they could have new coats, get their shoes repaired, buy a piece of meat, a cabbage . . .

The cab pulled up on the corner of Trinity Street and Falmouth Road. The cabby rapped on the roof with his whip. 'This is it.'

They pushed open the door and descended. Karl took another three sixpences from the Russian and handed them up to the driver who bit them, nodded, and was off again, disappearing into Dover Street, joining the other traffic. Karl looked at the building. There was a dirty brass plate on the wall by the door. He read: 'Seamen's Clinic.' He saw that the Russian was looking suspiciously at the plate, unable to understand the words. 'Are you a sailor?' Karl asked. 'Are you ill?'

'Be silent,' said Kovrin. 'Ring the bell. I'll wait here.' He put his hand inside his coat. 'Tell them that Kovrin is here.'

Karl went up the cracked steps and pulled the iron bell handle. He heard a bell clang loudly. He had to wait some time before the door was opened by an old man with a long white forked beard and hooded eyes. 'What do you want, boy?' said the man in English.

Karl said, also in English: 'Kovrin is here.' He jerked a thumb at the tall Russian standing in the rain behind him.

'Now?' The old man smiled in unsuppressed delight. 'Here? Kovrin!'

Kovrin suddenly sprang up the steps, pushing Karl aside. After a perfunctory embrace, he and the old man went inside, speaking rapidly to each other in Russian. Karl followed them. He was hoping to earn another half-sovereign. He heard little of what they said, just a few words – 'St Petersburg' – 'prison' – 'commune' – 'death' – and one very potent word he had heard many times before, 'Siberia'. Had Kovrin escaped from Siberia? There were quite a few Russians who had. Karl had heard some of them talking.

In the house, he could see that it was evidently no longer a doctor's surgery. The house, in fact, seemed virtually derelict, with hardly any furniture but piles of paper all over the place. Many bundles of the same newspaper stood in one corner of the hall. Over these a mattress had been thrown and was serving someone as a bed. Most of the newspapers were in Russian, others were in English and in what Karl guessed was German. There were also handbills which echoed the headlines of the newspapers: PEASANTS REVOLT, said one. CRUEL SUPPRESSION OF DEMOCRATIC RIGHTS IN ST PETERSBURG, said another. Karl decided that these people must be political. His father had always told him to steer clear of 'politicals', they were always in trouble with the police. Perhaps he should leave?

But then the old man turned to him and smiled kindly. 'You look hungry. Will you eat with us?'

It would be foolish to turn down a free meal. Karl nodded. They entered a big room warmed by a central stove. From the way in which the room was laid out, Karl guessed that this had been the doctor's waiting-room. But now it, too, stored bales of paper. He could smell soup. It made his mouth water. At the same time there came a peculiar sound from below his feet. Growling, thumping, clanking: it was as if some awful monster were chained in the cellar, trying to escape. The room shook. The old man led Karl and Kovrin into what had once been the main surgery. There were still glass instrument-cases along the walls. Over in one corner they had installed a big, black cooking range and at this stood a woman, stirring an iron pot. The woman was quite pretty, but she looked scarcely less tired than Karl's mother. She ladled thick soup into an earthenware bowl. Karl's stomach rumbled. The woman smiled shyly at Kovrin whom she plainly did not know, but had been expecting. 'Who is the boy?' she asked.

'Karl,' said Karl. He bowed.

'Not Karl Marx, perhaps?' laughed the old man, nudging Karl on the shoulder. But Karl did not recognize the name. 'Karl Glogauer,' he said.

The old man explained to the woman: 'He's Kovrin's guide. Pesotsky sent him. Pesotsky couldn't come himself because he's being watched. To meet Kovrin would have been to betray him to our friends . . . Give the boy some soup, Tanya.' He took hold of Kovrin's arm. 'Now, Andrey Vassilitch, tell me everything that happened in Petersburg. Your poor brother I have already heard about.'

The rumbling from below grew louder. It was like an earthquake. Karl ate the tasty soup, sitting hunched over his bowl at the far end of the long bench. The soup had meat in it and several kinds of vegetables. At the other end of the bench Kovrin and the old man talked quietly together, hardly aware of their own bowls. Because of the noise from the cellar, Karl caught little of what they said, but they seemed to be speaking much of killing and torture and exile. He wondered why nobody else seemed to notice the noise.

The woman called Tanya offered him more soup. He wanted to take more, but he was already feeling very strange. The rich food was hard to hold down. He felt that he might vomit at any moment. But he persisted in keeping it in his stomach. It would mean he would not need to eat tonight.

He summoned the courage to ask her what the noise was. 'Are

we over an underground railway?'

She smiled. 'It is just the printing press.' She indicated a pile of leaflets on the bench. 'We tell the English people what it is like in our country – how we are ground under by the aristocrats and the middle classes.'

'They want to know?' Karl asked the question cynically. His own experience had given him the answer.

Again she smiled. 'Not many. The other papers are for our countrymen. They give news of what is going on in Russia and in Poland and elsewhere. Some of the papers go back to those countries . . .'

The old man looked up, putting a finger to his lips. He shook his head at Tanya and winked at Karl. 'What you don't hear won't harm you, young one.'

'My father was a printer in Poland,' Karl said. 'Perhaps you have work for him. He speaks both Russian, Polish and Yiddish. He is an educated man.'

'There's little money in our work,' said Tanya. 'Is your father for the cause?'

'I don't think so,' said Karl. 'Is that necessary?'

'Yes,' said Kovrin suddenly. His red cheekbones burned a little more hotly. 'You must stop asking questions, boy. Wait a while longer. I think I will need to see Pesotsky.'

Karl didn't tell Kovrin that he didn't know where to find Pesotsky, because he might get another sum of money for taking Kovrin back to Whitechapel. Perhaps that would do. Also, if he could introduce his father to one of these people, they might decide to give him a job anyway. Then the family would be respectable again. He looked down at his clothes and felt miserable. They had stopped steaming and were now almost dry.

An hour later the noise from below stopped. Karl hardly noticed, for he was almost asleep with his head on his arms on the table. Someone seemed to be reciting a list to what had been the rhythm of the printing press.

'Elizelina Kralchenskaya – prison. Vera Ivanovna – Siberia. Dmitry Konstantinovitch – dead. Yegor Semyonitch – dead. Dukmasovs – all three dead. The Lebezyatnikovna sisters – five years prison. Klinevich, dead. Kudeyarov, dead. Nikolayevich, dead. Pervoyedov, dead. Petrovich, dead. And I heard they found Tarasevich in London and killed him.'

'That's so. A bomb. Every bomb they use on us confirms the

police in their view. We're always blowing ourselves up with our bombs, aren't we?' The old man laughed. 'They've been after this place for months. One day a bomb will go off and the newspapers will report the accident – another bunch of Nihilists destroy themselves. It is easier to think that. What about Cherpanski? I heard he was in Germany . . .'

'They rooted him out. He fled. I thought he was in England. His wife and children are said to be here.'

'That's so.'

Karl fell asleep. He dreamed of respectability. He and his father and mother were living in the Houses of Parliament. But for some reason they were still sewing coats for Mr Armfelt.

Kovrin was shaking him. 'Wake up, boy. You've got to take me to Pesotsky now.'

'How much?' Karl said blearily.

Kovrin smiled bitterly. 'You're learning a good lesson, aren't you?' He put another half-sovereign on the table. Karl picked it up. 'You people . . .' Kovrin began, but then he shrugged and turned to the old man. 'Can we get a cab?'

'Not much chance. You'd best walk, anyway. It will be a degree safer.'

Karl pulled his blanket round him and stood up. He was reluctant to leave the warmth of the room but at the same time he was anxious to show his parents the wealth he had earned for them. His legs were stiff as he walked from the room and went to stand by the front door while Kovrin exchanged a few last words with the old man.

Kovrin opened the door. The rain had stopped and the night was very still. It must be very late, thought Karl.

The door closed behind them. Karl shivered. He was not sure where they were, but he had a general idea of the direction of the river. Once there he could find a bridge and he would know where he was. He hoped Kovrin would not be too angry when he discovered that Karl could not lead him directly to Pesotsky. They began to walk through the cold, deserted streets, some of which were dimly lit by gas-lamps. A few cats screeched, a few dogs barked and a few voices raised in anger came from the mean houses by which they passed. Once or twice a cab clattered into sight and they tried to hail it, but it was engaged or refused to stop for them.

Karl was surprised at how easily he found London Bridge. Once across the sullen blackness of the Thames he got his bearings and

began to walk more confidently, Kovrin walking silently beside
him.

In another half an hour they had reached Aldgate, brightened by
the flaring lamps of the coffee-stall which stood open all night,
catering to the drunkards reluctant to go home, to the homeless, to
the shift workers and even to some gentlemen who had finished
sampling the low-life of Stepney and Whitechapel and were waiting
until they could find a cab. There were a few women there, too –
haggard, sickly. In the glare of the stall, their garishly painted faces
reminded Karl of the ikons he had seen in the rooms of the Russians
who lived on the same floor as his family. Even their soiled silks and
their faded velvets had some of the quality of the clothes the people
wore in the ikons. Two of the women jeered at Karl and Kovrin as
they passed through the pool of light and entered the gash of blackness which was the opening to the warren of alleys where Karl
lived.

Karl was anxious to get home now. He knew he had been away
much longer than he had expected. He did not wish to give his
parents concern.

He passed the dark and silent pub, Kovrin stepping cautiously
behind him. He came to the door of the house. His parents might be
sleeping now or they might still be working. They shared a room
above the workroom.

Kovrin whispered: 'Is this Pesotsky's? You can go now.'

'This is where I live. Pesotsky said he would meet me here,' Karl
told him at last. He felt relieved now that this confession was off his
chest. 'He owes me five shillings, you see. He said he would come
here and pay it. Perhaps he is waiting for us inside.'

Kovrin cursed and shoved Karl into the unlit doorway. Karl
winced in pain as the Russian's hand squeezed his shoulder high up,
near the neck. 'It will be all right,' he said. 'Pesotsky will come. It
will be all right.'

Kovrin's grip relaxed and he gave a huge sigh, putting his hand to
his nose and rubbing it, hissing a tune through his teeth as he
considered what Karl had told him. Karl pressed the latch of the
door and they entered a narrow passage. The passage was absolutely
dark.

'Have you a match?' Karl asked Kovrin.

Kovrin struck a match. Karl found the stump of candle and held it
out for Kovrin to light. The Russian just managed to light the wick
before the match burned his fingers. Karl saw that Kovrin had a gun

in his other hand. It was a peculiar gun with an oblong metal box coming down in front of the trigger. Karl had never seen a picture of a gun like it. He wondered if Kovrin had made it himself.

'Now where?' Kovrin said. He displayed the gun in the light of the guttering candle. 'If I think you've led me into a trap . . .'

'Pesotsky will come,' said Karl. 'It is not a trap. He said he would meet me here.' Karl pointed up the uncarpeted stairway. 'He may be there. Shall we see?'

Kovrin considered this and then shook his head. 'You go. See if he is there and if he is bring him down to me. I'll wait.'

Karl left the candle with Kovrin and began to grope his way up the two flights to the landing off which was the workroom. He had seen no lights at the window, but that was to be expected. Mr Armfelt knew the law and protected himself against it. Few factory inspectors visited this part of Whitechapel, but there was no point in inviting their attention. If they closed his business, where else would the people find work? Karl saw a faint light under the door. He opened it. The gas-jet was turned, if anything, a trifle lower. At the table sat the women and the children and the men, bent over their sewing. Karl's father looked up as Karl came in. His eyes were red and bleary. He could hardly see and his hands shook. It was plain that he had been waiting up for Karl. Karl saw that his mother was lying in the corner. She was snoring.

'Karl!' His father stood up, swaying. 'What happened to you?'

'It took longer than I expected, Father. I have got a lot of money and there is more to come. And there is a man I met who might give you a job as a printer.'

'A printer?' Karl's father rubbed his eyes and sat down on his chair again. It seemed he was finding it difficult to understand what Karl was saying. 'Printer? Your mother was in despair. She wanted to ask the police to find you. She thought – an accident.'

'I have eaten well, Father, and I have earned a lot of money.' Karl reached into his pocket. 'The Russian gave it to me. He is very rich.'

'Rich? You have eaten? Good. Well, you can tell me when we wake up. Go up now. I will follow with your mother.'

Karl realized that his father was too tired to hear him properly. Karl had seen his father like this before.

'You go, Father,' he said. 'I have slept, too. And I have some more business to do before I sleep again. That young man who came today. Has he returned?'

'The one who gave you the job?' His father screwed his eyes up and rubbed them. 'Yes, he came back about four or five hours ago, asking if *you* had returned.'

'He had come to pay me my money,' said Karl. 'Did he say he would be back?'

'I think he did. He seemed agitated. What is going on, Karl?'

'Nothing, Father.' Karl remembered the gun in Kovrin's hand. 'Nothing which concerns us. When Pesotsky comes back it will all be finished. They will go away.'

Karl's father knelt beside his mother, trying to wake her. But she would not wake up. Karl's father lay down beside his mother and was asleep. Karl smiled down at them. When they woke they would be very pleased to see the twenty-five shillings he would, by that time, have earned. And yet something marred his feeling of contentment. He frowned, realizing that it was the gun he had seen. He hoped Pesotsky would return soon and that he and Kovrin would go away for good. He could not send Kovrin off somewhere, because then Pesotsky would not pay him the five shillings. He had to wait.

He saw that a few of the others at the table were staring at him almost resentfully. Perhaps they were jealous of his good fortune. He stared back and they resumed their concentration on their work. He felt at that point what it must be like to be Mr Armfelt. Mr Armfelt was scarcely any richer than the people he employed, but he had power. Karl saw that power was almost as good as money. And a little money gave one a great deal of power. He stared in contempt around the room, at the mean-faced people, at his sprawled, snoring parents. He smiled.

Kovrin came into the room. The hand which had held the gun was now buried in his greatcoat pocket. His face seemed paler than ever, his red cheekbones even more pronounced. 'Is Pesotsky here?'

'He is coming.' Karl indicated his sleeping father. 'My father said so.'

'When?'

Karl became amused by Kovrin's anxiety. 'Soon,' he said.

The people at the table were all looking up again. One young woman said: 'We are trying to work here. Go somewhere else to talk.'

Karl laughed. The laughter was high-pitched and unpleasant. Even he was shocked by it. 'We will not be here much longer,' he said. 'Get on with your work, then.'

The young woman grumbled but resumed her sewing.

Kovrin looked at them all in disgust. 'You fools,' he said, 'you will always be like this unless you do something about it. You are all victims.'

The young woman's father, who sat beside her, stitching the seam of a pair of trousers, raised his head and there was an unexpected gleam of irony in his eyes. 'We are all victims.'

Kovrin glanced away. 'That's what I said.' He was disconcerted. He stepped to the door. 'I'll wait on the landing,' he told Karl.

Karl joined him on the landing. High above, a little light filtered through a patched fanlight. Most of the glass had been replaced with slats of wood. From the room behind them the small sounds of sewing continued, like the noises made by rats as they searched the tenements for food.

Karl smiled at Kovrin and said familiarly: 'He's mad, that old man. I think he meant you were a victim. But you are rich, aren't you, Mr Kovrin?'

Kovrin ignored him.

Karl went and sat on the top stair. He hardly felt the cold at all. Tomorrow he would have a new coat.

He heard the street door open below. He looked up at Kovrin, who had also heard it. Karl nodded. It could only be Pesotsky. Kovrin pushed past Karl and swiftly descended the stairs. Karl followed.

But when they reached the passage, the candle was still flickering and it was plain that no one was there. Kovrin frowned. His hand remained in the pocket of his coat. He peered into the back of the passage, behind the stairs. 'Pesotsky?'

There was no reply.

And then the door was flung open suddenly and Pesotsky stood framed in it. He was hatless, panting, wild-eyed. 'Christ! Is that Kovrin?' he gasped.

Kovrin said quietly. 'Kovrin here.'

'Now,' said Karl. 'My five shillings, Mr Pesotsky.'

The young man ignored the outstretched hand as he spoke rapidly to Kovrin. 'All the plan's gone wrong. You shouldn't have come here . . .'

'I had to. Uncle Theodore said you knew where Cherpanski was hiding. Without Cherpanski, there is no point in –' Kovrin broke off as Pesotsky silenced him.

'They have been following me for days, our friends. They don't know about Cherpanski, but they do know about Theodore's damned press. It's that they want to destroy. But I am their only link. That's why I've been staying away. I heard you'd been at the press and had left for Whitechapel. I was followed, but I think I shook them off. We'd better leave at once.'

'My five shillings, sir,' said Karl. 'You promised.'

Uncomprehending, Pesotsky stared at Karl for a long moment, then he said to Kovrin: 'Cherpanski's in the country. He's staying with some English comrades. Yorkshire, I think. You can get the train. You'll be safe enough once you're out of London. It's the presses they're chiefly after. They don't care what we do here as long as none of our stuff gets back into Russia. Now, you'll want Kings Cross Station . . .'

The door opened again and two men stood there, one behind the other. Both were fat. Both wore black overcoats with astrakhan collars and had bowler hats on their heads. They looked like successful businessmen. The leader smiled.

'Here at last,' he said in Russian. Karl saw that his companion carried a hatbox under his arm. It was incongruous; it was sinister. Karl began to retreat up the stairs.

'Stop him!' called the newcomer. From the shadows of the next landing stepped two men. They had revolvers. Karl stopped half-way up the stairs. Here was an explanation for the sound of the door opening which had brought them down.

'This is good cover, Comrade Pesotsky,' said the leader. 'Is that your name, these days?'

Pesotsky shrugged. He looked completely dejected. Karl wondered who the well-dressed Russians could be. They acted like policemen, but the British police didn't employ foreigners, he knew that much.

Kovrin laughed. 'It's little Captain Minsky, isn't it? Or have you changed your name, too?'

Minsky pursed his lips and came a few paces into the passage. It was obvious that he was puzzled by Kovrin's recognition. He peered hard at Kovrin's face.

'I don't know you.'

'No,' said Kovrin quietly. 'Why have they transferred you to the foreign branch? Were your barbarities too terrible even for St Petersburg?'

Minsky smiled, as if complimented. 'There is so little work for me in Petersburg these days,' he said. 'That is always the snag for a policeman. If he is a success, he faces unemployment.'

'Vampire!' hissed Pesotsky. 'Aren't you satisfied yet? Must you drink the last drop of blood?'

'It is a feature of your kind, Pesotsky,' said Minsky patiently, 'that everything must be coloured in the most melodramatic terms. It is your basic weakness, if I might offer advice. You are failed poets, the lot of you. That is the worst sort of person to choose a career in politics.'

Pesotsky said sulkily: 'Well, *you've* failed this time, anyway. This isn't the printing press. It's a sweatshop.'

'I complimented you once on your excellent cover,' said Minsky. 'Do you want another compliment?'

Pesotsky shrugged. 'Good luck in your search, then.'

'We haven't time for a thorough search,' Minsky told him. He signed to the man with the hatbox. 'We, too, have our difficulties. Problems of diplomacy and so on.' He took a watch from within his coat. 'But we have a good five minutes, I think.'

Karl was almost enjoying himself. Captain Minsky really did believe that the printing press was hidden here.

'Shall we begin upstairs?' Minsky said. 'I understand that's where you were originally.'

'How could a press be upstairs,' Pesotsky said. 'These rotten boards wouldn't stand the weight.'

'The last press was very neatly distributed through several rooms,' Minsky told him. 'Lead on, please.'

They ascended the stairs to the first landing. Karl guessed that the occupants of these rooms were probably awake and listening behind their doors. He once again experienced a thrill of superiority. One of the men who had been on the landing shook his head and pointed up the next flight of stairs.

The seven of them went up slowly. Captain Minsky had his revolver in his gloved hand. His three men also carried their revolvers, trained on the wretched Pesotsky and the glowering Kovrin. Karl led the way. 'This is where my father and mother work,' he said. 'It is not a printer's.'

'They are disgusting,' said Minsky to his lieutenant with the hatbox. 'They are so swift to employ children for their degraded work. There's a light behind that door. Open it up, boy.'

Karl opened the door of the workroom, fighting to hide his grin. His mother and father were still asleep. The young woman who had complained before looked up and glared at him. Then all seven had pushed into the room.

Minsky said: 'Oh, you do look innocent. But I know what you're really up to here. Where's the press?'

Now everyone put down their work and looked at him in astonishment as he kicked at the wall in which the fireplace was set. It rang hollow, but that was because it was so thin. There was an identical room on the other side. But it satisfied Minsky. 'Put that in here,' he told the man with the hatbox. 'We must be leaving.'

'Have you found the press, then?' Karl grinned openly.

Minsky struck him across the mouth with the barrel of his revolver. Karl moaned as blood filled his right cheek. He fell back over the sleeping bodies of his parents. They stirred.

Kovrin had drawn his gun. He waved it to cover all four members of the Secret Police. 'Drop your weapons,' he shouted. 'You – pick that hatbox up again.'

The man glanced uncertainly at Minsky. 'It's already triggered. We have a few moments.'

Karl realized there was a bomb in the box. He tried to wake his father to tell him. Now the people who had been working were standing up. There was a noisy outcry. Children were weeping, women shrieking, men shouting.

Kovrin shot Minsky.

One of Minsky's men shot Kovrin. Kovrin fell back through the door and Karl heard him fall to the landing outside. Pesotsky flung himself at the man who had shot Kovrin. Another gun went off and Pesotsky fell to the floor, his fists clenched, his stomach pulsing out blood.

Karl's father woke up. His eyes widened at what they saw. He clutched Karl to him. Karl's mother woke up. She whimpered. Karl saw that Minsky was dead. The other three men hurried from the room and began to run downstairs.

An explosion filled the room.

Karl was protected by his parents' bodies, but he felt them shudder and move as the explosion hit them. He saw a little boy strike the far wall. He saw the window shatter. He saw the door collapse, driven out into the darkness of the stairwell. He saw fire send tendrils in all directions and then withdraw them. The workbench had come to rest against the opposite wall. It was black and broken. The wall was naked brick and the brick was also black. Something was roaring. His vision was wiped out and he saw only whiteness.

He closed his eyes and opened them again. His eyes stung but he could see dimly, even though the gas-jet had been blown out. Throughout the room there was a terrible silence for a second or two. Then they began to groan.

Soon the room was filled with their groaning. Karl saw that the floor sloped where it had not sloped before. He saw that part of the outer wall had split. Through this great crack came moonlight. Black things shifted about on the floor.

Now the entire street outside was alive with noise. Voices came from below and from above. He heard feet on the stairs. Someone shone a lamp on to the scene and then retreated with a gasp. Karl stood up. He was unhurt, although his skin was stinging and he had some bruises. He saw that his father had no right hand any more and that blood was oozing from the stump. He put his head to his father's chest. He was still breathing. His mother held her face. She told Karl that she was blind.

Karl went out on to the landing and saw the crowd on both the upper and the lower stairs. The man with the lamp was Mr Armfelt. He was in his nightshirt. He looked unwell and was staring at the figure who leaned on the wall on the opposite side of the door. It was Kovrin. He was soaked in blood, but he was breathing and the strange gun was still in his right hand. Karl hated Kovrin, whom he saw as the chief agent of this disaster. He went and looked up into the tall Russian's eyes. He took the pistol from Kovrin's limp hand. As if the pistol had been supporting him, Kovrin crashed to the floor as soon as it was removed from his grasp. Karl looked down at him. Kovrin was dead. None of the watchers spoke. They all looked on as if they were the audience at some particularly terrifying melodrama.

Karl took the lamp from Mr Armfelt and returned to the room.

Many of the occupants were dead. Karl saw that the young woman was dead, her body all broken and tangled up with that of her father, the man who had said, 'We are all victims.' Karl sniffed. Minsky's body had been blown under the shattered bench, but Pesotsky had been quite close to the recess where Karl and his parents had lain. Although wounded, he was alive. He was chuckling. With every spasm, more blood gushed from his mouth. He said thickly to Karl: 'Thanks – thanks.' He waited for the blood to subside. 'They've blown up the wrong place, thanks to you. What luck!'

Karl studied the gun he had taken from Kovrin. He assumed that it was basically the same as a revolver and contained at least another five bullets. He held it in both hands and, with both his index fingers on the trigger, squeezed. The gun went off with a bang and a flash and Karl's knuckles were driven back into his face, cutting his lip again. He lowered the gun and picked up the lamp which he had placed on the floor. He advanced to Pesotsky and held the lamp over the body. The bullet had driven through one of Pesotsky's eyes and Pesotsky was dead. Karl searched through Pesotsky's blood-soaked clothes and found two shillings and some coppers. He counted it. Three shillings and eight-pence in all. Pesotsky had lied to him. Pesotsky had not possessed five shillings. He spat on Pesotsky's face.

At the sound of the shot, the people on the stairs had withdrawn a few paces. Only Mr Armfelt remained where he was. He was talking rapidly to himself in a language Karl did not recognize. Karl tucked the gun into the waistband of his trousers and turned Kovrin's corpse over. In the pockets of the greatcoat he found about ten pounds in gold. In an inner pocket he found some documents, which he discarded, and about fifty pounds in paper money. Carrying the lamp high he shone it on the blind face of his mother and on the pain-racked face of his father. His father was awake and saying something about a doctor.

Karl nodded. It was sensible that they should get a doctor as soon as possible. They could afford one now. He held out the money so that his father could see it all, the white banknotes and the bright gold. 'I can look after you both, Father. You will get better. It doesn't matter if you cannot work. We shall be respectable.'

He saw that his father could still not quite understand. With a shake of his head, Karl crouched down and put a kindly hand on his father's shoulder. He spoke clearly and gently, as one might address a very young child who had failed to gather it was about to receive a birthday present and was not showing proper enthusiasm.

'We can go to *America*, Father.'

He inspected the wrist from which most of the hand had been blown. With some of the rags, he bandaged it, stopping the worst of the bleeding.

And then the sobs began to come up from his stomach. He did not know why he was crying, but he could not control himself. The sobs made him helpless. His body was shaken by them and the noise he made was not very loud but it was the worst noise any of the listeners had heard that night. Even Mr Armfelt, absorbed in his hysterical calculations, was dimly aware of the noise and he became, if anything, even more depressed.

  – What do you think it can be? Something you ate? Do you want some aspirin?

  – Aspirin won't do anything for me. I don't know what causes a migraine. A combination of things, maybe.

  – Or merely a useful evasion, Karl. Like some forms of gout or consumption. One of those subtle diseases whose symptoms can only be transmitted by word of mouth.

  – Thanks for your sympathy. Can I sleep now?

  – What a time to get a headache. And you were just beginning to enjoy yourself, too.

What would you do? (6)

You live in a city.

A disaster has resulted in the collapse of society as you know it.

Public amenities, such as gas, electricity, telephones and postal services no longer exist. There is no piped water. Rats and other vermin proliferate in the piles of garbage which, uncollected, contaminate the city. Disease is rife. You have heard that things are equally bad in the country. There, strangers are attacked and killed if they try to settle. In some ways it is more dangerous in the country than it is in the city where gangs of predatory men and women roam the streets.

You aré used to city life. You have a house, a car and you have obtained several guns from a gunshop you broke into. You raid shops and garages for fuel and food. You have a water purifier and a camp stove. You have a wife and three young children.

Do you think it would be better to go out into the country and take your chances in the wild, or would you try to work out a way of living and protecting yourself and your family in a city with which you are familiar?

7. Calcutta Flies: 1911: Doing Business

Ten years ago, an observer going to India with a fresh mind for its problems saw two great engines at work. One was the British Government, ruling the country according to its own canons of what would be best for the people. Its system of education in Western science and thought was shaking the old beliefs and social traditions. By securing justice and enforcing peace, it had set men's minds free to speculate and criticise. For India's future it had no definite plan; its ambitions, to all outward seeming, were confined to a steady growth of administrative efficiency. The other engine was the awakening of a national consciousness. It was feeding on the Western ideas provided by the British Government and the noble army of Christian missionaries, adapting them to its own purposes, and building on them a rising demand that the people should be given a larger share in their own destiny. Our observer could not help being impressed by how far the two engines were from working in parallel. There was friction and a general feeling of unsettlement. In 1908 a cautious measure of political advance had been offered when Lord Minto was Viceroy and Lord Morley was his 'opposite number' in Whitehall. It was tainted, however, with an air of unreality which disquieted the officials and irritated the Indian politician. The cry grew loud for more rapid progress, 'colonial self-government' was the slogan, and the professional classes (chiefly the lawyers) with an English education were busy in a wide-spread movement for a change in the methods of government. As in all nationalist movements, there was an extreme wing, which leaned to direct action, rather than the slower constitutional modes of agitation. In Eastern hyperbole they wrote and harangued about British tyranny and the duty of patriots to rise and become martyrs for freedom. What they thus conceived in poetic frenzy was translated into sinister prose by others. Anarchists are never lacking in any crowded population, especially when hunger is the bedfellow of so many. In India the section of violence had got into touch with revolutionary camps in Europe and the United States, and sporadic outbursts from 1907 onwards, including attempts on the life of two Viceroys and a Lieutenant-Governor, indicated the existence of subterranean conspiracy. Public opinion condemned it, but did little to check vehemence of language which continued to inflame weak minds. The whole position was one of anxiety. Would it ever be possible to reconcile the two forces which were rapidly moving towards conflict?

The Rt. Hon. Lord Meston, KCSI, LLD, *The Dominions and Dependencies of the Empire: India*, Collins, 1924

— There! That's more like it, Karl! Ah! Better! Better! Now you're moving!

Karl bucks and bounces, gasps and groans. His muscles ache, but he forces his body to make dramatic responses to every tiny stimulus. The black man cheers him on, yelling with delight.

— Ah! sings Karl. Oh!

Ah! Oh!

Up and down and from side to side, whinnying like a proud stallion, he carries the black man round the hotel room on his back. His back is wet, but not from sperm or sweat, for, in spite of all his shouts of pleasure, the black man has not had an orgasm as far as Karl can tell. His back is wet with just a drop or two of blood.

— Now you're moving! Now you're moving! shouts the black man again.

— Hurrah!

Karl is twelve. An orphan. Half-German, half-Indian. In Calcutta. In 1911.

— Faster! Faster! The black man has produced a riding crop and with it he flicks Karl's bouncing buttocks. — Faster!

When Karl was fifteen, he left home to become a great painter. He returned home three months later. He had been turned down by the art school. His mother had been very sympathetic. She could afford to be.

— Faster! That's it! You're learning, Karl!

Karl is twelve. The red sun rises over red ships. Calcutta . . .

The riding crop cracks harder and Karl gallops on.

Karl was twelve. His mother was dead. His father was dead. His two sisters were sixteen and seventeen and he did not often see them. He embarrassed them. Karl was in business for himself and, all things considered, he was doing pretty well.

He worked the docks along the Hooghly. He described himself as

an agent. If something was wanted by the sailors or the passengers
off the ships, he would either get it for them or take them somewhere where they might obtain it. He did better than the other boys
in the same trade, for he was quite light-skinned and he wore a
European suit. He spoke English and German perfectly and was
fairly fluent in most other languages, including a fair number of
Indian dialects. Because he knew when to be honest and who to
bribe, he was popular both with customers and suppliers and people
coming from the big red steamers would ask after him when they
landed, having been recommended to him by friends. Because he
was well mannered and discreet, he was tolerated by most of the
Indian and British policemen on the docks (and he had done several
of them good turns in his time, for he knew the importance of
keeping in with the authorities). Karl was rumoured to be a
millionaire (in rupees), but, because of his overheads, he was, in
fact, worth only about a thousand rupees, which he banked with his
friend in Barrackpore, some fifteen miles away, because it was safer.
He was content with his relatively small profit and had worked out
that by the time he was twenty he would be quite rich enough to set
himself up in a respectable business of some kind in central Calcutta.

Karl's only concession to his Indian mother was his turban. His
turban was virtually his trademark and he was recognized by it
throughout Calcutta. It was a black turban, of gleaming silk. Its
single decoration was a small pin – an enamelled pin he had been
given by a rather eccentric English lady who had sought his services
a year or two back. The pin was white, gold and red and showed a
crown with a scroll over it. On the scroll was written *Edward VII*. It
had been made, the lady had told Karl, to commemorate the
Coronation. The pin was therefore quite old and might be valuable.
Karl felt it a fitting decoration for his black silk turban.

Earlier that morning, Karl had been contacted by a young sailor
who had offered to buy all the hemp Karl could procure by that
afternoon. He had offered a reasonable price – though not an especially good one – and Karl had agreed. He knew that the young sailor
had a customer in one of the European ports and that once his hemp
arrived in Europe it would be several times more valuable than it
was in Calcutta. But Karl was not worried. He would make his
profit and it would be satisfactory. Everyone would be happy. The
young sailor was English, but he was working on a French boat, the
Juliette currently taking on grain and indigo down at Kalna. The
young sailor, whose name was Marsden, had come up on one of the

river steamers.

Through the confusion of the dock strode Karl, walking as quickly as was sensible in the midday heat, dodging bicycles and donkeys and carts and men who were scarcely visible for the huge bundles on their backs. Karl was proud of his city, enjoying the profusion of different racial types, the many contrasts and paradoxes of Calcutta. When he was cursed, as he often was, he would curse back in the same language. When he was greeted by acquaintances he would give a little bow and salute them with cheeky condescension, aping the manner of the Lieutenant-Governor on one of his ceremonial processions through the city.

Karl swaggered a little as he crossed Kidderpore Bridge and walked across the Maidan. He imagined that London must look very much like this and had heard the Maidan compared to Hyde Park, although the Maidan was much bigger. The trees were mainly of the English variety and reminded Karl of the pictures he had seen of the English countryside. He passed close to the cathedral, with its Gothic spire emerging from a mass of greenery and a large sheet of water in the foreground. One of his customers, whom he had taken on a tour of the city the year before, had said it recalled exactly the view over Bayswater from the bridge spanning the Serpentine. One day Karl would visit London and see for himself.

He swaggered a little as he crossed the Maidan. He always felt more relaxed and at home in the better part of town. Near Government Houses, he hailed a rickshaw with a lordly wave and told the boy to take him to the junction of Armenian Street and Bhubab Road. It was really not much further to walk, but he felt in an expansive mood. He leaned back in his seat and breathed the spiced air of the city. He had told Marsden, the sailor, that he could get him a hundred pounds' worth of hemp if he wanted it. Marsden had agreed to bring a hundred pounds to Dalhousie Square that afternoon. It would be one of the largest single business deals Karl had pulled off. He hoped that his friend in Armenian Street would be able to supply him with all the hemp he needed.

His friend worked for one of the big shipping firms in Armenian Street. This friend was a messenger and made a number of trips in and out of Calcutta during the week. Almost every one of these trips yielded a certain supply of hemp which Karl's friend then stored in a safe place until contacted by Karl.

The rickshaw stopped at the corner of Bhubab Road and Karl descended to the pavement, giving the rickshaw boy – a man of about fifty – a generous tip.

The bustle in this part of town was of a different quality to that nearer the docks. It was more assured, more muted. People didn't push so much, or bellow at one, or shout obscene insults. And here, too, there were fewer people sharing considerably more money. Karl was considering Armenian Street as the site for his business when he opened it. It would probably be an import/export business of some kind. He began to walk, sighing with pleasure at the thought of his future. The bright sunshine and the blue sky served as a perfect background to the solid, imposing Victorian buildings, making them all the more imposing. Karl strolled in their shade, reading off their dignified signs as he passed. The signs were beautifully painted in black script, or Gothic gold or tasteful silver. There was nothing vulgar here.

Karl entered the offices of a well known shipping company and asked for his friend.

When he had completed his business in Armenian Street, Karl took out his steel railway watch and saw he had plenty of time to lunch before meeting the young sailor. Dalhousie Square was only a short distance away. Karl had, in fact, decided on one of his regular meeting places in St Andrew's Church – the Red Church as the Indians called it – which would be deserted that afternoon. He had chosen a spot not too far from Armenian Street because it was unwise to carry a full case of hemp around for too long. There was always the risk of an officious policeman deciding to find out what was in his case. On the other hand, St Andrew's was almost next door to the police headquarters and therefore one of the least likely places, so Karl hoped the police would reason, to choose for an illegal transaction.

Karl lunched at the small hotel called the Imperial Indian Hotel in Cotton Street. It was run by a Bengali friend of his and served the most delicious curries in Calcutta. Karl had brought many a customer here and his enthusiastic recommendations were always genuine. The customers, too, were well pleased. In return for this service, Karl could eat at the Imperial Indian Hotel whenever he wished.

He finished his lunch and passed the time of day with the manager of the restaurant before leaving. It was nearly three o'clock. Karl had arranged to meet Marsden at seven minutes past three. Karl always arranged to meet people at odd minutes past the hour.

It was one of his superstitions.

The curry had settled well on his stomach and he moved unhurriedly through the city of his birth. His suit was as clean and as well pressed as ever. His shirt was white and crisp and his black silk turban gleamed on his head like a fat sleek cat. In fact Karl himself was almost purring. In a short time he would have a hundred pounds in his pocket. Fifty of that, of course, would go immediately to his friend in Armenian Street. Then there were a few other expenses, such as the one he had just incurred during his chat with the manager of the hotel restaurant, but there would at the end of the day be about forty pounds to bank with his friend in Barrackpore. A worthwhile sum. His own business was not too far away now.

Dalhousie Square was one of Karl's favourite spots in the city. He would often come here simply for pleasure but when he could he mixed business with pleasure and became an unofficial tourist guide. As this was one of the oldest parts of Calcutta, he could show people everything they expected. The original Fort William had once stood here and part of it was now the customs house. Karl particularly enjoyed pointing out to the European ladies where the guard room of the Fort had been. This guard room had, in 1756, become the infamous Black Hole. Karl could describe the sufferings of the people more than adequately. He had had the satisfaction, more than once, of seeing sensitive English ladies faint away during his descriptions.

St Andrew's Scottish Presbyterian Church stood in its own wooded grounds in which there were two large artificial ponds (in common with the Anglo–Indians, Karl called them 'tanks') and the one drawback of the place was that it was infested with mosquitoes virtually all the year round. As Karl walked up the paved path between the trees, he saw a great cloud of flies swarming in the bars of light between the Grecian columns of the portico. The clock on the 'Lal Girja's' tower stood at six minutes past three.

Karl opened the iron gate in the fence and went up the steps, swatting at mosquitoes as he did so. He killed them in a rather chiding, friendly way.

He entered the relatively cool and almost deserted church. There was no service today and the only other occupant, standing awkwardly in the aisle between the pews of plain, polished wood, was the young sailor, Marsden. His face was red and sticky with sweat. He was wearing a pair of cream-coloured shorts, and a somewhat dirty white shirt. His legs and his arms were bare and the mosquitoes were delighted.

Marsden plainly had not wanted to make a noise in the church for fear of attracting someone's attention, so he had not slapped at the mosquitoes which covered his face, arms, hands and legs. Instead he was vainly trying to brush them off him. They would fly up in a cloud and settle immediately, continuing their feast.

'Good-afternoooon, Mr Marsden, sir,' said Karl, displaying the carpet bag containing the drug. 'One hundred pounds' worth, as promised. Have you the money?'

'I'm glad to see you,' said Marsden. 'I'm being eaten alive in here. What a place to choose. Is it always like this?'

'Usually, I'm afraid to say.' Karl tried to sound completely English, but to his annoyance he could still detect a slight lilt in his voice. The lilt, he knew, betrayed him.

The sailor held out his hand for the bag. Karl saw that red lumps were rising on virtually every spot of the man's bare skin. 'Come on, then, old son,' said Marsden, 'let's see if it's the genuine article.'

Karl smiled ingratiatingly. 'It is one hundred per cent perfect stuff, Mr Marsden.' He put the bag at his feet and spread his hands. 'Can I say the same about your cash, sir?'

'Naturally you can. Of course you can. Don't say you don't trust me, you little baboo! It's me should be worrying.'

'Then let me see the money, sir,' Karl said reasonably. 'I am sure you are an honourable man, but . . .'

'You're damned right I am! I won't have a bloody darkie . . .' Marsden looked round nervously, realizing he had raised his voice and it was echoing through the church. He whispered: 'I'll not have a bloody darkie telling me I'm a welsher. The money's back at the ship. I'd have been a fool to come here alone with a hundred quid on me, wouldn't I?'

Karl sighed. 'So you do not have the money on your person, Mr Marsden?'

'No I don't!'

'Then I must keep the bag until you bring the money,' Karl told him. 'I am sorry. Business is business. You agreed.'

'I know what we agreed,' said Marsden defensively. 'But I've got to be certain. Show me the stuff.'

Karl shrugged and opened the bag. The aroma of hemp was unmistakable.

Marsden leaned forward and sniffed. He nodded.

'How much money do you have with you?' said Karl. He was beginning to see that Marsden had been exaggerating when he had said he would buy as much as Karl could find.

Marsden shrugged. He put his hands in his pockets. 'I don't know. It's mainly in rupees. About four pounds ten.'

Karl sniggered. 'It is not a hundred pounds.'

'I can get it. Back at the ship.'

'The ship is nearly fifty miles away, Mr Marsden.'

'I'll give it you tomorrow.'

When Marsden jumped forward and grabbed up the bag, Karl didn't move. When Marsden pushed him aside and ran with the bag up the aisle, Karl sat down in one of the pews. If Marsden really did have four pounds ten, then at least Karl would have lost nothing on the deal. He would return the bag to his friend in Armenian Street and wait until he had a proper customer.

A short while later the young Sikh from Delhi came into the church. He was holding the bag. The Sikh had been staying at the Imperial Indian Hotel and had had trouble paying his bill. The manager of the restaurant had told Karl this and Karl had told the Sikh how he could earn the money to pay for his room. The Sikh evidently did not relish working for Karl, but he had no choice. He handed Karl the bag.

'Did he have enough money?' Karl asked.

The Sikh nodded. 'Is that all?'

'Excellent,' Karl told him. 'Where is Marsden now?'

'In the tank. He was probably drunk and fell in there. It happens to sailors, I hear, in Calcutta. He may drown. He may not.'

'Thank you,' said Karl.

He waited for the Sikh to leave and remained in the church for some minutes, watching the mosquitoes dancing in the light from the windows. He was a little disappointed, he had to admit. But sooner or later another deal would come, even if he had to work a trifle harder, and there was no doubt that his savings would increase, that his ambitions would be realized.

A priest appeared from behind the altar. He saw Karl and smiled at him. 'You're early, laddie, if you've come for the choir practice.'

– *You're learning, says the black man lasciviously. You see, I said you would.*

Karl smiles up at him and stretches. – *Yes, you said I would. It's funny . . .*

– *You were saying about that girlfriend of yours. The black man changes the subject.* – *How she became pregnant?*

– *That's right. Before the abortion reforms. It cost me the best part of two hundred pounds. Karl smiles.* – *A lot of uniforms.*

– *But the other two were cheaper? The two before?*

– *They got those done themselves. I was always unlucky. I couldn't use those rubber things, that was the trouble. I'd just lose interest if I tried to put one on.*

– *None of your children were born?*

– *If you put it like that, no.*

– *Let the next one be born. The black man puts his hand on the muscles of Karl's upper forearm.*

Karl is astonished at this apparent expression of human feeling. – *You're against abortion, then?*

The black one rolls over and reaches for his cigarettes on the bedside table. They are Nat Sherman's Queen Size Cigaretellos, an obscure American brand which Karl hasn't seen before. Earlier he has studied the packet with some interest. He accepts one of the slim, brown cigarettes and lights up from the tip of the black man's. He enjoys the taste.

– *You're against abortion, then? Karl repeats.*

– *I'm against the destruction of possibilities. Everything should be allowed to proliferate. The interest lies in seeing which becomes dominant. Which wins.*

– *Ah, says Karl, I see. You want as many pieces on the board as you can get.*

– *Why not?*

What would you do? (7)

You are a refugee fleeing from a government which will kill you and your family if they catch you.

You reach the railway station and in a great deal of confusion manage to get your wife and children on to the train, telling them to find a seat while you get the luggage on board.

After a while you manage to haul your luggage into the train as it is leaving the station. You settle it in the corridor and go to look for your family.

You search both ends of the train and they are not there. Someone tells you that only half the train left, that the other half is going to another destination.

Could they have got into the other half by mistake?

What will you do?

Pull the communication cord and set off back to the station, leaving your luggage on the train?

Wait until you reach the next station, leave your luggage there and catch the next train back?

Hope that your family will remain calm and follow you to your ultimate destination on the next available train?

8. Quiet Days in Thann: 1918: Mixed Meat

Never, probably in the history of the world, not even in the last years of the Napoleonic domination, has there taken place such a display of warlike passion as manifested itself in the most civilized countries of Europe at the beginning of August 1914. Then was seen how frail were the commercial and political forces on which modern cosmopolitanism had fondly relied for the obliteration of national barriers. The elaborate system of European finance which, in the opinion of some, had rendered war impossible no more availed to avert the catastrophe than the Utopian aspirations of international socialism, or the links with which a common culture had bound together the more educated classes of the Continent. The world of credit set to work to adapt itself to conditions which seemed, for a moment, to threaten it with annihilation. The voices of the advocates of a world-wide fraternity and equality were drowned in a roar of hostile preparation. The great gulfs that separate Slav, Latin, Teuton, and Anglo-Saxon were revealed; and the forces which decide the destinies of the world were gauntly expressed in terms of racial antagonism.

History of the War, Part One, published by *The Times*, 1915

– It's your turn now, says the black man. – If you like . . .

– I'm tired, says Karl.

– Oh, come now! Tired! Psychological tiredness, that's all! The black man pats him on the back. He gives Karl an encouraging grin, offering him the riding crop.

– No, says Karl. – Please, no . . .

– Well, I offered.

Karl is thirteen. His mother is twenty-nine. His father is dead, killed at Verdun in 1916. His mother has gone to live with her sister in a village near Thann, in Alsace . . .

– Leave me alone, says Karl.

– Of course. I don't want to influence you.

When Karl was thirteen he met a man who claimed to be his father. It was in a public lavatory somewhere in West London. 'I'm your dad,' the man had said. His stiff penis had been exposed. 'Are you still at school,

: 340 :

lad?' Karl had mumbled something and run out of the lavatory. He regretted his decision later because the man could have been his father, after all.

– Leave me in peace.

– You're a very moody chap, young Karl, laughs the black man.

He brings the riding crop down with a crack on Karl's back. Karl yells. He scrambles out of the bed and begins to get dressed. – That's it, he says.

– I'm sorry, says the black man. Please forgive me.

Karl is thirteen. He is now the provider for his mother and his aunt. The war continues not too far away. While it continues, Karl will survive . . .

– I misinterpreted you, that's all, says the black man. Please stay just a short while longer, eh?

– Why should I?

But Karl is weakening again.

Karl was thirteen. His mother was twenty-nine. His father was dead, killed in the war. His mother's sister was twenty-six, also a widow. Where they lived there were many reminders of the war. It had been fought around here for a while. Broken fences, smashed trees, craters filled with water, old trenches and ruins. Ploughmen did not like to plough the ground, for they always found at least one corpse.

Karl had found a gun. It was a good French rifle. He had found plenty of ammunition in the belt of the soldier. He had tried to get the soldier's boots, but the flesh inside them had swollen up too much. Besides, Karl was perfectly satisfied with the gun. With it, he was now able to earn a decent living. Few people in the villages around Thann could do that at present.

In a thick corduroy jacket and tweed knickerbockers secured below the knee with an English soldier's puttees, with a large German knapsack over his shoulder and the French rifle in the crook of his arm, Karl sat comfortably on a slab of masonry and smoked a cigarette, waiting.

It was close to sunrise and he had arrived at the ruined farmhouse about an hour earlier. Dawn was a yellow line on the horizon. He unpacked his German fieldglasses and began to scan the surrounding ground – mud, tree-stumps, ditches, trenches, craters, ruins . . . all were shadowy, all still. Karl was looking for movement.

He saw a dog. It was quite big, but thin. It sauntered along the edge of a ditch, wagging its feathery tail. Karl put down his fieldglasses and picked up his rifle. He adjusted the sliding rearsight, tucked the stock firmly into his shoulder, braced his feet on the mount of brick, took precise aim and squeezed the trigger of the rifle. The stock banged into his shoulder and the gun jumped. There was a report and smoke. Karl lowered the rifle and took out his fieldglasses. The dog was not quite dead. He stood up, a thumb hooked into the strap of the knapsack. By the time he reached it, the dog would be dead.

As he skinned the animal, Karl kept his eyes peeled for other quarry. It was thin on the ground, these days. But, if anyone could get it, Karl could. He sawed off the head with the bayonet he carried for the purpose. The butcher in Thann did not ask questions when he bought Karl's loads of 'mixed meat,' but he did not like to be reminded too closely of the type of animal he was buying.

A little later Karl shot two rats and the cat which had been hunting them. He was amused by this exploit.

He wished he could have told someone of it. But his mother and aunt were squeamish. They preferred to believe he was hunting pigeons. Sometimes he did shoot a pigeon. He would take that home and give it to his mother to cook. 'Part of the bag,' he would say. It was just as well to keep up appearances.

By midday Karl had done well. His knapsack was so heavy that he had trouble carrying it. He lay in a trench which was overgrown with a rich variety of weeds and grasses and smelled delicious. The early autumn day was warm and Karl had been amazed to see a pair of hares. He had killed one, but the other had fled. He was hoping it would reappear. When he had it, he would go home. He had not eaten that morning and was both tired and hungry.

The rims of the glasses were beginning to irritate his eyes when he caught a movement to the south and adjusted the focus quickly. At first he was disappointed. It wasn't the hare, only a man.

The man was running. Sometimes he fell down, but picked himself up again immediately, running on. His back was bowed and he waved his arms loosely as he ran. Karl could now see that he was in uniform. The uniform was probably grey. It was covered in mud. The man was hatless and had no weapons. Karl hadn't seen a soldier in this part of the world for well over a year. He had heard the gunfire, as had everyone else, but otherwise his particular village had seen no action for ages.

The German soldier came closer. He was unshaven. His eyes were red. He gasped as he moved. He seemed to be running away. Surely the Allies had not broken through the German line? Karl had been certain it would hold for ever. It seemed to have been holding for almost as long as he could remember. The thought unsettled him. He had been happy with the status quo and wasn't sure if he looked forward to any change.

More likely the German soldier was a deserter. A silly place to desert, round here. Still . . .

Karl yawned. Another quarter of an hour and he'd leave. He hung his fieldglasses round his neck and picked up his rifle. He sighted down the barrel, aiming at the German soldier. He pretended he was in the war and that this was an attack on his trench. He cocked the bolt of the rifle. There were thousands of them attacking now. He squeezed the trigger.

Although he was surprised when the German threw up his arms and shouted (he could hear the shout from where he lay) he did not regret his action. He raised his fieldglasses. The bullet had struck the soldier in the stomach. A careless shot. But then he hadn't been aiming properly. The soldier fell down in the long grass and Karl saw it waving. He frowned. The waving stopped. He wondered whether to go home or whether to cross the field and have a look at the soldier. Morally, he should look at the soldier. After all, it was the first time he had killed a human being. He shrugged and left his bag of mixed meat where it was. The soldier might have something useful on him, anyway.

With his rifle over his shoulder, he began to plod towards the spot where his man had fallen.

– *Is it morning yet? asks Karl, yawning.*
  – *No. A long time until morning, Karl.*
  – *The night seems to be lasting for ever.*
  – *Aren't you glad?*
  He feels a strong hand in his crotch. It squeezes him gently but firmly. Karl's lips part a little.
– *Yes, says Karl, I'm glad.*

What would you do? (8)

You are a white man in a town where the people are predominantly black.

Because of indignities and insufficient representation of their cause, the black people, militant and angry, seize control of the town.

They are met with violence from some of the whites and they respond in turn, lynching two white officials against whom they have particular grievances.

But now the people have become a mob and are out for white blood. The mob is approaching your part of the town, smashing and burning and beating whites. Some of the whites have been beaten to death.

You cannot contact your black friends and ask for their help because you don't know exactly where they are.

Would you hide in the house and hope that the mob didn't bother you?

Would you try to take your chances on the street and hope to find a black friend who would vouch for you?

Would you go to the aid of other white people defending themselves against the mob? Would you then try to make everyone calm down?

Or would you simply help your fellow-white people kill the black people attacking them?

Or would you join the black people attacking the whites and hope to win acceptance that way?

9. The Downline to Kiev: 1920: Shuffling Along

Official verification came to hand yesterday of the report recently published of the ex-Tsar's violent end at Ekaterinburg at the hands of his Red Guards. The message has been transmitted as follows through the wireless stations of the Russian Government:

Recently Ekaterinburg, the capital of the Red Ural, was seriously threatened by the approach of the Czecho-Slovak bands. At the same time a counter-revolutionary conspiracy was discovered, having for its object the wresting of the ex-Tsar from the hands of the Council's authority by armed force. In view of this fact the Council decided to shoot the ex-Tsar. This decision was carried out on July 16. The wife and son of Romanoff have been sent to a place of security. Documents concerning the conspiracy, which were discovered, have been forwarded to Moscow by a special messenger. It had been recently decided to bring the ex-Tsar before a tribunal to be tried for his crimes against the people and only later occurrences led to delay in adopting this course. The Russian Executive Council accept the decision of the Rural Regional Council as being regular. The Central Executive Committee has now at its disposal extremely important material and documents concerning the Nicholas Romanoff affair – his own diary, which he kept almost to the last day, diaries of his wife and children, his correspondence, amongst which are letters by Gregory Rasputin to Romanoff and his family. All these materials will be examined and published in the near future.

News of the World, Sunday, 21 July 1918

Seated before the mirror, Karl examines his flesh. Neither the harsh neon light over the mirror, nor the mirror itself, are flattering. Karl pouts his lips and rolls his eyes.

– I don't think you're a Nigerian at all, now. Your accent changes all the time.

– We all change our accents to suit our circumstances. *In the mirror their eyes meet. Karl feels cold.*

We are all victims.

He is fourteen. His mother and his father were killed in an explosion in a café in Bobrinskaya.

Karl's friend puts friendly hands on Karl's shoulders. – What would you like to do now? . . .

He is fourteen. Sitting on a flat car, hanging on for dear life as the train roars across the plain. The plain is dead. It consists of nothing but the blackened stalks of what was once wheat. The wheat has been deliberately burned.

The sky is huge and empty.

Karl shivers.

– Any ideas?

The train moves to meet the sullen bank of grey cloud on the horizon. It is like the end of the world. The train carries death. It goes to find more death. That is its cargo, its destiny.

At several points on the train – on the locomotive bellowing ahead, on the rocking carriages, the bucking open trucks – black flags flap like the wings of settling crows.

It is the Ukraine.

And Karl shivers.

Karl was fourteen. His mother and father had been thirty-five when they were killed by the bomb. They came from Kiev but had been driven out during one of the pogroms. They had thought it safer to stay with their relatives in Bobrinskaya. Someone had set a bomb off in a café and Karl had gone to Alexandria where he had met the army of von Bek, the Nihilist. He had joined that army. He had been in several battles since then and now he had a machine gun of his own to look after. He loved the machine gun. He had secured the stand to the flat car with big horseshoe nails. It was an English machine gun, a Lewis. His greatcoat was English, too. It was leather and had a special pocket in front shaped like a revolver. During their last battle, near Golta, he had managed to acquire a revolver. They had been beaten at that battle. They were now making for Kiev because the railway line direct to Alexandria had been blown up to cut off their retreat. Von Bek's black banners flew everywhere on the train. Some of the banners bore his slogan: Anarchy Breeds Order. But most were plain. Von Bek had been in a bad mood since Golta.

Over the rattle of the train and the roar of the locomotive came the sounds of laughter, of song, of an accordion's whine. Von Bek's army lounged on every available surface. Young men, mainly, their clothes were evidence of a hundred successful raids. One wore a tall silk hat decorated with streaming red and black ribbons. His body was swathed in a sleeveless fur coat with the skirt hacked off to give his legs freedom. He wore green Cossack breeches tucked into red leather boots. Over his coat were criss-crossed four bandoliers of bullets. In his hands was a rifle which, intermittently, he would fire into the air, laughing all the time. At his belt was a curved sabre and stuck in the belt were a Mauser automatic pistol and a Smith and Wesson .45 revolver. Bottles were passed from hand to hand as they thundered along. The young man in the top hat flung back his head and poured wine over his bearded face and down his throat, breaking into song as the accordion began to play the army's familiar melody, 'Arise young men!' Karl himself joined in with the sad, bold last lines. 'Who lies under the green sward?' sang the man in the top hat. 'We heroes of von Bek,' sang Karl, 'saddle rugs for shrouds.'

There was a great cheer and peaked caps, sheepskin hats, derby hats, stocking caps and the caps of a dozen different regiments were waved or thrown through the steam from the engine. Karl was proud to be of this reckless company which cared nothing for death and very little for life. The cause for which they fought might be doomed but what did it matter? The human race was doomed. They at least would have made their gesture.

There was not a man on the train who was not festooned with weapons. Sabres and rifles and pistols were common to all. Some sported ornate antique weapons, broadswords, officers' dress swords, pistols inlaid with gold, silver and mother of pearl. They wore boaters, solar topees, extravagant German helmets, wide-brimmed felt hats, panamas and every variety of clothing. Near Karl and manning one of the other machine guns, a fat Georgian was stripped to the waist, wearing only a pair of gentleman's blue riding breeches and boots decorated with silver thread. Around his neck he had wound a long feather boa. He was hatless, but had on a pair of smoked glasses with gold rims. At his belt were two military holsters containing matched revolvers. The Georgian claimed that they had belonged to the Emperor himself. Sharing a bottle with the Georgian was a sailor from Odessa, his vest open to the navel, displaying a torso completely covered in pink and blue tattoos showing dragons, swords and half-dressed ladies all mixed up together. The freshest of the tattoos ran across his breastbone, a Nihilist slogan – Death to Life. A boy, younger than Karl, wearing a torn and blood-stained surplice, clutching a cooked chicken in one hand, jumped down from the top of the box-car behind them and swayed towards the sailor, offering him half the chicken in exchange for the rest of the wine. In his other hand he held an enormous butcher's cleaver. The boy was already nine parts drunk. He was a Ukrainian Jew called Pyat.

The train hooted.

Balancing on the carriage ahead, an old man, with a student cap perched on his white hair hooted back. He steadied himself by means of a Cossack lance around which was tied a torn black skirt. Painted on the skirt was a yellow sunrise. The old man hooted again, before falling on his side and rolling dangerously close to the edge of the roof. The lance remained where he had stuck it. The old man lost his cap and began to laugh. The train took a bend. The old man fell off. Karl saluted the tumbling figure as it disappeared down a bank.

On the curve, Karl could see the front section of the train where von Bek himself sat. The flat-wagons on both sides of him were piled with gun-carriages, their dirty steel and brasswork shining dully beneath a sun which now only made occasional appearances through the looming clouds. A truck near to the engine was full of shaggy horses, their backs covered by Jewish prayer-shawls in place of blankets. Von Bek's chosen Heroes sat all around their leader, their feet dangling over the sides of the wagons, but none sat near him. Karl had an impression of nothing but legs. There were legs in riding boots, legs in puttees made from silk dresses or red plush or green baize ripped from a billiard table, feet in yellow silk slippers with velvet pompoms bouncing on them, in felt shoes, in laced boots, in sandals and in brogues, or some completely naked, scratched, red, horny, dirty. No songs came from von Bek's guard. They were probably all too drunk to sing.

On von Bek's wagon a huge, gleaming black landau had been anchored. The landau's door was decorated with the gilded coat of arms of some dead aristocrat. The upholstery was a rich crimson morocco leather. The shafts of the landau stuck up into the air and on each shaft flapped a black banner of Nihilism. On each corner of the wagon was placed a highly polished machine gun and at each machine gun squatted a man in a white Cossack cap and a black leather greatcoat. These four were not drunk. Von Bek himself was probably not drunk. He lay against the leather cushions of the landau and laughed to himself, tossing a revolver high into the air and catching it again, his feet in their shining black boots crossed indolently on the coach box.

Feodor von Bek was dying. Karl realized it suddenly. The man was small and sickly. His face was the grey face of death. The black Cossack hat and the gay, embroidered Cossack jacket he wore emphasized the pallor of his features. Over his forehead hung a damp fringe of hair which made him look a little like some pictures of Napoleon. Only his eyes were alive. Even from where he sat Karl could see the eyes – blazing with a wild and malevolent misery.

Feodor von Bek tossed the revolver up again and caught it. He tossed it and caught it again.

Karl saw that they were nearing a station. The train howled.

The platform was deserted. If there were passengers waiting for a train, they were hiding. People normally hid when von Bek's army came through. Karl grinned to himself. This was not an age in which the timid could survive.

The train slowed as it approached the station. Did von Bek intend to stop for some reason?

And then, incongruously, a guard appeared on the platform. He was dressed in the uniform of the railway line and he held a green flag in his right hand. What a fool he was, thought Karl, still sticking to the rule book while the world was being destroyed around him.

The guard raised his left hand to his head in a shaky salute. There was a terrified grin on his face, an imploring, placatory grin.

The front part of the train was by now passing through the station. Karl saw von Bek catch his revolver and cock it. Then, casually, as his landau came level with the guard, the Nihilist fired. He did not even bother to aim. He had hardly glanced at the guard. Perhaps he had not really intended to hit the man. But the guard fell, stumbling backwards on buckling legs and then crumpling against the wall of his office, his whole body shuddering as he dropped his flag and grasped at his neck. His chest heaved and blood vomited from between his lips.

Karl laughed. He swung his machine gun round and jerked the trigger. The gun began to sing. The bullets smashed into the walls and made the body of the guard dance for a few seconds. Karl saw that the placatory smile was still on the dead man's face. He pulled the trigger again and raked the whole station as they went through. Glass smashed, a sign fell down, someone screamed.

The name of the station was Pomoshnaya.

Karl turned to the young Ukrainian who had opened a fresh bottle of vodka and was drinking from it in great gulps. He had hardly noticed Karl's action. Karl tapped him on the shoulder.

'Hey, Pyat – where the hell is Pomoshnaya?'

The Ukrainian shrugged and offered Karl the bottle.

The station was disappearing behind them. Soon it had vanished.

The tattooed sailor, his arm around a snub-nosed girl with cropped hair, a Mauser in her hand, took the bottle from Pyat and placed it against the girl's thin lips. 'Drink up,' he said. He peered at Karl. 'What was that, youngster?'

Karl tried to repeat his question, but the train entered a tunnel and thick smoke filled their lungs, stung their eyes and they could see nothing. Everyone began to cough and to curse.

'It doesn't matter,' said Karl.

– You're still looking a bit pale, says Karl's friend, fingering his own ebony skin. – Maybe you could do with another bath?

Karl shakes his head. – It'll be hard enough getting this lot off. I've got to leave here sometime, you know. It's going to be embarrassing.

– Only if you let it be. Brazen it out. After all, you're not the only one, are you?

Karl giggles. – I bet you say that to all the boys.

What would you do? (9)

You have been told that you have at most a year to live.
Would you decide to spend that year:

(a)   enjoying every possible pleasure?
(b)   doing charitable works?
(c)   in some quiet retreat, relishing the simpler
        pleasures of life?
(d)   trying to accomplish one big thing that you will
        be remembered for in times to come?
(e)   putting all your resources into finding a cure
        for the illness you have?

Or would you simply kill yourself and get the whole thing
over with?

10. Hitting the High Spots on W. Fifty-Six: 1929: Recognition

Trapped at sea in a violent thunderstorm, the U.S.S. *Akron*, largest and finest dirigible airship in the world, crashed off the Barnegat Lightship at 12:30 o'clock this morning with 77 officers and men aboard. Among them was Rear Admiral William A. Moffett, chief of the Bureau of Aeronautics.

Only 4 of the 77 were known to have been saved at 5 o'clock this morning. At that time the wreckage of the stricken airship was out of sight in the storm and darkness from the German oil tanker *Phoebus*, which first reported the catastrophe. A northwest wind blowing about 45 miles an hour was blowing the wreckage off shore and made rescue operations doubly difficult.

No hint of the cause of the disaster was contained in the fragmentary and frequently confusing reports received from the *Phoebus*, but it was considered highly likely that the great airship was struck by lightning.

New York Times, 4 April 1933

You were bound to get depressed after all that excitement, says Karl's friend. – What about some coffee? Or would you rather I sent down for some more champagne?

He grins, making an expansive gesture.

– Name your poison!

Karl sighs and chews at his thumbnail. His eyes are hooded. He won't look at the black man.

– All right, then how can I cheer you up?

– You could fuck off, says Karl.

– Take it easy, Karl.

– You could fuck off.

– What good would that do?

– I didn't know you were interested in doing good.

– Where did you get that idea? Don't you feel more a person now than you felt before you came with me through the door? More real?

– Maybe that's the trouble.

– You don't like reality?

– *Yes, maybe that's it.*
– *Well, that isn't my problem.*
– *No.*
– *It's your problem.*
– *Yes.*
– *Oh, come on now! You're starting a new life and you can't manage even a tiny smile!*
– *I'm not your slave, says Karl. I don't have to do everything you say.*
– *Who said you had to? Me? The black man laughs deridingly. – Did I say that?*
– *I thought that was the deal.*
– *Deal? Now you're being obscure. I thought you wanted some fun.*
Karl is fifteen. Quite a little man now.
– *Fuck off, he says. – Leave me alone.*
– *In my experience, the black man sits down beside him, that's what people always say when they think they're not getting enough attention. It's a challenge, in a way. 'Leave me alone.'*
– *Maybe you're right.*
– *Darling, I'm not often wrong. The black man once again puts his arm around Karl's shoulders.*
Karl is fifteen and in his own way pretty good-looking.
He's dating the sweetest little tomato in the school.
– *Oh, Jesus!*
Karl begins to weep.
– *Now that's enough of that, says his friend.*

Karl was fifteen. His mom was forty. His dad was forty-two. His dad had done all right for himself in his business and just recently had become president of one of the biggest investment trusts in the nation. He had, to celebrate, increased Karl's allowance at his fifteenth birthday and turned a blind eye when Karl borrowed his mother's car when he went out on a date. Karl was a big boy for his age and looked older than fifteen.

In his new tuxedo and with his hair gleaming with oil, Karl could have passed for twenty easily. That was probably why Nancy Goldmann was so willing to let him take her out.

As they left the movie theatre (*Gold Diggers of Broadway*), he whistled one of the tunes from the film while he gathered his courage together to suggest to Nancy what he had been meaning to suggest all evening.

Nancy put her arm through his and saved him the worst part:

'Where to now?' she asked.

'There's a speakeasy I know on West Fifty-Six.' He guided her across the street while the cars honked on all sides. It was getting dark and the lights were coming on all down Forty-Second Street. 'What do you say, Nancy?' They reached his car. It was a new Ford Coupe. His dad had a Cadillac limousine which he hoped to borrow by the time he was sixteen. He opened the door for Nancy.

'A speakeasy, Karl? I don't know . . .' She hesitated before getting into the car. He glanced away from her calves. His eyes would keep going to them. It was the short, fluffy skirt. You could almost see through it.

'Aw, come on, Nancy. Are you bored with speakeasies? Is that it?'

She laughed. 'No! Will it be dangerous? Gangsters and bootleggers and shooting and stuff?'

'It'll be the dullest place in the world. But we can get a drink there.' He hoped she would have a drink, then she might do more than hold his hand and kiss him on the way home. He had only a vague idea of what 'more' meant. 'If you want one, of course.'

'Well, maybe just one.'

He could see that Nancy was excited.

All the way up to W. Fifty-Six Street she chattered beside him, talking about the movie mostly. He could tell that she was unconsciously seeing herself as Ann Pennington. Well, he didn't mind that. He grinned to himself as he parked the car. Taking his hat and his evening coat from the back, he walked round and opened the door for Nancy. She really was beautiful. And she was warm.

They crossed Seventh Avenue and were nearly bowled over by a man in a straw hat who mumbled an apology and hurried on. Karl thought it was a bit late in the year to be wearing a straw hat. He shrugged and then, on impulse, leaned forward and kissed Nancy's cheek. Not only didn't she resist, she blew him a kiss back and laughed her lovely trilling laugh. 'Did anyone ever tell you you looked like Rudy Vallee?' she said.

'Lots of people.' He smirked in a comic way and made her laugh again.

They came to a gaudy neon sign which flashed on and off. It showed a pink pyramid, a blue and green dancing girl, a white camel. It was called the Casa Blanca.

'Shall we?' said Karl, opening the door for her.

'This is a restaurant.'

'Just wait and see!'

They checked their hats and coats and were shown by an ingratiating little waiter to a table some distance from the stand where a band was backing someone who looked and sounded almost exactly like Janet Gaynor. She was even singing 'Keep Your Sunny Side Up'.

'What happens next?' said Nancy. She was beginning to look disappointed.

The waiter brought the menus and bowed. Karl had been told what to say by his friend Paul who had recommended the place. 'Could we have some soft drinks, please?' he said.

'Certainly, sir. What kind?'

'Uh – the strong kind, please.' Karl looked significantly at the waiter.

'Yes, sir.' The waiter went away again.

Karl held Nancy's hand. She responded with a funny little spasm and grinned at him. 'What are you going to eat?'

'Oh, anything. Steak Diane. I'm mad about Steak Diane.'

'Me, too.' Under the table, his knee touched Nancy's and she didn't move away. Of course, there was always the chance that she thought his knee was a table leg or something. Then, when she looked at him, she moved her chin up in a way that told him she knew it was his knee. He swallowed hard. The waiter arrived with the drinks. He ordered two Steak Dianes 'and all the trimmings'. He lifted his glass and toasted Nancy. They sipped together.

'They've put a lot of lemon in it,' said Nancy. 'I guess they have to. In case of a raid or something.'

'That's it,' said Karl, fingering his bow tie.

He saw his father just as his father saw him. He wondered if his father would take the whole thing in good part. The band struck up and a couple of thinly dressed lady dancers began to Charleston. He saw that the lady dining with his father was not his mother. In fact she looked too young to be anybody's mother, in spite of the make-up. Karl's father left his place and came over to Karl. 'Get out of here at once and don't tell your mother you saw me here tonight. Who told you about this place?' He had to speak loudly because the band was now in full swing. A lot of people were clapping in time to the music.

'I just knew about it, Dad.'

'Did you? Do you come here often, then? Do you know what kind of a place this is? It's a haunt of gangsters, immoral women, all kinds of riffraff!'

Karl looked at his father's young friend.

'That young lady is the daughter of a business associate,' said Mr Glogauer. 'I brought her here because she said she wanted to see some New York nightlife. It is not the place for a boy of fifteen!'

Nancy got up. 'I think I'll get somebody to call me a cab,' she said. She paused, then took her drink and swallowed it all down. Karl ran after her and caught her at the checking desk. 'There's another place I know, Nancy,' he said.

She stopped, pulling on her hat and giving him a calculating look. Then her expression softened. 'We could go back to my place? My mom and pop are out.'

'Oh, great!'

On the way back to Nancy's place in the car she put her arms round his neck and nibbled his ear and ruffled his hair.

'You're just a little boy at heart, aren't you?' she said.

His knees shook. He had heard that line earlier tonight and he could guess what it meant.

He knew he would always remember this day in September.

– Thanks, Karl accepts the cup of coffee his friend hands him. – How long have I been asleep?

– Not long.

Karl remembers their scene. He wishes it hadn't happened. He was behaving like some little fairy, all temperament and flounce. Homosexual relationships didn't have to be like that now. It was normal, after all. Between normal people, he thought. That was the difference. He looked at his friend. The man was sitting naked on the edge of a chest of drawers, swinging his leg lazily as he smoked a cigarette. His body really was beautiful. It was attractive in itself. It was very masculine. Oddly, it made Karl feel more masculine, too. That was what he found strange. He had thought things would be different. He kept being reminded of some quality he had always felt in his father when his father had been at home.

– Did you dream anything? asked the black man.

– I don't remember.

What would you do? (10)

You are married with a family and you live in a small apartment in the city, reasonably close to your work.

You learn that your mother has become very ill and can no longer look after herself.

You hate the idea of her coming to live with you in your already cramped conditions, particularly since she is not a very nice old woman and tends to make the children nervous and your wife tense. Your mother's house is larger, but in a part of the world which depresses you and which is also a long way from your work. Yet you have always sworn that you will not let her go into an old people's home. You know it would cause her considerable misery. Any other decision, however, would mean you changing your way of life quite radically.

Would you sell your mother's house and use the money to buy a larger flat in your own area? Or would you move away to a completely different area, perhaps somewhere in the country, and look for a new job?

Or would you decide, after all, that it would be best for everyone if she did go into a retirement home?

11. Shanghai Sally: 1932: Problems of Diplomacy

In Shanghai is one of the most extraordinarily gruesome sights in the world. I have never seen anything to approach it. Parts of Chapei and Hongkew, where fighting was hottest, are in ruins paralleling those of the Western front in France. The Japanese looted this area, which comprises several square miles, not merely of furniture, valuables, and household possessions, but of every nail, every window wire, every screw, bolt, nut, or key, every infinitesimal piece of metal they could lay hands on. Houses were ripped to pieces, then the whole region set on fire. No one lives in this charred ruin now. No one could. The Japanese have, however, maintained street lighting; the lighted avenues protrude through an area totally black, totally devoid of human life, like phosphorescent fingers poking into a grisly void.

What is known as the Garden Bridge separates this Japanese-occupied area with one rim of the International Settlement proper. Barbed wire and sandbags protect it. Japanese sentries representing army, navy, and police stand at one end. British sentries are at the other. I have seen these tall Englishmen go white with rage as the Japanese, a few feet away, kicked coolies or slapped old men. The Japanese have life-and-death power over anyone in their area. Chinese, passing the Japanese sentries, have to bow ceremoniously, and doff their hats. Yet the Japanese – at the same time they may playfully prod a man across the bridge with their bayonets – say that they are in China to make friends of the Chinese people!

Lest it be thought that I exaggerate I append the following Reuter dispatch from Shanghai of date March 30, 1938:

'Feeling is running high in British military circles here today as a result of an incident which occurred this morning on a bridge over the Soochow Creek . . . Japanese soldiers set upon and beat an old Chinese man who happened to be on the bridge, and then threw him over into the water. The whole action was in full view of sentries of the Durhams, who were on duty, at one end of the bridge. The British soldiers, unable to leave their posts,

were compelled helplessly to watch the old man drown,
while the Japanese soldiers laughed and cheered.'
John Gunther, *Inside Asia*, Hamish Hamilton, 1939

*– We protect ourselves in so many foolish ways, says Karl's friend. – But
let the defences drop and we discover that we are much happier.*

– I don't feel much happier.

– Not at present, perhaps. Freedom, after all, takes some getting used to.

– I don't feel free.

– Not yet.

– There is no such thing as freedom.

– Of course there is! It's often hard to assimilate a new idea, I know.

– Your ideas don't seem particularly new.

– Oh, you just haven't understood yet, that's all!

*Karl is sixteen. Shanghai is the largest city in China. It is one of the
most exciting and romantic cities in the world. His mother and father came
here to live two years ago. There are no taxes in Shanghai. Great ships
stand in the harbour. Warships stand a few miles out to sea. Anything can
happen in Shanghai.*

*– Why do people always need a philosophy to justify their lusts? Karl
says spitefully. – What's so liberating about sex of any kind?*

– It isn't just the sex.

Black smoke boils over the city from the north. People are complaining.

– No, it's power.

– Oh, come, come, Karl! Take it easy!

*Karl Glogauer is sixteen. Although a German by birth, he attends the
British school because it is considered to be the best.*

– Who do you like best! asks Karl. – Men or women?

– I love everyone, Karl.

Karl was sixteen. His mother was forty-two. His father was fifty.
They all lived in the better part of Shanghai and enjoyed many
benefits they would not have been able to afford in Munich.

Having dined with his father at the German Club, Karl, feeling
fat and contented, ambled through the revolving glass doors into
the bright sunshine and noisy bustle of the Bund, Shanghai's main
street and the city's heart. The wide boulevard fronted the harbour
and offered him a familiar view of junks and steamers and even a
few yachts with crisp, white sails, sailing gently up towards the sea.
As he creased the crown of his cream-coloured hat he noticed with

dissatisfaction that there was a spot of dark grease on the cuff of his right sleeve. He adjusted the hat on his head and with the fingers of both hands turned down the brim a little. Then he looked out over the Bund to see if his mother had arrived yet. She had arranged to meet him at three o'clock and take him home in the car. He searched the mass of traffic but couldn't see her. There were trams and buses and trucks and cars, rickshaws and pedicabs, transport of every possible description, but no Rolls-Royce. He was content to wait and watch the passing throng. Shanghai must be the one place in the world where one never tired of the view. He could see people on the Bund of virtually every race on Earth: Chinese from all parts of China, from beautifully elegant businessmen in well tailored European suits, mandarins in flowing silks, singing girls in slit skirts, flashily dressed gangster types, sailors and soldiers, to the poorest coolies in smocks or loincloths. As well as the Chinese, there were Indian merchants and clerks, French industrialists with their wives, German ship-brokers, Dutch, Swedish, English and American factory-owners or their employees, all moving along in the twin tides that swept back and forth along the Bund. As well as the babble of a hundred languages, there was the rich, satisfying smell of Shanghai, a mixture of human sweat and machine oil, of spices and drugs and stimulants, of cooking food and exhaust fumes. Horns barked, beggars whined, street-sellers shouted their wares. Shanghai.

Karl smiled. If it were not for the present trouble the Japanese were having in their sector of the International District, Shanghai would offer a young man the best of all possible worlds. For entertainment there were the cinemas, theatres and clubs, the brothels and dance-halls along the Szechwan Road. You could buy anything you wanted – a piece of jade, a bale of silk, embroideries, fine porcelain, imports from Paris, New York and London, a child of any age or sex, a pipe of opium, a limousine with bullet-proof glass, the most exotic meal in the world, the latest books in any language, instruction in any religion or aspect of mysticism. Admittedly there was poverty (he had heard that an average of 29,000 people starved to death on the streets of Shanghai every year) but it was a price that had to be paid for so much colour and beauty and experience. In the two years that he had been here he had managed to sample only a few of Shanghai's delights and, as he neared manhood, the possibilities of what he could do became wider and wider. No one could have a better education than to be brought up in Shanghai.

He saw the Rolls pull in to the curb and he waved. His mother, wearing one of her least extravagant hats, leaned out of the window and waved back. He sprang down the steps and pushed his way through the crowd until he got to the car. The Chinese chauffeur, whose name Karl could never remember and whom he always called 'Hank', got out and opened the door, saluting him. Karl gave him a friendly grin. He stepped into the car and stretched out beside his mother, kissing her lightly on the cheek. 'Lovely perfume,' he said. He flattered her as a matter of habit, but she was always pleased. It hardly occurred to him to dislike anything she chose to do, wear or say. She was his mother, after all. He was her son.

'Oh, Karl, it's been terrible today.' Frau Glogauer was Hungarian and spoke German, as she spoke French and English, with a soft, pretty accent. She was very popular with the gentlemen in all the best European circles of the city. 'I meant to do much more shopping, but there wasn't time. The traffic! That's why I was late, darling.'

'Only five minutes, Mama.' Karl looked at his Swiss watch. 'I always give you at least half an hour, you know that. Do you want to finish your shopping before we go home?' They lived in the fashionable Frenchtown area to the west, not too far from the race course, in a large Victorian Gothic house which Karl's father had purchased very reasonably from the American who had previously owned it.

His mother shook her head. 'No. No. I get irritable if I can't do everything at my own pace and it's impossible this afternoon. I wish those Japanese would hurry up and restore order. A handful of bandits can't cause that much trouble, surely? I'm sure if the Japanese had a free hand, the whole city would be better run. We ought to put them in charge.'

'There'd be fewer people to manage,' said Karl dryly. 'I'm afraid I don't like them awfully. They're a bit too heavy-handed in their methods, if you ask me.'

'Do the Chinese understand any other methods?' His mother hated being contradicted. She shrugged and pouted out of the window.

'But perhaps you're right,' he conceded.

'Well, see for yourself,' she said, gesturing into the street. It was true that the usual dense mass of traffic was if anything denser, was moving more slowly, with less order, hampered by even more pedestrians than was normal at this hour. Karl didn't like the look of the lot of them. Really villainous wretches in their grubby smocks and head-rags. 'It's chaos!' his mother continued. 'We're having to go half-way round the city to get home.'

'I suppose it's the refugees from the Japanese quarters,' said Karl. 'You could blame the Japs for the delays, too, Mother.'

'I blame the Chinese,' she said firmly. 'In the end, it always comes down to them. They are the most inefficient people on the face of the Earth. And lazy!'

Karl laughed. 'And devious. They're terrible scamps. I'll agree. But don't you love them, really? What would Shanghai be without them?'

'Orderly,' she said, but she was forced to smile back at him, making fun at herself for her outburst, 'and clean. They run all the vice-rings, you know. The opium-dens, the dance-halls . . .'

'That's what I meant!'

They laughed together.

The car moved forward a few more inches. The chauffeur sounded the horn.

Frau Glogauer hissed in despair and flung herself back against the upholstery, her gloved fingers tapping the arm of the seat.

Karl pulled the speaking tube towards him. 'Could you try another way, Hank? This seems impassable.'

The Chinese, in his neat grey uniform, nodded but did nothing. There were carts and rickshaws packing the street in front of him and a large truck blocking his way back. 'We could walk,' said Karl.

His mother ignored him, her lips pursed. A moment later she took out her handbag and opened the flap so that she could look into the mirror set inside it. She brushed with her little finger at the right eyelid. It was a gesture of withdrawal. Karl stared out of the window. He could see the skyscrapers of the Bund looming close behind them still. They had not gone far. He studied the shops on both sides. For all that the street was crowded, nobody seemed to be doing much business. He watched a fat Indian in a linen suit and a white turban pause outside a shop selling the newspapers of a dozen countries. The Indian picked his nose as he studied the papers, then he selected an American pulp magazine from another rack and paid the proprietor. Rolling the magazine up, the Indian walked rapidly away. It seemed to Karl that some more mysterious transaction must have taken place. But then every transaction seemed like that in Shanghai.

The Rolls rolled a few more feet. Then the chauffeur saw an

opening in a sidestreet and turned down it. He managed to get half-way before a night-soil cart – the 'honey-carts' as the Chinese called them – got in his way and he was forced to brake quite sharply. The driver of the cart pretended not to notice the car. One wheel of his cart mounted the sidewalk as he squeezed past. Then they were able to drive into the sidestreet which was barely wide enough to accommodate the big Phantom.

'At least we're moving,' said Frau Glogauer, putting her compact back into her bag and closing the clasp with a snap. 'Where are we?'

'We're going all round the world,' said Karl. 'The river's just ahead, I think. Is that a bridge?' He craned forward trying to get his bearings. 'Now, that must be north . . . My God!'

'What?'

'Chapei. They must have set fire to it. The smoke. I thought it was clouds.'

'Will it mean trouble – here, I mean?' asked his mother, taking hold of his arm.

He shook his head. 'I've no idea. We're pretty close to the Japanese concession now. Maybe we should go back and speak to father?'

She was silent. She liked to make the decisions. But the political situation had never interested her. She always found it boring. Now she had no information on which to base a decision. 'Yes, I suppose so,' she said reluctantly. 'That was gunfire, wasn't it?'

'It was something exploding.' Karl suddenly felt an intense hatred for the Japanese. With all their meddling, they could ruin Shanghai for everybody. He took up the speaking tube. 'Back to the Bund, Hank, as soon as you can get out of here.'

They entered a wider thoroughfare and Karl saw the crowds part as if swept back by invisible walls. Through the corridors thus created a Chinese youth came running. Hank had pulled out into the street and now the car was blocking the youth's progress.

Behind the youth came three little Japanese policemen with clubs and pistols in their hands. They were chasing him. The youth did not appear to see the car and he struck it in the way that a moth might strike a screen door. He fell backwards and then tried to scramble up. He was completely dazed. Karl wondered what to do.

The Japanese policemen flung themselves on to the youth, their clubs rising and falling.

Karl started to wind down the window. 'Hey!'

His mother buried her face in his shoulder. He saw a smear of powder on his lapel. 'Oh, Karl!'

He put his arm around his mother's warm body. The smell of her perfume seemed even stronger. He saw blood well out of the bruises on the Chinese boy's face and back. Hank was trying to turn the car into the main street. A tug went past on the river, its funnel belching white smoke which contrasted sharply with the oily black smoke rising over Chapei. It was strange how peaceful the rest of the tall city looked. The New York of the Orient.

The clubs continued to rise and fall. His mother snuffled in his shoulder. Karl turned his eyes away from the sight. The car began to reverse a fraction. There was a tap on the window. One of the Japanese policemen stood there, bowing and smiling and saluting with his bloody club. He made some apology in Japanese and grinned widely, shaking his free hand as if to say, 'Such things happen in even the best-run city.' Karl leant over and wound the window right up. The car pulled away from the scene. He didn't look back.

As they drove towards the Bund again, Karl's mother sniffed, straightened up and fumbled in her handbag for a handkerchief. 'Oh, that awful man,' she said. 'And those policemen! They must have been drunk.'

Karl was happy to accept this explanation. 'Of course,' he said. 'They were drunk.'

The car stopped.

– *There is certainly something secure, says Karl, about a world which excludes women. Which is not to say that I deny their charms and their virtues. But I can understand, suddenly, one of the strong appeals of the homosexual world.*

– *Now you're thinking of substituting one narrow world for another, warns his friend. – I spoke earlier of broadening your experience. That's quite different.*

– *What if the person isn't up to being broadened? I mean, we all have a limited capacity for absorbing experience, surely? I could be, as it were, naturally narrow.*

Karl feels euphoric. He smiles slowly.

– *No one but a moron could be that, says the black man, just a trifle prudishly.*

What would you do? (11)

A girl you know has become pregnant.

You are almost certainly the father.

The girl is not certain whether she wants the baby or not. She asks you to help her to decide.

Would you try to convince her to have an abortion?

Would you try to convince her to have the baby?

Would you offer to support her, if she had the baby?

Would you deny that the baby was yours and have nothing further to do with the girl?

If she decided to have an abortion and it had to be done privately, would you offer to pay the whole cost?

Would you tell her that the decision was entirely up to her and refuse to be drawn into any discussion?

12. Memories of Berlin: 1935: Dusty

King Alexander of Yugoslavia was assassinated at Marseilles yesterday. M. Barthou, the French Foreign Minister, who had gone to the port to greet the King, was also murdered.

The assassin jumped on the running board of the car in which the King, who had only just landed, was driving with M. Barthou, General Georges, and Admiral Berthelot, and fired a series of shots. The General and the Admiral were both wounded. The murderer, believed to be a Croat, was killed by the guard.

King Alexander was on his way to Paris for a visit of great political importance. It was to have been the occasion of an attempt to find means, through French mediation, of improving relations between Yugoslavia, the ally of France, and Italy, as preliminary to a Franco-Italian rapprochement.

The Times, 10 October 1934

A policy of keeping the United States 'unentangled and free' was announced here today by President Roosevelt in his first public utterance recognizing the gravity of war abroad . . .

The general advance of the Italian armies from Eritrea has begun. At dawn today 20,000 men in four columns crossed the Mareb River which forms the Ethiopian boundary. Groups of light tanks operating ahead covered the crossing. Airplanes hovered overhead and long range guns fired occasional shells to discourage opposition. Italian planes bombed Adowa and Adigrat . . .

New York Times, 2 and 3 October 1935

The Italian government is capable of almost any kind of treason.

Adolf Hitler, 9 August 1943

He looks up into the cloudy eyes of his friend. – You seem quite pale, he says. – Why doesn't anything happen? Karl wipes his lips.
– That's none of your business, says the black man. – I feel like a drink.

Do you want one? He turns and goes to the table where the waiter has arranged a variety of drinks. — What do you like?

I don't drink much. A lemonade will do.

— A glass of wine?

— All right.

Karl accepts the glass of red wine. He holds it up to a beam of moonlight. — I wish I could help you, he says.

— Don't worry about that.

— If you say so. Karl sits down on the edge of the bed, swinging his legs and sipping his wine. — Do you think I'm unimaginative?

— I suppose you are. But that's nothing to do with it.

— Maybe that's why I never made much of a painter.

— There are lots of different kinds of imagination.

— Yes. It's a funny thing. Imagination is man's greatest strength and yet it's also his central weakness. Imagination was a survival trait at first, but when it becomes overdeveloped it destroys him, like the tusks of a mammoth growing into its own eyes. Imagination, in my opinion, is being given far too much play, these days.

— I think you're talking nonsense, says the black man. It is true that he looks paler. Perhaps that is the moonlight, too, thinks Karl.

— Probably, agrees Karl.

— Imagination can allow man to become anything he wants to be. It gives us everything that is human.

— And it creates the fears, the bogeymen, the devils which destroy us. Unreasoning terror. What other beast has fears like ours?

The black man gives him an intense glare. For a moment his eyes seem to shine with a feral gleam. But perhaps that is the moonlight again.

Karl is seventeen. A dupe of the Duce. Escaped from Berlin and claiming Italian citizenship, he now finds himself drafted into the Army. You can't win in Europe these days. It's bad. There is pain . . .

There is heat.

— Are you afraid, then? asks Karl's friend.

— Of course. I'm guilty, fearful, unfulfilled . . .

— Forget your guilts and your fears and you will be fulfilled.

— And will I be human?

— What are you afraid of?

Karl was seventeen. His mother had gone. His father had gone. His uncle, an Italian citizen, adopted him in 1934. Almost immediately Karl had been conscripted into the Army. He had no work. He had been conscripted under his uncle's new name of Giombini, but they knew he was a Jew really.

He had guessed he would be going to Ethiopia when all the lads in the barracks had been issued with tropical kit. Almost everyone had been sure that it would be Ethiopia.

And now, after a considerable amount of sailing and marching, here he was, lying in the dust near a burning mud hut in a town called Adowa with the noise of bombs and artillery all around him and a primitive spear stuck in his stomach, his rifle stolen, his body full of pain and his head full of regrets. His comrades ran about all round him, shooting at people he couldn't see. He didn't bother to call out. He would be punished for losing his rifle to a skinny brown man wearing a white sheet. He hadn't even had a chance to kill somebody.

He regretted first that he had left Berlin. Things might have quietened down there eventually, after all. He had left only because of his parents' panic after the shop had been smashed. In Rome he had never been able to get used to the food. He remembered the Berlin restaurants and wished he had had a chance to eat one good meal before going. He regretted, too, that he had not been able to realize his ambitions, once in the Army. A clever lad could rise rapidly to an important rank in wartime, he knew. A bomb fell near by and the force of it stirred his body a little. Dust began to drift over everything. The yells and the shots and the sounds of the planes, the whine of the shells and the bombs, became distant. The dust made his throat itch and he used all his strength to stop himself from coughing and so make the pain from his wound worse. But he coughed at last and the spear quivered, a sharp black line against the dust which made everything else look so vague.

He watched the spear, forcing his eyes to focus on it. It was all he had.

You were supposed to forget about wordly ambitions when you were dying. But he felt cheated. He had got out of Berlin at the right time. Really, there was no point in believing otherwise. Friends of his would be in camps now, or deported to some frightful dungheap in North Africa. Italy had been a clever choice. Anti-Semitic feeling had never meant much in Italy. The fools who had gone to America and Britain might find themselves victims of pogroms at any minute. On the other hand the Scandinavian countries had seemed to offer an alternative. Perhaps he should have tried his luck in Sweden, where so many people spoke German and he wouldn't have felt too strange. A spasm of pain shook him. It felt as if his entrails were being stirred around by a big spoon. He had become so conscious of his innards. He could visualize them all – his lungs and his heart and his ruined stomach, the yards and yards of offal curled like so many pink, grey and yellow sausages inside him; then his cock, his balls, the muscles in his strong, naked legs; his fingers, his lips, his eyes, his nose and his ears. The black line faded. He forced it back into focus. His blood, no longer circulating smoothly through his veins and arteries, but pumping out of the openings around the blade of the spear, dribbled into the dust. Nothing would have happened in Germany after the first outbursts. It would have died down, the trouble. Hitler and his friends would have turned their attention to Russia, to the real enemies, the Communists. A funny little flutter started in his groin, below the spear blade. It was as if a moth were trying to get into the air, using his groin as a flying field, hopping about and beating its wings and failing to achieve take-off. He tried to see, but fell back. He was thirsty. The line of the spear shaft had almost disappeared and he didn't bother to try to focus on it again.

The distant noises seemed to combine and establish close rhythms and counter-rhythms coupled with the beating of his heart. He recognized the tune. Some American popular song he had heard in a film. He had hummed the same song for six months after he had seen the film in Berlin. It must have been four years ago. Maybe longer. He wished that he had had a chance to make love to a woman. He had always disdained whores. A decent man didn't need whores. He wished that he had been to a whore and found out what it was like. One had offered last year as he walked to the railway station.

The film had been called *Sweet Music*, he remembered. He had never learned all the English words, but had made up words to sound like them.

> *There's a tavern in the town, in the town,*
> *When atroola setsen dahh, setsen dahh,*
> *Und der she sits on a luvaduvadee,*
> *Und never never sinka see.*
> *So fairdeewell mein on tooday . . .*

He had had ambitions to be an opera singer and he had had ambitions to be a great writer.

The potential had all been there, it was just a question of

choosing. He might even have been a great general.

His possible incarnations marched before him through the dust.

And then he was dead.

– You could be anything you wanted to be. His friend kisses his shoulder.

– Or nothing. Could I be a woman and give birth to five children? Karl bites the black man.

The black man leaps up. He is a blur. For a moment, in the half-light, Karl thinks that his friend is a woman and white and then an animal of some kind, teeth bared. The black man glowers at him. – Don't do that to me!

And Karl wipes his lips.

He turns his back on his friend. – Okay. You taste funny, anyway.

What would you do? (12)

You are a priest, devoutly religious, you are made miserable by the very idea of violence. You are, in every sense, a man of peace.

One morning you are cutting bread in the small hall attached to your church. You hear screams and oaths coming from the church itself. You hurry into the church, the knife still in your hand.

The soldier of the enemy currently occupying your country is in the act of raping a girl of about thirteen. He has beaten her and torn her clothes. He is just about to enter her. She whimpers. He grunts. You recognize the girl as a member of your parish. Doubtless she came to the church for your help. You shout, but the soldier pays no attention. You implore him to stop to no avail.

If you kill the soldier with your knife it will save the young girl from being hurt further. It might even save her life. Nobody knows the soldier has entered the church. You could hide the body easily.

If you merely knock him out – even if that's possible – he will almost certainly take horrible reprisals on you, your church and its congregation. It has happened before, in other towns. Yet you want to save the girl.

What would you do?

13. At the Auschwitz Ball: 1944: Strings

The war in Europe has been won; but the air of Europe smells of blood. Nazis and Fascists have been defeated; but their leaders have not yet been destroyed. It is still touch-and-go even now, whether the surviving Nazis are to have another chance of power, or whether they can be made harmless for ever by their swift arraignment as war criminals. And make no mistake this is not simply a matter for self-evident criminals such as Goering, Rosenberg and those others guilty of outstanding crimes, or responsible for the orders which caused major atrocities.

I have before me about twenty dossiers from small, unimportant French villages, and some from better-known places. They are unemotional accounts based on the evidence of named witnesses, of events which occurred during the German occupation. The Massacre of Dun Les Plages on June 26, 1944; the destruction of the village of Manlay on July 31, 1944; the treatment and murder in the Gestapo barracks at Cannes – and so it goes on. Sometimes the names of the local Nazis responsible have been discovered and named; often not.

The full horror of these cold indictments are revealed by the photographs which accompany them. It is difficult to describe them. Two or three of the mildest only are reproduced here. The Nazis took delight in having themselves photographed with their victims while these were in their agony of outrage and torture. It is not a simple crime that is depicted, but a terrible degradation of man. All the most horrible instincts which survive in our subconscious have come brutally out into the open. It is no relapse into savagery, because no savages ever behaved with such cold, unfeeling, educated brutality and shamelessness.

These dossiers are French. But the same story is repeated in every country the Germans occupied, and also from those countries which allied themselves with the Nazis. Arrests, deportations, questionings and punishment were all carried out with a deliberate maximum of brutality accompanied by every conceivable carnal licence. Like the concentration camps, these methods aimed at the destruction of confidence in democratic values; at inducing a total surrender to the Nazi terror.

They succeeded for a time – probably more than most people who have never lived under Nazi domination care to believe. That fear and horror of the Nazi bully has not yet been eradicated. The war will not be over until all the outraged millions of once-occupied Europe enjoy full confidence that democratic Governments can protect their rights, and that those who have offended are punished and broken. The Nazis mobilised the *Untermensch*, the sub-human, into their ranks. The wickedness he worked is a vivid memory, and it must be exorcised before Europe can have peace.

Picture Post, 23 June 1945

– *Don't try that with me, you little white bastard! Karl displays his arms.*
 – *I'm a black bastard now.*
 – *We can soon change that.*
 – *Oh, hell, I'm sorry, says Karl. – It was just an impulse.*
 – *Well, says his friend grimly, you're certainly losing your inhibitions now, aren't you.*

Karl is eighteen. He is very lucky, along with the other members of the orchestra. His mother told him there was a point to learning, that you never knew when it came in useful, fiddle-playing. And it was beautifully warm in the barracks. He hoped they would dance all night.
 – *Come back to bed, says Karl. – Please . . .*
 – *I thought you were a nice, simple, uncomplicated sort of chap, says the black man. – That's what attracted me to you in the first place. Ah, well – it was my own fault, I suppose.*

Karl is eighteen and playing Johann Strauss. How beautiful. How his mother would have loved it. There are tears in his eyes. He hoped they would dance for ever! The Oswiecim Waltz!
 – *Well, I'm not at my best says Karl. – I wasn't when you met me. That's why I was in the Roof Garden.*
 – *It's true, says his friend, that we hardly know each other yet.*

Karl was eighteen. His mother had been given an injection some time ago and she had died. His father had probably been killed in Spain. Karl sat behind the screen with the other members of the orchestra and he played the violin.

That was his job in Auschwitz. It was the plum job and he had been lucky to get it. Others were doing much less pleasant work and it was so cold outside. The big barrack hall was well heated for the Christmas dance and all the guards and non-commissioned officers, their sweethearts and wives, were enjoying themselves thoroughly, in spite of rations being so short.

Karl could see them through a gap in the screen as he and the others played *The Blue Danube* for the umpteenth time that evening. Round and round went the brown and grey uniforms; round and round went the skirts and the dresses. Boots stamped on the un-carpeted boards of the hall. Beer flowed. Everyone laughed and joked and sang and enjoyed themselves. And behind the leather upholstered screen borrowed for the occasion the band played on.

Karl had two pullovers and a pair of thick corduroy trousers, but he hardly needed the second pullover, it was so warm. He was much better off than when he had first come to the camp with his mother. Not that he had actually seen his mother at the camp, because they had been segregated earlier on. It had been awful at first, seeing the faces of the older inmates, feeling that you were bound to become like them, losing all dignity. He had suffered the humiliation while he summed up the angles and, while a rather poor violinist, had registered himself as a professional. It had done the trick. He had lost a lot of weight, of course, which was only to be expected. Nobody, after all, was doing very well, this winter. But he had kept his dignity and his life and there was no reason why he shouldn't go on for a long while as he was. The guards liked his playing. They were not very hot on Bach and Mozart and luckily neither was he. He had always preferred the lighter gayer melodies.

He shut his eyes, smiling as he enjoyed his own playing.

When he opened his eyes, the others were not smiling. They were all looking at him. He shut his eyes again.

– *Would you say you were a winner? asks Karl's friend.*

    – *No. Everything considered, I'd say I was a loser. Aren't we all?*

    – *Are we? With the proper encouragement you could be a winner. With my encouragement.*

    – *Oh, I don't know. I'm something of a depressive, as you may have noticed.*

    – *That's my point. You've never had the encouragement. I love you, Karl.*

    – *For myself?*

    – *Of course. I have a lot of influence. I could get your work sold for good*

prices. *You could be rich.*
  – *I suppose I'd like that.*
  – *If I got you a lot of money, what would you do?*
  – *I don't know. Give it back to you?*
  – *I don't mean my money. I mean if your work sold well.*
  – *I'd buy a yacht, I think. Go round the world. It's something I've*
always wanted to do. I went to Paris when I was younger.
  – *Did you like it?*
  – *It wasn't bad.*

What would you do? (13)

You own a dog. It is a dog you inherited from a friend
some years ago. The friend asked you to look after it for a
short while and never returned.

Now the dog is getting old. You have never cared much
for it, but you feel sympathetic towards it. It has become
long in the tooth, it makes peculiar retching noises, it has
difficulty eating and sometimes its legs are so stiff you
have to carry it up and down stairs.

The dog is rather cur-like in its general demeanour. It
has never had what you would call a noble character. It is
nervous, cowardly and given to hysterical barking.

Because of the stiffness in its legs you take it to the
veterinary clinic.

The dog has lived several years beyond its expected life-
span. Its eyes are failing and it is rather deaf.

You have the opportunity to ask the veterinary to destroy the dog. And yet the dog is in no pain or any particular discomfort most of the time. The vet says that it will
go on quite happily for another year or so. You hate the
idea of witnessing the dog's last agonies when its time does
come to die. You have only a faint degree of affection for
it. It would really be better if the vet got it over with now.

What would you say to the vet?

---

14. The Road to Tel Aviv: 1947: Traps

ATIYAH: I have three comments to make. First, concerning what Reid said about Palestine having belonged to the Turks. Under Turkish suzerainty the Arabs were not a subject people, but partners with the Turks in the empire. Second, on what I considered was the false analogy – when Crossman said the Jews were unlucky in that they were, as he put it, the last comers into the fields of overseas settlement. He mentioned Australia. I would point out that the Arabs in Palestine do not belong to the same category as the aborigines of Australia. They belong to what was once a highly-civilized community, and before what you call overseas settlement in Palestine by the Jews was begun, the Arabs were reawakening into a tremendous intellectual and spiritual activity after a period of decadence, so there can be no comparison between the two cases.

CROSSMAN: Tom, what do you think were the real mistakes of British policy which led up to what we all agree is an intolerable situation?

REID: The British Government during the first World War had induced the Arabs, who were in revolt against the Turks, to come in and fight on the allied side. We made them a promise in the McMahon Declaration and then, without their knowledge, invited the Jews to come in and establish a national home. That was unwise and wicked. As I understand it, the idea of the British Government was that the Jews should come in and gradually become a majority. That was a secret understanding and was doubly wicked.

Picture Post, Palestine: Can deadlock be broken? Discussion between Edward Atiyah, Arab Office; Thomas Reid, MP; R. H. S. Crossman, MP, and Prof. Martin Buber, Prof. Sociology, Jerusalem University, 12 July 1947

– *What does money mean to you, Karl?*

– *Well, security, I suppose, first and foremost.*

– *You mean it can buy you security. A house, food, the obvious comforts, power over others.*

– *I'm not sure about power over others. What has that to do with security?*

– Oh, it must have something to do with it.

At nineteen, Karl is bent on vengeance and the regaining of his rights. He has a .303 Lee Enfield rifle, some hand grenades, a bayonet and a long dagger. He wears a khaki shirt and blue jeans. On his head is a burnouse. He stands on the bank overlooking the winding road to Tel Aviv. He lifts his head proudly into the sun.

– You can keep yourself to yourself, says Karl with a grin. – Can't you.

– As long as others do. The dweller in the suburbs, Karl, must pursue a policy of armed neutrality.

– I was brought up in the suburbs. I never saw it like that. I don't know what things are like in Nigeria, mind you . . .

At nineteen, Karl has a girl whom he has left behind in Joppa. There are five friends with him on the road. He sees a dust-cloud approaching. It must be the jeep. With the veil of his burnouse, Karl covers his mouth against the dust.

– Much the same, says Karl's friend. – Much the same.

Karl was nineteen. His mother had been gassed, his father had been gassed. At least, that was as far as he knew. He had been lucky. In 1942 he and his uncle had managed to sneak into Palestine and had not been caught as illegal immigrants. But Karl had soon realized the injustice of British rule and now he belonged to the Irgun Tsva'i Leumi, pledged to drive the British out of Palestine if they had to kill every single British man, woman or child to do it. It was time the Jews turned. There would never be another pogrom against the Jews that was not answered in kind. It was the only way.

He squinted against the glare of the sun, breathing with some difficulty through the gauze of his headdress. The air was dry, dusty and stale. There was no doubt about the single jeep droning along the road from Abid to Tel Aviv. It was British. He gestured down to his friend David. David, too, was masked. David, too, had a Lee Enfield rifle. He handed up the fieldglasses to Karl. Karl took them, adjusted them, saw that there were two soldiers in the jeep – a sergeant and a corporal. They would do.

Further along the road, in the shade of a clump of stunted palms, waited the rest of the section. Karl signalled to them. He swept the surrounding hills with his glasses to check that there was no one about. Even a goatherd could prove an embarrassment, particularly if he were an Arab. The parched hills were deserted.

You could hear the jeep quite clearly now, its engine whining as it changed gear and took an incline.

Karl unclipped a grenade from his belt.

The others left the shade of the palms and got into the ditch behind the bank, lying flat, their rifles ready. Karl looked at David. The boy's dark eyes were troubled. Karl signalled for David to join him. He pulled the pin from the grenade. David imitated him, unclipping a grenade, pulling out the pin, holding down the safety.

Karl felt his legs begin to tremble. He felt ill. The heat was getting to him. The jeep was almost level. He sprang up, steadied himself on the top of the bank and threw the grenade in a gentle, graceful curve. It was a beautiful throw. It went straight into the back seat of the jeep. The soldiers looked astonished. They glanced back. They glanced at Karl. The jeep's pace didn't slacken. It blew up.

There was really no need for the second grenade which David threw and which landed in the road behind the remains of the jeep.

The two soldiers had been thrown out of the wreckage. They were both alive, though broken and bleeding. One of them was trying to draw his side-arm. Karl walked slowly towards him, his .303 cocked. With a casual movement of his foot he kicked the pistol from the sergeant's hand as the man tried to get the hammer back. The sergeant's face was covered in blood. Out of the mess stared two blue eyes. The ruined lips moved, but there were no words. Near by, the corporal sat up.

The rest of the group joined Karl.

'I'm glad you weren't killed,' Karl said in his guttural English.

'Aaah!' said the corporal. 'You dirty Arab bastards.' He hugged his broken right arm.

'We are Jews,' said David, ripping his mask down.

'I don't believe it,' said the corporal.

'We are going to hang you,' said Karl, pointing at the palms, visible beyond the bank.

David went to look at the jeep. The whole back section was buckled and one of the wheels was off. Some piece of machinery still gasped under the bonnet. David reached into the jeep and turned the engine off. There was a smell of leaking petrol. 'It's not much use to us,' said David.

'What do you bloody mean?' said the corporal in horror. 'What the fuck do you bloody mean?'

'It's a message,' said Karl, 'from us to you.'

Michael Moorcock

– I've made up my mind, says Karl's friend as he busily massages Karl's buttocks. – I'm going to take you with me when I go home. You'll like it. It isn't everyone I meet I'd do that for.

Karl makes no reply. He is feeling rather detached. He doesn't remember when he felt so relaxed.

What would you do? (14)

You are very attracted to a girl of about seventeen who is the daughter of one of your parents' friends. The girl lives with her parents in the country. You take every opportunity to see her (you are not much older than her, yourself) but although you take her out to formal parties a couple of times and to the cinema once, you can't be sure how she feels towards you. The more you see of her the more you want to make love to her. But you realize she is quite young and you don't want to see yourself in the role of the seducer. You would feel perfectly happy about it if she made the first move. But she is shy. She plainly likes you. Probably she is waiting for you to make the first move. You are passing through the part of the world where she and her parents live and you decide to visit the house and ask if you can stay the night, as it's quite late. You rather hope that, at last, you will be able to find an opportunity to make love to the girl.

You arrive at the house. The door is opened by the girl's mother, an attractive woman in her early forties. She is very welcoming. You tell her your story and she says that of course you can stay, for as long as you like. She regrets that you will not be able to see her husband because he is away for some days on a business trip. Her daughter is out – 'with one of her boyfriends'. You feel disappointed.

You have dinner with the mother and you and she drink quite a lot of wine. The mother makes no doubt about the fact that she finds you attractive. After dinner, sitting together on a couch, you find that you are holding hands with her.

You have a mixture of feelings. She is attractive and you do feel that you want to make love, but you're rather afraid of her experience. Secondly, you feel that if you sleep with her, it will complicate the situation so much that you will never have an opportunity to make love to her daughter, whom you feel you could easily fall in love with. You also need the mother's good will.

Would you get up from the couch and make an excuse in order to go to bed? Would you make love to the mother up to a point and then claim that you were too drunk to go further? Would you pretend to be ill? Would you give in completely to your desires of the moment and sleep with the mother, in spite of the inevitable situation which this would lead to? Would you hope that the daughter would be so intrigued by your having slept with her mother that she would make it clear that she, too, wanted to sleep with you (you have heard that such things happen)? Or would you feel that the whole problem was too much, leave the house and resolve never to see any member of the family ever again?

15. Big Bang in Budapest: 1956: Leaving Home

In the Troodos hills in the west of Cyprus, the job is being carried out by Number 45 Commando of the Royal Marines, together with two companies of the Gordon Highlanders. The Commando arrived in Cyprus last September; its headquarters are now in Platres, near Troodos. Its commanding officer, Lt.-Col. N. H. Tailyour, DSO, recalled its record to date. 'In early November we took the first haul of EOKA arms. We shot and captured the brother of the Bishop of Kyrenia (who was deported with the Archbishop) while he was trying to break through a cordon with some important documents . . . So far we have killed two men . . . We have been ambushed seven times, and lost one marine killed and seven wounded.' A lot more has happened since then.

Picture Post, 7 April 1956

'My daughter was one of the ten people who went into the Radio building. They were asked to wait on the balcony while the business was discussed. The students below thought they had been pushed out. They tried to crush through the door and the police opened fire. I did not see my daughter fall down. They said she fell and the security police carried her away. She may not be dead. Perhaps it were better she were.'

Hungarian woman, Picture Post, 5 November 1956

Picture Post brings you this week the most dramatic exclusive of the war in Egypt – the first documentary record of life behind the Egyptian lines after the invasion of Port Said. How this story was obtained by correspondent William Richardson and photographer Max Scheler is in itself one of the remarkable stories of the campaign. While the fires at Port Said still burned, Richardson was at the British front line at El Cäp watching the Egyptians dig in 1,000 yards south. Three weeks later he stood at those same Egyptian positions watching the British across the lines and getting a briefing on the campaign from Brigadier Anin Helmini, one of Nasser's most brilliant young generals. Yet to negotiate that 1,000 yards between the British and Egyptian lines Richardson had to travel some 5,600 times that distance, flying from Port Said to Cyprus and from there to Athens and Rome. There the Egyptian Embassy granted him a visa after he told them he had been in Port Said and wanted to see both sides. In a month, he was accredited to three forces – British, Egyptian and United Nations, a total of 12 nationalities in uniform.

Picture Post, 17 December 1956

– *Is your only pleasure making me feel pleasure? Karl asks.*
– *Of course not.*
– *Well, you don't seem to be getting any fun out of this. Not physical, anyway.*
– *Cerebral pleasures can be just as nice. It depends what turns you on, surely?*
Karls turns over. – There's something pretty repressed about you, he says. – Something almost dead.
– *You know how to be offensive don't you? A short time ago you were just an ordinary London lad. Now you're behaving like the bitchiest pansy I ever saw.*
– *Maybe I like the role.*
Karl is twenty. He scents escape at last. He has survived through the war, through the Communist takeover. Now there is a way out. He prays that nothing will happen to frustrate his plans this time . . .
– *And maybe I don't. When I said you could have anything you wanted I didn't mean a bra and suspender belt. The black man turns away in disgust.*
– *You said anything was worth trying, didn't you? I think I'd look rather nifty. A few hormone jabs, a pump or two of silicone in my chest. I'd be a luscious, tropical beauty. Wouldn't you love me more?*
Karl is twenty. His brain is sharp. He tears up his party membership card. Time for a change.
– *Stop that! orders Karl's friend. – Or I won't bother. You can leave now.*
– *Who's being narrow-minded, then!*

Karl was twenty. Both his mother and his father had been killed in the pre-war pogroms. He had survived in Budapest by changing his name and keeping undercover until the war was over. When the new government was installed, he became a member of the Communist party, but he didn't tell his friends. That would have been pointless, since part of his work involved making discreet enquiries for the Russian-controlled security department on the Westbahnhof.

Now he was working out his best route to the Austrian border. He had joined with his fellow-students in the least aggressive of the demonstrations against the Russians and had established himself as a patriot. When the Russians won – as they must win – he would be in Vienna on his way to America. Other Hungarians would vouch for him – a victim, like themselves, of Russian imperialism.

Earlier that day he had contacted the hotel where the tourists were staying. They told him that there were some cars due to leave for Austria in the afternoon by the big suspension bridge near the hotel. He had described himself as a 'known patriot' whom the secret police were even now hunting down. They had been sympathetic and assured him of their help.

Lenin Street was comparatively quiet after the fighting which, yesterday, had blasted it into ruins. He picked his way through the rubble, ducking behind a fallen tree as a Russian tank appeared, its treads squeaking protest as they struck obstacle after obstacle.

Karl reached the riverside. A few people came running up the boulevard but there didn't seem to be anyone behind them. Karl decided it was safe to continue. He could see the bridge from here. Not far to go.

There came the sudden slamming cacophony of automatic cannon a few blocks to the east; a howl from a hundred throats at least; the decisive rattle of machine guns; the sound of running feet. From out of a street opposite him Karl saw about fifty freedom fighters, most of them armed with rifles and a few with tommy-guns, dash like flushed rats on to the boulevard, glance around and then run towards the bridge. He cursed them. Why couldn't they have fled in the other direction?

But he decided to follow them, at a distance.

On the suspension bridge he saw some tanks. He hoped they had been immobilized. Bodies were being thrown over the side into the Danube. He hoped they were Russian bodies. He began to look for the cars. A new Citroën, green, one of the tourists had told him, and a Volkswagen. He peered through the gaps in the ranks of the running men. He began to run himself.

And then the automatic cannon started once more. This time it was directly ahead and it was joined by the guns of the tanks. The freedom fighters fell down. Some got up and crawled into doorways, firing back. Karl fell flat, rolling to the railings and looking to see if there was a way down to the river. He might be able to swim the rest of the distance. He looked across the Danube. He could still make it. He would survive.

Tanks came towards him, he made a vain attempt to get through the railings and then lay still, hoping they would think him dead.

More rifle and tommy-gun fire. More Russian gunfire. A shout. A strangled scream.

Karl opened his eyes. One of the tanks was on fire, its camouflaged sides scorched, its red star smeared with blood. The tank's driver had tried to get out of his turret and had been shot to pieces. The other tanks rumbled on. The fighting became more distant. Karl glanced at his watch. Not more than five minutes before the cars left.

He got cautiously to his feet.

A Russian's head appeared in the turret behind the corpse of the driver. The man's flat features were tormented. He was doubtless badly wounded. He saw Karl. Karl put up his hands to show that he was unarmed. He smiled an ingratiating smile. The Russian aimed a pistol at him. Karl tried to think what to do.

He felt the impact as the bullet struck his skull. He went back against the railings and collapsed without seeing the Danube again.

– You seem to think I'm trying to corrupt your morals or something. You've got hold of the wrong end of the stick. I was simply talking about expanding your range of choices. I don't know what to make of you, Karl.

– Then we're even.

– I might have to change my mind about you. I'm sorry, but that's the way it is. If I'm to adopt you, it will be on very strict terms. I don't want you to embarrass me.

– That goes for me, too.

– Now, don't be insolent, Karl.

What would you do? (15)

You live in a poor country, though you yourself are comparatively rich.

There is a famine in the country and many of the people are starving. You want to help them. You can afford to give the local people in the village about fifty pounds. But the number of people in the village is at least two hundred. If each receives part of the money you have, it will buy them enough to live on for perhaps another four days.

Would you give them the money on condition it was spent on the people most in need? Or on condition that it was spent on the children? Or would you select a handful of people you thought deserved the money most? Or would you hand it over to them and ask them to divide as they saw fit?

16. Camping in Kenya: 1959: Smoke

Here is the grim record as far as it can be added up in figures: more than a thousand Africans hanged for serious crimes, 9,252 Mau Mau convicts jailed for serious offences, and 44,000 'detainees', guilty of lesser Mau Mau offences, in rehabilitation prison camps. In these camps, in carefully graded groups, Mau Mau adherents are re-educated as decent citizens . . . To make return possible mental attitudes have to be changed . . . Perhaps 'soul-washing' is not too strong a word for an organized process aimed at teaching civilized behaviour and the duties, as well as the rights, of citizenship . . .

Soldiers and police have won the long battle of the bush against ill-armed men fighting for what they believe to be a good cause. All but the broken remnants, under their broken leader Dedan Kimathi, have been killed or rounded up. The battle to turn Mau Mau adherents into decent citizens goes well.

But the battle to remove the underlying causes, social and economic, of the anti-white hate that created Mau Mau, will go on for long years. There, too, a hopeful beginning has been made. Princess Margaret's visit marks not just the end of a long nightmare, but the beginning of a new era of multi-racial integration – and of fairer shares for the African – in lovely Kenya.

Picture Post, 22 October 1956

If the Malayan and Korean campaigns had drawn most attention during the early part of the 1950s, the British Army had had much to do elsewhere. In Kenya the Mau Mau gangs, recruited from the Kikuyu tribe, had taken to the dense rain forests from which they made sorties to attack Europeans and Africans. The Kikuyu were land hungry. Their discontent was used to further the aspirations of urban Africans for political independence. Over eight years, 1952–60, British battalions, batteries and engineer squadrons, supported by small but intensely-worked communications and administrative teams, broke the movement in alliance with a devoted police and civil government organization, many of them Africans or

Asian settlers. Only when this had been done was the cause of Kenyan independence advanced.

Brig. Anthony H. Farrar-Hockley, DO, MBE, MC, Arthur Baker, 1970 Ch. 32: *After the War, History of the British Army* ed. Brig. Peter Young and Lt.-Col.

J. P. Lawford

— You're right. There's no such thing as innocence, says Karl.

— Absolutely. It's as abstract as 'justice' and 'virtue' – or, for that matter, 'morality'.

— Right. There's certainly no justice!

— And far too much morality!

They laugh.

— I didn't realize you had blue eyes, says Karl, astonished.

— They're only blue in some lights. Look, I'll turn my head. See?

— They're still blue.

— What about this? Green? Brown?

— Blue.

Karl had reached his majority. He's twenty-one. Signed on for another seven years' stint in the Mob. There's no life like it!

— You're just telling me that, says his friend anxiously. – How about now?

— Well, I suppose you could say they looked a bit greenish, says Karl kindly.

— It's envy, old chap, at your lovely big bovine brown tones.

— Give us a kiss.

Twenty-one and the world his oyster. Cyprus, Aden, Singapore. Wherever the British Army's needed. Karl is a sergeant already. And he could do the officer exam soon. He's used to commanding, by now. Twice decorated? No sweat!

— Where?

— Don't make me laugh.

Karl was twenty-one. His mother was forty-five. His father was forty-seven. They lived in Hendon, Middlesex, in a semi-detached house which Karl's father, who had never been out of work in his life, had begun to buy just before the war. His father had been doing indispensable war work and so had not had to serve in the Army (he was a boiler engineer). His father had thoughtfully changed his name to Gower in 1939, partly because it sounded too German, partly because, you never knew, if the Germans won, it sounded too Jewish. Not, of course, that it was a Jewish name. Karl's dad denied any such suggestion vehemently. It was an old Austrian name, resembling a name attached to one of the most ancient noble houses in Vienna. That's what Karl's grandfather had said, anyway. Karl had been called after his grandad. Karl's father's name was English – Arnold.

Karl had been in the Army since he had joined up as a boy-entrant in 1954. He had seen a lot of service since then. But for the past two years he'd been out in Kenya, clearing up the Mau Mau business, which seemed to drag on for ever. Off duty, it was a smashing life. The worst of the terrorism was over and it wasn't nearly so dangerous as it had been. Karl had an Indian girlfriend in Nairobi and he got there as often as he could to fuck the shit out of her. She was a hot little bitch though he had a sneaking suspicion she'd given him his last dose of crabs. You could never tell with crabs, mind you, so he gave her the benefit of the doubt. What a muff! What tits! It gave you a hard-on just thinking about them. Lovely!

The jeep pulled up at the gates of the compound. Another day's work was beginning. Karl was part of the special intelligence team working closely with the Kenya Police in this area, where there was still a bit of Mau Mau mischief. Privately, Karl thought it would go on for ever. They didn't have a hope in hell of governing themselves. He looked at the inmates behind the barbed wire. It made you smile to think about it. Offering it, that was different, if you had to keep them under control. Of course you can have independence – in two million bloody years! Ho, ho, ho!

He scratched his crotch with his swagger stick and grinned to himself as his driver presented their pass. The jeep bumped its way over the uneven mud track into the compound.

The Kikuyu prisoners stood, or sat, or leaned around, looking with dull eyes at the jeep as it pulled up outside the main intelligence hut. Some distance away, squatting on the ground, were about a hundred natives listening to Colonel Wibberley giving them their usual brainwashing (or what would be a brainwashing if they had any brains to wash, thought Karl. He knew bloody well that you released the buggers as decontaminated only to get half of them back sooner or later with blood on their bloody hands). Oh, what a horrible lot they were, in their reach-me-down flannel shorts, their tattered shirts, their old tweed jackets, their bare scabby feet, some of them with silly grins all over their ugly mugs. He saluted Private Peterson who was on guard outside the hut as usual. He already felt like an officer.

'Morning, sarge,' said Peterson as he passed. Bastard!

Corporal Anderson, all red and sweaty as usual, was on duty at the desk when Karl entered. Anderson always looked as if he'd just been caught in the act of pulling his plonker – shifty, seedy.

'You are an unwholesome little sod, Corporal Anderson,' said Karl by way of greeting. Corporal Anderson tittered. 'What's new, then? Blimey, couldn't you get a stronger bulb, I can't see for looking.'

'I'll put a chit in, sarge.'

'And hurry up about it. Is old Lailu ready to talk yet?'

'I haven't been in there this morning, sarge. The lieutenant . . .'

'What about the bleeding lieutenant?'

'He's away, sarge. That's all.'

'Bloody good fucking thing, too, little shit-faced prick, little upper-class turd,' mumbled Karl to himself as he went through the papers on his desk. Same problem as yesterday. Find out what Lailu knew about the attack on the Kuanda farm a week ago. Lailu had been in the raid, all right, because he'd been recognized. And he'd used to work at the farm. He claimed to have been in his own village, but that was a lie. Who could prove it? And he'd been in the camp more than once. He was a known Mau Mau. And he was a killer. Or knew who the killers were, which was the same thing.

'I'll have a word with him, I think,' said Karl, sipping the tea the corporal brought him. 'I'll have to get unpleasant today if he don't open his fucking mouth. And I'll have him all to my fucking self, won't I, corp?'

'Yes, sarge,' said corp, his thick lips writhing, his hot, shifty eyes seething, as if Karl had caught him out at some really nasty form of self-abuse.

'Ugh, you are horrible,' said Karl, automatically.

'Yes, sarge.'

Karl snorted with laughter. 'Go and tell them to take our little black brother into the special room, will you?'

'Yes, sarge,' Corporal Anderson went through the door into the back of the hut. Karl heard him talking to the guards. A bit later Anderson came back.

'He's ready, sarge.'

'Thank you, corporal,' said Karl in his crisp, decisive voice. He put his cigarettes and matches in the top pocket of his shirt, picked up his swagger stick and crossed the mud floor to the inner door.

'Oh,' he said, hesitating before entering, 'if our good lieutenant should come calling, let me know would you, corporal?'

'Yes, sarge, I get you.'

'And don't pick your nose while I'm gone, will you, corporal?'

'No, sarge.'

Karl thought about that little Indian bint in Nairobi. He'd give a lot to be taking her knickers down at this moment, getting her legs open and fucking the arse off of her. But duty called.

He whistled as he walked along the short, dark passage to the special room. It was bleeding hot in here, worse than a bloody native hut. It stank of fucking Kikuyu.

He gave the guard at the door of the special room his officer's salute, with the swagger stick touching the peak of his well set cap.

He went into the special room and turned on the light.

Lailu sat on the bench, his bony knees sticking up at a peculiar angle, his eyes wide and white. There was a lot of sweat in his thin moustache.

'Hello, Mr Lailu,' said Karl with his cold grin, 'how are you feeling this fine summer morning? A bit warm? Sorry we can't open a window for you, but you can see for yourself, there isn't one. That's probably against fire regulations. You could complain about that. Do you want to complain to me, Mr Lailu?'

Lailu shook his black head.

'Because you've got your rights, you know. Lots and lots of rights. You've heard the lectures? Yes, of course you have, more than once, because you've been here more than once, haven't you, Mr Lailu?'

Lailu made no response at all to this. Karl went up to him and stood very close, looking down on him. Lailu didn't look back. Karl grabbed the man's ear and twisted it so that Lailu's lips came together tightly. 'Because I remember my trademark, you see, Mr Lailu. That little scar, that's not a tribal scar, is it, Mr Lailu? That little scar isn't a Mau Mau scar, is it? That is a Sergeant Gower scar, eh?'

'Yes, boss,' said Lailu. 'Yes, boss.'

'Good.'

Karl stepped back and leaned against the door of the special room. 'We're going to keep everything informal, Mr Lailu. You know your rights, don't you?'

'Yes, boss.'

'Good.'

Karl grinned down on Lailu again. 'You were at the Kuanda farm last week, weren't you?'

'No, boss.'

'Yes you were!' Karl began to breathe quickly, the swagger stick held firmly in his two hands. 'Weren't you?'

'No, boss. Lailu not Mau Mau, boss. Lailu good boy, boss.'

'Yes, a good little liar.' The swagger stick left Karl's right hand almost without him thinking about it. It struck Lailu on the top of his head. Lailu whimpered. 'Now I won't do that again, Lailu, because that's not the way I work, is it?'

'Don't know, boss.'

'Is it?'

'No, boss.'

'Good.' Karl took out his packet of Players and selected one. He put the cigarette between his lips and he put the packet carefully back into his pocket. He took out his matches and he lit the cigarette so that it was burning just right. He put the matches back in his pocket and neatly he buttoned the pocket. He drew a deep puff on the cigarette. 'Smoke, Lailu?'

Lailu trembled all over. 'No, boss. Please.'

'Shit, Lailu? You look as if you feel like one. Use the pot over there. Get them manky pants down, Lailu.'

'Please, boss.'

Karl moved quickly. It was always best to move quickly. He grabbed the top of the Kikuyu's shorts and ripped them down to his knees, exposing the shrivelled, scarred genitals.

'Oh, I have been here before, haven't I, Lailu?'

— *That's better, says Karl.*

— *You're insatiable, says his friend admiringly. I've got to admit it, for all your faults.*

— *What's the time? Karl asks. — My watch has stopped.*

— *It must be coming up for morning, says his friend.*

What would you do? (16)

You and your sister have been captured by your enemies. They are brutal enemies.

They want information from you concerning your friends. They say they will make you responsible for your sister's safety. If you tell them all they wish to know she will go free. If you do not they will humiliate, terrorize and torture her in every way they know.

You are aware that should they catch your friends they will do the same thing to at least some of them, perhaps all of them.

Whom will you betray?

17. So Long Son Lon: 1968: Babies

Quite apart from the enormous present importance of South Vietnam and our actions there, I have often reflected – as one who was tempted to become a professional historian – that the story of Vietnam, of South-East Asia, and of American policy there forms an extraordinarily broad case history involving almost all the major problems that have affected the world as a whole in the past 25 years. For the strands of the Vietnam history include the characteristics of French colonial control compared to colonial control elsewhere, the end of the colonial period, the interrelation and competition of nationalism and communism, our relation to the Soviet Union and Communist China and their relationships with each other, our relation to the European colonial power – France – and at least since 1954 – the relation of Vietnam to the wider question of national independence and self-determination in South-East Asia and indeed throughout Asia . . .

. . . So all over South-East Asia there is today a sense of confidence – to which Drew Middleton again testified from his trip. Time has been bought, and used. But that confidence is not solid or secure for the future. It would surely be disrupted if we were, in President Johnson's words, to permit a Communist take-over in South Vietnam either through withdrawal or 'under the cloak of a meaningless agreement.' If, on the contrary, we proceed on our present course – with measured military actions and with every possible non-military measure, and searching always for an avenue to peace – the prospects for a peaceful and secure South-East Asia now appear brighter than they have been at any time since the nations of the area were established on an independent basis.

William P. Bundy, *The Path to Vietnam*: An address given before the National Student Association convention held at the University of Maryland, 15 August 1967, United States Information Service, American Embassy, London, August 1967

'We were all psyched up, and as a result when we got there the shooting started, almost as a chain reaction. The majority of us had expected to meet VC combat troops, but this did not turn out to be so . . . After they got in the village, I guess you could say that the men were out of control.'

G. I. Dennis Conti

'They just kept walking towards us . . . You could hear the little girl saying, "No, no . . ." All of a sudden, the GIs opened up and cut them down.'

Ron Haeberle, reporter

'It's just that they didn't know what they were supposed to do; killing them seemed like a good idea, so they did it. The old lady who fought so hard was probably a VC. Maybe it was just her daughter.'

Jay Roberts, reporter – Seymour M. Hersh, *'My Lai 4*: a Report on the Massacre and Its Aftermath', *Harper's Magazine*, May 1970

Mr Daniel Ellsberg will surrender tomorrow in Boston where he lives. He was charged on Friday with being unlawfully in possession of secret documents, and a warrant was issued for his arrest. Since he was named on June 16, by a former reporter of the 'New York Times,' as the man who provided the paper with its copy of a Pentagon report, Mr Ellsberg and his wife have been in hiding. The Pentagon is about to hand over its Vietnam study to congress for confidential perusal. On Saturday the Justice Department sought to convince the court that indiscriminate publication of further documents from the study would endanger troops in South Vietnam and prejudice the procedures for obtaining the release of prisoners.

Guardian, 28 June 1971

– You're not slow, are you? says Karl's friend. – And to think I was worried. Now I think I'll get some sleep.

– Not yet, says Karl.

– Yes, now. I'm not feeling too well, as it happens.

– You are looking a big grey. Karl inspects the black man's flesh.

Compared with his own skin, it is quite pale.

Karl is twenty-two and it's his last few months in the army. The past five months have been spent in Vietnam. Although he's seen only one VC in that time, he's tired and tense and fearful. He jokes a lot, like his buddies. There is heat, sticky sweat, jungle, mud, flies, poverty, death, but no Viet Cong. And this is a place reputedly thick with them.

– I'll be all right when I've rested, says Karl's friend. – You've worn me out, that's all.

Karl reaches out the index finger of his right hand and traces his nail over his friend's lips. – You can't be that tired.

Twenty-two and weary. A diet of little more than cold C-rations for weeks at a stretch. No change of clothing. Crashing around in the jungle. For nothing. It wasn't like the John Wayne movies. Or maybe it was. The shit and the heat – and then the action coming fast and hard. The victory. The tough captain proving he was right to drive the men so hard, after all. The bowed heads as they honoured dead buddies. Not many could stop the tears . . . But so far all they had was the shit and the heat.

Karl's friend opens his lips. Karl hasn't noticed before that his friend's teeth are rather stained.

– Just let me rest a little.

Karl was twenty-two. His mother was forty-five. His father was forty-four. His father managed a hardware store in Phoenix, Arizona. His mother was a housewife.

Karl was on a big mission at last. He felt that if he survived the mission then it would all be over and he could look forward to going home, back to his job as his father's assistant. It was all he wanted.

He sat shoulder to shoulder with his buddies in the shivering chopper as it flew them to the combat area. He tried to read the tattered *X-Men* comic book he had brought along, but it was hard to concentrate. Nobody, among the other members of his platoon, was talking much.

Karl's hands were sweating and there was dark grease on them from the helicopter, from his rifle. The grease left his fingerprints on the pages of the comic book. He tucked the book into his shirt and buttoned it up. He smoked a joint handed to him by Bill Leinster who, like two-thirds of the platoon, was black. The joint didn't do anything for him. He shifted the extra belt of M16 ammo to a more comfortable position round his neck. He was overloaded with equipment. It would almost be worth a battle to get rid of some of the weight of cartridges he was carrying.

He wondered what would be happening in Son Lon now. The hamlet had already been hit by the morning's artillery barrage and the gunships had gone in ahead. The first platoon must have arrived already. Karl was in the second platoon of four. Things would be warming up by the time he landed.

The note of the chopper's engine changed and Karl knew they were going down. He thought he heard gunfire. He wiped the grease off his hands on to the legs of his pants. He took a grip on his M16. Everyone else was beginning to straighten up, ready themselves. None of the faces showed much emotion and Karl hoped that his face looked the same.

'After what they did to Goldberg,' said Bill Leinster in a masculine growl, 'I'm going to get me a lot of ears.'

Karl grinned at him.

The chopper's deck tilted a little as the machine settled. Sergeant Grossman got the door open. Now Karl could hear the firing quite clearly, but he could only see a few trees through the door. 'Okay, let's go,' said Sergeant Grossman grimly. He sprayed a few rounds into the nearby trees and jumped out. Karl was the fifth man to follow him. There were eight other helicopters on the ground, a patch of mud entirely surrounded by trees. Karl could see four big gunships firing at something ahead. Two more big black transports were landing. The noise of their rotors nearly drowned the noise of the guns. It seemed that the first platoon was still in the landing zone. Karl saw Sergeant Grossman run across to where Lieutenant Snider was standing with his men. They conferred for a few moments and then Grossman ran back. Snider's platoon moved off into the jungle. After waiting a moment or two Grossman ordered his men forward, entering the line of trees to the left and at an angle to where Snider's men had gone in. Karl assumed that the VC in this area had either been killed or had retreated back to the hamlet. There was no firing from the enemy as yet. But he kept himself alert. They could be anywhere in the jungle and they could attack in a dozen different ways. He suddenly got a craving for a Coors. Only a Coors in a giant-size schooner, the glass misted with frost. And a Kool, enjoyed in that downtown bar where his father's friends always drank on Saturday nights. That was what he'd have when he got home. The firing in front intensified. The first platoon must have met head-on with the VC. Karl peered through the trees but could still see nothing. Sergeant Grossman waved at them to proceed with increased caution. The comic book was scratching his stomach. He regretted putting it in there. He glanced back at Bill Leinster. Leinster had the only grenade launcher in this team. Karl wondered if Leinster shouldn't be ahead of them, with the machine gunner and the sergeant. On the other hand, their rear might not be protected by the squad supposed to be flanking them and there was no cover on either side, as far as he knew, though technically there should have been. You could be hit from anywhere. He began to inspect the ground for mines, walking carefully in the footprints of the man in front of him. Sergeant Grossman paused and for a second they halted. Karl could now see a flash of red brick through the trees. They had reached the hamlet of Son Lon. There was a lot of groundfire.

Suddenly Karl was ready. He knew he would do well on this mission. His whole body was alert.

They moved into the hamlet.

The first thing they saw were VC bodies in black silk pyjamas and coolie hats. They were mostly middle-aged men and some women. There didn't seem to be too many weapons about. Maybe these had been collected up by the first platoon.

Two or three hootches were burning fitfully where they had been blasted by grenades and subsequently set on fire. A couple of the red brick houses bore evidence of having been in the battle. Outside one of them lay the bloody corpse of a kid of around eight or nine. That was the worst part, when they used kids to draw your fire, or even throw grenades at you. More firing came from the left; Karl turned, ducking and ready, his rifle raised, but no attack came. They proceeded warily into the village. Leinster, on command from Grossman, loaded his grenade launcher and started firing into the huts and houses as they passed, in case any VC should still be in there. It was menacingly safe, thought Karl, wondering what the VC were waiting for. Or maybe there hadn't been as many slopes in the hamlet as Captain Heffer had anticipated. Or maybe they were in the paddy-fields on the left and right of the village.

Karl really wanted to fire at something. Just one VC would do. It would justify everything else.

They entered the centre of the village, the plaza. Lieutenant Snider and his men were already there, rounding up civilians. There were a lot of bodies around the plaza, mainly women and children. Karl was used to seeing corpses, but he had never seen so many. He was filled with disgust for the Vietnamese. They really had no human feelings. They were just like the Japs had been, and the Chinese in Korea. What was the point of fighting for them?

One of the kids in the group which had been rounded up ran forward. He held a coke bottle in his hand, offering it to the nearest soldier. The soldier was Henry Tabori. Karl knew him.

Tabori backed away from the boy and fired his M16 from the hip. The M16 was an automatic. The boy got all of it, staggering backwards and falling into the gang of villagers. Some of the women and old men started to shout. Some fell to their knees, wringing their hands. Karl had seen pictures of them doing that. Lieutenant Snider turned away with a shrug. Tabori put a new magazine into his rifle. By this time the other five men were firing into the ranks of civilians. They poured scores of rounds into them. Blood appeared on the jerking bodies. Bits of chipped bone flew.

Karl saw Sergeant Grossman watching the slaughter. Grossman's face was thoughtful. Then Grossman said: 'Okay, Leinster. Give it to 'em.' He indicated the huts which had so far not been blasted. Leinster loaded his grenade launcher and began sending grenades through every doorway he could see. People started to run out. Grossman shot them down as they came. His machine-gunner opened up. One by one the other boys started firing. Karl dropped to a kneeling position, tucked his rifle hard against his shoulder, set the gun to automatic, and sent seventeen rounds into an old man as he stumbled from his hootch, his hands raised in front of his face, his legs streaming with blood. He put a fresh magazine into the rifle. The next time he fired he got a woman. The woman, with a dying action, rolled over on to a baby. The baby wasn't much good without its mother. Karl stepped closer and fired half his magazine into the baby. All the huts and houses were smoking, but people kept running out. Karl killed some more of them. Their numbers seemed to be endless.

Grossman shouted for them to cease firing, then led them at a run out of the plazas and along a dirt road. 'Get 'em out of the huts,' Grossman told his men. 'Round the bastards up.'

Karl and a negro called Keller went into one of the huts and kicked the family until they moved out into the street. There were two old men, an old woman, two young girls, a boy and a woman with a baby. Karl and Keller waved their rifles and made the family join the others in the street. They did not wait for Grossman's orders to fire.

Some of the women and the older girls and boys tried to put

themselves between the soldiers and the smaller children. The soldiers continued to fire until they were sure they were all dead. Leinster began to giggle. Soon they were all giggling. They left the pile of corpses behind them and some of them swaggered as they walked. 'We sure have got a lot of VC today,' said Keller, wiping his forehead with a rag.

Karl looked back. He saw a figure rising from the pile of corpses. It was a girl of about thirteen, dressed in a black smock and black pyjamas. She looked bewildered. Her eyes met Karl's. Karl turned away. But he could still see her eyes. He whirled, dropped to one knee, took careful aim, and shot her head off. He thought: They've all got to die now. What have they got to live for, anyway? He was putting them out of their misery. He thought: If I don't shoot them, they'll see that it was me who shot the others. He reached up and pulled his helmet more firmly over his eyes. It was not his fault. They had told him he would be shooting VC. It was too late, now.

They left the hamlet and were on a road. They saw a whole lot of women and children in a ditch between the road and a paddy-field. Karl was the first to fire at them. Leinster finished them off with his grenades. Only Karl and Leinster had bothered to fire that time. Nobody looked at anybody else for a moment. Then Grossman said: 'It's a VC village. All we're doing is stopping them from growing up to be VC.'

Leinster snorted. 'Yeah.'

'It's true,' said Sergeant Grossman. He looked around him at the paddy-fields as if addressing the hundreds of hidden VC he thought must be there. 'It's true. We've got to waste them all this time.'

Another group of men emerged on the other side of the paddy-field. They had two grenade launchers which they were firing at random into the ground and making the mud and plants gout up.

Karl looked at the corpses in the ditch. They were really mangled.

They went back into the village. They found a hut with three old women in it. They wasted the hut and its occupants. They found a two-year-old kid, screaming. They wasted him. They found a fifteen-year-old girl. After Leinster and another man called Aitken had torn her clothes off and raped her, they wasted her. Karl didn't fuck her because he couldn't get a hard-on, but he was the one who shot her tits to ribbons.

'Jesus Christ!' grinned Karl as he and Leinster paused for a moment. 'What a day!'

They both laughed. They wasted two water-buffalo and a cow. Leinster blew a hole in the cow with his launcher. 'That's a messy cow!' said Karl.

Karl and Leinster went hunting. They were looking for anything which moved. Karl was haunted by the faces of the living. These, and not the dead, were the ghosts that had to be exorcized. He would not be accused by them. He kicked aside the corpses of women to get at their babies. He bayoneted the babies. He and Leinster went into the jungle and found some wounded kids. They wasted the kids as they tried to stumble away.

They went back to the village and found Lieutenant Snider talking to Captain Heffer. They were laughing, too. Captain Heffer's pants were covered in mud to the thigh. He had evidently been in one of the paddies.

The gunships and communications choppers were still thundering away overhead. Every two or three minutes you heard gunfire from somewhere. Karl couldn't see any more gooks. For a moment he had an impulse to shoot Lieutenant Snider and Captain Heffer. If they had turned and seen him, he might have done so. But Leinster tapped him on the shoulder, as if he guessed what he was thinking, and jerked his thumb to indicate they should try the outlying hootches. Karl went with him part of the way, but he had begun to feel tired. He was hoping the battle would be over soon. He saw an unshattered coke bottle lying on the ground. He reached out to pick it up before it occurred to him that it might be booby-trapped. He looked at it for a long time, struggling with his desire for a drink and his caution.

He trudged along the alley between the ruined huts, the sprawled and shattered corpses. Why hadn't the VC appeared? It was their fault. He had been geared to fight. The sound of gunfire went on and on and on.

Karl found that he had left the village. He thought he had better try to rejoin his squad. They ought to retain military discipline. It was the only way to make sense of this. He tried to go back, but he couldn't. He dropped his rifle. He leant down to pick it up. On either side of him the rice paddies gleamed in the sun. He reached out for the rifle, but his boot caught it by accident and it fell into a ditch. He climbed into the ditch to get the rifle. He found it. It was covered in slime. He knew it would take him an age to clean it. He realized that he had begun to cry. He sat in the ditch and he shook with weeping.

A little later Grossman found him.

Grossman kneeled at the side of the ditch and patted Karl's shoulder. 'What's the matter, boy?'

Karl couldn't answer.

'Come on, son,' said Grossman kindly. He picked Karl's slimy rifle out of the ditch and slung it over his own shoulder. 'There isn't much left to do here.' He helped Karl to his feet. Karl drew a deep, shuddering breath.

'Don't worry, kid,' said Grossman. 'Please . . .'

He seemed to be begging Karl, as if Karl were reminding him of something he didn't want to remember.

'Now, you stop all that, you hear? It ain't manly.' He spoke gruffly and kept patting Karl's shoulder, but there was an edge to his voice, too.

'Sorry,' said Karl at last as they moved back to the village.

'Nobody's blaming you,' said the sergeant. 'Nobody's blaming nobody. It's what happens, that's all.'

'I'm sorry,' said Karl again.

– But we have got to blame somebody sooner or later, says Karl. – We need victims. Somebody's got to suffer. 'Now lieutenant, will you kindly tell the Court just what you had to do with the Human Condition? We are waiting, lieutenant? Why are we not as happy as we might be, lieutenant? Give your answer briefly and clearly.'

– What the hell are you talking about? says his friend, waking up and yawning.

– I didn't say anything, says Karl. – You must have been dreaming. Do you feel better?

– I'm not sure.

– You don't look it.

What would you do? (17)

You have been travelling in the desert.

There has been an accident. Your car has overturned and the friend with whom you were travelling has been badly hurt. He is almost certain to die.

Would you remain with him and hope that rescue would come soon?

Would you leave him what water you have, making him as comfortable as possible and setting off to find help, knowing he will probably be dead by the time you return?

Would you decide that, since he was as good as dead, you might as well take the water and food with you, as it will give you a better chance?

Would you remain in the shade of the wreck, knowing that this would be the wisest thing to do, but deciding not to waste your water on your dying friend?

18. London Life: 2000: City of Shadows

One of the happiest answers recorded of living statesmen was that in which a well known minister recommended to an alarmed interrogator the 'study of large maps'. The danger which seems so imminent, so ominous, when we read about it in a newspaper article or in the report of a speech, grows reassuringly distant when considered through the medium of a good sized chart.

Walter Richards, *Her Majesty's Army: Indian and Colonial Forces*: A Descriptive Account, J. S. Virtue & Co., 1890

If SNCC had said Negro Power or Colored Power, white folks would've continued sleeping easy every night. But BLACK POWER! Black! That word. BLACK! And the visions came of alligator-infested swamps arched by primordial trees with moss dripping from the limbs and out of the depths of the swamp, the mire oozing from his skin, came the black monster and fathers told their daughters to be in by nine instead of nine-thirty. The visions came of big BLACK bucks running through the streets, raping everything white that wore a dress, burning, stealing, killing. BLACK POWER! My God, the niggers were gon' start paying white folks back. They hadn't forgotten 14-year-old Emmett Till being thrown into the Tallahatchie River. (We know what you and that chick threw off the Tallahatchie bridge, Billy Joe) with a gin mill tied around his ninety-pound body. They hadn't forgotten the trees bent low with the weight of black bodies on a lynching rope. They hadn't forgotten the black women walking down country roads who were shoved into cars, raped, and then pushed out, the threat of death ringing in their ears, the pain of hateful sex in their pelvis. The niggers hadn't forgotten and they wanted power. BLACK POWER!

Julius Lester, *Look Out, Whitey! Black Power's Gon' Get Your Mama*, Grove Press, 1969

– It's dawn, says Karl. – At last! I'm starving!
– You're beautiful, says his friend. – I want you for always.

– *Well* . . .

– *Always.*

– *Let's have some breakfast. What's the time? Do they serve it yet?*

– *They serve it whenever you want it, whatever you want.*

– *That's service.*

– *Karl?*

– *What?*

– *Please stay with me.*

– *I think I'll just have something simple. Boiled eggs and toast. Christ, can you hear my stomach rumbling?*

Karl is fifty-one. Lonely. All as far as he can see, the ruins stretch away, some black, some grey, some red, outlined against a cold sky. The world is over.

Karl's friend seizes him by the wrist. The grip hurts Karl, he tries to break free. Karl blinks. The pain swims through him, confusing him.

An old fifty-one. A scrawny fifty-one. And what has he survived for? What right has he had to survive when others have not? There is no justice . . .

– *Karl, you promised me, last night.*

– *I don't remember much of last night. It was a bit confused, last night, wasn't it?*

– *Karl! I'm warning you.*

Karl smiles, taking an interest in his fine, black body. He turns one of his arms this way and that as the dawn sunshine glints on the rich, shiny skin. – *That's nice*, he says.

– *After all I've done for you*, says his friend, almost weeping.

– *There's no justice*, says Karl. – *Or maybe there is a very little. Maybe you have to work hard to manufacture tiny quantities of justice, the way you get gold by panning for it. Eh?*

– *There's only desire!* His friend hisses through savage, stained teeth. His eyes are bloodshot. – *Karl! Karl! Karl!*

– *You're looking even worse in the daylight*, says Karl. – *You could do with some breakfast as much as me. Let's order it now. We can talk while we eat.*

Karl will be sixty-one. His mother will have been dead long-since, of cancer. His father will have been dead for nine years, killed in the Wolverhampton riots of 1993. Karl will be unemployed.

He will sit by the shattered window of his front room on the ground floor of the house in Ladbroke Grove, London. He will look out into the festering street. There will be nobody there but the rats and the cats. There will be only a handful of other human beings left in London, most of them in Southwark, by the river.

But the wars will be over. It will be peaceful.

Peaceful for Karl, at any rate. Karl will have been a cannibal for two of the years he has been home, having helped in the destruction of Hong Kong and served as a mercenary in Paris, where he will have gained the taste for human flesh. Anything will be preferable to the rats and the cats. Not that, by this time, he will be hunting his meat himself; he will have lost any wish to kill the few creatures like him who will haunt the diseased ruins of the city.

Karl will brood by the window. He will have secured all other doors and windows against attack, though there will have been no attack up to that time. He will have left the wide window open, since it will command the best view of Ladbroke Grove.

He will have been burning books in the big fireplace to keep himself warm. He will not, any longer, be reading books. They will all depress him too much. He will not, as far as it will be possible, think any more. He will wish to become only a part of whatever it will be that he is part of.

From the corners of his eyes he will see fleeting shadows which he will think are people, perhaps even old friends, who will have come, seeking him out. But they will only be shadows. Or perhaps rats. Or cats. But probably only shadows. He will come to think of these shadows in quite an affectionate way. He will see them as the ghosts of his unborn children. He will see them as the women he never loved, the men he never knew.

Karl will scratch his scurvy, unhealthy body. His body will be dying much faster now that the cans have run out and he will no longer be able to find the vitamins he has used before.

He will not fear death.

He will not understand death, just as he will not understand life.

One idea will run together with another.

Nothing will have a greater or a lesser value than another thing. All will have been brought to the same state. This will be peace of a particular kind. This will be security and stability of a particular kind. There will be no other kind. All things will flow together. There will be no past, no present. No future.

Later Karl will lie like a lizard, unmoving on the flat table, his rifle forgotten beside him, and he will stare out at the ruins as if he has known them all his life, as if they, like him, are eternal.

★

They eat breakfast.

– It's a lovely morning, says Karl.

– I am very rich, says his friend. – I can let you have all you want. Women, other men, anyone. Power. You can satisfy every desire. And I will be whatever you want me to be. I promise. I will serve you. I will be like a genie from the lamp bringing you your heart's every whim! It is true, Karl! *The sickly eyes burn with a fever of lust.*

– I'm not sure I want anything at the moment. *Karl finishes his coffee.*

– Stay with me, Karl.

Karl feels sorry for his friend. He puts down his napkin.

– I'll tell you what we'll do today. We'll go back to the roof garden. What about it?

– If that's what you want.

– I'm very grateful to you, in a way, says Karl.

Michael Moorcock

What would you do? (18)

Your father has been to hospital at his doctor's request, because he has been suffering pain in his chest, his stomach and his throat. The hospital has told him that he has a form of rheumatism and prescribes certain kinds of treatment.

You receive a request from your father's doctor to visit him.

The doctor tells you that your father is actually suffering from inoperable cancer. He has cancer of the lung, of the stomach and of the throat. He has at very most a year to live.

The doctor says that the decision whether to tell your father of this is up to you. He, the doctor, can't accept the responsibility.

Your father loves life and he fears death.

Would you tell your father the whole truth?

Would you offer him part of the truth and tell him that he has a chance of recovering?

Would you think it better for your father's peace of mind that he know nothing?

19. In the Roof Garden: 1971: Happy Day

The prosecution today won its fight to try Capt. Ernest L. Medina on murder charges, but decided not to seek the death penalty.

International Herald Tribune, 26–7 June 1971

Karl and his friend stood together by the railing, looking at the view over London. It was a beautiful, warm day. Karl breathed in the scents of the flowers, of the store below, of the traffic beyond. He felt contented.

His friend's pale, blue eyes were troubled. He looked thin and his silk suit hardly seemed to fit any longer. He had put on several rings and, when he tapped his fingers nervously on the rails, they seemed to be the only part of him that had any life.

'Are you sure you know what you're doing, Karl?' said his friend.

'I think so. Honestly, it would be for the best now. It couldn't last.'

'I could do so much for you still. If you knew who I really was, you'd believe me.'

'Oh, I've seen your pictures. I didn't want to put you out by mentioning it. I didn't recognize you at first, that was all.'

'I offered you an empire, and you've chosen a cabbage patch.'

Karl grinned. 'It's more my style, boss.'

'You can always change your mind.'

'I know. Thank you.'

Karl's friend was reluctant to say good-bye, but he was too miserable to attempt to summon any further strength and try to persuade Karl.

Karl adjusted the hat he had bought for himself on the way up. 'I think I'll go down and buy a suit somewhere now,' he said. 'Adios!'

The white man nodded and turned away without saying good-bye.

'Look after yourself,' said Karl. 'Get some sleep.' With a spring in his step, he walked through the Woodland Garden to the exit. The two middle-aged ladies were there as usual. A fat tourist came out of the lift and bumped into him. The tourist cursed him and then apologized almost at the same time. He was evidently embarrassed.

'Don't worry, boss,' said Karl, flashing him a grin. 'That's okay.'

He took the lift down, changed as usual at the third floor, went down to the ground floor, bought himself a newspaper and studied the lists of runners for the day's races.

A middle-aged man in a check suit and wearing a smart bowler, with a white handle-bar moustache, smelling of tobacco, asked: 'What are you planning to do?' He was genuinely interested. He had his own paper open at the racing page. 'Any tips?'

'I'm feeling lucky today.' Karl ran his slender brown finger down the lists. 'What about Russian Roulette, two-thirty, Epsom?'

'Right. And thank you very kindly.'

'It's all right, man.'

The punter laughed heartily and slapped Karl on the back. 'I'll say that for you fellows, you know how to keep cheerful. Cheerio!'

Karl saluted and left the store, crossing the High Street and walking up Church Street, enjoying the morning. At Notting Hill he stopped and wondered if he should go straight back to Ladbroke Grove. The suit he wanted had just taken shape in his mind.